McCARTER TOOK THE FLIGHT RECORDER AND SLID IT ACROSS THE TABLE TO PROPENKO

"Here, this is your first job. Take this and—"

Propenko's scarred fist slammed down on the flight recorder. Bits of thick plastic armor flew in all directions. He scooped up the little black box's innards and made a fist around them. Technology cracked and popped.

The Russian went to the sink, turned on the tap and flicked on the garbage disposal. He dropped the shattered remnants down the drain and the flight recorder of Drone 1 met its final mastication.

McCarter noted that the Russian's leg seemed to be bothering him a lot less.

Everyone froze as the lights suddenly went out and the garbage disposal spun to a grinding, snapping halt. For a moment the only sound was the running tap. The lights of the neighbors on the surrounding hillsides and the lights of the city below didn't flicker. Someone had cut the safe house's power.

"Gear up," McCarter ordered. "We're about to get hit."

DON PENDLETON'S

STONY

AMERICA'S ULTRA-COVERT INTELLIGENCE AGENCY

MAN®

CITADEL OF FEAR

A GOLD EAGLE BOOK FROM
WORLDWIDE®

TORONTO • NEW YORK • LONDON
AMSTERDAM • PARIS • SYDNEY • HAMBURG
STOCKHOLM • ATHENS • TOKYO • MILAN
MADRID • WARSAW • BUDAPEST • AUCKLAND

Recycling programs
for this product may
not exist in your area.

First edition June 2015

ISBN-13: 978-0-373-80451-1

Citadel of Fear

Special thanks and acknowledgment to
Charles Rogers for his contribution to this work.

Printed in U.S.A.

CITADEL OF FEAR

CHAPTER ONE

Poland, Gulf of Gdansk

"I have movement," Gary Manning reported.

David McCarter, leader of Phoenix Force, looked up into the scudding rain of the Baltic Sea in winter. "Able Team gets all the soft jobs..." he muttered. "What do you see, Gummer?"

Manning spoke from his sniper hide three hundred meters back. They were in Baltic marshlands and he held the only high ground, but it was barely ten meters above sea level. "Three trucks, as reported. I make them Russian civilian Zil half-tons. Canvas tops."

T. J. Hawkins checked his weapon. He mostly approved of the Polish kit. The Beryl rifle was basically a Russian AK but sexier and built to NATO standards. The young soldier peered out into crepuscular dawn across the gulf and took in the lights of Kaliningrad across the border as they came on in the predawn. "You know, I still don't quite get how that's Russia."

Calvin James checked his weapon a final time, as well. "It's an *oblast*, Hawk."

"A what?"

"An exclave federal subject of Russia."

"You know I love it when you talk all smart 'n' stuff," Hawkins declared.

Calvin James waited for it.

Hawkins sighed. "Okay, what's an exclave?"

James made the young warrior work. "What's the difference between the Latin prefixes *en* and *ex*?"

"Ex! Like exoskeleton! Outside! Like sci-fi body armor, and bugs!"

James nodded grudgingly. "Someone give that Wal-Mart-shopping, cornbread-fed Son of the South a cigar."

Hawkins beamed. "Yeah, but why is it Russia? I mean, shouldn't it be part of Poland or one of the Balticstans?"

Rafael Encizo snorted. "Did he just say Balticstan?"

"That piece of property has gone back and forth more than a few times historically," Calvin James explained. "But the last time it traded hands? The Soviets took it from the Nazis, in World War II, and they didn't give it back. To anybody."

Hawkins nodded sagely. "They have a habit of that."

"That they do. It's the Russian Federation's only western seaport that doesn't freeze over in winter. They aren't going to give it back to anyone anytime soon."

Hawkins looked to their leader. "So what are we doing here again?

McCarter watched the trucks approach down the one-lane road through the misty marsh forest. They were a dozen klicks outside the Polish city of Elbag. The land was flat, dank, forested with twisted trees right out of a horror movie and mostly undeveloped. The Kaliningrad *oblast* was indeed Russia's westernmost outpost, and had a massive military presence. Not unsurprisingly, the *oblast* also had a massive Russian organized crime presence, and served as a launch point for Russian *mafiya* endeavors into Western Europe.

This stretch of coast was a well-known smugglers' route. McCarter knew that big money was paid on both sides of the border to keep the salty, dark, cold and windswept stretch of wetlands clear of Polish state police and customs.

Phoenix Force had rather neatly stopped a terrorist attack a week ago in Prague. McCarter had been rather pleased with himself and his team. However, Stony Man Farm had picked up some very strange and seemingly related chatter within hours of the strike. Strange enough that Aaron "the Bear" Kurtzman, the Farm's cybernetics genius, had used the dreaded word *anomalous*.

The Farm had tracked the weapons through the black market web and their path had led to the Gdansk smuggling route and Kaliningrad. All signs pointed to something going on tonight.

McCarter scowled into the misting rain. Phoenix Force had once again been reduced to sticking their necks out and seeing who tried to chop their heads off. It was the Englishman's least favorite method of investigation.

"With any luck we're tying up loose ends, Hawk," McCarter replied.

"I got a feeling we're just getting started."

McCarter nodded wearily into the wind. "And you're not alone in that, are you, old son?"

"He called me old son."

"You know? One day you are going to go one right proper Charlie too far."

"What the hell does that mean?"

James answered. "It means, young blood, that one day, you are going to be all full of piss and vinegar, and say 'you love it when I talk all black and stuff' to me, and our fearless leader shall sit back and laugh at what happens to you."

Hawkins looked back and forth as every senior Phoenix Force member save Manning grinned at him in the gloom. "That's not right. That's wrong. I'd never say something like that."

Phoenix Force, including Manning over the com link, spoke as a unit. "Yes, you would."

"That's just wrong—"

Manning interrupted him with, "One mile, within range of my rifle, waiting on green light."

"Roger that, Gummer," McCarter replied. "Wait on my signal unless you get sudden inspiration."

"Copy that."

Encizo flipped up the sight on his grenade launcher. "Three trucks, how do you want to play it?"

"Well, I suppose I could step down there, step out in front and ask for an inspection."

The Cuban grunted in amusement. "You don't speak Russian or Polish."

"But I do know a lorryful of Russian swearwords, and the word stop. Then it would be up to you lot and we all play it by ear."

James gave the Phoenix Force leader a bemused look. "Wow."

"You've got a better plan, then?"

"No, not all." James grinned. "I'm all in."

Manning's voice dropped low over the link. "Guys?"

The convoy had stopped at approximately three hundred meters.

Hawkins stared at the three idling trucks. "Now why do you think they did that?"

McCarter's brows bunched. "Don't say it…"

Encizo said it. "I got a bad feeling."

"They know we're here," James confirmed.

Manning's voice grew concerned across the link. "Does anyone else hear that?"

McCarter strained his senses over the sound of the idling trucks in the distance.

Hawkins's head snapped up. "Aw, hell."

McCarter heard it. It was low and sounded off in the fog, which told him that it was actually high. It sounded like a distant gardener's Weed-Eater whirring from on high. Hawkins raised his weapon skyward. "It's an RC helicopter"

"And it has a bloody infrared camera," McCarter snarled. "And it bloody well has us! Fish?"

Encizo opened the action on the Pallad grenade launcher slaved beneath the barrel of his rifle. He took out the fragmentation grenade and slid in a fléchette round. "Hey, Hawk."

"Yeah?"

"Go out in that clearing behind us. Do a little duck tolling. Maybe entice that eye in the sky to come down and take a closer look at you."

"Oh, for…" Hawkins popped to his feet and ran at a crouch into the clearing.

Encizo shouldered his weapon. "Cal, a little light on the subject, if you please."

Calvin James clicked an illumination-round rifle grenade over his muzzle. "Say when."

The other members of Phoenix Force watched as Hawkins squelched across the wet glade one way and then came back the other. He suddenly crouched and ran to his left.

"Would you describe those as furtive movements?" James asked.

Manning spoke across the link. "I'd describe it as—"

"Now!" Encizo shouted and estimated the shot. "Nine o'clock!"

James snapped up his rifle and fired. The rifle bucked and the illumination round burst skyward. The low clouds, fog and predawn murk lit up and the small remote-controlled helicopter found itself starkly illuminated at five hundred feet. It appeared to be a fairly standard quadcopter with four rotors. It hovered in place for a moment like a deer in the headlights. James suspected the nonmilitary-grade night-vision camera's lens had temporarily solarized.

The spy-copter was blind.

Like a cockroach when the kitchen lights came on, it suddenly tried to scuttle away. In this case by accelerating straight upward.

Encizo raised his weapon and fired. The 40 mm Pallad belched pale yellow smoke and sent fifty steel darts screaming skyward in an expanding swarm. The RC chopper tilted crazily as fléchettes speared into its plastic fuselage and tore apart its starboard rotors.

McCarter grunted in appreciation. "Nice shot, Fish."

The little unmanned aircraft suddenly dipped with only its portside rotors to support it and spun violently toward the earth like a falling maple seed on meth.

"Hawk," McCarter ordered, "be a good lad. Find that and mark it for retrieval. Everyone else hold position."

"Be a good lad…" Hawkins muttered. Nevertheless the soldier slogged out of the slough and into the trees.

Encizo opened the smoking breech on his weapon and slid in a frag. "So what do you think they're up to?"

McCarter kept his eyes and his muzzle pointed at the trucks in the mist. Above the tableau, the illumination grenade guttered as it descended on its parachutes. "They just lost their drone and are watching the end of the light show."

"If I were them? I'd attack right now."

The canvas covering of the lead truck suddenly popped off like a magic trick. The truck was armed with twin-mounted 23 mm automatic antiaircraft cannons.

Encizo shook his head. "Why don't you just spit in the wind, Cal?"

Hawkins trotted through the trees clutching his prize. "What's—"

"Down!" McCarter ordered.

"Jesus!" Hawkins threw himself down. "They brought artillery!"

"And aerial reconnaissance," James reminded.

"Who are these guys!" Encizo snarled.

McCarter roared as the twin cannons hammered into life, sending high-explosive shells into the trees. Shrapnel from the high-explosive fragmentation rounds tore through the foliage over McCarter's head. It was only a matter of moments before Phoenix Force got shredded. "Gummer!"

"Gimme a second! The cab is in the way!"

Encizo fired his 40 mm. The round detonated well off target as it hit a tree branch shrouded in fog. "Goddamn it…"

McCarter, James and Hawkins hugged mud. Encizo reloaded. The twin 23 mms thundered like giant jackhammers and continued to give the forest a haircut as they sought out human targets.

Manning did his math and found his shot. It was lost in the cacophony of cannon fire but from his little hillock his bullet drew a deadly line through the lead truck's windshield, rear window and the cannon operator's skull. The gunner rubbernecked and oozed out of his seat. The cannons went silent and oozed smoke. Armed men spilled out of the trucks. McCarter decided he'd had enough of this ambush. "Counter attack! By twos! Fish, on me!"

McCarter and Encizo jumped up and advanced through the trees straight at the enemy. They fired on rapid semiauto and reaped the men deploying across the open road. McCarter dropped to one knee beside a tree as his weapon slammed open empty. "Reloading!"

"Reloading!" Encizo echoed.

"Coming through!" James bellowed.

"Coming through!" Hawkins shouted.

The two soldiers leapfrogged McCarter's and Encizo's positions, firing as they went. James put a burst though the window of one of the trucks as it tried to back up. The truck lurched as the driver fell against the wheel. James dropped to one knee. "Reloading!"

Encizo fired his weapon empty. "Reloading!"

"Coming through!" McCarter and Encizo advanced, relying on their optics and shock and awe. The enemy expected to chop their prey to pieces with the cannon or at the very least pin them down and then flank them. They had not expected a counter-assault. The enemy fired wildly on full auto and appeared to be in full panic mode. Manning's sniper rifle reached out unseen for men who had taken cover behind the trucks. The rear truck was reversing and some of Phoenix's assailants were running for their lives to get to it and get in. "Fish!"

Encizo instinctively knew what McCarter wanted. He dropped to one knee. "Grenade!" His 40 mm fired and his grenade flashed and smoked and perforated the truck's cab and its occupants. The rear truck ground to a halt.

The enemy found themselves pinned.

McCarter was getting the feeling these guys were gangsters rather than real soldiers. His boots hit pavement and the last bullet in his magazine pushed a man into the ditch by the side of the road.

"Reloading!"

Encizo fired off three more rounds and knelt again. "Reloading!"

James and Hawkins charged forward. "Coming through!"

McCarter slammed in a fresh magazine as the twin 30 mm antiaircraft cannons suddenly traversed. McCarter swung up his rifle one heartbeat too slow. He had just enough time to see the new gunner's teeth flash in the gloom as he smiled and told McCarter goodbye. The cannon operator tumbled out of his seat as Manning's long-range rifle said so long first.

James and Hawkins fired their rifles empty and knelt out in the open, counting on their comrades. "Reloading!"

McCarter and Encizo advanced, firing. "Coming through! Flank the road!"

McCarter and Encizo reached the bumper of the first truck and gave covering fire as Hawkins ran across the road.

Manning shouted over the com, "Watch out! Second truck!"

Rubber screamed as tires spun against the slick road surface.

"He's ramming!"

McCarter leaped back. Encizo was a second too late. The middle truck rear-ended the lead and moved it six feet. Encizo was at the end of the chain and the bumper sent him flying. "Fish!" The truck tilted as its rear axle snapped. The Cuban did a spectacular reverse somersault across the pavement and collapsed prone by the side of the road. "Fish!"

James burst out of the trees. He grabbed Encizo by his straps and hauled him back. Tracers flew between the tree trunks in angry streaks. James jerked three times and fell. Gears ground as the middle truck went in reverse to position itself for a second ramming attack. "Cal! Fish!"

Calvin James's voice was ragged over the line. "We can fight!"

"Covering fire!" McCarter vaulted up the steel bumper and onto the hood of the truck. He emptied his rifle on full-auto as he went over the top and leaped to the tilted truck bed. The second truck's tires screamed and bit in. The truck lurched forward to ram. McCarter tossed his empty rifle and swung into the gunner's seat. He kicked the traversing pedals and brought up the muzzles of the twin cannons.

The truck driver stared into the twin 23 mms and stood

on his brakes; the truck started to hydroplane. McCarter snarled and squeezed the trigger. The bastard should have stayed on course. The cannons came to life and ripped the truck apart from stem to stern. The truck was instantly reduced to burning wreckage, but the wreckage had the good taste to swerve and slam into a tree by the side of the road. This conveniently left the third truck wide-open.

McCarter gave truck number three both barrels. The truck broke apart like a beer can. McCarter traversed and scoured the underbrush on both sides of the road. He eased his finger off the trigger. The misty road was eerily lit in orange by the burning trucks. The road was littered with bodies. For McCarter the loudest sound was the ticking of his red-hot cannon barrels and the misting rain sizzling off them. The Phoenix Force leader spoke quietly into the com. "Sound off."

Phoenix Force came back in the affirmative. James and Encizo sounded worse for wear.

"Hold positions," McCarter bellowed like a boss. He used a choice phrase in Russian he had picked up in his travels. "Surrender or die!"

Two men hesitantly rose from the wet, their hands raised. On the other side of the road a rifle clattered out onto the wet pavement. A large, bald man came out with a pronounced limp.

McCarter kept his hands on his cannons' firing grips. He jerked his head at the road and the three men went to their knees. "Fish, you all right?"

"I got my wind, my ribs and my lungs knocked out of me. It'll be a miracle if nothing isn't broken."

"Cal?"

"I got it about one-sixteenth as bad as Fish. I took three to the chest, but my armor held."

"Hawk, Fish, sweep the area. Gummer, hold position and keep an eye on the road. Cal, on me with our friends."

Phoenix moved.

Cal came forward and admired the cannons. "Well played, team leader. Well played."

"Thanks. Check our pals, would you?"

James strode up upon the prisoners. The three kneeling men regarded the large black man with mixed fear and hostility. "Anyone speak English?" he asked. Three sullen glares was the only response. James clicked the Polish-issue bayonet onto his rifle. "You boys sure?"

The big, bald, wounded man spoke. "I speak."

"Good, that's real good." James shot him a winning smile. "Russian, huh?" The man's shoulders sagged. His leg was clearly paining him. James continued to smile and continued to keep the brutal-looking man kneeling in place. "What's your name?"

The man seemed to search for strength.

"For the next forty-eight hours you're mine. So, what would you like me to call you?"

The man closed his eyes. "Nikita."

"Okay, Nick. Can I call you Nick? Good." James took a big, deep breath of the misty, salty, dank Gdansk dawn. He sighed happily. "So, how are you enjoying Poland?"

Nick's accent was very thick. "I hate fuckin' place."

"Rather be back in Kaliningrad, would you?"

Nick sighed fatalistically. "Never should have left Orsk."

"Orsk?" James grinned. "I killed a whole bunch of guys in Orsk once."

Nick didn't bat an eye. "I believe."

James looked at the other two. One was tall and skinny and one was tall and fat; they looked related. "Do those two speak English?"

Nick glanced at the men. They glared back. "No."

"Who are they?"

"Hammerhead scum."

Hammerhead was Russian slang for low-level *mafiya* enforcers and, to James's eye, they fit the bill. As had their distinct nonmilitary behavior during the entire battle. James suspected if he stripped them, the two men would be covered in Russian prison tattoos. He regarded Nick shrewdly. He had an inkling Nick wouldn't be. "If they're hammerhead scum, I think that makes you *podryadchik*."

Nick flinched.

Cal knew he'd hit pay dirt. *Podryadchik* was Russian for someone who was paid to do something for someone else. It was their word for contractor. Nick was former Russian military, probably special forces of one stripe or another, and was likely in private security, and now, it seemed, private wet work.

"What were you before you got saddled with these *mafiya* wing-nuts? Alfa-Tsenter? Moran group? RSB?"

James studied the man's reactions and compared them to everything he had revealed in the past sixty seconds. James started reading him like a book. "Nah, you're a good Russian boy. You love your homeland. And that's where you do your best work. I bet you were Viking Group."

Nick twitched again. James knew from past experience that Viking Group specialized in private security within Russia.

"You didn't like this job from the get-go. You knew going into Poland was a mistake. But the money was real good, wasn't it?"

"Screw you," Nick responded. But he didn't seem to have much heart in it.

"I'll take that as a yes."

Nick mumbled something in Russian that sounded very fatalistic.

"You know something, Nick. I like you."

"I do not like you at all."

"Of course you like me. You love me. But I'm a pillar of Nubian manhood, and that's left a boy from Orsk a little confused."

One corner of the Russian's mouth quirked in amusement despite himself.

"Aw, you smiled!" The black Phoenix Force pro took out a pack of Marlboros. Nick blinked. James had given up smoking long ago, but a good deal of the planet hadn't. In many of the world's neighborhoods a pack of cigarettes was a perfectly acceptable small bribe or gift, and as an interrogator the offer of a smoke was often very useful in breaking the ice and bonding with a subject. It was Calvin James's experience that most Russians smoked like chimneys.

As predicted, Nick gazed upon the pack longingly.

James shook the pack with an expert hand and put a cancer stick between Nick's lips. He put the point of his bayonet between Nick's collarbones and his finger on the trigger as he dug out a lighter. James lit the cigarette. Nick stopped short of sagging in relief. James lit one for himself to complete the bonding experience, and hated himself for enjoying the opportunity. The two soldiers spent a few moments smoking silently in the Polish dawn.

"Nick?"

Nick breathed out blue smoke. He savored the cigarette as if he suspected it was his last. "Yes?"

"You seem like an okay Ivan to me."

"Thank you."

"So I tell you what I'm going to do—despite the fact you tried to blow me apart with an antiaircraft gun."

"This was nothing personal."

"I know. Neither was killing most of your friends."

"These men were not my friends."

"I know. So you know what I'm going to do?"

"No. I do not know what you are going to do. I find you very unpredictable."

"You're a charmer. Here's what I'm going to do. I'm going to patch up that leg. I'm going to give you a shot of morphine and something to eat, and I'm going to let you live. The question is, do you want me to let you live here, handcuffed to that cannon after we drop a dime on Polish state security and anonymously tell them that there has been an armed Russian incursion across the Kaliningrad border. Or..."

"Or what?"

"Would you rather come with me?"

Nick looked as though he was getting a migraine.

"Maybe see Orsk again?" James cajoled. "Me? I'm going to Sweden. Want to go to Sweden with me?"

Nick turned pale, gray, bloodshot eyes on Calvin James. "I have never been on Swedish holiday with pillar of Nubian manhood."

James turned to McCarter. "I like him! Can I keep him?"

McCarter got on the horn. "*Dragonslayer*, we need extraction. One guest."

Right now the Stony Man chopper wore civilian clothes and currently bobbed upon the waves on pontoons just outside Poland's three-mile international limit around the Gdansk Gulf.

"Copy that, we have room. Let me warm up the engines," Jack Grimaldi returned from the chopper. "ETA ten minutes. You got an LZ for me?"

"It should be light by the time you get here. Right next to my signal is a glade. Hawk will be standing in it waving his arms. It's mostly muck, but with the pontoons you should be able to land just fine."

"Copy that. How did it go?"

"They were expecting us." McCarter glanced at the

twin barrels of the ZSU-23-2 cannons. He had grown rather fond of them. "And, Jack?"

"Yeah?"

"I think they were expecting you, as well."

CHAPTER TWO

The Game Room

"Jesus, who are these guys?" Junior Pyle leaned back from his massive, multiscreened console. Rong leaned back from his own console as he watched the men disappear into the woods with their prisoner. "Got to be the same guys as last week. Got to be."

"No doubt," Kun agreed.

"Yeah, no doubt." Pyle kept his hands on the joysticks of the second drone. Drone 2 flew at a height where its rotors could not be heard and, in what was left of the gloom, not seen. Neither the Russians nor their opponents knew about Drone 2.

Pyle zoomed the camera to maximum but despite its sophistication and power, at this height the resolution was not great and the men were moving under the trees. "Listen, it's going to be light in minutes and they'll be able to see Drone 2 with optics. I can't get a good picture of these guys without going low enough to let them shoot at us." He was keenly aware of the fact that he had lost Drone 1.

"We were supposed to kick these guys' asses. Our asses got handed to us." Rong chewed his lip unhappily. "The Magistrate is not going to be amused."

The three men contemplated the Magistrate's possible ire; two with fear and one in personal disappointment. All three men were in their twenties and from Silicon Valley, Seoul and Hong Kong. Each man had run the computer world high-tech gamut from software engineer to hacker to gamer and game designer. They were some of the best cybernetic experts in the business, sought after by top-end, high-tech companies worldwide.

They had been lured, and then very handsomely remunerated, into become experts in the rapidly advancing field of high-tech mercenaries. A private army specializing in unconventional warfare and crime, including cyber crime prevention, which they found boring, and cyber crime commitment, which was proactive, fun, far more profitable and had perks two of the trio had never even dreamed about.

These men were the advantage most criminals or opponents in low-intensity conflicts did not have and could not afford. Most modern militaries had men like them, but nowhere near as good, and had much less exciting toys. However, Junior Pyle was right and all three men knew it. They had gotten their asses handed to them.

Kun smiled. The Korean was dressed immaculately in a retro, light blue suit. A 007 aficionado would have recognized it as Sean Connery's gray, tropical-weight suit from the film *Dr. No*, and Kun had styled his hair to match right down to a tousled spit curl. Hardly anything Kun owned besides his high-tech equipment was not custom made and straight out of a James Bond movie. He found himself amused. "These guys are real, genuine, badasses."

"Speaking of badasses…" Rong looked and dressed like a skateboarder. His hair was at that hedgehog look of an Asian male who had a missed a lot of haircuts but not yet grown it long enough so that it would fall over into a shag. It was a look he assiduously cultivated and had currently dyed orange. "They took Propenko, alive."

Junior Pyle dressed as though he thought he was still in college or wanted to be the lead singer of an Emo band or both with the tattoos, piercings and black hair, black T-shirts and black jeans to match.

Pyle and Rong were certifiable, card-carrying computer geeks and Kun was a certifiable sociopath. But the three young men were all at the pinnacle of their fields and their power and, having dropped out of their civilian fields, had become urban legends. Pyle was very unhappy. "Does this mean the Russian mafia is going to kill us?"

"No." Rong sighed. "But Propenko probably will. He looked straight into my camera before he went across the border and told me not to mess this up."

Propenko had no idea who the three cyber warriors were or even where they were, but Propenko was a trained investigator and a very violent man. The team had chosen him for this mission and they had not picked him out of a hat.

Rong's and Pyle's grommets tightened at the idea of a displeased Magistrate and the big Russian filled with thoughts of revenge.

Kun contemplated the Walther PPK in his shoulder holster happily. He still hadn't gotten around to shooting anybody with it yet. As with the best of sociopaths, Kun genuinely wasn't afraid of anything or anybody, but he did have certain goals and objectives that he wished to achieve. He was a realist in these matters, and being on the wrong side of Propenko qualified as a genuine obstacle and not one to be taken lightly. "Money makes Propenko come. Money makes him go away."

"Unless he goes surly Russian on us," Pyle countered.

"Well…" Kun smiled again. Pyle was blissfully unaware of the fact that Kun disliked him intensely and intended to skin him alive. "They have our drone."

Rong regained his good humor. "So how do you want to play it?"

All three men were genuine geniuses. All three men knew that Kun was the one who could think outside the box. Both in cyber warfare and in the outside world, which neither Rong nor Pyle functioned all that well in.

Kun contemplated. He liked Rong. Rong, like Pyle, was equally unaware that, because Kun liked him, he intended to kidnap Rong, shackle Rong, encase Rong in latex and do unspeakable things to him. Kun was already secretly interviewing replacements for both his partners in cyber space.

Kun returned to the matters at hand. They had several options. "The copter is programmed to return to its launch point if it loses contact. We have to assume these assholes know this. We will need to move. However, I do not believe they have the tech to open her up and read her programming on them at the moment. They will need to go to a safe house first."

Pyle's equipment peeped and a window popped up on one of his screens. Data started rapidly scrolling south. "Polish state security channels are lighting up. I think these guys actually made the call themselves."

"Interesting," Kun mused. "They were ambushed outside Kaliningrad—and they do not know how—and it is they who have called the state police. They will want to get out of Poland without flying across it, and they certainly will not want to fly east. I think they'll head straight north. It's a short shot across international waters into Sweden. They'll have something cozy set up there."

Rong grinned. "Sweet."

Kun considered the equipment he had personally installed in Drone 1. "Let's play a game."

Pyle actually raised his hand as if he were in school. "What about the Magistrate? Who's gonna tell him?"

"The Magistrate has been watching our feed the entire time and listening to our conversation."

Rong and Pyle collectively dropped their jaws.

"I will speak with him later and give him a full debriefing." Unlike his compatriots, Kun was not afraid of the Magistrate. Kun loved the Magistrate as his personal god.

Kun rose and walked to the end of the Game Room. He opened the door and looked down the steps at a pair of security men smoking and watching the sunrise. Kun lit himself an unfiltered Turkish cigarette and watched the sun rise for a moment, as well. From the outside, the Game Room appeared to be a standard container vessel. The Game Room currently sat mounted on the trailer of a Russian Kamaz tractor-truck. "Hey, guys?"

The two Russian gangsters turned.

Kun nodded at the sun rising over Kaliningrad. "Let's get back into Russia."

Kalmar, Sweden

"Nikita Propenko." Aaron Kurtzman made an impressed noise over the link. "You landed yourself a real, genuine, Russian badass."

McCarter sat in the master bedroom of the safe house with a laptop and satellite rig. "Right. Viking Group." McCarter allowed himself a little smugness. "We know."

"Right. But do you know what he did before he went private?"

"Spetsnaz?" McCarter proposed. "He's a tough son of a bitch, I'll give him that. The only thing he wasn't immune to was Cal's charms."

"Who is?" The Stony Man cybernetics genius's voice held a chuckle. "But your boy Propenko was Saturn Detachment."

"Doesn't ring a bell." McCarter frowned. "Saturn Detachment sounds a bit dark, then, doesn't it?"

"*Dark* is one word for it. Saturn Detachment was the Moscow Department of the Federal Penitentiary Service—FSIN. Saturn is FSIN's special-purpose unit."

"The Russians have a penal special-purpose unit?" McCarter asked.

"Saturn Detachment was formed in 1992 as part of the Moscow Department of Punishment Execution, the UIN, under the Ministry of the Interior."

"Department of Punishment Execution?" Most days McCarter woke up thinking nothing could surprise him anymore. Leading Phoenix Force and having conversations with Aaron Kurtzman consistently proved him wrong. "You know? The Soviets did have a certain Orwellian sense of style about them. I'll give them that."

"Well, when the Soviet Union fell, like a lot of Soviet organizations, the UIN changed their name and shuffled ministries. They're still known by everyone as Saturn, but they were officially renamed the Federal Penitentiary Service and operate under the auspices of the Russian Ministry of Justice."

"That does sound a little less Kafkaesque, but I intend to work this guy, Bear. Short version, what is Saturn?"

"They're nickname in Russia is Jail Spetsnaz."

"Jail Special Forces?" McCarter found himself surprised again. "Now there is something you don't hear every day."

"You are aware of the reputation of Russian prisons?" Kurtzman queried.

McCarter had fought the Russian *mafiya* many times. From everything he knew or had gleaned, Russian federal penitentiaries were a nasty place to be.

David McCarter thought he had an inkling but asked, anyway. "So just what does Jail Spetsnaz do, exactly?"

"Their official tasks are preventing crimes in detention facilities, antiriot actions in detention facilities, hostage rescue in detention facilities, counter terrorism actions in detention facilities, high-value prisoner transfers, personal security for Ministry of Justice and court officials, and—here is where it gets interesting—search and arrest of escaped criminals. Think of them as the most violent, messed-up version US Federal Marshals imaginable.

"By the way, your boy Propenko? For a number of years he did undercover operations in several Russian federal detention facilities. I leave it to you to decide what kind of balls a man has to have to go undercover in a federal prison."

McCarter knew one man. His name was Mack Bolan. And no story Bolan told about the experience had been pretty. "Right. So Propenko is a real, genuine, Russian badass, then."

"He's airborne-trained, specifically to parachute into a prison in a riot situation, and the Russian police equivalent of a designated marksman. After the third time he was shot he took some time off and acted as UIN academy hand-to-hand-combat instructor. Turns out he was a Russian sambo champion. He was going to go to the Olympics in Sochi but he got shot again."

"The man has a résumé."

"You have no idea. He also earned the Russian Federation's Ministry of Justice's maximum achievement certification in penal psychological warfare." Kurtzman paused at that. "You be the judge of what that means…"

"It means I'm glad I shot him and even gladder that he fell in love with Cal."

"Yeah, that was for the best…" Kurtzman agreed.

"Right, going to go make our Captain Penal Power an offer he can't refuse, then."

"David, this man has operated undercover in Russian supermax prisons. I want you to consider the fact that he may have deliberately decided to let himself be captured so that he could find out who you and Phoenix Force are, kill the entire team except you, torture you for everything you know and then extract back into the Russian Federation and report to whoever is running him."

"The thought had occurred, but thanks. I'll be right back."

McCarter walked down the narrow, wood-paneled stairs. For giant Viking people, Swedes had strangely narrow homes. Nonetheless the house just about fell off the hillside and had a panoramic view of the black Baltic nighttime sea, which was pretty spectacular with the full moon reflecting off it.

James and Propenko sat in the kitchenette playing speed chess. Propenko seemed to be halfway through a bottle of Swedish black market *brännvin*, wood-cellulose "burned wine." McCarter raised an eyebrow at the Chicago native. "Is the prisoner drinking wood alcohol?"

"Yeah, for the past hour, mixed with morphine I gave him." James sighed heavily at the chessboard. "I only won my first game five minutes ago. I think the drugs are kicking in."

"Ha!" Propenko finished his move and slammed the timer. His injured leg was bound and stretched out on a chair; his right hand was handcuffed to the sink. The Russian's words were definitely starting to slur. "American pussies..."

James raised one hand to the side of his face and mouthed, "We may need another bottle."

McCarter nodded. "How you doing, Nick?"

Propenko scowled at James. "Nubian has admirable qualities."

The black Phoenix Force medic nodded demurely, made a move and tapped his timer.

The Russian lifted a grudging chin at McCarter. "I have always admired English."

"Good to know."

Propenko scowled down the stairs behind him. "Fish chained me to sink. I do not like Cubans."

McCarter smiled. "My apologies."

Propenko grunted. "Gummer is sniper. I have not met rifleman I have not liked."

Manning called down the skylight from his perch on the roof. "Thanks!"

"And Hawk?" McCarter asked.

"He is too good-looking to be soldier." Propenko made an extremely bold move with his knight and nearly broke the chess timer as he slammed it down. "Maybe he is not hawk. Maybe he is fruit rabbit."

Hawkins's head snapped up from the dining-room table. As the most tech savvy member of Phoenix Force he was doing a preliminary disassembly on the enemy drone. "Hey!"

James raised a diplomatic finger. "Not that there's anything wrong with that."

McCarter smiled at Propenko, but he wasn't fooled. Not for a minute. "Listen, old son, I like you."

"I am liking you, too, English."

"So let me tell you how I see it... I think you have a liver the size of a fifty-year-old speed bag with the cracks and scars to match. I think you're going to be dead in five years, but right now I think you're still a nasty piece of work, and in your line of work you are at the prime of your powers.

"You're a right bloody charmer, and not a quarter as sodding drunk as you're pretending to be. I think you might have it in mind to snap that handcuff after me and my friend there are slightly more relaxed and do something terrible. Then you do the rest of us up a treat and start rooting around for intel. And, I think you've done it before."

The palest, coldest, soberest Russian eyes McCarter had ever seen regarded him unblinkingly. "So?"

"So convince me to keep you around."

"And if I do not?"

McCarter drew his pistol. Phoenix Force had been forced to toss their weapons into the Baltic when they'd entered into Swedish airspace. Sweden was a neutral country with their own cottage arms industry and, unlike many European nations, was not awash in surplus or black market weapons. The CIA had managed to get them some very archaic armaments that had "disappeared" from a Swedish reserve armory. McCarter pointed something that looked strangely like a German Luger at Propenko's right leg. "Then I shoot you in the other leg and I still keep you around."

Propenko sipped wood alcohol.

McCarter pushed. "So?"

The only thing colder and clearer than the Russian's eyes was his smile. His voice was suddenly cold and clear, as well. "So convince me to let you keep me around with one wounded leg rather than two."

McCarter gave a grudging noise of admiration. "Who do you work for?"

"That information is confidential."

"Do you still work for them?"

Propenko gave a very Russian shrug. "I believe the contract terminated when you smashed mission."

"But you were paid?"

"I was. Half in front. Mission did not succeed. Back half will not be—" he belched "—be forthcoming."

McCarter allowed himself a smile.

Propenko eyed the bottle of *brännvin* ruefully. "Swedish fire-piss, I must be getting old."

"And you won't help me in my mission against your previous employers?"

"Do I work for you? Do I have contract?" Propenko swirled the wood alcohol in his teacup and pursed his lips judiciously. "Have I been paid?"

Hawkins made a noise. "The balls on this guy..."

Propenko slowly turned his head to regard Hawkins. "Would you like to see them, Fruit Rabbit?"

"If he calls me Fruit Rabbit one more time..."

"*Dah*. And?"

McCarter brought the conversation back on line. "So your job was to kill us?"

"Sustain your attempted ambush, destroy you and collect information."

"Collect information?"

"You would be interrogated."

"By you?"

"By me. But I would start with Fruit Rabbit."

Hawkins shot to his feet. "That's it!"

Propenko kept his eyes on McCarter. "All evidence collected since Great Patriotic War says that with English? It is being more effective to make him watch torture of one of his men, then torture English himself."

"Lovely. Right, then. Listen, I'm in a bit of a hurry. How much?"

"How much what?" Propenko asked.

"To put you on the payroll."

"The payroll?"

"My payroll. You contract is terminated with these people after I smashed your mission and captured you. You're currently unemployed, Nick. You want a job or do you want to go back to Orsk?"

Propenko's pale eyes narrowed. "You wish to employ me against former employers? This is not strictly honorable."

"They're terrorists. Work against them or for them."

"I am not aware of this."

"I'm betting on that, Nick."

"I am willing to entertain these ideas, but I must warn you. People I worked for apparently had ability to mint own money," Propenko replied.

"Fine. Then double."

Propenko blinked. "You do not know yet how much I am paid."

"Make up a number—but, be a good lad and do try not to go stark ravers about it."

"You do not work for British Intelligence," Propenko declared.

McCarter sipped liquor.

"You do not work for American Intelligence."

McCarter neither confirmed nor denied.

"Who are you?"

McCarter spit in his palm and held out his hand. "Your boss."

Propenko slammed his hand into McCarter's. The Russian had a grip like a clam but he stopped just short of the bone-breaker. "Unless you move, you must expect attack before dawn. I am surprised it has not happened already."

"How much?"

"We talk money later. Now? I will be needing to lose handcuffs and get gun."

"One condition."

"And, so?"

McCarter nodded toward Hawkins. "His name is Hawk." He tossed the Swedish M-40 pistol onto the table. "Uncuff him."

CHAPTER THREE

The War Room

Aaron Kurtzman observed as T. J. Hawkins operated on the Unmanned Aerial Vehicle thousands of miles away in Scandinavia. Kurtzman would have preferred to have done the surgery himself, but security protocols dictated the little UAV helicopter traveled no farther until they could make sure they weren't bringing a Trojan horse into the Farm's precincts.

Kurtzman secretly wished Hermann "Gadgets" Swartz was in the operating theater, but Hawkins wasn't bad. The UAV was a standard quad-motor helicopter with four equidistant rotors on stalks sticking out of the main body. This one had a very powerful and sophisticated camera that was night-vision capable. Hawkins had separated the motors and the camera; they were amazing pieces of technology.

"Here we go…"

Gummer leaned in carefully. He was the team's explosives expert and this was the point where everyone wondered if the UAV would blow sky-high. Hawkins carefully separated the two halves of the fuselage as if it were the shell of a crab.

Kurtzman leaned forward in his wheelchair and peered at the feed from Sweden on his screen.

The guts of the UAV were extremely interesting.

Much like a crab shell, nothing was attached to the top. All the good stuff was attached to the bottom half.

Hawkins looked into the camera. "Bear, I don't know what half this stuff is."

Gary Manning sat back, nodding to himself. "I don't see a booby trap. If there are any explosives in there, they are tiny and made to wipe the equipment instead of kill anyone who might be tampering."

"Wait a minute, before you two touch anything else." Kurtzman took control of the camera on his end and began panning and scanning the UAV's internal organs.

The power supply system was easy to spot and very impressive. It was a flat stack and Kurtzman suspected this UAV would have double the range and endurance of a standard commercial model of comparable size. He had to admit he had never seen a CPU like the one he beheld mounted in a UAV like this. Most similar models were equipped with a simple GPS that allowed them to return to their launch point if they lost contact with their human operator. The sophistication of this drone's CPU implied to the Stony Man cybernetics whiz that the drone was capable of making a number of decisions autonomously and could operate in independent search, patrol or mapping functions.

Kurtzman was also willing to bet that this machine was capable of being operated by, or cooperating with, other autonomous drones operating as autonomous units. In effect, this baby was capable of engaging in independent small- and large-unit actions without the benefit of a human operator in control.

It was an incredibly sophisticated piece of machinery.

Kurtzman leaned back in his chair. It was a very strange thing to be shot down out of the sky during an engagement with Russian *mafiya* thugs. Of course the *mafiya* thugs had showed up with antiaircraft artillery. It all led to the inescapable conclusion that there was a much larger game afoot.

Hawkins pointed his screwdriver at a small, yellow, rectangular casing that almost seemed off in a corner by itself. It didn't appear to be connected to the UAV's power supply, CPU, engine or guidance units. "What do you figure the little yellow box is?"

"I figure that little yellow box is the little black box."

"A flight recorder?" Manning offered. "On a little rig like this?"

"You're right," Kurtzman agreed. "You don't usually see that on a UAV this size. But it's not attached to anything and it hasn't blown up. A drone is the same as any other vehicle. You don't want the flight recorder attached to anything else in the system. You want it to independently record what happens in case the vehicle gets lost, shot down, captured or, most important, hacked and hijacked."

"So it's on right now?" Hawkins asked.

"I suspect its transponder is pinging away."

As a demolitions man, Manning knew something about electronics. He eyed the little yellow box. "So the bad guys know where we are? Even here?"

"Depends on the range. That is a pretty small unit and you have flown it across the Baltic. It's not like you left it where it fell in Gdansk. Then again? Just about everything inside that rig appears to be about ten times more powerful than any standard, comparable commercial model UAV. Heck, a lot of its electronics are more sophisticated than similar-size stuff the United States military issues to our troops, including Special Forces. This fellow is not standard issue anywhere. It's made to look like a commercial rig, but it was made custom from top to bottom, to customer specifications, and that customer had money to burn."

"So the bad guys know where we are?" Hawkins asked again.

Kurtzman made a judgment call. "Normally, I would say no, unless of course the bad guys have their own satellite talking to it."

McCarter leaned in to the conversation. "You think these guys have their own satellite?"

"I would bet they have one. Or, given the level of sophistication, they can access someone else's satellite and the owners don't know about it."

Hawkins tried one more time. "So the bad guys know where we are?"

"Oh, I'd bank on it," Kurtzman confirmed. "Speaking of which, did you get the guns?"

Hawkins had taken the elite trajectory from United States Army to United States Army Ranger to Delta Force before he had taken a meeting with Mack Bolan and company. All of his life, guns were artillery pieces. Firearms were weapons. He had given up trying to explain this to Kurtzman. Hawkins often had to remind himself that despite the man's utter brilliance, Kurtzman was, and always would be, a civilian. "The guns arrived, Bear. Swedish steel is good steel." Hawkins made a face. "Too bad they're fifty years old…"

"Short notice?" Kurtzman vaguely milled his hands. "Sweden?"

"They're charmingly retro," quipped Calvin James from where he sat in an armchair assiduously cleaning and oiling his weapon. "I've met some old-timers at the SEAL meets who've told stories about being issued Swedish Ks." He made a face that matched Hawkins's. "In Nam—"

"Retro is right," Hawkins grunted.

The Swedish K submachine guns had no optics, laser designators, suppressors or tactical lights. They looked as though they belonged in a Bond film; nothing later than early Roger Moore, and Sir Roger probably would have scowled at them. They only operated on rock and roll and didn't even have a safety. Though that part Hawkins perversely kind of liked. He also kind of liked the fact that the models the CIA had procured were so old they had the original adapter for Finnish 50-round magazines. Hawkins got back to the matter at hand. He turned to McCarter. "So, boss. Do I do anything about the black box or not?"

McCarter leaned over the table and peered at the little yellow question of the day. "Bear, what do you think?"

"My guess is they have been able to track you, and they had all day to cross the Baltic or organize something in your neighborhood. If you want to move, they'll be able to track you. Maybe you want to do that and set a trap? Or you could remove it, put it on a train to nowhere and send the bad guys on a wild-goose chase, then maybe we can take a stab at tracking them."

It wasn't a bad plan and McCarter had considered it. However, in his opinion, Phoenix Force had already frittered away a day crossing the Baltic and hanging out in Sweden. He had to admit the food and rest had been welcome and that as an asset Nikita Propenko got more interesting by the minute. "Or I could destroy the black box right now, let our opponents know we found it and force the bloody sons of bitches to act before they lose us."

"There is that," Kurtzman conceded.

McCarter decided. "Hawk, gut it."

Hawkins unbolted the little yellow box from the UAV fuselage. He held it up and almost dropped it as it made a single, plaintive, electronic peep. "Bear?"

Kurtzman sighed. The cat was out of the bag. "If I had to guess, someone, somewhere, is now aware that the flight recorder has been removed from the UAV body."

"Then the jig is up and an attack is imminent." McCarter took the flight recorder and slid it across the table to Propenko. "Here, this is your first job. Take this and—"

The bottom of Propenko's scarred fist slammed down

on the flight recorder like a hammer. Bits of thick, weather-sealed plastic armor flew in all directions.

McCarter nodded. "And do something like that."

Propenko scooped up the little black box's innards and made a fist around them. Little bits of technology cracked and popped. The Russian rose, went to the sink, turned on the tap and flicked on the garbage disposal. Propenko dropped the shattered remnants down the drain and the flight recorder of Drone 1 met its final mastication. Mc-Carter noted that not only had the Russian's English gotten better but his leg seemed to be bothering him a lot less.

Everyone froze as the lights suddenly went out and the garbage disposal spun to a grinding, snapping halt. For a moment the only sound was the tap water trickling. The lights of the neighbors on the surrounding hillsides and the lights of Kalmar below didn't flicker a single watt. Someone had cut the safe house's power. Propenko turned the tap off.

"Gear up," McCarter ordered. "We're about to get hit."

Phoenix Force's armament might have been archaic but they still had their mission night-vision gear, armor and com equipment.

Jack Grimaldi's voice shouted across the link. "Two choppers just flew by! Low and fast and inbound on your position. They have door gunners and they are not Swedish Coastal Patrol!"

Encizo spoke from his lookout point in the loft. "I see them. Coming in hot."

McCarter spoke into the com. "Jack, get airborne."

Grimaldi was on the beach. He had flown Phoenix Force in illegally below Swedish air control radar and was three klicks south. He was about to rise and announce himself to Swedish airspace. "ETA five!"

McCarter nodded to himself. Phoenix Force was going to have to take the shot. He highly suspected the enemy ground teams were already on top of them. "Well, lads, they didn't sick the local bobbies on us, so it looks like they're spoiling for a fight. Let's knock one down! Backyard! Everyone except you, Fish. I think they'll sweep the main level."

"What if they sweep the loft?"

"Then you're screwed, mate!"

"Yeah, yeah, yeah..."

"All right. Backyard! Behind the chimney! Brick and mortar are our best friends! Watch your leads. They'll be flying over the house and nap of the earth up the mountainside. We might get a good shot. Go for the second bird!"

Phoenix flowed out the back door. The safe house's backyard was little more than a carved-out flat space with a brick barbecue attached to the chimney and a hot tub and a sauna. Beyond that the mountain ran almost straight up. The sound of rotors beat against the hillside. Multiple machine guns ripped into life and echoed over Kalmar. Bullets tore through the little mountain house, shattering glass and ripping wood. McCarter smiled as the rotors beat overhead. The enemy wasn't hovering and firing. Someone had told them what had happened in Gdansk. They were making fast gun runs.

The two choppers swung up the mountainside in echelon bare meters above the treetops of the near-vertical forest.

Grimaldi's voice came over the link. "These boys aren't bad."

"Screw 'em," Hawkins snapped.

"Rear target!" McCarter bellowed over the overwhelming rotor noise overhead. "Fire!"

Six stone-cold soldiers opened up. The two choppers were little more than thundering shadows save that they were commercial copters and their running lights flying straight up the mountain and barely overhead made for perfect target frames.

The chopper flying wing position took three hundred and fifty 9 mm rounds up his ass in the space of three seconds. The helicopter slewed and made a stuttering *whirp-whirp-whirp* noise as broken engine parts and severed hydraulic lines failed. The lead chopper summitted and disappeared into Sweden.

"Up yours, dude," Hawkins swore. He and the rest of the team slammed in fresh 50-round magazines.

The stricken copter nosed up to apex in the starlight. It suddenly auto-rotated and nosed downward. Sparks and smoke belched out of it and the helicopter began wildly swinging down the mountainside, still barely above the tree line and suicidally straight at the safe house.

Hawkins reassessed. "Aw, damn…"

Behind them Phoenix Force heard glass and wood breaking as the enemy team hit the house.

Fire exploded out of the kamikaze helicopter as it came on like doomsday.

McCarter roared. "Forward! Forward! Forward! Hug trees!"

Phoenix Force ran forward. Olympic synchronized swimmers would have admired how they vaulted the hot tub and the tiny, motorized-current lap pool. As a unit they each found a beautiful pine tree, ran just past it and then fell against it.

The burning helicopter plowed into the back of the safe house. Rotors snapped, fuel tanks ruptured, the house's natural gas tank detonated and the world went orange. McCarter had ordered his teammates to hug trees. They were mostly cringing as heat washed up the mountainside and black smoke followed in billowing waves. James had taken cover behind the sauna but the sauna was now on fire. Encizo burst from the house and was vaguely smoking as he ran out and hurled himself into the stationary lap pool.

McCarter watched the tail rotor of the enemy chopper slowly turn as heat rose through it. The chopper's blackened tail boom tilted through the roof of the burning house where the chimney used to be. The house was burning out of control. McCarter spoke into his link. "Jack, do we have movement?"

"You have ashes settling," Grimaldi returned. "Flawless victory."

"Phoenix, sound off!"

Everyone complied from behind their smoldering tree. Encizo rose from the lap pool and shot a thumbs-up.

McCarter surveyed his team. "Where's Nick?"

James and Manning snapped up their K guns to watch their flanks.

Propenko limped out of the burning safe house, the enemy UAV's fuselage halves clamped beneath his arm trailing scorched wires and guts. "I am figuring you are still wanting this."

"You bet, bubba!" Hawkins said.

McCarter was duly impressed but stayed on mission. "Jack?"

"Lead chopper is gone. I wanted a piece of him but he has headed straight north into the Swedish hinterland. You want me to pursue or do you want extraction?"

There was very little way Phoenix Force could wander down the mountain after a gunfight, ghost helicopter crash and a flaming cabin. McCarter could already hear police and emergency vehicle sirens down in Kalmar proper.

"Jack? We need extraction now."

"Where to? Swedish police channels are blowing up, much less Swedish air traffic control. My range is severely limited. Norway? Denmark? Pick a Baltic republic. They are all about incursions!"

"Poland," McCarter decided.

Grimaldi was unusually flabbergasted. "You want me to fly you back across the Baltic into Poland?"

"Right back to Gdansk," McCarter affirmed, and he felt good about it. "It's the last thing any idiot we are dealing with will ever expect."

CHAPTER FOUR

The Annex, Stony Man Farm

"Wow!" Akira Tokaido proclaimed. "Just...wow."

The insides of the little UAV Phoenix Force had captured in Gdansk were even more impressive in person. Phoenix Force had managed to get the unmanned vehicle's remains delivered to the United States Embassy in Stockholm and a private courier jet had gotten them to the United States in just under twenty-four hours. Tokaido, Kurtzman, Huntington Wethers and "Gadgets" Schwarz might as well have been in an operating theater.

The slightly scorched and smoke-stained patient had taken half a dozen steel fléchettes, but the damage had done nothing to mar the UAV's majesty in the eyes of everyone assembled. Save one. Able Team happened to be in-house and Carl "Ironman" Lyons stood like a stone Buddha as the geek talk flew fast and thick. He finally began to lose patience with all the oohing and ahhing.

"So, can Phoenix trace any of it?" Lyons inquired. The Able Team leader was the one Stony Man member who had been a policeman rather than a soldier before he had been tapped by the Farm. He had risen to the rank of detective, and he was very good at it. "Can I?"

Wethers stood tall and stretched from all the hunching over the table. The distinguished, brilliant, black university professor was a key member of the Stony Man Farm cybernetics team. If you were one of the bad guys, Hunt

Wethers turning his mind upon you and your operation as a problem that needed solving probably meant your ass. "Not exactly, Carl."

"What do you mean, not exactly?"

"It means, technically, these components are untraceable."

Lyons blinked. "What, it's a People's Republic knockoff and there are no serial numbers? We've dealt with that before. There's a factory someplace that manufactured this stuff, and they will have left their stink all over it."

Wethers shook his head. "Not this time."

"You're saying there's no factory?"

"Not precisely, no."

"It wasn't manufactured?"

"No."

Lyons shrugged. "You're saying some closet-case, geek genius just built it in his garage out of pipe cleaners, bubble gum and baling wire? Hunt, even pipe cleaners, bubble gum and baling wire have a trail. I know, I've followed them."

"You're exactly right, Carl. Except that this exceptional little machine was not manufactured or cobbled together by some—" Wethers rolled his eyes "—geek genius in his garage."

"You're saying it was conjured out of thin air?"

"Exactly!" Wethers smiled happily as if Lyons were a student who was slowly but surely bringing his grades up and just might graduate on time. "Every last piece of that UAV, from stem to stern, motors to rotors, GPS, CPU— you name it—guidance, flight controls and the fuselage itself, were all conjured out of thin air."

Lyons's blond brows slowly bunched as he chewed all this over. "You're saying it was printed."

"Carl, you get an A."

"Thanks, Prof." The Able Team leader surveyed what

he considered to be a shot-down toy helicopter. He was aware of the burgeoning world of 3-D printing, but mostly over the hysterics surrounding the idea of people being able to print their own guns. He hadn't found the single-shot, .22-caliber zip guns the size of a small megaphone all that impressive, but he knew the technology involved was growing by leaps and bounds and revolutionizing a lot of industries. "The whole thing?"

"Every component save the wiring was put together one micron-thin layer at a time."

"So we can trace the wires?"

"Oh, yeah." Tokaido nodded absently as he tried to make the UAV's CPU communicate with his laptop. The young hacker frowned. The CPU's encryption was fighting him. To his chagrin it was holding its own. Whoever had designed the CPU, its programming and encryption was starting to disturbingly remind Tokaido of himself. "The wires came from China."

"That's a start?"

Schwarz looked at his Able teammate wryly. "Carl, do you have any idea how many meters of wire the PRC manufactures per year?"

"Millions?" Lyons ventured.

"Billions."

"Oh."

"This specific component wire could have been bought in any Radio Shack in America or, for that matter, any place that sells wire on planet earth. I myself happen to own reams of it. Trying to trace the wire is a nonstarter, buddy. Sorry."

Lyons gazed down upon the remains of the immaculately conceived UAV. The detective part of his mind had already leapfrogged past the wire. "So this was an expensive proposition?"

Kurtzman shook his head at the wreckage in admiration. "Carl? You have no idea."

"Give me an idea."

"All right. The United States military has all sorts of unmanned vehicles, aerial, terrestrial and aquatic vehicles both surface combatant and submersibles. But this baby? Every last piece is custom designed and printed. You could not get Congress to pass a spending budget that included something like this. The Europeans? Forget it. The Chinese or the Russians? Maybe, just maybe, if they were really that motivated, but they would probably have to subcontract the work and why bother? They've got their own unmanned vehicles, not as good as ours—at least not yet. But again, why wouldn't they just use commercial parts and if the UAV got captured just deny everything? It's what they do. Someone cared enough to make this baby from scratch."

Lyons leaned over the table. "Cal shot this bird down over Gdansk, and it was watching a bunch of Russian *mafiya* assholes that had been sent to wipe out Phoenix, except they didn't know who Phoenix was or they wouldn't have been so stupid."

Kurtzman agreed. "Exactly."

Lyons's instincts spoke to him. "This is a private venture, a very well-funded private venture, and they've got an agenda we haven't even begun to fathom."

"That sounds about right," Wethers agreed.

Lyons nodded to himself. "Somewhere there is a money and a technology trail. Whoever these guys are they used Russian muscle in Gdansk. That's where the money trail starts. Where's David and Phoenix now?"

Barbara Price, Stony Man's mission controller, stepped into the room. "They're about to sneak into Russia."

Kaliningrad, Moskovsky District

IT WAS A BEAUTIFUL, sunny day in the Russian Federation *oblast*. The past three days of misting rain had stopped and the sun had broken out.

McCarter, Manning and Propenko were not in a very beautiful part of town. The Kaliningrad *oblast* was almost the Russian version of Okinawa. The exclave was a small landmass overloaded with naval bases, air bases and army bases. That many military men crammed into such a small amount of acreage required a great deal of off-duty entertainment.

In the Moskovsky District the strips that provided neon-lit clubs with strippers and liquor quickly gave way to the back streets that provided prostitutes and drugs. Those gave way to the rotting back alleys that provided shooting galleries and the worst of streetwalkers.

McCarter and his two-man team walked through the worst part of town at high noon. The area, much like most of its denizens, was decidedly unattractive in direct sunlight. Spent needles and cigarette butts littered the gutters. Russia did not believe in recycling, so no bums collected the sea of empty liquor bottles. Garbage and human sewage was openly dumped in the streets, and snarling, sprung-ribbed mongrel dogs ate the parts they could digest. Given the smell and the swarm of flies, McCarter was fairly certain one of the soiled-newspaper-covered bums they had passed was dead.

The plan was fairly simple. Phoenix Force had deliberately left Propenko's two remaining associates alive and sent an anonymous call to Polish State Security forces. The Polish State Police had arrived to find a fairly massive, recent battleground, a sea of bodies and weapons, and two Russian mobsters handcuffed to a truck. Polish gun-control laws were fairly lax compared to a great deal of Europe, but owning and operating antiaircraft guns was strictly illegal. Poles as a general rule had very little love for Russians, much less Russian gangsters without visas but with automatic cannons. The Polish state justice system was not particularly known for its leniency; it was, however, known for being utterly corrupt.

Neither Phoenix Force nor Propenko was surprised to learn that Ilya and Artyom Gazinskiy had made the Polish equivalent of bail and disappeared. Using Occam's Razor, the obvious answer was that whoever had bailed them out had most likely had them killed. However, Ilya and Artyom were Kaliningrad *mafiya* born and raised. They would have connections and, for a short time, possibly even people who would protect them. The question was where would they go to ground?

Propenko had not hired the Gazinskiy brothers. Rather, they had been bequeathed onto him by money-hemorrhaging parties unknown. Still, he had run the Gazinskiys in the Gdansk operation, listened to them drink and shoot their mouths off, and he felt as though he had a pretty firm idea of where they might be found if they were to be found at all.

That would be the worst part of the Moskovsky District.

Walking across the Polish/Russian Federation *oblast* border and walking to Kaliningrad had been a very bold move, but even in a militarized area like the *oblast*, borders were mostly long and unguarded things. In the city of Kaliningrad the team was simply three very dangerous-looking men in a very dangerous part of town. No one gave them a second look. In fact, most of the local denizens immediately cast their gaze down and refused to make eye contact.

Propenko pointed at a sagging, grimy, prewar, three-story tenement. All the windows were boarded up. It didn't have a neon sign or even a red light. However, over the door faded red paint in a very sloppy version of western graffiti read $$$Luffy-Land$$$.

"Luffy?" McCarter inquired.

"Ilya and Artyom brag about how they are 'pimping large' when not kicking ass. This is establishment. Luffy-Land."

Manning stared at the hideous, rotting building. He could almost swear the spavined structure was staring back, malevolently. "Why is Luffy written in English instead of Cyrillic?"

Propenko kept a remarkably straight face. "Classier."

"I thought you said they didn't speak English," McCarter mentioned.

"I lied. They speak better than me."

"Thanks."

"This serves, easier for you to interrogate, and I lied for them. This may be enough to make them trust for a few minutes. Gives us advantage. They only dealt with Nubian. Gummer was sniper, not seen. You, English, were mostly being smoke-obscured man behind cannons. We may be able to be lying our way in."

Manning nodded reluctantly at McCarter. "He keeps making sense. I'll give him that."

"How's your leg, Nick?" McCarter asked.

"Not bleeding again yet. Nubian does good work."

McCarter once again reconsidered that Propenko had marched twenty kilometers with a hole in his leg. "That he does."

The Russian gave McCarter an interested look. "What is plan?"

McCarter was pretty sure Propenko had a plan but the Russian was interested in seeing what his new boss was made of. "Oh, let's just walk right in."

"That was my plan, also."

McCarter walked up the short flight of sagging steps.

Manning and Propenko fanned out to either side to form a three-man wedge. The establishment was *mafiya*-owned and protected and it was the middle of the day. The door wasn't locked and no bouncer guarded the entrance. Mc-Carter and his team walked through the tiny foyer and entered Luffy-Land. Manning had seen the insides of bad bordellos from Bangkok to Tijuana. He looked around and was appalled.

"Oh, for God's sake..." Manning muttered.

Propenko nodded. "Yes."

It wasn't just that it was a bad bordello. Luffy-Land was an affront to all five senses. If Manning had possessed a sixth sense he was pretty sure the place's aura would be urine yellow and thrown-up lime green, and he was pretty sure he could feel it pulsing against his skin, and sticking. The smell reminded Manning of a rugby locker room if the players mostly didn't shower but wore perfume and smoked unfiltered cigarettes.

An interior wall had been knocked down to form the main "hospitality area." The decor consisted mostly of old torn movie posters taped over old torn and peeling paisley-pink wallpaper and old tattered couches. There were a few stolen Russian military folding tables and chairs for drinking and playing cards. Bad Russian rap with too much bass thudded from somewhere deeper in the building, and some sort of Slavic soap opera played on a big-screen TV on the wall.

Hardly anyone was around. A few of the ladies of the house sat drinking straight vodka and watching television just in case some soldier or sailor managed to sneak off base for some afternoon delight. If one's idea of love in the afternoon were middle-aged, Baltic women's rugby players in pancake makeup spilling out of 1980's vintage Jane Fonda workout wear, right down to the headbands and leg warmers, Luffy-Land might just be heaven. The working girls instantly picked up on the fact that the three very dangerous-looking men were not clients. They gave McCarter and his team a few heartbeats of bored and exhausted interest before returning to the TV and liquor.

"Gazinskiy brothers, pimpin' large," Manning mused.

Propenko made a noise. "Yes."

McCarter walked right up to the zinc bar. A huge, bald, sagging bull of a man in a white tracksuit sat watching a European League basketball game on a small TV. He had sleepy eyes but eyed McCarter with keen interest. His right hand disappeared under the bar. *"Dah?"* he grunted.

McCarter grunted back. "Ilya. Artyom."

Propenko took a cigarette from a pack of CCCPs lying on the bar without it being offered and lit up. The bartender looked as if he might say something and then thought better of it. Manning just leaned against the bar and glared. McCarter gave the bartender a dead "don't make me repeat myself" look. The bartender nodded again. *"Dah."* He jerked his head at one of the girls. "Roona!"

Roona sighed and scratched what looked like bed bug bites. She rose with a sigh to do the bartender's bidding. The bartender's right hand reappeared empty. He rose and took three cans of Baltika beer out of the cold case. He looked at the trio before him, frowned and reached up for some rather cleaner glasses and poured. The music in the back of the building suddenly got louder as a door opened. Ilya and Artyom Gazinskiy emerged, accompanied by three men even larger and goonier-looking than themselves. McCarter was bemused that both men wore $$$Luffy-Land$$$ logo T-shirts and he thought about acquiring one for Hawkins. Ilya's eyes bugged at the sight of Propenko. Ilya's fatter brother, Artyom, fired off a stream of surprised swearwords.

Propenko snarled. "Speak in English."

The Gazinskiy brother blinked.

"We want no one besides us to understand this conversation."

Ilya shrugged and spoke with a thick accent. "Hey, Nika, whatever you say, man. What happened to you? I thought you are maybe being in Guantanamo, or dead. And who are these guys? Friends of yours?"

McCarter and Manning drank beer and continued to stare at the Gazinskiy crew as though they were bugs.

"Mission went very bad, Ilya. I got shot and I have lost great deal of money."

"Hey, man. Hey!" The fat Gazinskiy held up his hands placatingly. "We all lost money! Me and Ilya? We lost friends!"

"I lie for you. Tell them you are idiot hammerheads not speaking English. You get picked up and slapped around a bit by Polish police. Then you make bail and twenty-four hours you are back in Luffy-Land dripping in beer and whores. Me? I had to kill some people and walk back. My leg hurts and I hate Poland."

"Hey, Nika. Me and Arty fought hard. We did not give up until they turned our own damn cannons on us."

"This I know. How you made bail when you are found at battle scene hand-cuffed to antiaircraft cannon in Poland? This I do not know."

McCarter glanced around Luffy-Land dryly and managed a TV-worthy Russian accent. "Girls did not pass hat."

Manning laughed unpleasantly.

The Gazinskiy brothers pulled back slightly. The Gazinskiy goon squad bristled and glanced back and forth at each other. They did not understand what was being said but they did not like seeing their bosses intimidated. Artyom was becoming both scared and angry. "Hey! Who are these guys?"

McCarter continued. "You did not make call. You were surprised. Who is bailing you out?"

Artyom stabbed out an accusing finger. "Listen! You—"

"I am listening, but I am not hearing answer."

Ilya grew some backbone. "You don't come into our place! Make us speak English!"

McCarter smiled without an ounce of warmth. "I already have."

The brothers Gazinskiy blinked in unison.

Propenko's already gravelly voice dropped a dangerous octave. "Who bails you out?"

Artyom made an unhappy noise. "We were told not to talk about it."

"Yes." McCarter nodded at the wisdom of this. "Who told you not to talk about it?"

Artyom threw a desperate look at Propenko. "Listen, I do not think you want to be screwing with these people."

Propenko glanced at McCarter and Manning and spoke the truth. "I know for fact you do not want to mess with these men."

Manning noted that Ilya was staring at McCarter, and the Russian's brows slowly knitted as if he was mentally doing long division counting on his fingers. It had been a decent ploy, but things were about to go FUBAR. Manning smiled and punched Ilya in the throat.

Gazinskiy the Elder did a short, remarkable imitation of a seagull squawk-and-flap and fell to the grimy floor. Propenko instantly followed suit. He shot the heel of his hand forward and made a credible attempt to shove Gazinskiy the Younger's nose into his brain. The Gazinskiy bullyboy brigade seemed to have spent more time stomping drunken sailors and looking tough than in getting in real fights; seeing their bosses fall in the space of two seconds left them hesitating for one more. It cost the one closest to Manning a kneecap. It cost the one closest to Propenko a left eye.

The last remaining goon screamed something defiant in Russian. He pulled up his tracksuit jacket with his left hand and went for his gun with his right. McCarter slapped a hand over each of the Russian's wrists and gave him the Danish Kiss.

McCarter was happy to acknowledge the English had not invented the head butt, but he was rather insistent that they had perfected it. English soccer hooligans would have squealed in delight as a cranium of the United Kingdom met a skull of the Russian Federation and the hammerhead dropped like a cow that had just reached the end of the slaughter chute.

McCarter ignored the dancing lights as he caught motion behind him. The bartender swung. McCarter had known a lot of bartenders who kept baseball or cricket bats behind the bar. He had about one heartbeat to note that this was the first bat he had seen that had been scored with shallow, cross-hatching saw cuts and filled with several dozen safety razor blades. He stepped into the blow, caught the bartender's wrist and heaved his sagging bulk over the bar. He kept the weapon as the barman landed badly in a clatter of bar stools.

McCarter regarded the hideous bludgeon he had acquired. "Nice hate stick, old son. You just earned yourself an appointment with your old Doc Marten, and the doctor is in." McCarter gave the bartender his boots until the big man was reduced to twitching, bleeding and wheezing.

The floor of Luffy-Land was a sea of broken, moaning, screaming Russians. None of the girls had moved an inch or batted an eye, much less screamed. They seemed to have found the spectacle slightly more interesting than their soap opera. They watched avidly to see what might happen next.

McCarter turned to his team and held up the razor-enhanced baseball bat. "Did you see this?"

Propenko grunted. "I have seen this. In Vladimir Central Prison. It was used for rectal purposes."

Manning gazed heavenward. "Could have gone my whole life…"

Propenko held out his hand.

McCarter handed him the hate stick. The Russian went and took a knee on Artyom's chest. "I told you. You do not want to screw with these men. Now, answer their questions."

Artyom bubbled and gasped around his shattered septum and the blood filling his mouth. "Listen, Nika, we can—"

"Do not talk to me." Propenko glanced back at McCarter. "Talk to him."

Artyom babbled. *"Christos…"*

"Do not talk to Jesus. These men are your god. God helps those who help themselves." The Prison Spetsnaz officer spit on the razor club meaningfully. "Help yourself, Artyom. Help your brother. While you still can."

Artyom Gazinskiy whimpered and began helping himself and his brother.

CHAPTER FIVE

The Annex

Akira Tokaido sang to himself. "Money, money, money, muh-nee… Money!"

Kurtzman and Wethers exchanged weary looks of mutual sympathy.

"Boy couldn't carry a tune in a bucket…" Kurtzman muttered.

Wethers glanced over at the young Japanese-American hacker. One of these days someone was just going to have to tell him that ponytails for computer geeks had gone out of fashion. "And he has exactly as much rhythm as one would expect…"

However, Kurtzman admitted to himself, Tokaido's instincts were correct. When you lacked a face, a fingerprint or a smoking gun—though Phoenix had rather boldly latched onto a pair of smoking automatic cannons—you followed the money trail.

The brothers Gazinskiy had told a fascinating tale and almost none of it made any sense. It would have been clear to a child that the Gazinskiy boys were tools and nothing more. No one would miss them.

Nikita Propenko was a power tool—a tool of a higher order—but even if he died badly and in public, little more would happen than a few dangerous men in Moscow drinking a shot of vodka in his name, shaking their heads and muttering "He never should have gone into Poland."

Propenko had been offered a big fee, big enough to tempt him from his lucrative private work in Russia and its former republics. They had hired a small army of hammerheads but they had also hired a very dangerous and disciplined man to run them. The cannons had been his idea and he had enough pull to buy artillery on the black market. Anyone other than Phoenix Force would have been wiped out, captured or extracted, taking heavy casualties every step of the way. Propenko had demanded cold, hard Euros.

The Gazinskiy brothers, besides being low-rent muscle and peddlers of extremely low-rent flesh, were also low-rent cyber criminals. They had a fairly lucrative sideline running online scams in former stan-suffixed Russian republics where entire rural areas were just starting to explore the internet and connectivity.

The Gazinskiys had accepted bitcoins as payment.

The Central Bank of the Russian Federation had issued a statement stating that it considered the exchange of bitcoins for goods, services or currencies a "dubious activity." This was a veiled threat, but both an admonition and an admission that the Russian Federation currently had almost no ability to regulate it or control bitcoin transactions.

Bitcoins were the first, real, online alternate currency and, despite many national governments trying to crack down on their use, they were still the choice of cyber geeks who wanted their transactions off the grid, as well as cyber criminals that wanted the same.

The Gazinskiy brothers had used their massive infusion of bitcoins to buy and sell drugs in Kaliningrad without the Russian *mafiya* "made men" above them knowing about it. Bitcoins were the currency of the cyber savvy; the technology behind them and the people running it continuing to evolve faster than governments and traditional financial institutions could adapt. The jury was out as to whether they were an abomination, the way of the future or little more than a temporary blip on the world economic radar. What they offered was anonymity and transactions at the rate of high-speed cable that left regulators scrambling.

Akira Tokaido was the kind of man who left entire intelligence agencies, state security services and militaries scrambling in his wake. This was just his game. His current problem was that he was not cracking government agencies, terrorist cells or databases; he was fighting people exactly like himself.

He was relishing the challenge.

"Money, money, money, muh-nee…" Tokaido howled tonelessly. "Money!"

"Akira?" Kurtzman asked.

"No, these guys are good, really good." Tokaido stared at the lines of code scrolling down his massive main screen. His cursor moved across the streams like the planchette of an Ouija board. "This is going to take a while."

"No, Akira, I mean—"

"Could you shut up?" Wethers finished.

Tokaido gave Wethers a vaguely hurt look and shoved in his ear buds. He went back to examining data and began nodding his head. Without thinking his lips started moving. "Money, money…"

Kurtzman stared at Wethers helplessly. "Phoenix still at Luffy-Land?"

Wethers cracked his first smile of the day, and it had been a long day. "Word is they're getting us T-shirts."

"Didn't know it was a franchise."

Wethers considered the file they had compiled on their subjects. "Mrs. Gazinskiy raised herself some ambitious boys, if not bright ones."

"Phoenix has put the Gazinskiys to work. They've put out the word that Propenko is alive, very pissed off and wants either payback or to get paid." Kurtzman grinned. "Now we wait to see who comes knocking and whether they're carrying checkbooks or more automatic cannons."

"They've worked with less," Wethers pointed out.

Kurtzman was very well aware of that, but Kaliningrad was a bad neck of the woods to get caught in.

The exclave was very nearly a militarized city-state and while Phoenix could run roughshod over the local criminals, if police and military got involved they would be met with an overwhelming force that would take a very dim view of them if they were captured. Calvin James would stick out like a sore thumb. They had snuck him in under cover of night, but if he stepped out in daylight it would be like a unicorn sighting. The Kaliningrad *oblast* was one very white wood.

Wethers knew exactly what the Stony Man cybernetics chief was thinking. He was thinking it, too. He was also trying to think positively.

"Plus, the bad guys absolutely got shut down in Sweden. Propenko is claiming to have killed some people and escaped. He is the only solid lead they have to work with at the moment. Whoever hired him will be very interested in debriefing him."

"Which may include torturing the living hell out of him and his new friends."

"There is that, but Propenko has a very heavy reputation. I think there is a decent chance they might even rehire him, and his new friends."

Kaliningrad, Luffy-Land

CALVIN JAMES REPORTED from the roof. "We've got company. A limousine and she's riding low. I'm saying she's armored. Two SUVs riding escort on the limo's twelve and six."

"Copy that," McCarter replied. "It's showtime."

While Phoenix had waited, they had checked on the apartment Propenko had been renting. Nothing was missing, but the Russian reported that someone with a fair degree of skill had searched the place. Propenko had filled a bag with clothes and guns and gear.

Kaliningrad wasn't exactly the fashion capital of Paris or Milan, but he'd bought the most expensive off-the-rack suits available for Phoenix Force. McCarter, Manning and Propenko looked decently dapper and decidedly dangerous. McCarter had decided to stay with the three-man team he had presented to the Grazinskiys and to keep James and Encizo as unseen aces in the hole.

The limo pulled to a halt outside. Two men each jumped out of the backs of the SUVs and one man raced to open the limo's door. A man about six feet tall and nearly five feet wide emerged.

Propenko grunted as he peered through one of the boarded-up windows.

"Someone of note?" McCarter asked as he peered through his opening.

"Gospodin Gaz," the Russian affirmed. "Minor *mafiya* royalty."

McCarter had operated with and against Russians many times and this was far from his first time operating on Russian Federation soil. He knew a fairly extensive range of Russian words and phrases. *Gospodin Gaz* roughly translated into "Mr. Gas."

McCarter considered the brutal, Mack-truck-built man emerging from the limo. "Glorified bagman," he mused.

"Correct. Gaza has moved far up food chain from simple collections."

McCarter was fairly certain he didn't want to know but asked, anyway. "Why do they call him Mr. Gas?"

"Back in day, when collection proved difficult? They

send Gaz. He comes with a can of gasoline. Perhaps for place of business. Perhaps for house. Perhaps for you."

"Nice," Manning commented.

"He did five-year stint in Siberian maximum hard-labor colony. He ran it for four and a half."

McCarter eyed Propenko. "You two have run into each other before?"

"We are acquainted." The Russian blew cigarette smoke and shrugged. "Gaz also known for loyalty and dealing square. Sometimes he is called in as third party during difficult negotiations."

McCarter watched the Russian mobster, flanked by his five men, lumber up the steps. None of the guards wore tracksuits or gold chains. They dressed well and smelled more ex-military than musclemen or hammerheads. Save one, who was smaller, wiry like a terrier and seemed as agitated as one.

"So this could be a positive development."

Propenko lit himself a CCCP. "Perhaps."

The doorbell rang.

McCarter glanced at the brothers Gazinskiy. They sat forlornly on a couch. The ladies of the establishment had been sent home and the hammerheads had been carted off to a non-licensed infirmary that dealt with these kinds of situations. Ilya wore a neck collar and the shattered remnants of Artyom's septum were held together by medical tape. McCarter nodded at Artyom.

The nasally impaired gangster got up and went to the door. McCarter and Propenko went to the bar. Manning stayed off to one side and smiled at Artyom.

"Not one word," Manning warned.

Artyom flinched and answered the door. Gaz's men flowed into Luffy-Land, forming a skirmish line. Gaz ignored the Gazinskiys and walked up to the bar. Propenko slid the pack of cigarettes down the zinc bar. "Let us speak English."

Up close, Gaz was a very ugly man. Someone had flattened his nose the way Manning had flattened Artyom's, but he had never had it fixed. His thick-fingered hands were red and scarred. The mobster's ugly face was blotched from years of heavy drinking. His thick, gray hair was Soviet-era cosmonaut. He smiled to reveal yellowed, crooked teeth and shrugged as if the matter was of no importance. "Sure, Nika. If it pleases you." He lit a cigarette. "You look good."

"You look as I remember you."

"I will take this as compliment. Piles are killing me."

"Too much easy living?" McCarter asked.

The Russian eyed McCarter.

McCarter noted that the Russian seemed utterly unperturbed and didn't ask Propenko about his new friend.

Gaz grinned but his eyes were cold. "I had plenty hard labor in Siberia. Enough for lifetime." Gaz deigned to glance at the Gazinskiy brothers sitting obediently on the couch. The mobster waved his cigarette to encompass Luffy-Land. "Speaking of soft life, you boys going into business? I tell you, Gazinskiys not made-men. Never will be, but they are paid up. Not sure Luffy-Land is worth headache for you."

McCarter glanced around Luffy-Land's dubious charms. The wiry guy was mad-dogging him but McCarter ignored him. "No, but it got us a meeting with you, *Gospodin*."

Gaz made a noise. McCarter had just called him "sir."

"Call me Gaz. my friends do."

"Offer you a beer, Gaz?"

"Always!" Gaz raised a scarred eyebrow. "Unless there is something stronger?"

McCarter went behind the bar and poured three shots of

Absolut. His was barely a splash. The three men downed them amiably.

Gaz smacked his lips. "So, Nika, word is you are unhappy."

"None of us are happy," McCarter remarked.

The young, skinny, agitated Russian took a step out of the skirmish line. "Who is this guy? Who cares if he is unhappy? He owes us money! He owes us blood!"

McCarter gave Gaz a patient look. Gaz sighed and spoke too low for the skinny man to hear. "That is the *Pan* Dory."

McCarter nodded sympathetically. *Pan* was an ancient Slavic honorific for "royalty." Dory was the diminutive for the Russian given name Dorofei. Russian honorifics and given name diminutives were never mixed, except with great affection or even greater condescension. Gaz had just sneered and called the man "The Little Lord."

McCarter began to see the situation very clearly. "He is supposed to be learning from you?"

"Supposed to be. Father ranks rather high in certain circles in Kaliningrad."

"And Luffy-Land is part of the little kingdom his father has given him," McCarter concluded.

"Yes. I am afraid Gazinskiy brothers earn for Dory. You have taken Luffy-Land. As I say, we have slight problem."

"Slight problem?" Dory stalked forward. "We have big problem! Who are these pricks?"

Manning stepped forward and intercepted him.

"And who is this smiling…" Dory trailed off.

McCarter was smiling at Dory. It was the special smile he reserved for intimidating unpleasant people. The smile that convinced very bad people that he was considering killing them and the deciding factor would be the next thing that came out of their mouth.

Dory met Manning's gaze, blinked first and closed his mouth.

Gaz started dropping knowledge. He nodded at Propenko. "You know this man, and his reputation, Dory?"

"That is Nika—"

"Yes. Well, Nika Propenko is now mercenary and now doing jobs outside Russian Federation. Things went bad in Poland, and I am thinking he call upon his new Western friends." Gaz put his hands on his chest and made an attempt at looking personally hurt by this development. "Instead of calling on old friends and homeboys."

Propenko dragged deeply on his cigarette. "Hard to know who to trust."

Dory regained a tiny amount of outrage. "Propenko brings foreign mercenaries into a place I control?" He shot a nervous, angry look at Manning. "And this smiling asshole is—"

Manning spoke the German he had been raised with. "Your worst nightmare."

Gaz's head snapped around. "German?"

Manning smiled menacingly. *"Jah."*

McCarter watched wheels turn in Gaz's mind.

The Berlin Wall had officially fallen in 1989. Before it had, East Germany had been an Orwellian nightmare. Their secret police and border guards had made the same services of their Soviet overlords look like mild-mannered milquetoasts, and in the Eastern bloc, East German organized crime was the worst of the worst and feared out of all relation to their numbers and actual influence. In Russia, even to this day, German was the language of the enemy. In Russian criminal circles, a smiling man speaking German was the Slavic version of the white devil.

Propenko had been doing work for criminals and parties unknown of late, and the fact that he had escaped from Poland, come back and kicked ass in Kaliningrad was causing shock waves. That he appeared to have a Nazi devil on a leash only added to the wampum he was walking with.

"Nika, my friend," Gaz asked, "what is it you and your friends want?"

"Money," McCarter suggested.

"Payback," Propenko snarled.

Manning dropped the dead smile and shrugged. "A job?"

Gaz shoved out his shot glass and McCarter poured. The Russian leaned in and spoke low. "Listen, despite certain discrepancy and—" he looked back at Dory "—disrespect, we can make this work out." Gaz looked at McCarter warily and turned back to Propenko. "Forgive me, Nika. But you act like this man is your superior."

Propenko simultaneously lied through his teeth and told the stone-cold truth at the same time. "The last time I took job from man in West?" He lifted his chin at McCarter. "I worked for him. He got me out of jam."

Gaz chain-lit another cigarette. "I believe you. Your reputation is known. You say you want payback?"

"I was shot, captured and interrogated. Torture was amateurish, lightweight, Western. But as fighters these men were unbeatable."

"You say you escaped?"

"I got myself out of that situation and made it across border. It beat being handcuffed to truck and waiting for Polish police."

"I am a middleman, Nika, but I have been informed that certain parties would like to know much more about what happened in Poland. It was suggested that perhaps I scoop you up and bring you to them, or perhaps even show up with can of gasoline. I suggested I talk to you first."

"Thank you."

Gaz glanced at McCarter and Manning. "I am thinking I made correct choice. Tell me, Nika. These men who captured you and interrogated you... You think you can find them again? It will be worth great deal of money."

"Perhaps. But if I can't?" It was Propenko's turn to glance at McCarter and Manning. "These men can."

War Room, Stony Man Farm

"SO WE'RE BAIT," Carl Lyons concluded.

It was a simple plan, but from where Lyons sat it sucked. Able Team was to go to Europe, to essentially pose as Phoenix Force to fool the enemy, while the real Phoenix Force led the enemy straight to Able Team.

"That's about it," Price confirmed. "I discussed it with Hal, and he agrees we're boxed in." Price was referring to Hal Brognola, Director of the Special Operations Group. Brognola was fully engaged running interference in Washington, DC, but was in constant touch with his mission controller. "Risky, yes, but it's our best bet. And he's got the President's go-ahead."

Rosario Blancanales shrugged and looked at Schwarz. "Wouldn't be the first time we're the cheese in the mousetrap."

All three members of Able Team were seated at the War Room conference table with Price and Kurtzman.

Price outlined the plan. "When the bad guys went after Phoenix the first time, they had eyes in the sky. We think they will again, and we think they are going to make one hell of an attempt at capturing you. Whoever is behind all this is extremely well-funded, has access to the absolute latest technology and seems to be up to something. The good news is we are as much a mystery to them as they are to us. And, after Gdansk and Karmal, the first two rounds go to the Farm. Whoever these people are, they must be in pretty desperate need to find out who we are and fast. The flip side of that is we have to expect the next fight to get real nasty."

Schwarz considered the technology he had been examining for the past twenty-four hours. "This sure stinks like a trap."

"A trap within a trap within a trap," Kurtzman agreed. "It's very Russian. The advantage we have is that it is a trap on both sides, and Phoenix Force will be sort of a reverse Trojan horse on the inside. I think the most likely scenario is that Phoenix and whomever the bad guys send along with them will be cannon fodder and a diversion. You need to expect to get hit by a second force, and expect them to come in with overwhelming force. Given the tech they put in their UAVs, we have to expect they have access to satellite imaging and absolutely top-notch ground surveillance. So will we. It will be a question of who catches who watching who first."

Blancanales thought it was the worst plan in the world except that no one was coming up with anything better. He turned to his mission controller. "What is Phoenix's disposition going to be?"

Price started laying out details. "David is sticking with a three-man team of him, Manning and Propenko going in. The good news for you is that Cal and Hawk will be seconded to Able Team."

Schwarz pumped his fist. "Yes!"

"Jack will involve *Dragonslayer* and he will be armed. The bad guys must think we are some sort of clandestine operation—they probably won't be expecting a gunship. Of course, given what happened in Karmal, we have to expect they may have air power, as well."

Blancanales perked up hopefully.

"Does that mean we get Rafe, as well?" Lyons asked.

"You do. We have reason to suspect the Russian force they give Propenko will be considered expendable. When it hits the fan, we think there is a good chance they will follow Propenko wherever he leads. So you and Phoenix may end up with a small army of your own. And, yes, Encizo will be on your team."

Lyons brought up the question of the day. "There was already a mysterious battle on the Polish-Kaliningrad border. Don't you think the Polish police and border patrol are pretty stirred up as it is?"

"If it comes down to a pitched battle, you will have to expect Polish security forces to come in fast and hard," Price admitted.

Blancanales spoke for himself and the team. "This sucks."

"This is our best shot to get something real on the bad guys—on the ground, eyes in the sky or in cyber space. The good news is we are positioning you absolutely primo gear. The bad news?" Barbara Price stared fondly at her boys. "You need to be in Poland in twelve hours."

CHAPTER SIX

Kaliningrad. Warehouse District.

Propenko snapped his team to attention. He scowled over the nine men standing in line as if he might just condescend to let them lick his boots, but only the soles. He shook his head in disgust and pointed at McCarter. "This man is God! I am prophet! Do you have any questions?"

None did.

Manning smiled and spoke low to McCarter. "Nice touch."

Gaz the Bagman had turned out to indeed be a bag of money.

Rather than accept bully boys from Moscow, Propenko had taken the money and privately gone shopping. It had been a risk, but McCarter had gone along with it. Propenko had used his personal connections and found ten Russian military policemen of the Western Military District, special *oblast* unit, who were more than willing to make some cash on the side. Save that one was missing; McCarter was pleased with the transaction.

All of the assembled men had the Russian Federation equivalent of fast-reaction-team training and all of them spoke English. Several were local boys and spoke Polish. All had proved themselves as tough, capable and utterly corruptible soldiers. Being utterly corrupt military police in Fortress Kaliningrad, they had easily been able to acquire high-quality weapons and gear. They had brought a truckload of body armor, night-vision goggles, com gear and stubby, Kashtan submachine guns with sound suppressors and red-dot sights. As well, there was an assortment of grenades, though, the Phoenix Force leader knew, they were less than lethal flash-stuns and sting-ball, blunt-trauma weapons.

McCarter and Manning had helped themselves. It was good kit, but it was light, "slender gear'" as McCarter's father would have said.

Every scenario the group had run ended up with the real enemy force coming in hard and heavy. Phoenix Force would have to rely on the reinforced Able Team and *Dragonslayer* to make up the difference.

Propenko strode up to McCarter and saluted. "They are ready for your inspection."

"You said you'd hired ten."

"I did."

"Where is our missing military policeman?"

"Do not know. Missing man is youngest. Perhaps he is late, or screw up getting off duty tonight."

"Well, then, we'll just have to make do, won't we?" McCarter scanned his squad. "They seem likely enough, I'll give them that."

"Good news is they are Russian boys. They have seen far too many action movies and shows on cable television. Trained from childhood to think officer with English accent is best of best. They will think you are James Bond or General Montgomery or both if you let them believe. I suggest you do."

"Right." McCarter strode forth and stopped just short of being a Monty Python skit as he laid it on thick. "Right! Listen here, you communist heathens!"

Several of the men smirked.

McCarter allowed it. He wanted cohesion and camaraderie on this one. Propenko could instill blind fear and obedience if the situation warranted. "The situation is simple. There happen to be some right bloody bastards in Poland who don't belong there, and there are men in Moscow with money. Manna from bloody heaven, amounts of money, my lads!

"The pricks in Poland, who are squatting there quite unreasonably, have given the men in Moscow grief, added insult on top of injury, and cost them blood and money. The men in Moscow have shown the infinite good taste and wisdom to hire me. I have sent forth Mr. Propenko, and he has hired you. I am informed you are all Military Police—Voennaya Politsiya, VP—Western District, special unit. The best of the best! You know how to conduct a raid, how to kick ass and know how to take prisoners and collect evidence! The money men in Moscow would dearly love to speak with these men, so alive if possible. I am informed we will have satellite and ground level intelligence."

The Russians nodded and made affirmative noises.

"You are all being issued communication gear. All battle instructions will be in English. This is Operation Red Wolf. We are Wolf Pack."

The Russians liked the sound of it.

McCarter snarled. "Wolf Pack! Sound off!"

The Russians shouted out in domino effect. "Wolf One. Wolf Two. Wolf Three. Wolf Four, Wolf..."

"Memorize it," McCarter ordered. "From now on we have no names. I am Alpha." McCarter snapped his head toward Propenko. "He is Lobo."

Wolf One was a black-haired, bearded, buff individual and he gave Manning a wary look. "Him?"

"He is Werewolf. He will be operating independently, with the biggest bloody rifle you have ever seen. If all goes well, we go in tonight. Until then, I am told we have been given unlimited privileges at Luffy-Land."

Several Wolf Pack men made smothered throw-up noises. Others laughed.

"Right!" McCarter nodded at a table covered with steaming aluminum takeout dishes. "We have cots and Kazak barbecue. I personally recommend you stay here, eat your fill, check your weapons and sleep if you can. If we get the go-ahead? It will all happen very fast."

The men nodded and started to break up.

Propenko roared something Old Testament in Russian. The nine men snapped to attention.

McCarter gazed long and hard at his squad. The nine men absolutely refused to meet his gaze. McCarter suddenly pumped his fist and bellowed as only an old-school British Officer could. "Wolf Pack!"

The squad roared in return. "Wolf Pack!"

"Right! Fall out!"

The men fell out nodding and making enthusiastic noises. They seemed excited about the plan and thankful to be a part of it.

Outside the warehouse a motorcycle screamed to a halt. A lanky, blond young man came running in breathlessly laden with two heavy, bulging, XL gear bags. Propenko already had a face like a skull. Filled with fury, it was a death's head to behold. He rounded on the young VP soldier. He didn't yell. The young man went pale as Propenko read him the riot act in a guttural hiss only the two of them could hear.

"Mr. Propenko!" McCarter shouted.

Propenko snapped around. *"Dah!"*

"Bring that man to me!"

Propenko escorted the man into McCarter's presence. McCarter nodded at Gary Manning, who drew his pistol. Propenko shoved the man to his knees. The nine Russians stared in sudden shock and apprehension at their young comrade.

"Mr. Propenko. Who the bloody hell is this and what is he doing in my warehouse?"

"The late one." Propenko glared bloody murder at the young man. "The...how do you say? The rookie!"

McCarter's voice suddenly dropped to a frighteningly conversational tone. "And where have you been, my good man?"

Manning pointed his pistol at the young man's head.

The young man gulped. "Ukov, Maksim. Reporting for duty! Regretting delay!"

"You weren't talking to someone, were you? Perhaps telling them you were coming here?"

"No, sir. I am told we are perhaps performing raid. Perhaps snatch-and-grab. I was acquiring materials."

"What materials?"

Maksim Ukov shrugged off his pack straps and opened one of the bags. "Gas masks and—"

"What the bloody hell do I need gas masks for?" McCarter thundered, though he was secretly grateful for them.

Ukov showed some guts and managed a sly look. "In case we use these?"

The young Russian opened up his other bag. It was full of light blue grenades the size and shape of tallboy beer cans and covered with Cyrillic writing.

Propenko squinted at the munitions and made a noise of approval.

"Mr. Propenko?" McCarter inquired.

Propenko showed a rare smile. "Blue Blitz."

McCarter was aware of it. "Knock-out gas."

Manning lowered his pistol.

Ukov grinned hopefully. "Thirty cartridges, if it pleases?"

McCarter gazed down at the young Russian. "Well, you romantic schemer, you."

Gulf of Gdansk

ABLE TEAM WAITED, along with three members of Phoenix Force, for the imminent attack. Carl Lyons looked over their defenses one more time. The situation wasn't as bad as it could be. Barbara Price had once again done very well for them with very little. The Polish duck-hunting lodge was more than a hundred years old. The walls were made of heavy stone-and-mortar masonry. The windows were narrow, could almost be described as firing slits and had heavy shutters to resist Baltic storms. The front, side and back doors were incredibly thick, iron-bound oak that looked as if they might be petrifying rather than weathering. Most of the house was bulletproof up to .30 caliber. The main approach to the lodge was a bit of raised single-lane road with wetlands overgrown with small trees on either side. The house sat on an acre or two of raised land with larger willows and alders forming a tiny forest. Behind the house the land fell away into a genuine fen that turned into a duck hunter's dream of a swamp that drained into the gulf.

It was cold and wet and wretched, but it was defendable.

The lay of the land was in the Stony Man team's favor, and out in the fen sat Jack Grimaldi in *Dragonslayer*. The chopper still wore her pontoons but she had machine guns slaved atop each one of them and rocket pods on stalks on either side of the fuselage. All of the equipment was mounted with explosive bolts and could be ejected into the marsh with the press of a button.

Encizo had built a cheery fire and his teammates chewed duck jerky and dunked black bread into steaming mugs of black tea with lemon and honey. Lyons lifted his chin as the wind moaned against the shutters. He almost felt bad for Calvin James. The Navy SEAL was somewhere out there in the wind, rain, darkness and muck watching the main approach to the lodge. It was a shit detail, but of course that was what SEALs did.

Lyons clicked his com unit. "How's it hanging, Cal? Cold as a well digger's ass?"

"Gdansk is God's country," James replied dryly. "I'm coming back."

"Copy that." Lyons looked to Schwarz and checked his watch. Schwarz sat by his laptop and a small array of communications and security gear. He'd spent the day putting surveillance gear and some unpleasant surprises for trespassers around the manse. "How are we doing?"

"We have two more hours of satellite window, then we are going to have a half-hour gap before the Farm can get eyes on us again. We've—" Schwarz sat straight as his computer pinged a message from McCarter.

Coming in hard

"We've got Wolf Pack on the way!" Schwarz announced.

Lyons strode over and messaged back.

Come and get it

Kurtzman's window popped up on Schwarz's screen. "Able. Be advised. You have major movement to the north and south."

Lyons leaned over and looked at the satellite image. They had heat signatures, and a lot of them. "Wolf Pack is coming in from the east."

"Affirmative."

"Where the hell did these guys come from?"

Kurtzman wasn't happy. The bad guys had snuck under his radar. "It's like they popped up out of the earth."

Lyons wasn't happy, either. The bad guys had managed to get into the swamp behind them. "So we have to assume Wolf Pack has been compromised."

"We always did."

"And they are heading into cross fire."

"That is correct. I already informed them."

"Tell Jack to get airborne, message McCarter and tell him to plan B as hard as he can."

"Copy that."

The Able Team leader took up his weapon. "Able! Gear up! Here it comes!"

The Game Room

PYLE SAT HUNCHED in front of his massive screen. His fingers hammered his keyboard. "They're communicating!"

"With whom?" Kun asked.

"It's scrambled. They have to be bouncing it off a satellite."

"How many satellites could be giving them real-time imaging and intelligence?"

"No. It's communication. It could be being bounced from multiple—"

"That is not what I asked you."

Pyle flinched and, nervous habit, tugged at his nose ring. "You think they're piggy-backing?"

"Currently, somewhere on this planet," Kun stated what to him was completely obvious, "there is a room much like this one. Inside it there are men, much like us. They are our real enemies. We are not taking advantage of poor native criminals or guerilla fighters in Africa or a 'Stan' country. We have encountered another genuine player. I am not sure whether they are state-sponsored, rogue or deniables. Regardless, we have a real game on hour hands."

Pyle called up his file on all satellites and their orbits. "Checking."

Rong sat in front of three screens swiping his fingers across them to pull up and expand images. This was the action, and absolutely the part of his job he loved. It was a cross between a strategy game and a first-person shooter, but the blood and the stakes were real. Not for him, but nevertheless it gave him a thrill as none other. Seventy-two hours ago, the first Battle of Gdansk, as Rong liked to call it, was the first battle he had ever lost since moving from online gaming to gaming with human lives in the Game Room. That loss still stung. A lot.

He watched the enhanced thermal images of Propenko and the meat shields sweeping toward the lodge in a very professional manner and felt a glimmer of foreboding. "I don't like this Alpha, International Man of Mystery bastard, him or his Wolf Pack. I don't like them at all."

Kun watched his screens. He didn't like Alpha and his Wolf Pack, either, except for the fact that he loved them. Kun loved challenges. He lit a cigarette, reached into his mini-fridge and mixed himself the single vodka martini he would allow himself until the battle was over. Kun normally didn't care for alcohol or its effects, as it dulled his senses for the experiences he enjoyed the most, but in battle the prop was important to him. His team perked up at the sight of him mixing it.

Junior Pyle grinned. He and Rong, on the other hand, were stopping just short of main-lining energy drinks through an IV. "Here we go!"

"In case of trouble, or when the bell tolls," Rong gleefully intoned. "Have no fear, because Bond has Seoul."

Kun loved Rong and what he was going to do to him even more.

Rong broke the mood. "Shit!"

"What?"

"Wolf Pack just stopped moving."

Kun swiped his screen and expanded his view of the skirmish line that had suddenly stopped. "They know."

"What do we do?"

Kun spoke a sentence that pleased him very much. "Let the Wolf Pack have it. Give them all of it."

Heat signatures popped up in the thermal imaging as engines roared into life.

Wolf Pack

McCARTER READ THE message about the enemy moving in from north and south. The question now was would he be able to weld Wolf Pack to his will. He'd held up his fist and the pack's fighting line halted. He took a brief meeting with Manning and Propenko and then addressed the men. "Lads? We are righteously rogered!"

The Russians vaguely rippled in place. They clutched their weapons and made unhappy noises as they didn't quite understand but feared the sum of all fears.

"Men? We are betrayed. We have enemy units coming in with overwhelming force from the north and the south."

Engines stuttered and belched into life in the surrounding fen in agreement.

Russian swearwords snarled out of the trees.

Propenko raised his voice for the first time. "English is battle language!"

"They have armor! God!"

"Who said that?" McCarter roared.

"We're screwed!"

McCarter recognized Maksim's voice. "Mr. Propenko. Bring that man to me." Propenko loped into the alders and seized Maksim by his hair. He dragged the young man screaming into McCarter's presence by one hand almost effortlessly while he withdrew his knife with the other. Maksim screamed.

"English!" Propenko hissed.

"We are dead!"

McCarter took a risk and tapped his Farm-issue phone. "Ironman, we have armor on the move."

"Copy that. We have eyes on."

"We are counterattacking to the south. Get Jack airborne and—" Gunfire crackled in the direction of the Baltic.

Jack Grimaldi broke across the line. "I'm getting shot at!"

Schwarz confirmed the worst. "We have satellite. You have four armored vehicles. They are coming straight through the swamp and not stopping for shit. They must be amphibious. They can follow us right into the Gulf!"

McCarter listened to the sound of amphibious armored vehicles splashing, grinding and snapping their way through the wet forest as though it didn't exist. Heavy machine guns opened fire and traversed through the trees reaping branches and shuddering trunks.

Manning hugged muck again. "Déjà vu, anybody?"

McCarter ate mud and listened to the incoming fire and his instincts. They spoke to him. Once again the enemy eyes in the sky could see them, but their soldiers on the ground could not. Their fire was being directed and it was incoming fire from antiquated com-bloc amphibious vehicles without stabilized weapons wallowing through a swamp. The moment they got up onto the road or the raised bit of the hunting lodge's land proper, everything would change for the worse.

Worst case they would get up on dry land and ram right through the walls of the lodge while they disgorged assholes out their back hatches.

McCarter growled at Maksim and snatched grenades out of his pack. "You! You godless heathen! You're with me!" His voice boomed in command. "Werewolf! Lobo!

We're taking out their armor! Wolf Pack! One Blue Blitz each! Wait for my signal! If you don't get the signal in five minutes? Drop gas and make for the lodge, or disperse and make a run for the border! Your choice!"

The Wolf Pack rode on the cusp of panic.

The pack saw their Alpha male leap up and charge into the teeth of the enemy armor.

McCarter slapped his phone onto the Velcro strap on his wrist and shouted into his com link. "I need eyes!"

The Farm provided. In the thermal satellite imaging the cold of the swamp was white and gray and the heat images of the four armored vehicles wallowing forward through the swale were black. All McCarter could see was the stuttering orange flash of their guns, but that was enough to pick his path and avoid their fire. The closer he got the more certain he became. He ran along the slightly firmer mud just below the raised road and Maksim loped on McCarter's six with the strength and agility of youth.

"What do you want me to do?" the Russian shouted.

"You'll know." McCarter put his submachine gun in his left hand and used his trigger finger to pull the pin on the Blue Blitz in his right. Manning was right; it was déjà vu all over again. McCarter found himself charging through the cold, Polish wetness at vehicles chain-sawing through the trees with automatic weapons seeking his life. The armored vehicles suddenly hit their headlights.

It was the worst mistake they could make.

McCarter had seen the like many times. They were very old MT-LBs. The armored vehicles had treads like a tank and their armored bodies were long, wide and low, and had a distinct "frog that had been stepped on" silhouette about them. These APCs were designed to cross soft ground where tanks and jeeps would fail, and swim short distances if needed. Their problem was that they were sixty-year-old technology and exactly the kind of armored vehicle one could buy on the black market in Eastern Europe and Russia. They were perfect for raiding a duck lodge at two o'clock in the morning in Gdansk. Their 14.5 mm heavy machine guns were a few hairbreadths short of being cannons in their own right.

The MT-LBs and their operators were not ready for the leader of Phoenix Force leading his own personal Russian wolf pack. The long, low shovelnose of the vehicles was far easier to run up than the front of a semi-truck. It formed a very convenient assault ramp if you were the sort of person who charged armored vehicles head-on. McCarter vaulted from the muddy berm onto the prow of the armored personnel carrier. Someone inside shouted in alarm. The turret turned but McCarter was already inside its arc of fire and they had left their hatches open for firing and deployment.

McCarter opened his right hand.

The cotter pin of the Blue Blitz grenade pinged away and the hissing cylinder dropped down the open commander's hatch. Men with guns popped up out of the hatches as expanding gas plumed from the vehicle's every orifice. McCarter ran across the hull top and dropped into the swamp.

Maksim held his breath and leaped atop the vehicle. His silenced submachine gun cracked every head foolish enough to burst out of a hatch. The APC slewed as the driver succumbed to the gas and plowed into a berm. Maksim finished his deck run and jumped into the fen beside McCarter. McCarter pulled the pin on another gas grenade. The enemy had deployed their vehicles two by two, one pair flanking each side of the road. He watched as the wingman swerved and crushed stunted trees. "Tell me that wasn't fun."

Maksim's teeth flashed in the dark. "You're great!"

"Stay out of the headlights, we have one more."

The Game Room

"WHAT THE HELL?" Pyle shook his head as a second armored unit came to a mysterious halt and then a third. "Nothing hit them. Nothing! They're not on fire or blowing up and there are no visible firing signatures. I mean what the hell?"

Kun pondered the conundrum of his stalling armor attack. The com link was blowing up north and south. Save for his armored vehicles, there was only silence.

Rong zoomed and expanded his screen to maximum. It made the image a little fuzzy and the mist around the tanks was getting thicker by the second. He joined Pyle in the head-shaking business. "It looks like they're smoking like chimneys, but their heat signature hasn't changed."

"Gas," Kun surmised.

"Gas?" Pyle frowned. "Tear gas can't stop a tank."

"It can if someone tosses a grenade into the cabin. But in that case the men would be abandoning ship as if the hold was filled with angry bees. This is not tear gas."

Rong's jaw dropped. From his view from above, the black, motionless armored vehicles with their shovel noses suddenly looked disturbingly like coffins. "Poison gas?"

"I find that difficult to believe." Kun considered his options. Each MT-LB held a squad of eight men. Operation Gdansk Deux had just lost almost all of its assault force without inflicting a single casualty on the enemy. The men to the north were mostly snipers whose job it was to keep the men in the lodge pinned down. Wolf Pack's job had been to tear apart the frontal assault like good little meat shields and make the men in the lodge expend most of their ammo. Then the armored wave would go in, ram down the walls and forcibly extract the targets. Then Mr. Paulus would zip-tie them hand and foot, lay them one by one in front of the tank treads, feetfirst, and ask them questions while the eleven-ton vehicles steamrolled up their bodies in six-inch segments. To Kun's knowledge, no one had ever stayed salty by the time the treads hit their hipbones. When the interrogation was over, the process had the added benefit of turning the bodies into mulch, which was easily disposed of, particularly in a swamp. It was a good plan; Kun had come up with it, and he had been relishing watching the last part in particular, in person.

The plan had gone to hell in a handbasket.

Kun tapped his private com line to Mr. Paulus. "Deux Leader, this is Game Master, do you copy?"

"Copy, Game Master."

"The plan has gone to hell."

Mr. Paulus's Slavic accent was clipped and hard. "Copy that, Game Master."

"I believe the MT-LBs have been gassed."

"Yes, I have retrieved three of my men. All show signs as if they are drunk or on drugs. The Russians brought knockout gas. The concentrations inside the vehicles may have been lethal."

Kun knew there was no such thing as knockout gas. Blue Blitz and its few siblings in the genre of war gases were anesthetics and, as any anesthesiologist would tell you, turning off someone's higher brain functions without dangerously affecting lower ones like respiration and heart rate was a tricky business. In practical use in riots and hostage situations, knockout gas had extremely mixed results. In battle there was hardly ever a specialist checking your vitals and asking you to count backward from one hundred as he monitored your vitals. "Can your remaining men get past it?"

"We must assume they have more gas, and we are not equipped with gas masks. We must assume if the enemy is using gas then they have gas masks. This will grant them a great deal of autonomy of action we will not have."

Kun loved listening to Mr. Paulus talk. "Recommendations?"

"Bring in the helicopters. Have them hover over the armor to disperse the lingering gas clouds."

"Do we have anyone left who knows how to drive an MT-LB?"

"Myself. We will open all the hatches and blast out the gas. Then choppers hover over us as we full assault."

Wolf Pack

"IRONMAN, THIS IS ALPHA." McCarter stared up through the trees into the night through his Russian Federation NVGs. They were bulky and nowhere near as good as Farm equipment. "I hear rotor noise and it is not *Dragonslayer*."

"Copy that."

"Multiple rotors. At least two birds, running without lights. They seem to be hovering over the road."

"Copy that, Alpha."

"Farm, do we have eyes?" McCarter asked.

"Twenty minutes until next window," Kurtzman reported.

"Sometimes—" Propenko suddenly grinned beneath his goggles "—man must just go see for himself."

McCarter had to admit the Russian prison commando was growing on him. "Right, then. Ironman, we're going to go have a boo, as Gummer would say."

"Copy that, Alpha."

"Lobo, Maksim, with me!" McCarter glared at the oldest, grizzled Russian in Wolf Pack. "You—Grigory! Take Wolf Pack to the lodge. Ironman is now your commander."

"Dah." Grigory sliced his hand toward the lodge and Wolf Pack melted away north through the twisted, Baltic swamp trees. McCarter and his Russians ran south back along the banks to the battle scene they had just left.

"Sons of bitches!" Propenko declared.

The two helicopters hovered over both sides of the road, hammering the air with their rotor wash. The remaining Blue Blitz clouds were shredding apart. None of the enemy had gas masks but well more than a dozen men were doing triage. They had stacked close to twenty men who would never wake up into a dead pile like cordwood. Another dozen-plus men were being slapped around and having cold, Polish swamp water flung in their faces.

"Ironman, this is Alpha. The enemy is regrouping. Two helicopters. And will counterattack at half platoon strength." McCarter watched one of the vehicles belch blue smoke and crank back into life. "Armor is reengaging!" The helicopters rose over the tree line and McCarter could see door gunners hanging on chicken straps and weapons attached to the skids. "I have two gunships."

"Alpha, I recommend you pull back to the lodge. Get some stone between you and them."

One of the helicopters broke off, dipped its nose and thundered toward the lodge. "Ironman, you have—"

The helicopter ripped around in a tight U-turn and the glare of its spotlight slammed into angry, incandescent life and illuminated McCarter and his team. The Phoenix leader knew satellite surveillance had finally found them. "Disperse and regroup!"

McCarter's team bolted in three directions.

Soviet heavy machine guns hammered into life and young Maksim twisted and fell as he was hammered apart. McCarter grimaced and emptied his weapon up into the aircraft. The slow, silent, subsonic bullets weren't exactly antiaircraft material but they sparked against the fuselage and caught the helicopter's attention. The chopper's nose and its spotlight spun in McCarter's direction.

Propenko knew the drill and emptied his weapon into the chopper's tail as it turned. The chopper pilot panicked and took the better part of valor. The gunship swung out over the trees away from the incoming fire so it could pick its own advantageous gun run. McCarter drew grenades. He hurled a flash bang at the MT-LB as it lurched up the embankment and hit the road and threw another. The grenades detonated with a sound like cannon shells. Like chopper pilots, armor drivers could be convinced they were being hit heavy, and sometimes sparks and thunder rattling off their hull and smoke clouding their periscopes could make them panic.

Whoever was driving wasn't having it.

The machine gun turret turned and tried to finish what the first chopper had started. McCarter threw himself down as the second chopper rose and began lacing the tree line with tracer fire. "A little help, then!"

Grimaldi shouted across the link. "*Dragonslayer* inbound!"

The MT-LB went incandescent as it turned on its infrared searchlight and the turret swept around.

McCarter squinted through his NVGs, flicked his selector to semi-auto and popped off three quick shots. The searchlight of death shattered and died. The armor kept lumbering forward without headlights or searchlights.

"Bastard…" McCarter emptied his magazine into the armored vehicle to attract its attention. Sparks spattered off the hull and it didn't give a single shit. The armored vehicle literally seemed to come alive as it grabbed onto solid road and charged forward. About a score of men were charging behind it. "Ironman, this is Alpha. You have incoming armor! One vehicle. Infantry behind."

"Copy that! Gummer?" Lyons inquired.

Gary Manning sounded positively smug. "Oh, I see him."

Manning happened to be on the roof of the lodge with a Polish Tor .50-caliber anti-matériel rifle. He muttered

happily to himself. "No chance, that's what you got…"
He squeezed the trigger and half a second later his armor-
piercing round shrieked six inches below the MT-LB's
turret proper. The machine gun suddenly drooped very
convincingly as if the gunner's life had been torn out
of his body. Manning worked the very large bolt of his
weapon and went for the driver. The driver's heavy steel
shutter suddenly dropped down and Manning recognized
the spark spray of a remarkable ricochet. He ignored the
shuttered windows and hatches and began punching holes
through the vehicle's rooftop.

The MT-LB swerved off the road and dropped down
the embankment and temporarily out of Manning's sight.
The Canadian sharpshooter worked his bolt. "Yeah, you
run, eh." He raised his sights for the sky as the helicopter
pair swung in for the kill.

"Here they come."

CHAPTER SEVEN

Able Team

Led by Carl Lyons, the Stony Man warriors erupted out of the lodge. Upstairs Calvin James worked his bolt and fired, but trying to maneuver a thirty-five-pound rifle and track helicopters in evasive action was problematic.

By the same token James had forced the enemy helicopters into evasive action and he had also forced the remaining enemy armor to take a dive off the road and back into the swamp where it belonged. He'd punched three holes in the lead chopper before it had banked away. He fired again and chastised himself as he saw his tracer streak off just behind its tail. "I can't hit a chopper with this thing unless it's coming straight in!"

The lead chopper came in machine guns firing. Wolf Pack fired their submachine guns from the trees on the grounds, but the chopper just wasn't being intimidated again. A missile hissed off one of its weapon stalks and screamed in for the lodge.

The Stony Man warriors had already left the building.

Except for James, who happened to be on the roof. "Damn!"

Lyons raised his Polish RPG and fired. It was an antipersonnel round rather than antitank. And rather than a shaped-charge war-head designed to pierce steel, it was a fragmentation weapon rocket that detonated right after launching and hurled five hundred steel wedding rings at

250 miles per hour. It was made to take out charging infantrymen. The accompanying literature suggested the rocket would also be effective against light, low-flying aircraft.

The lead chopper took five hundred steel rings in the face.

The helicopter's windshield shattered and the pilot, copilot and their controls were ripped apart. The helicopter spun out of control into swamp. Its missile continued with soulless, silicon accuracy and hit the lodge. Lyons felt the heat wash and bits of stone peppering his back. He dropped his smoking rocket tube and unslung his rifle. The Able Team leader spun and went full auto at the second chopper. "Pol!"

"On it!" Blancanales returned.

The second chopper came in guns blazing and rippled off four missiles in apparent panic or rage.

James's voice rose across the link. "Damn!"

The missiles hit the lodge in a salvo and exploded. Fire roared in all directions and stone and mortar folded inward like a house of cards. Lyons shouted in the closest thing he was capable of to distress. "Cal!"

"Cal!" Hawkins roared.

Leaping from the top of the burning building, James tossed his massive anti-materiel rifle and wind-milled his arms and legs as he fell through the fire-lit space. He had chosen his trajectory with terrible care.

Encizo focused on the incoming chopper, swung up his RPG and fired. The second chopper took several hundred steel rings through its tail boom and skidded violently through the sky. Lyons, Encizo, Schwarz, Hawkins and Wolf Pack tracked the aircraft with their weapons and filled the ethers with lead.

The helicopter spun in gigantic, dragonfly-like rage and pointed its nose and its four remaining missiles at the lodge frontage. Able Team, Phoenix Force and Wolf

Pack fired their weapons dry and scattered as the machine guns tore into life.

Dragonslayer dropped out of the sky like vengeance from on high.

The machine guns mounted atop her pontoons strobed and tracers ripped into the offending chopper. *Dragonslayer* chopped the enemy aircraft into pieces. The offending chopper spun out of control and Grimaldi orbited it in a tight dance of death, pouring in fire. The hostile helicopter auto-rotated out of the sky and hit the trees bursting in flaming wreckage.

"Four enemy choppers in forty-eight hours," Encizo commented. "Is that a record?"

"Not for Able," Lyons said.

"Five if you count the UAV," Manning added.

"Maybe," Lyons conceded.

Dragonslayer shuddered and tottered like an airborne drunk as she landed awkwardly on the road. Grimaldi spoke over the link. "My girl has taken hits. I am leaking fluids and have red lights across the board. Are we done here?"

"Able!" Lyons called. "Phoenix! Sound off!"

Both teams sounded off.

"Wolf Pack!"

Manning responded. "Maksim, Grigory and Karpin are dead. Where is Alpha?"

Lyons spoke low across the link. "Alpha?"

"The bastard in the tank has made a run for it," McCarter responded. "I'm on it. Wait for my signal."

Armor 1

MR. PAULUS BURNED straight for the Gulf of Gdansk. He took no chances but he drove aggressively. Saplings in his path snapped and he crushed fields of reeds and flattened mud bars. For longer and longer stretches he found himself buoyant and swimming. He took a chance and tapped his private communications link. "Game Master, this is Deux Leader. Do you copy?"

"Deux Master this is Game Master. I copy."

"Copy that, Deux Leader. What is your status?

"I am in Armor 1, heading due north, and require extraction."

"Copy that, Deux Leader. How many men are you extracting with?"

"None." Paulus paused. He had not bothered to respond or to pick up any of the men in the swamp north of the lodge, and he was ninety-nine percent sure that this was the answer Game Master wanted. He was seventy-five percent sure that Game Master still considered him a valuable asset worth saving, if the risk was minimal.

"I am fully amphibious," Paulus continued. "I am currently crossing the wetlands and heading for the gulf. Send me a boat."

There was an answering pause on the other end of the link.

Paulus had a hunch where Game Master and the Game Room might be at the moment, and if he was right they could very well send him a boat. "Once I am in open water, I will open all hatches and scuttle Armor 1."

"Continue course, Deux Leader. I am reacquiring you."

"Copy that." Paulus lit himself a cigarette as his fate was decided. The interior of Armor 1 was still filled with the acrid, nutty smell of the Blue Blitz gas and it was making him slightly woozy. He cranked open the armored shutters in front of the driver and commander's windows, then risked stopping the vehicle to heave up the two hatches over the troop compartment. He pulled the dead gunner out of the mini turret and hauled him back into the troop compartment.

Paulus slid behind the wheel and rolled on. The MT-LB could do about twenty miles per hour off road and just under four swimming with its tracks. The vehicle lurched and bobbed and slowed to a crawl. This comforted him because now all he was hitting was weeds and water. The dawn was just starting to rise and he took off his night-vision goggles. Pearly light showed through the holes the sniper had punched in the hull. The salt marsh expanse emptied of trees and he entered open territory. Paulus was in dangerous ground but he was almost there. Even if he was refused extraction he felt he had a very good chance of extracting himself into Kaliningrad or parts of Poland where he had friends. His phone peeped.

"Deux Leader, we have eyes on you, but we need our orbital assets to continue monitoring the battle site. However, we are tracking you via GPS. The enemy has no one following you, no assets currently in the air. Continue your course. The morning tide is just starting to go out, no swell. You will be met by a small boat. ETA fifteen minutes."

"Copy that, Game Master. Continuing course."

Paulus continued on. As the sun rose in the distance he could see tiny whitecaps out on the Baltic. With a sigh of relief he hit the open water of the gulf. He considered his flask of Slivovitz but didn't start celebrating quite yet. The sight of a small Rigid Hulled Inflatable Boat tearing across the water in his direction almost made him feel like allowing himself a snort.

His phone pinged and he recognized a new but safe signal. Paulus tapped the icon and accepted it. "This is Deux Leader."

"Deux Leader, this is Chariot. We have you in sight. Cut your engines. Prepare to open your rear troop compartment doors and scuttle Armor 1, but wait for my signal."

"Copy that, Chariot."

Paulus cut the MT-LB's V-8 diesel. Armor 1 ceased powered-forward momentum and bobbed disturbingly upon the water like an eleven-ton iron cork that had been designed to ford rivers and mud and never, ever sail upon open water. He unlimbered his large frame from the driver's seat and moved back into the bloodstained troop cabin.

Paulus heard the engine of the RHIB approaching. His com link chimed. "Deux Leader, this is Chariot. We are about to come alongside. When Armor 1 sinks it will probably go fast. Once you open the troop compartment we recommend you immediately extract out of the commander's hatch so you don't go down with it."

"Copy."

"All right, on my signal, get ready—" The man in Chariot suddenly shouted across the link, "Deux Leader! You have a hitchhiker! You have—"

Paulus heard the chuffing and click-click-clicking of a sound-suppressed weapon firing right over his head. He also heard screaming and suddenly the screaming and the throttle of the boat went dead.

Armor 1 continued to gently bob in the calm water and the sudden silence.

Paulus drew his stainless-steel Czech .357 Magnum revolver.

A fist rapped on the steel roof above. Paulus recognized an English accent. "Hey, you in there! Come on up, then! Let's talk!"

The click of Paulus cocking the hammer on his Alfa revolver was very loud in the calm. "Why don't you come down?"

"Got you dead to rights, mate," the voice advised.

Paulus began very slowly making his way to the machine gun turret. "They will send another boat. Perhaps you want to start swimming?"

"Why would I swim when I am the owner of a brand-new boat?"

"Well..." Paulus folded his frame into the gunner's position in the turret. "There is that."

"You sound Serbian."

Paulus flinched. "You sound English."

"Two mighty nations," the Englishman agreed. "Come up on deck. I think we can work this out."

"You won't shoot?" Paulus put one hand on the manual traverse.

"I'll do you one better. I'll offer you a deal. And it will beat the bloody hell out of sending you to the bottom of the Baltic."

"You win!"

"I like the sound of that," the Englishman replied.

Paulus peered through the turret sight. A large, sandy-haired man with a mustache squatted on his heels over the starboard troop compartment hatch. He was holding a sound-suppressed submachine gun. It irked Paulus that the man had ridden him the entire time. It irked him more that he highly suspected the enemy had tracked him the entire time. Paulus took his revolver by the barrel and tossed it up the port hatch.

"Thanks, mate. Now, nice and slow."

Paulus put his hand on the machine gun's trigger. "Don't shoot!"

"Slow, easy and hands first. You and I will be right as rain, mate."

"I am coming. Don't shoot." Paulus spun the manual traverse and the barrel of the PKT machine gun swung toward the Englishman like an accusing finger of doom. Paulus hissed as the man up top adroitly leaped. He hit his inclination wheel but the man had already disappeared from view. The top of the turret thudded slightly as someone alighted on top of it.

The Englishman was right above him. "Now, that was unkind."

"Come on down, English," Paulus snarled. "I have more guns. In fact, I have a knife. Perhaps I will just open the troop compartment doors and sink us. See which one of us has better sub-aqueous warfare training. Maybe we will see which one of us can hold his breath the longest. What do you say?"

Paulus's stomach tightened as he heard the ping of a cotter pin fly away and the Englishman above announce doom. "Say good night."

A blue, cylindrical grenade clattered to the troop compartment floor and began spewing thick white gas. Paulus gasped and accidentally took some of it in. He held his breath as he withdrew his knife and wormed out of the turret. The man above kicked down both hatches with a clang and Blue Blitz gas expanded to fill the closed interior of the armored vehicle in a solid cloud. Paulus held his breath as long as he could and tried to reach the rear doors. His breath burst from his lungs and he couldn't stop himself from inhaling a chunk of the nearly solid atmosphere of the armored vehicle's interior. He fell to the steel floor of the troop compartment with loosened limbs and cursed in Serbian.

McCarter glanced at his watch and waited a full thirty seconds. The RHIB was drifting away but he decided to attend to that later. He hurled open the hatches and stepped away as they funneled gas into the Polish morning. McCarter spent a few moments hyperventilating, took a deep breath and then dropped down into the cramped compartment. He ignored the particulate stinging his eyes and grabbed the armored man lying on the floor. With immense effort he shoved the limp man up the hatch like a collapsing sausage. McCarter checked to make sure his opponent was still breathing. He held his breath as he dived back down into the gas and retrieved the man's pack sitting in the commander's seat. McCarter reemerged and gasped for breath on the aft end of the floating armored vehicle.

The good news was the rain had stopped.

He got on the horn with the Farm. "Tell me you saw where that boat came from."

Kurtzman's voice came back. "A container vessel, just outside the Polish territorial limit. We are tracking it."

"I have one prisoner. I think he was the man in command on the ground. And I have a boat."

"I suggest you head straight out to sea. We will arrange for someone to pick you up."

"Copy that."

"Find anything useful?" Kurtzman asked.

McCarter rummaged through the unconscious man's pack. "I have a cell phone. I have a tablet. I have his com gear."

"Nice. Try to keep all that dry," Kurtzman suggested.

McCarter watched the enemy boat and the two dead men piloting it drifting away. He considered the hundred-meter swim in the black, Baltic winter waters. He stopped rummaging through the pack as he found a flask. He opened it and smelled Slivovitz. He capped the flask then raised it to the sleeping Serb. "Cheers, mate. This'll come in handy when we have something to truly celebrate."

McCarter smiled ruefully and shucked off his boots.

The Game Room

"JESUS CHRIST!" Junior Pyle was bouncing around in his chair. "They got Mr. Paulus! Jesus! They took him alive! Oh, Jesus! Oh, Jesus."

Rong stared at his bank of screens and watched the commandeered RHIB zip back into the delta. "If they have the boat, they can follow it back to us."

"They already know where we are," Kun said. "They are very likely tracking us by satellite as we speak."

"Jesus. Oh, Jesus…"

Kun frowned. He was not a religious man. However his parents in Seoul had converted to Mormonism and his upbringing had left an ingrained dislike of people swearing and taking the Lord's name in vain. "You need to stop saying that," Kun advised.

Pyle shut his mouth.

Rong perceived he was still in Kun's good graces. "So what do we do?"

"We take it to the next level." Kun tapped an icon on his screen to signal he wanted immediate extraction. He tapped another icon and rang up the Game Room's personal security provider. "Mr. Ji-Hoon?"

A chat window popped open. Ji-Hoon was Korean, like Kun, and six foot four. He had a face like a rounded-off anvil and a Korean-Elvis haircut. In his youth as a member of the Blue Dragon Second Marine Division his facial nerves had been damaged by a concussion grenade thrown by a North Korean infiltration team on the DMZ. This left his normal facial expression a cipher-like blank that most people found vaguely disturbing. When he smiled it did not reach his eyes; his smile scared the hell out of people. He'd done a tour of duty in the second Iraq war and after his stint had taken on contractor work in Afghanistan. Ji-Hoon had gone on to private security work in Asia, developing a formidable reputation as a discreet yet brutal "fixer" of private, personal and business situations. "Yes, boss?"

"We have a problem."

"Yeah, I kind of liked that Serbian prick, too."

Kun smiled. Ji-Hoon was one of the few people whose swearing and salty behavior he enjoyed. Ji-Hoon had spent a lot of time around American soldiers and had taken on many of their mannerisms when he spoke English. Kun also liked the fact that Ji-Hoon had no qualms whatsoever about helping him out with the acquirement, physical assistance and disposal phases of the extracurricular activities that Kun enjoyed in his spare time. He also liked it when he called him boss. "You wouldn't mind killing Mr. Paulus, would you?"

Ji-Hoon shot a dead smirk. "I didn't like him that much."

Mr. Paulus was a high-level associate that the Magistrate, via Kun, had used on several occasions. Paulus did not know enough, but he knew far too much. As a high-level field asset Mr. Paulus had been subdermally implanted with a radio frequency identification microchip. The GPS-enabled chip was an incredibly expensive piece of technology. It would take an MRI to find, but once the GPS tracking went active it was a signal the enemy could follow, as well.

Kun was very certain the enemy on the ground had no ability to do so. He glanced around the Game Room. Kun was becoming more certain by the minute that his adversaries were close enough to his own technological and intellectual level to be genuinely dangerous. He was one hundred percent certain they had access to military-grade observation and tracking satellites.

Kun bitterly regretted his decision to not implant one into Propenko based on financial reasons.

Then again, Kun was rather certain that in the very near future, if not now, Mr. Paulus and Captain Propenko would be in very close proximity. "Mr. Ji-Hoon?"

"Yes, boss."

"I am activating GPS tracking on Mr. Paulus. Would you take care of that?"

"Love to."

"And I would dearly love to have one or more of these

people who are causing us so much trouble alive if possible. We have had three firefights with them, lost all of them, and we still have absolutely no idea who they may be."

"That could be a little harder, but I will see what I can do, boss."

"Thank you, Mr. Ji-Hoon."

"No problem, boss. What about your personal security situation?"

"We are extracting."

"Fly safe, boss."

"Thank you." Kun cut the link. He rose as he heard men working on top of the Game Room. He nodded at Pyle and Rong. "We are out of here."

Kun walked to the door of the Game Room. The ocean breeze hit him as he opened it and lit a cigarette. Kun stepped out onto the deck of the feeder ship *Maria Cecilia*. The container vessel was in international waters off the Gulf of Gdansk. The ill-fated RHIB the *Maria* had launched was directly traceable to the ship. There was no doubt at all the enemy was watching the *Maria Cecilia* as it steamed away. Kun knew he had a small window of opportunity while there was nothing the enemy could actively do about it. They could try an assault with their single helicopter and stolen boat, and part of Kun hoped they would try.

He suspected they were stealing off into the dawn with their prizes.

It was time for the Game Room to do the same. Kun looked up at the men on top of the Game Room attaching lift cables to its corners. A crewman held up his hand and spread his fingers. "Five minutes."

Kun looked over at the Sikorsky S-64 Sky crane heavy-lift helicopter that had appeared like magic out of four false, connected, forty-five-foot containers. More crewmen were attaching the maximum lift lines to its under-carriage. The *Maria Cecilia's* manifest listed neither the Game Room nor any of its inhabitants, nor the heavy lift helicopter. Of course, sailors talked, but then, container vessels actually had very small crews. They would all be dead from an outbreak of food poisoning via the galley within hours, and the *Maria Cecilia* would hit rocks off Denmark the autopilot had been hacked to take a course for and sink and the Game Room would be long gone.

Kun smiled. Let the enemy track that. Meanwhile, he would be tracking Mr. Paulus, and his enemy.

CHAPTER EIGHT

Świnoujście, Poland

Aaron Kurtzman happily read the prisoner's résumé over the link. "Goran Paulus, sergeant in the Yugoslavian People's Republic Army, rose to the rank of captain in the Serbian army after the war and the breakup of Yugoslavia. Is reported to have involved in some very ugly goings-on as a merc in the Congo. Since then he's developed something of a reputation as private contractor in Eastern European and the former Soviet republics."

Goran Paulus sat zip-tied to a chair and didn't bother to confirm or deny. "Goran?" McCarter asked. "Can I call you Goran? You and I have shared a gunfight, an amphibious armored vehicle ride, a gas grenade and a romantic swim in the Baltic. I feel like we know each other."

Goran Paulus squeezed his eyes shut and furrowed his brow as though he were in severe pain. Blue Blitz appeared to leave one with one hell of an anesthetic hangover.

McCarter and James examined their subject. He was sort of like Propenko. The Russian had been in some terrible situations, been given terrible decisions to make and done terrible things. The Serb, on the other hand, was simply a terrible person. McCarter was not in a sympathetic mood, but he wanted answers. "I know!" McCarter pointed at Paulus happily. "You need a cigarette."

Paulus's eye's slammed open against his will at the idea. Phoenix Force watched the wheels turn in the suffering Serb's mind. Grimaldi had picked up McCarter and his prize and managed to wobble *Dragonslayer* out over international waters and head west. The Farm had set up a safe house in Świnoujście. It was a port and resort city in the extreme northwest of Poland with the Baltic to the north and the Szczecin Lagoon to the south. It was winter and many of the summerhouses were unoccupied. Paulus had slept through the flight. Able Team had pulled a fade and were in a beachside hotel a block away with a scope-sighted rifle's view of the safe house. Wolf Pack had extracted into Kaliningrad with their pockets full of Euros.

Propenko had stayed along for the ride.

McCarter nodded at the Russian. Propenko put a CCCP between the Serb's lips and lit it with a match. "Paulus," he said commiseratingly. "I know you by reputation. Perhaps you know me the same way. I suggest you talk to this man."

Paulus blew smoke. "You are all dead men."

McCarter kept grinning. "Do you know how many times I've been told that?"

Paulus shifted his cigarette to the other side of his mouth. "I do not know. Many?"

Propenko lit himself a cigarette and read the Serb. "He is Slav, like me. I tell you. He expects to die. Us, them, or his own. They come, and he does not come back alive."

"Is that true?" McCarter asked.

Paulus dragged deep on his cigarette, savoring it like a man facing the firing squad.

"Nick, I think you're right." McCarter leaned in on Paulus. "Now, you, old son? I think the cavalry might be coming, but coming to cut your head off rather than save you, and I think they would love to put me in that chair and the only cigarettes they'll be giving me are the ones they shove burning into my eyeballs to make me talk.

The question facing both of us is how could they possibly know where we are?"

"He's microchip tagged." Calvin James took out his wasp-waisted, Vietnam-era Gerber Mark II dagger. "Get the reader. I'll dig it out of him."

Paulus jerked backward in his seat. Against his will his eyes shot toward his left hand where it was zipped to the arm of the chair. The hand was a common place to put a microchip tag. The skin was thin and someone using it as an ID could swipe their hand beneath a reader. In a tracking mode emergency, with a little determination and a sharp knife, the user could remove the device himself.

The Phoenix Force medic had no technology that could detect such a device, but James was a master interrogator and he had made his subject give himself away. He sheathed his knife and made Paulus an offer. "I have a scalpel and forceps in my med kit. You want it out?"

"Perhaps that would be for best." Paulus agreed.

James looked at McCarter. The Phoenix Force leader weighed the options. The enemy had probably been tracking Paulus since they had loaded the Serb aboard *Dragonslayer*, and Phoenix Force had been in the safe house for several hours now. The enemy almost certainly knew exactly where Phoenix Force was. They didn't know Able Team was within rifle range. Propenko had made a brilliant turnaround.

McCarter was willing to take a guarded chance on the Serb. "You tell me everything you know. If I even suspect you are holding back, my friend here will inject you with sodium pentothal. You already have Blue Blitz in your system. I suspect you'll babble like a brook, but I don't have time to put on my Wellies and wade through the muck in your mind. Neither do you. You give me all the pertinent information and our friend will take out that RFID tag leaving your hand intact, and I'll give you a thousand Euros, a false ID, a rail pass and let you run. If we get attacked before we're done here I expect you to fight like a brave—for us. We clear, sunshine?"

"Clear as crystal," Paulus said.

McCarter nodded at James. "Tell you what, go ahead and cut him. We don't want to be in a bloody operating theater later if the enemy hits us."

James reached into his medical kit and took out his minor surgery tools. McCarter snapped open his tactical knife and cut the zip tie holding Paulus's right hand. The Serb flexed it and looked at his left. McCarter inclined his head at James and the scalpel in his hand. "Best to keep it restrained for the moment."

Paulus rolled his eyes at what was about to happen. "Perhaps that would be best."

McCarter pulled Paulus's flask of Slivovitz from his pocket and held it out to the preoperative Serb. "Cheers, mate. For the pain."

Stony Man Farm

KURTZMAN'S ATTENTION leaped from screen to screen. Goran Paulus had some fascinating tales to tell. He'd given up every last detail of his past five missions and the names of everyone he had worked with. On two occasions he had done some very dirty work for shadow employers with incredible technology and toys, and apparently more money than God. The Stony Man operatives ran these stories and compared them with the debriefings Propenko had given them. The Swedish government was treating the attack in Karmal as some sort of terrorist action, and the NSA had received information about the makes, models, serial numbers and registrations of the two downed helicopters.

Kurtzman had been counting on getting some interesting intel once the *Maria Cecilia* made port.

He found himself disturbed by the sinking of the container ship and the loss of all hands.

Kurtzman had dealt with enemies from cannibal savages to slavers, drug and criminal cartels, terrorist cells, renegade intelligence agencies, shadow governments and right on up to those who had acquired weapons of mass destruction and were willing to see the whole world burn in the name of revenge, or worse, the name of their deity. He preferred them all to what he was looking at. It was the opponents who simply eliminated human life as if it flicking the beads of an abacus that made him wonder if humanity was going to make it to the next millennium.

Nevertheless he had lived to see the turn of the last millennium and had been pleasantly surprised. As he looked around at his team he reminded himself that there were still a few guys wearing white hats running around.

"Akira, how are we doing on the money angle?"

"You want the good news or the bad news first?" the young genius replied.

Kurtzman was simply glad Tokaido hadn't started singing again. "The bad news?"

"These guys are good. Real good. Ghost-in-the-machine good. They don't leave tracks."

The Stony Man cybernetics leader was buoyed by the fact that Tokaido didn't seem upset. "The good news?"

"Since we don't have a trail, we need to look at the evidence and come up with a pool of suspects."

"We have a pool of suspects?"

"We got nothing. No clue whatsoever who is behind all this. Positively anonymous."

Kurtzman's brow furrowed. Nonetheless he noted Tokaido still didn't seem worried. "So?"

"So, failing a pool of suspects, we need a pool of possible pawns. Pawns who can move a lot of money, either willingly or while being duped, and we need to tie them to what we've observed so far."

Huntington Wethers looked up the work he was doing on the battle in Karmal, Sweden. "You have a pool of possible pawns?"

Tokaido was almost gleeful. "Hundreds!"

Wethers gave Tokaido his "professor dealing with a brilliant but wayward student" look. "And, so, anyone stand out in particular?"

"Oh, there're a couple I have my eye on…" Tokaido teased.

"Akira?" Kurtzman asked.

"Yes, Bear?"

"Hunt and I are old men. We're going to be dead soon. Would you care to share who your number one suspect is?"

Tokaido punched a key and a window popped up on both Kurtzman and Wethers's screens.

"Oh, my." Wethers managed a smile. "Demetrios Papastathopoulos."

Tokaido nodded enthusiastically. "Yeah, try saying that ten times fast."

"Well," Kurtzman conceded, managing a smile of his own. "You picked a real gem."

"Indeed I did," Tokaido gloated.

Kurtzman was well aware of Demetrios Papastathopoulos. He scanned the file Tokaido had been compiling on the man. His nickname was "the Warlord of Wall Street." He was the son of a Greek shipping magnate who had gone on to earn a Harvard MBA and then into corporate finance. Kurtzman shook his head at the leering man in the picture.

Demetrios Papastathopoulos had shortened his name to Demi Papas. Cosmetic enhancements had given him

Ronald Reagan's hair, Jack Nicholson's grin and the Botox features of a Stepford Wife. He wrote books and appeared on radio and cable talk shows. He referred to himself in the third person as "Big Papa" and his catch phrase was "Do what your Papa tells you." Papas had his own cult-of-personality-media empire. His specialty in making his billions was suddenly lunging in and buying controlling stock in a company, forcing it to freakishly buy or sell even more of its stock to or from him or his puppets, and then get out while the company flopped and gasped like a fish that had been yanked up out the water and thrown on the bank to die.

Kurtzman believed very firmly in venture capitalism. He believed in the adage "nothing ventured, nothing gained." In his other life, he had served a consultant to major corporations. The majority of businessmen he'd worked with, and he wouldn't work with the other kind, wanted to see their investments and companies grow. Even the so-called vampire capitalists at their worst bought a failing company for a pittance and then sold off all its assets. Men like Demi Papas damaged and destroyed perfectly good companies. They manipulated ones, zeroes and ledgers while the dreams of entrepreneurs and working men and women died. Men like Papas built, created or rescued nothing. In Aaron Kurtzman's view, men like Demi Papas were the scum of earth.

A part of Kurtzman hoped and prayed, and indeed salivated at the possibility that Papas was indeed their target and the Farm would bring him and his corporate cult down.

Tokaido was reading Kurtzman's mind. "So what do you think?"

"If we can ever get Able out of Poland, I think they should pay Big Papa a visit and make him an offer he can't refuse."

Świnoujście safe house

"Phoenix, we have no movement," Blancanales reported.

"Copy that, Able," McCarter replied. He had been in three battles with a very dangerous and still unknown opponent. Having Able Team on his six was a comfort and one hell of an ace in the hole. He glanced over to the kitchen table where Propenko and Paulus were sipping Slivovitz out of little cordial glasses, smoking and having some sort of deep conversation in Russian. The RFID was out of the Serb's hand and now resided in McCarter's pocket. With some reluctance McCarter had returned Paulus's revolver to him and issued the Serb a Kashtan submachine gun and six loaded magazines.

McCarter wandered over with Rafael Encizo in tow. The Phoenix Force leader looked at the bandage on Paulus's left hand. "How are we doing?"

Paulus flexed his fingers and winced slightly as he made a successful fist. "Your man Cal does good work."

"That he does," McCarter agreed. "He's patched me up right many a time."

Propenko poured himself another finger of plum brandy. "We have been discussing mission similarities. We are certain his controller and mine were the same, but I was one level lower, so I had no direct contact. We know his controller, Game Master, was operating out of container vessel off Polish coast. On my operation on Kaliningrad border, I have strong impression Game Master was close by, as well."

"That implies a mobile base," Encizo said. "A ship as a mobile command center makes some sense, since you can operate in international waters or scoot into the territorial waters of friends if things get hot. Still, if you get followed back to it, as we followed them to the *Maria Ce-*

cilia's launch, you are a pretty easy target to track by satellite, and scuttling an entire feeder ship is a bit drastic."

James called from the couch, "Less drastic if you can extract your whole base off of the ship."

Paulus blinked. Propenko nodded. "They had best of best of equipment. I do not believe they sank Game Room to bottom of Baltic."

"It was a feeder ship. A container vessel," Encizo ventured. "The Game Room is an intermodal shipping container."

"Shipping container." Paulus mulled the idea over.

"Sure," Encizo continued. "In Iraq we would ship equipment over in containers, then clean them out, add bunks and chemical toilet and turn them into barracks. I've racked Zs in one more than once. A standard forty-footer would give you more than two thousand square feet of internal volume, and they make bigger ones. You can stack them and snap them together like Legos if you need more space. Infinitely customizable. You can put it on a container ship, a railroad car, a medium-size transport plane or the flatbed of a semi. Given our theory that it's a mobile command center, the interior is going to be some command consoles and some very sophisticated electronics. Mostly empty space and not that heavy. I'll bet anything they sky-craned it off the *Maria Cecilia*."

"This makes sense." Propenko nodded.

McCarter agreed. "It's not bad. But I don't think a heavy-lift helicopter would have the range to fly out to the *Maria Cecilia* and then fly back. I'm saying they had a chopper with them on the boat rather than call it in."

Paulus frowned. "They hid Game Room and sky-crane?"

"They have ISO high-cube containers that are extra tall," Encizo explained. "As well as ones whose sides open for oversize or out-of-gauge cargo."

McCarter looked over at the couch. "You getting all this, Cal?"

"Getting it and forwarding it to base about as fast as you all are saying it."

McCarter was rather pleased they had figured this out before Kurtzman and his team back at the Farm. "Hawk?"

Hawkins was already tapping away on his tablet. "Looking up sky-crane helicopters that can carry a forty-foot, high-cube container or bigger. Most choppers that can do it are military. Most militaries don't sell them surplus— you always have huge, heavy things that need transporting. They fly them until the rotors fall off or mothball them."

"Commercial models?"

"They make them, but as you can imagine it's a limited market." Hawkins looked up. "Hey, Cal! Tell—"

"Already on it," James finished.

McCarter's phone beeped. It was Lyons. "Able, this is Phoenix."

"Phoenix, be advised you have a small craft about two miles offshore of your position. It's loitered for about sixty seconds."

James had already jumped up from the couch. He peered out the window with a pair of laser range-finding binoculars through a slit he had cut in the curtains. The momentary sunshine had disappeared and wind and rain lashed the windows and the deck outside. It was very Baltic-in-winter weather. James observed a fishing boat rolling in the whitecaps. It had a cabin and he made it out to be around thirty feet plus with something tarped on the back deck. "Lousy day for it," James observed. He pressed the button on his optics and got the range. "Fishing boat, big enough to be sport-fishing charter, just over 4,000 meters offshore."

McCarter tapped his phone. Manning was on the roof of the safe house next to the chimney in the wind and rain with his rifle. He was covered by a tarp that implied work was being done on the roof. "I have eyes on, craft is— Christ!"

James snarled as the tarp came off in the back of the boat, exposing a large launch tube and sighting unit on a tripod. Upstairs Manning's rifle began cracking; a boat was a big target, but two miles was long range for a .30-caliber rifle firing at a boat in pitching seas. James broke from the window as fire blasted out of both ends of the launcher and a missile came spiraling toward the safe house trailing smoke. "Incoming! Everyone down! Down! Down!"

Propenko and Paulus upended the heavy oak table as a shield. McCarter rammed his shoulder into the thin slats of the pantry door and hurled himself inside. He grunted as Encizo flung himself on top of him. Hawkins was on the couch next to the window. With an impressive show of strength he turned the couch over on top of himself. James rather spectacularly vaulted into the air, got one foot onto the top of the Slavic table fortress and performed a magnificent dive over the kitchen island. Up on the roof Manning slung his rifle as he watched the missile hiss toward him head-on with deceptive speed.

The missile exploded like a supernova fifty meters in front of the beach house. Every window in the house burst inward.

Manning rolled down the back roof as every shingle on the seaward side flew into the air like a giant, flaming game of 52 Card Pick-up. The blast wave slapped away most of the chimney and took a stab at literally ripping the roof off. The roof bucked underneath him and then partially buckled. Manning suddenly ran out of roof and found himself falling while blindly blinking at flashing afterimages behind his eyes. The lid of the barbecue "broke" his fall, and the Canadian warrior slid off the top of the barbecue and flopped to the concrete slab of the back patio. He laid there mostly blind, totally deaf and being rained on.

"Jesus…"

CHAPTER NINE

Able Team

"Jesus!" Blancanales exclaimed. The blast had rattled their windows from six hundred meters away. Hermann Schwarz blinked away the spots dancing in front of his eyes. "That was a thermobaric! These guys aren't playing around!"

Lyons hefted his weapon. "They are playing around."

"You're right," Blancanales admitted. If the fuel-air warhead had hit the house it would have blown most of it sky-high. The people killed by the initial blast wave would be the lucky ones. The victims who had found some kind of shelter inside would find the intense, sustained heat wave channeling through the rooms, hallways and ventilations system sizzling any flesh it came in contact with, and the sudden, hot, violent vacuum it created in its wake would literally rip their lungs out. Any who had avoided that would find themselves burned, blinded, their eardrums ruptured, suffer massive concussion damage to the brain and find themselves gasping in an environment in which every last bit of oxygen had been burned away and the local atmosphere reduced to super-hot carbon dioxide, ash and a toxic mix of left over ethylene and propylene oxide fuel residue that would be as lethal as any war gas or chemical weapon known in modern warfare.

The enemy had chosen instead to detonate the warhead

in the open air fifty meters from the safe house, turning the weapon into the equivalent of a massive stun grenade.

Schwarz gazed out over the water. "The boat is coming straight in at full throttle."

"They've had time to put this together, so there'll be a ground team, as well." Lyons hit his com. "*Dragonslayer*, this is Able, did you see that?"

"Yes, sir, I did. What happened?"

"Phoenix just got hammered. We have a boat at sea firing rockets and expect to encounter ground support. Can you give us air support?"

"I am leaking oil and hydraulic fuel like a sieve and she is flying like a pig. I was really counting on the Farm arranging some air transport to get the girl to a military base in Germany where I can get some real repairs done."

"Can she fly?"

"She can, but who knows for how long."

"Do the machine guns still work?"

"Hardly been fired," Grimaldi replied.

"And if you fall into the Baltic, you still have pontoons?" Lyons suggested.

"You know you're awfully cavalier with other people's helicopters," the ace Stony Man pilot observed. "Heating up the engines now. Airborne in five or less."

"Copy that." Lyons ran for the back door. "Gadgets! Take the van. Get Phoenix on their feet and load them up. Pol, with me!"

Able deployed out the back.

Świnoujście was a seaside resort and it was winter. The rental agencies had fallen over themselves to set Able Team up. Lyons and Blancanales mounted their BMW G650 motorcycles and rooster-tailed mud in their wake as they burned down the wet access road for Phoenix Force's safe house.

The safe house looked like hell.

Rather than just setting the house ablaze from within, the superheated blast wave had slapped it. Some parts of a house were much more flammable than others, so the safe house had developed multiple small fires across its frontage. The chimney had collapsed and smoke was pouring out the shattered windows. Lyons and Blancanales screamed up the back drive and skidded to halt by the patio.

Gary Manning lay on the concrete gasping like a goldfish, making small, spastic and spectacularly unsuccessful attempts to rise.

Lyons and Blancanales dropped their bikes. "Gummer!" Lyons vaulted the fallen Canadian who appeared to be breathing and not burned or bleeding. "We'll be right back!"

Manning blinked and made an "ack!" noise. Whether it was a reply or just his current state of being was debatable. Lyons and Blancanales moved into the house. The fire alarm was shrieking. Just about every single last thing in the house that wasn't nailed down had fallen or broken. It looked as though God had picked up the little Polish beach house, shaken it like a Magic 8 Ball, thrown it down in disgust at the answer he'd received and then made a halfhearted attempt to set it on fire before walking away. There was a saying that a house resembled its owners. Phoenix Force and company were in bad shape.

Propenko and Paulus lay unconscious behind the shattered remnants of the dining table they had sheltered behind and were looking pretty shattered themselves.

Calvin James rose from behind the kitchen island with a nosebleed. "We got—aw…" James's knees went rubbery like a boxer who had taken a surprise left hook. His eyes rolled and he took three collapsing steps to his left and fell against the refrigerator, where he slid down the door and sat against his will.

"Cal! Where are—?"

McCarter emerged from the shattered pantry, mostly holding up Encizo.

"You all right?" Lyons asked.

"My team's a mess. Status?"

"Gadgets is bringing up the van. *Dragonslayer* is inbound. The enemy boat is closing in real quick. Their guys on the ground haven't showed themselves yet but I feel them. God help us if they have air assets, as well." Lyons scanned the room. "Where's Hawk?"

As he approached the shattered front porch, the worse things got. Several ceiling beams had fallen, and two of them were burning. One burning beam was pinning down and scorching an upside-down couch. The couch was jerking violently.

Lyons strapped on his gloves and heaved away the burning beam. He upended the couch to reveal a remarkably unscathed T. J. Hawkins, who stared up at him from the fetal position.

"Nice fort, kid. You want some chairs, blankets and stuffed animals to go with that?"

"You know?" Hawkins grinned at Lyons. "Up yours, Blondie."

Lyons nodded. It looked as if Hawkins was the last Phoenix Force member who could fight. "Gear up. We're going down to the beach and giving these pricks some grief."

"About goddamn time if you ask me." Hawkins rolled to one knee and scooped up his slightly scorched rifle. He glanced back at the rest of Phoenix Force. McCarter, Encizo and James were pulling a dead last in six-legged race for the back patio and it was difficult to see who was holding up whom. Lyons and Blancanales were dragging a boneless Slav each.

"Boss?" Hawkins called.

McCarter shouted back raggedly. "Get some, Hawk!"

Hawkins grabbed a vest full of magazines and munitions and a com unit. "Let's do it."

"On my six," Lyons ordered. He strode out to the blackened remains of the fallen front balcony. Smoke rose up from the burning wreckage below and a bit of the balcony crumpled like scorched paper beneath his boot. The rain sizzled against the embers. Lyons took one step back, gazed at the soggy, ruin-strewed bit of hill beneath him and jumped off. His boots hit hillside. Mud and sparks flew and he was running through the trees. Lyons heard Hawkins hit behind him. "On your six!"

Lyons ran for the beach. With any luck the smoke had obscured his and Hawkins's ejecting from the front of the house. Luck wasn't holding. The enemy boat was roaring in as though it was going to beach itself and the machine gun it had mounted over the wheelhouse in the intervening minutes began ripping through the coastal pines. The rocket launcher on the prow looked big even at this distance and it had to have been reloaded.

Lyons found a good, thick tree and began firing around it. The range was too long for the stubby Polish carbine. He raised his aim and hoped for pot shots. The Able Team leader knew they weren't within range of Hawkins's grenade launcher. "*Dragonslayer!* We need something!"

Lyons could hear the chopper malfunctioning over the link. Grimaldi's voice was tight with concern for his team and his sick bird. "Two minutes. Hold on."

"Hawk, let them come to us. *Dragonslayer* is inbound."

Hawkins's 40 mm grenade launcher thumped. "Popping smoke screen."

Lyons kept firing. Through his optic he could see the gunner and loader on the rocket launcher. His bullets were landing nowhere close and they didn't seem to care. The loader slammed the gunner on the shoulder. The gunner leaned his face into the electro-optical viewer of his sight and traversed the weapon down from the house to the trees. "Get down!" Lyons shouted.

Manning's voice croaked across the link. "What I don't owe this guy..."

Lyons watched as the optical sight and range-finding unit shattered and the man behind it slumped. The launch tube rose to vertical. The loader leaped for the weapon desperately but it fired. Back blast enveloped the loader and the boat's forward fishing deck. The rocket shot skyward for the heavens. The rocket reached its apex and the low-lying, scudding rain clouds pulsed like pudding with the thermobaric blow.

"Go!" Lyons ran for the beach at full sprint.

The boat swerved out of its ball of smoke and once again bore straight for the beach. The machine gunner got back behind the triggers of his gun. Four men with rifles spilled out of the cabin. They filled the rails and started firing. Unfortunately for them, if they were in range, they were also in rifle range of Lyons and Hawkins. The enemy gunmen were also on a pitching boat. They compensated by spraying on full-auto. Lyons and Hawkins simultaneously flicked their weapons to semi and began judging the rolling of the boat. Hawkins fired and a gunman fell into the sea. Lyons fired and his bullet sparked off the boat's rail. Hawkins fired again and another man fell backward with the pitch of the boat and rolled against the wheelhouse spraying blood across the deck. Lyons fired and missed. Hawkins fired and his target fell across the rail as though he was seasick, but the only thing coming out of his mouth was blood. "Three..." Hawkins commented.

Lyons watched the prow rise as it took a wave on the chin and the man who appeared to be seasick slid into the gray water. The prow dropped down and he fired at the remaining gunman. His target sprawled backward onto the foredeck that was already swimming in blood. "Yeah, I'm more a close-quarters guy," Lyons said into his com as the boat began to veer off. "Gummer, this is Ironman, can you take the guy at the wheel?"

"Yeah." A bullet appeared in the bridge window and cracks spider-webbed away from it. The boat continued to turn. "Probably…" A second bullet smashed through the window and weatherproof pane collapsed in a fractured sheet. "Maybe…" The boat turned broadside and the starboard bridge porthole blew inward. The engine died as whoever was skippering death gripped the throttle and fell backward. "Yeah, I got it." The ghost boat bobbed powerless upon the waves. The machine gunner hid behind the wheelhouse with one hand on his weapon firing blind bursts into the trees. "How do you feel about him, Ironman?"

"I like the way he cringes just fine. Just don't let him off his station."

"Copy that."

"Copy that." Hawkins gazed from his chewed-up tree trunk to Lyons. "You Able guys are all rough trade and stuff."

Dragonslayer came skidding around the headland. The chopper wasn't wobbling per se but neither was her flight the usual flawless, oil-on-glass glory that was Jack Grimaldi at the stick. He was clearly fighting his controls and his voice was tight over the com. "This is *Dragonslayer*. What's the status of the guy on the boat?"

"He's Ironman's," Hawkins reported. "You might tell him to get away from that machine gun."

Dragonslayer hovered slightly astern of the craft and dipped her nose to lay the muzzles of both her machine guns squarely on the lonesome gunner. He took the hint and put up his hands. He looked at the prow swimming in blood and the blackened stern deck and chose the ladder to go kneel on in surrender.

"Phoenix Leader, this is Ironman," Lyons reported. "Got you a boat and a prisoner."

"Copy that, Ironman," McCarter replied.

"You got any sign of the enemy ground team?"

"No, and I don't like it."

McCARTER DIDN'T LIKE it at all.

"Gummer! Anything?"

"No movement, Phoenix Leader," Manning replied.

"What about you, Jack?"

"I got nothing seaward. Be advised I don't think I can carry both teams and two prisoners."

McCarter calculated. "Right. Get Ironman and Hawk onto the boat. Have them take it up the coast a ways. Pick the first beach with a road access and land. We'll extract up top with the van and the motorcycles and meet you. You'll take the wounded and the rest of us will extract by sea. Bear?"

"Copy, Phoenix Leader."

"*Dragonslayer* is in shit shape. We need any friendly ship with a helipad within range."

"Already on it, USS *Coronado* has broken from maneuvers off the German coast and is steaming at full speed toward your position. ETA two hours. They are aware of the fact that this is a mission of US national security and no questions asked."

"Thanks, Bear."

James and Schwarz, having loaded Encizo and Propenko into the van, had come back for Paulus.

McCarter looked up into the leaden, raining skies hopefully. "Do we have satellite?"

"Ten more minutes, Phoenix Leader."

"Copy that." McCarter spit at the taste of smoke in his

mouth. He could hear the sound of sirens in the distance and he was feeling awfully exposed. "We are extracting now. We'll—"

McCarter's voice sank at the sound of a grenade launcher thump-thump-thumping in rapid fire out of the trees. "Down!"

The grenades hit. McCarter felt more blast and heat and a part of him recognized that these were offensive blast grenades rather than frags. The enemy ground game was awfully late in coming, and the Phoenix Force leader suddenly had a terrible inkling as to why. He rose, spraying his rifle into the trees. "The van! The van! The van!"

James and Manning began firing to cover Schwarz as he sprinted for the van. The grenade launcher slammed three times anew from the trees.

"Got you!" Manning snarled as his rifle cracked.

"Gadgets!" McCarter shouted.

Schwarz veered and hurled himself over the barbecue.

The three grenades hit and the world went Guy Fawkes Day for McCarter and his team as the three white-phosphorus grenades sprayed superheated gas and burning phosphorus streamers in all directions.

All three grenades had landed with excellent accuracy between the combined forces of Able Team and Phoenix Force and the van Encizo and Propenko lay inside.

"Fish!" James leaped up and despite his condition began a broken run skirting the expanding cloud. Running through it would be a death sentence. McCarter flanked the other side of the cloud bellowing aloud and through his com. They had loaded Encizo and Propenko's gear in with them. McCarter prayed that one or both of them might be able to rouse themselves. "Rafe! Nick! You have to fight! They're coming for you! You have to fight!"

McCarter prayed for gunfire as he rounded the horrible hot cloud. He raised his rifle and then lowered it as all he saw were the taillights of the van disappearing in the trees. He grit his teeth and crouched as James skidded up next to him.

"Tires! McCarter ordered. McCarter raised his own aim and fired a burst through back of the van high and on the driver's side. James fired and sparks screamed off the left rear fender.

The van disappeared around a bend.

McCarter hit his com. "Bear, this is Phoenix Leader. The enemy has Fish and Propenko. They are in the van. License plate Zulu-November-5-9-4. I need an anonymous to the local police that it is stolen and associated with this incident. Advise that it has bullet holes in it."

Kurtzman's voice was tight. Any capture of Farm personnel was a sum-of-all-fears situation. "Be advised, you have local police units scrambling."

"Copy that." McCarter looked over as James fell to his knees clutching his head. His nose hadn't stopped bleeding, but nothing was currently leaking out of his eyes or ears.

Grimaldi called across the com. "What do you want me to do?"

Kurtzman answered him. "Be advised. The next town over has launched its police helicopter. Polish Coastal Patrol is responding."

McCarter considered what remained of his battered team and available assets. He had two slightly scorched motorcycles. "Jack, you're going to take our injured and get out of here." McCarter went and lifted his bike up. "Ironman, Hawk, I need you now. Gadgets, we're taking the bikes and pursuing, two by two. We may have to go through town or residential. Lose your rifles—handguns and grenades only." McCarter checked the load in his pistol. "Bear, tell me you have something—anything."

"Five more minutes until satellite window." Kurtzman's voice was grim but filled with resolve. "And I am in communication with Fish's phone. Until the enemy makes him unlock it, or if they have very sophisticated detection equipment, they will not know that I have activated his GPS."

CHAPTER TEN

The Room

Rafael Encizo sat handcuffed to a chair in his underwear. Propenko didn't wear underwear and all he wore was the bandage around his leg that he had bled through again. A camera and a laptop sat on a folding table and the camera's red light was on. Four men who looked like mercs and smelled like gunpowder were in the room with them. One of the men was just finishing a very slow walk around Encizo with a very sophisticated camera.

Encizo knew he was being photographed from all angles and the images were going to run against all available data bases the enemy had. Everything Encizo and Propenko had on them when they had been loaded into the van was on a separate table.

Encizo was aware that there was a fifth man behind him who had not chosen to reveal himself or to speak.

Propenko grinned at the cameraman. "What? No pictures of me?" He looked down at himself with pride that reality backed up. "This is internet worthy!"

The cameraman walked up and jammed his thumb into the bullet hole in Propenko's leg. He slowly twisted it back and forth and corkscrewed his thumb down into the wound; he filmed it while he did. Save for his leg tensing, Propenko did a remarkable job of not appearing to care.

The man stood and spoke for the first time with some kind of eastern European accent. "What is going to happen to you, Nikita Propenko? This is illegal to post on the internet, but many bad people, including a number who you put in prison, will pay great amounts of money to buy a copy of it on the black market." He matched Propenko smile for smile and nodded at the Russian's wedding tackle. "Perhaps you would like to say goodbye to it. You will be parting soon. Perhaps I will make you kiss it after you part with it. Perhaps I will make you eat it."

Propenko sighed. "If I had ruble for every time…"

Encizo took stock of the situation. He was still a little shaken from the blast but he was fairly certain he didn't have a concussion. The enemy had seen fit to stun and blindfold him before taking him out of the van. He had smelled trees. He hadn't smelled the sea and, despite being in fairly bad shape, he was certain the ride had been less than half an hour. He and Propenko were in an empty, windowless room, but it did not have the lingering smell of released bowels and fear that the average torture chamber maintained. Nor did it smell of bleach or disinfectant. It appeared to an interior room and one that had been recently cleared out for the two current guests of honor.

None of this meant that it couldn't swiftly turn into an abattoir as Propenko's new friend had just implied. Encizo had looked at the table containing their gear once. The only things missing were their pistols and knives. He had seen his phone and noted that it had been opened and been ignored since. Unless the enemy had tampered with it there was a very good chance the Farm was tracking him. The enemy had undoubtedly turned it off. What they did not know was that this was a Farm-issue phone. It looked and mostly functioned like the Apple product Encizo personally preferred, but it had a number of very interesting modifications and capabilities the smartest smartphone on the market lacked.

One of those functions: even when it was outwardly

turned off, there were several parts that were always on. One such part was much like the RFID Calvin James had removed from Paulus's hand. The chip in Encizo's phone sat, waiting, passively listening, 24/7, with the patience of silicone for a certain coded signal from the Farm. When that signal was received it would activate the GPS tracking function, all the while leaving the phone apparently dead.

Another interesting function was that once the signal from the Farm was received, they owned the phone. They could turn any aspect of it on they wished, and the phone would lie there like a brick. The included the speaker and the camera. The camera was currently pointed at the ceiling.

Encizo didn't bother to resist as another man walked up to him. The man hit an app on his cell phone and one by one began pressing the fingertips of Encizo's fingers to the screen and electronically fingerprinting them. He straightened, nodded at the unseen man in the back of the room and hit Send.

The man in the back spoke. "Now, Propenko is dead. That's a fact. There is very little we really think we can learn from him we don't already know. You, on the other hand?" he said to Encizo. "You, we really want to get to know better. So I am going to make this very simple for you. You are going to get to watch what we do to Propenko. We'll have to make it a quick and dirty job, but dirty it will be. This will let you know that we are serious. Then I am going to have a number of questions for you.

"Any time I start having a problem with your answers we will begin the same procedures we performed on Propenko on you, though more slowly and carefully. The good news is, if you are helpful, at a certain point I will put a bullet in Propenko's head and end his suffering. Even better news? Impress me, and you might even leave this room alive. We might go for a little ride together, and I might introduce you to some people who will wish to have several long conversations with you. How does that sound?"

"Sounds great," Propenko offered. "Torture him, and I will talk."

Encizo laughed. So did the man behind them. "They say you're as tough as they come, Propenko, say you've been tortured before and not broken, but I'm just betting it wasn't blow torches and physical dismemberment."

He returned his attention to Encizo. "Now, listen, mystery man, I won't kid you, you will still probably end up as mulch someplace. It will all be out of my hands at that point. But, you might survive another day or three. During that time you can try to plot your escape, pray somebody will come rescue you, you might even get fed once or twice. And, like they say, every day above ground... Think about it."

The hidden man raised his voice to the other four men in the room. "Gentlemen, extraction is coming soon, and we are on a tight schedule. Let's get to work!"

McCarter scanned the cabin as the driving rain pounded down through the forest. The cabin was a "great sodding affair" in McCarter's personal parlance. The structure was two stories high and constructed of logs as big around as beer kegs and looked as if they'd do quite elegantly for stopping subsonic pistol bullets. There was a small carriage house made of beams and boards that looked like it could easily hold three vehicles.

The Stony Man operatives caught their breath and watched. Once the Farm had given them the coordinates, they had abandoned their bikes and gone for a very long, hard run through the woods and rain. The Farm had gotten eyes on the place approximately an hour ago and nothing had gone in or out since.

Kurtzman had activated Encizo's phone receiver, as

well, and was monitoring the conversation inside. So far it wasn't sounding good.

Kurtzman spoke in McCarter's ear bud. "We have three voices so far. All speaking English. One Slavic and unidentified. One we can't figure out, and Propenko is pulling his World's Toughest Ivan routine again. They're talking torture, and by the sound of the conversation Fish is in the room and isn't talking. We're pretty sure we heard him laugh once, speech recognition software cannot confirm. Be advised we are losing satellite window in fifteen minutes and counting."

"Copy that, Bear." McCarter tried to push his senses into the house but nothing was moving except the rain, and it was going to be dark soon. "These guys have had some time to plan this, so we have to figure they have a drone flying around. We also have to figure their bloody mobile Game Room is somewhere nearby, as well. I think they intended to hammer us and take whoever was still alive off in the boat. We have that boat and sent them packing in a van full of holes, so they've gone to ground in their own safe house and must be arranging alternate extraction."

Lyons nodded. "How do you want to play it, David?"

McCarter considered his ad hoc team. Since it was a Phoenix Force man who was missing, McCarter had silently been acknowledged as team leader. The mix had a few advantages. While Phoenix Force had been scrambling all over Poland by land, sea and air, Able Team had flown into Poland in first class and had had time to arrange primo gear to the bait house. A lot of that gear had been lost in the burning beach house and men riding motorcycles double through city streets couldn't carry most of what was left. What Lyons and Schwarz did have were sound suppressors for their pistols.

"Two-man teams. Carl with me. Gadgets with Hawk. You will be taking point and, with luck, their sentries."

Lyons and Schwarz nodded and screwed the suppressors onto the USP tactical pistols the CIA had managed to smuggle to the hunting lodge in Gdansk.

Lyons vastly preferred his .357 Python but he would save that for the torturers once he got inside.

McCarter flicked the safety off.

"You want to check the garage?" Hawkins asked.

McCarter watched as the curtains of the upstairs lodge opened briefly and the shape of a head appeared for the second time in five minutes. "Someone is expecting someone, and getting a little antsy."

"Gotta be expecting a helicopter," Schwarz said. "That thermobaric burst must have set every dog in town barking. Then the fire? Polish police will be setting up checkpoints all over the place. If these guys have a ground extraction plan, it had better be nothing short of awesome."

McCarter nodded. Schwarz had a point. The cabin was something of a monstrosity. Big enough to have its own gravel drive, with a frontage large enough to land three *Dragonslayers,* and the town of Świnoujście was close enough to Germany to throw a rock at.

Kurtzman spoke urgently. "Phoenix Leader, you need to hear this."

McCarter listened as the Stony Man cybernetics genius patched his phone into the receiver in Encizo's phone. Propenko had raised his voice but as though he was talking to an idiot child. "Fool! You do not cut off! You crush! Crushing much more painful. You think showing me finger scares me? Pussy!"

"Farm, this is Phoenix Leader. We are going in now. Going in hard."

The curtain upstairs opened again. Lyons and Schwarz both fired a single shot. Two holes appeared in the pane and the face snapped way from the window with the blows.

McCarter broke into a run across the dead ground. "Make the call."

THE MAN WHO had jammed his thumb into Propenko's leg wound tossed Propenko's left little finger into Encizo's lap. The Cuban shrugged at the man as though he was feeble. "What am I supposed to do with that? My hands are tied."

Propenko glanced at his four-fingered left hand. The torturer had taken off the digit at the root with the deftness of a surgeon. "If you cut, you use shears. Long, slow squeeze, and you do one joint at time."

The man blinked and looked toward the unknown man at the back of the room.

"You want me to do it?" Encizo suggested.

The voice spoke. "Very well, let's lop off Propenko's Johnson, and then let's feed it to laughing boy. Tie it off first. I don't want him bleeding to death."

"Tie it off? Look at me!" Propenko looked around the room. "Did you bring rope?"

The voice spoke. "Darius?" One of the men looked up from Propenko's hand. "Go out to the shed and get Branko some shears."

Darius slung a rifle over his shoulder and left the room. Branko raised his bloody knife. "Do we wait?"

"No," the voice responded. "Let's speed this up and—" Encizo's phone rang.

The voice dropped low. "Branko, I told you turn both men's phone off."

Branko flinched. "I did! I swear!"

"You know? I believe you. Take the call, but don't say anything."

"But it's locked. I—"

"It isn't now. Put it on speaker. The camera can flip to

selfie, so hold it sideways and put it down on the table facing away from everyone."

Branko picked up the phone as though it was a snake and awkwardly tapped to take the call. He set the phone down so that if faced empty wall on both sides.

The unseen man shouted out jovially. "Hi, there!"

Kurtzman's voice was scrambled as he spoke back. "You ready to surrender?"

"Absolutely not!"

"You, Branko, finger fetish. Surrender right now and I give you my word we'll keep Propenko away from you. You don't? We give you to him."

"You should have killed me," Propenko advised. "You should kill me now."

Encizo gauged his enemies. Branko looked a little panicky. The other two men were tense but still frosty and picked up their rifles.

The unseen man sounded absolutely unconcerned. "I could put a bullet through the back of Propenko's head. I could do the same to your friend. Or I could put one through Propenko's skull just to show you that I'm serious."

"People who cut off parts of people are deadly serious, I've already granted you that. What we both know is that it all comes down to the one man in the room who really knows. He's the one you wanted intel from. You kill Propenko? Well, we've all grown rather fond of him, and that will make us rather angry at you."

Propenko nodded. "Thank you."

"You're welcome. Now," Kurtzman continued, "you kill the guest of honor, all negotiations end and we take the cabin by force. When we do, I suggest you put your gun in your mouth before we get hold of you. Any hope of making any kind of deal for yourself is off the table."

"You sound very First World to me, and I do not believe you and your people are the torturing kind."

"The term has fallen out of favor, but it's called extraordinary rendition. You will be extra-judicially transferred from the chair you are sitting in now to the one Propenko is occupying."

"I think you—"

"And as for our people being torturers? It will be a shame to lose Propenko, but we've had Goran Paulus warming up in the bullpen to deal with just this exact situation."

The unseen man had no immediate response.

"You want to surrender now?"

"I think we beat your team pretty savagely. I think your assets in Poland are at the end of their rope. Your helicopter was in shit shape last I heard, and I just don't hear rotors or see anyone fast-roping down into the trees. I am going to kill Propenko, and my men and I are walking out with your friend. If anyone interferes...he dies."

Encizo spoke coldly. "Where do you think your buddy Darius is? Spanking his monkey in the shed?"

The door behind him suddenly opened and slammed shut. The lock clicked. The jaws of Branko and the other two mercs dropped in sudden abandoned horror. The door facing Encizo and Propenko smashed open. Encizo squeezed his eyes shut and vainly wished he could cover his ears as the grenade bounced into the room.

McCarter's voice boomed. "Go! Go! Go!"

The stun grenade went off like a bomb inside the confines of the small room.

McCARTER AND LYONS charged through the door. Lyons figured the guy with the knife was Branko and he did him a favor by putting two .357 Magnum slugs in his chest. McCarter put one in the chest and one in the head of one rifleman. The other man threw down his rifle and screamed for mercy in a language other than English.

McCarter took a step forward and booted him savagely in the groin. The man fell, clutching himself, and McCarter finished it by putting his heel through the man's front teeth. Encizo shouted in the way that temporarily deafened people do who unconsciously assume everyone is deaf, as well. "Back door! He rabbitted!"

McCarter got on the horn. "Hawk! Gadgets! We have at least one man loose in the house. Probably the guy in charge." The Stony Man teams had run a cursory sweep of the house, and Lyons and Schwarz had shot four more men, but the team was only four men, as well, and it just wasn't enough to hold down a cabin this size, much less hold the perimeter. "He'll be making for the carriage house and the vehicles."

"On it," Schwarz called.

Kurtzman came over everyone's link. "Be advised. Two vehicles have left the main route and are heading toward the cabin."

Hawkins's shout could be heard on and off the link. "He's out the front! Heading straight down the drive for the road!"

McCarter scooped up Branko's knife and cut Encizo's right-hand tie. Encizo took the knife. "Go. Nick and I are fine."

McCarter and Lyons sprinted for the front of the cabin. He could see Hawkins tearing down the drive after a large man running into the trees. The two team leaders burst from the cabin at a dead sprint but Hawkins was younger and faster.

The former Delta Force operative suddenly reappeared running as though hell was on his heels. "Holy Christ!"

A Humvee burst out of the trees. The vehicle was painted Polish military dark green and bore military markings and the Polish white-and-red flag on the doors. McCarter saw it all in one flash. The enemy was going

to drive straight through every police checkpoint out of
Świnoujście. Given the level of sophistication the enemy
had, their papers would appear to be in order and their orders to be let through would be the Polish military equivalent of God on High.

Hawkins broke right as he hit the grounds. The Humvee mounted a machine gun and the gunner traversed for
Hawkins. McCarter and Lyons both began emptying their
pistols at the gunner. He jerked as he took hits. The driver
floored it and came straight on for the two team leaders.
A Polish military truck burst onto the drive behind it. It
swerved for Hawkins while the Humvee came on.

Schwarz charged between McCarter and Lyons. "Grenade!"

The Humvee driver stood on his brakes as Schwarz
hurled his munition. The flash-bang stood no chance of
breeching the vehicle, but the driver experienced a thun-
derclap and an explosion of sparks on his hood. The vehicle
swerved wildly. McCarter and Lyons stood their ground and
finished emptying their pistols through the windshield. The
Humvee throttled down as the driver died at the wheel. The
Phoenix Force leader turned just in time to see Hawkins go
down under the wheels of the truck. "Hawk!"

Schwarz roared in dismay. "Hawk!"

Lyons dropped his empty .357 Magnum and slapped
leather for his silenced weapon. McCarter and Schwarz
slammed in fresh magazines.

The truck turned and tore back for the road.

Hawkins was nowhere in sight.

"You brilliant little punter." McCarter felt a ray of hope.
"Fire, but raise your aim."

The remaining Stony Man warriors fired off shots that
struck above and to either side of the fleeing truck. Mc-
Carter's faith was rewarded as Hawkins's boots appeared
beneath the rear bumper.

The military truck had more than two feet of road clearance and Hawkins's legs bounced dangerously up and down as he was dragged. Hawkins's lower torso appeared as he played a very dangerous game of traversing the bottom of the truck hand over hand while it was in motion. His face appeared as he got his hands on the steel bumper. He grinned maniacally backward and nearly lost everything including his skull as the truck hit a bump as it left the drive and hit the road. He kept one hand on and swiftly regained the other. The team kept firing. The last thing McCarter saw was Hawkins doing a sudden, violent leg lift with a half twist and just managing to hook a heel over the bumper steel and completely get his body off the ground. The truck swerved around the curve and was gone.

Schwarz slapped in a fresh magazine and lowered his smoking weapon. "I take back everything I ever said about him."

"I don't. He's an idiot." Lyons picked up his Python and wiped dirt off the brushed stainless steel. "A beautiful idiot, mind you."

McCarter felt a slight glow of pride. "You can't have him. He's mine. Check the Humvee. See if anyone is hiding in the back." The Phoenix Force leader spoke into his phone. "Farm, this is Phoenix Leader. Propenko and Fish are secure. No casualties. We have one enemy prisoner. Their leader escaped in a Polish military truck."

Lyons stood next to the Humvee and made the cutting motion across his throat with his hand.

Kurtzman was grim. "I have eyes on the truck, and I am going to lose my satellite window in ninety seconds. He hits the main road and he is gone."

"Funny you should mention that." McCarter and his team began walking back to the cabin. "There has been an unexpected development."

CHAPTER ELEVEN

Piast Canal

T. J. Hawkins was cold, wet and exhausted. The insane glee at how pleased he was with himself allowed him to glow from within. The truck had not burned for the German border or doubled back east for what could be described as the Polish mainland. The magnetic sensor in his phone's compass app told him he was heading south. Google Earth and his GPS had informed him they were paralleling the Piast Canal and heading straight toward the Oder Lagoon.

It was ironic that despite being wet and shivering, he was very thirsty. He clicked off his phone. His Farm-issue device looked like a Droid Turbo but had nearly twice the battery power and life. However he had been using it a lot and he had no idea when he would be able to recharge. He had nothing to report at the moment and the Farm was tracking him. They would contact him if something came up. The cab was separated from the truck bed and the bed was covered with canvas with no window inside. The enemy had managed to pick up only one man so there had been no reason to check the back.

Hawkins considered his assets. They consisted of his phone, his pistol, one spare magazine and his tactical knife. He'd found two boxes of Polish army uniforms undoubtedly meant as disguises for the kidnap team. Changing into dry clothes had been a terrible temptation but he didn't speak Polish and if he was caught in Polish fatigues he could technically be shot as a spy. Most likely it would cause him immense amounts of trouble that would include detainment and could take days for the Farm to fix. Wet and cold wasn't going to change anytime soon.

The truck suddenly ground to a halt.

Hawkins rolled over the back gate, hit mud and rolled under the rear bumper. "Hello, old friend," he muttered. Peering forward he could see the vast expanse of the Oder Lagoon and the lights of the port of Stettin and the smaller cities and towns ringing the lagoon and dotting its many islands. He could also distinguish the large black shape of an offshore ship with its lights out.

The truck was on a slightly raised turn-out overlooking the water. Hawkins noted a small, old-fashioned motor launch sitting at rest on the shore. The truck's lights went out and the two men in the cab jumped out. Three men came forward from the launch while a fourth stayed behind the wheel. Two of the men had rifles and flanked the third man like guards, but they kept their weapons slung. In the gloom the men were mostly dark shapes, but the guy who had jumped out the driver's side was huge.

The big man suddenly laughed as the two groups met. "Well, that went for shit."

The leader from the Lagoon side spoke. "Anyone else make it out?"

"Anyone else contact you?"

"No."

"Then I doubt it. These Russian and Serb mercs you keep giving me are ass-kickers and leg-breakers, but not exactly escape-and-evasion, secret-agent types. Unlike the competition, I might add."

"Any chance you were followed?"

"Oh, we played all sorts of games on the road, doubling

back, crisscrossing over the canal roads. No way we were tailed."

"They found you at the cabin," the other man suggested.

"Yeah, yeah, they did. But they were zeroing in on the asshole's phone GPS, and it was the last of their team that could still stand up. When we hit the grounds in the Hummer and the truck, there were only three guys."

"We saw only two on the camera when they assaulted the interrogation room. Then your prisoner freed himself and Propenko and shut off the camera. So I agree, four or five men, tops." The man made a bemused noise. "Propenko is still alive."

"Yeah, and now he will be actually, genuinely, pissed off."

Hawkins stared out onto the water. The conversation was mildly amusing but he had bigger fish to fry. He figured he had zero chance of sneaking aboard the launch and six to one was long odds in a gunfight. Hawkins also had a very sneaky suspicion the motionless ship out on the water was his quarry's next destination. He had another sneaky, rather gleeful suspicion that the mythological Game Room might be one of the containers on board the ship. Containers ships were big and had small crews; there would be lots of places to hide. It would be his second stowaway ride of the day. How awesome would that be?

Of course, if he swam out there and the launch puttered off into the dark in the opposite direction, he would be the moron of the century.

It was also the middle of winter on the northern edge of Poland and he was already freezing. Climbing aboard the ship once he got there would be another matter entirely. Hawkins smiled to himself. Somewhere in the back of his mind, he heard Calvin James expressing the idea that this was the sort of thing that Navy SEALs did in their sleep and that Delta Force guys were all secretly pussies who, once they stopped being Rangers, slept in beds and ate off plates and only showed up when all the real work had been done.

Hawkins made his decision.

He went Ranger silent as he moved backward from under the truck and circled wide. With practiced speed he shucked his boots and tied them around his neck. The Farm phone was highly water resistant but he didn't take any chances and stuffed it and his tactical knife down a boot each. He reluctantly tossed his pistol. It was two pounds of steel he didn't want to swim with and he suspected there would be guns on board. He silently loped down to the beach and stepped into the water.

Hawkins froze as the launch flashed its lights twice.

In the sudden light he saw a white rope girding the side of the launch with a series of blue floats hanging from it about two feet above the water line.

As the men on shore began walking toward the launch, Hawkins threw caution to the wind and slid under the water. The cold hit him hard and he fought it by swimming as fast as he ever had under water. The distance was thirty meters and he counted his breaststrokes. He felt his lungs burning way too quickly and his strokes slowing. Hawkins lost his timing. Just as he was about to come up for a peek, he saw stars as his head thumped into the side of the launch. He narrowly avoided inhaling a lungful of water and stayed under. No one seemed to have noticed. He pulled a *Creature from the Black Lagoon* slow rise and it took every ounce of will he had not to gasp aloud.

There was no pier, the shore was rocky and the men had to wade out at chest height to get to the launch. Hawkins had guessed right; they were approaching the other side of the boat. He grabbed the float line and let his breathing return to normal as the five men boarded and threw blankets around their shoulders. Hawk smelled coffee and hated them.

The motor kicked into life and Hawkins found himself on a reverse Nantucket sleigh ride across the Oder Lagoon. The ride was mercifully short but the question looming closer like the sheer sides of the ship was what he was going to do once they got there.

He was like a dog chasing a car, but he was about to catch a container vessel.

If they lowered a gangway or a ladder he would just have to take the launch once it broke off and follow. That might be enough. He would be seen come daylight, but by the same token he could contact the Farm and hopefully within the next couple of hours they could reestablish satellite eyes on the ship. Of course, the enemy had slipped away from them the last time they had done that.

Hawkins really, really, really wanted on that ship.

The launch came alongside. Hawkins wasn't that nautical but examining how much shore light it blocked from end to end it was maybe the same size as the *Maria Cecilia* or a little bigger. It also had its own cranes, which that told him it was probably another feeder vessel. That seemed to be the Game Room's MO. As a mobile operation they didn't want to be stuck on a big vessel dependent on shore cranes and the good will of the port authority.

Hawkins sank under the water as the launch was hailed from above. Long moments passed. He put his hand against the hull of the launch and felt and heard clinks and clanks and the thud of feet.

Hawkins figured it out. The container had lowered cables. The launch had cleats and they were securing the boat to winch it aboard. They were doing it efficiently and without lights. Hawkins rose and took the float rope in both hands, wondering if his numb fingers had the strength to hold on. Someone up top shouted something in German or Polish or Slobovian, for all Hawkins knew, and the launch suddenly left the water.

Hawkins rose with it.

No one noticed the hitchhiker. Men up top and on the launch shouted things at each other that Hawkins figured was "Easy!" and "Steady as she goes!" He felt his grip weakening.

The launch providently rose past an open, darkened gangway that girded most of the ship's side. Hawkins risked everything. He kicked his frozen legs back, let go with one hand and swung out for the rail like an ancient and arthritic orangutan. God provided and the launch swung inward toward the ship to add to his momentum. Hawkins let go as he nearly passed the gangway and fell. The rail brutally slammed under both his armpits.

He clung to the rail for long moments, waiting, but the launch kept rising. Men called out but their tones of voice didn't change and no one turned on a light. Hawkins climbed over the rail with slothlike slowness and collapsed to the steel deck gasping.

"I am a god," he declared.

T. J. Hawkins stood and went hunting for warmth, shelter and hot coffee.

Stony Man Farm

KURTZMAN FELT guardedly pleased with the world. Losing Encizo had been a stomach-dropping experience and he had expected the worst. The fiasco had turned into, as Akira Tokaido declared it, "Flawless victory."

Aaron Kurtzman allowed himself a small smirk. Flawless wasn't quite the way he would have described it. Hawkins's hobo excursion across northern Poland had been one piece of blind luck after another. However, Kurtzman also had to give Hawkins credit. One whole hell of a lot of balls had been involved, as well. The feeder ship *Belle Nymphe* had passed northward through the Piast Canal flying under Italian registry, and the Game Room, if it was on board—and that was still a mighty big if—was once again in the Baltic Sea and operating in international waters. Kurtzman's every instinct told him it was.

The question was what to do about it.

Phoenix Force had extracted to the Littoral Combat Ship USS *Coronado*. Even without any passengers, Grimaldi had been forced to land *Dragonslayer* on the water and Phoenix had been reduced to towing it with the boat they had stolen. Kurtzman couldn't imagine the look on the captain of the *Coronado's* face when he had picked up a boat whose prow was covered in blood, her stern blackened by fire and pulling a helicopter on pontoons through the waves. What he thought of the passengers would be another thing entirely.

Phoenix Force had been beat up pretty badly.

Gary Manning had cracked ribs from barbecue diving. Calvin James was having balancing issues. The good news was he wasn't displaying any other classic concussion symptoms and the ship's surgeon aboard the *Coronado* believed it was an inner ear issue from being hit by the pressure wave and should resolve itself. Explosions were capricious.

David McCarter had come out of the blast apparently without a scratch but now he was developing a cough. Whether that was a mild burn from breathing in the superheated air, breathing in some very nasty leftover chemicals or whether he had caught a cold running around in the rain for three days was yet to be determined.

Rafael Encizo had been knocked unconscious and that was always a bad sign but they were monitoring him in sick bay.

Goran Paulus was also in bad shape. He definitely had

some bleeding in the brain and was in and out of consciousness. The Serb would be of no use as an intelligence asset or an extra gun for the foreseeable future.

That left Propenko.

Kurtzman genuinely smiled. He had been knocked unconscious by the blast, as well, and showed no signs of damage whatsoever. The surgeon had informed the Russian that reattaching his finger was really out of his and his staff's purview. They could fly him to a hospital in Germany but because the injury was starting to get old and the finger had not been kept in a sterile condition, there would be no guarantee of success. Propenko had declared his intention to use it for bait and inquired if there was any saltwater tackle aboard the *Coronado*.

Kurtzman was really starting to wonder if Nikita Propenko had been born in the Highlands of Scotland four hundred years ago and the only way to kill him would be to cut off his head and take his power. With Hawkins off on his own, Phoenix Force was down a man. Propenko had offered to continue his services, for pay of course, and first crack at the unseen man from the cabin.

Hot food, hot showers and rack time was the best solution for Phoenix Force at the moment while the *Coronado* kept an extremely loose tail on the *Belle Nymphe* and her flight mechanics oohed and ahhed and did what they could for *Dragonslayer* under Jack Grimaldi's watchful eye.

Able Team was another story entirely. They were right as rain. After a deep but hurried strategy session, Price had opted to set the teams on separate courses.

Able Team was on a military flight out of Germany heading back to the United States. Carmen Delahunt, the other member of his team, and Huntington Wethers were feverishly working out role camouflage for them that could stand up to some professional scrutiny. Rather than wading through swamps in Poland, they were going to be wallowing through the mire of Wall Street.

Stony Man's cybernetics chief looked over at the portside screen at his workstation. Up in one corner, the inset photo of Demi Papas grinned at him. Kurtzman grinned back.

The Farm had been compiling a very large set of files on the man, and they kept getting more and more interesting. Some qualified as damning, morally, if not quite legally, yet Kurtzman's team was working away on it.

Demi Papas regularly boasted on television that he could sell water by the river, and in his books he often spoke about how his alpha personality was just as or even more important than his business acumen to his success. He professed that there were a lot of guys who had a lot of weapons on Wall Street. Papas said it was better to turn yourself into a "perfect weapon" and he used himself as the template ad nauseam.

Kurtzman was very interested to see what would happen when Wall Street's "Perfect Weapon" met the planet's premier psychological warfare expert in the shape of Rosario Blancanales. Throwing Carl Lyons and Hermann Schwarz into the mix was just icing on the cake.

Aaron Kurtzman loved his job and the challenges it presented, though they were often very stressful and could run the gamut from the tragic to the genuinely frightening.

He had a feeling that this next phase of the operation might qualify as genuine fun.

Kurtzman checked his watch.

Able Team would be landing in New York in two hours.

CHAPTER TWELVE

Wall Street

Schwarz scanned the screens in front of him. He sat in the van surrounded by his security suite. "This Papas prick? His stuff is absolutely top-notch."

"Can you beat it?" Blancanales asked.

Schwarz gave Blancanales a look.

Lyons checked the loads in his Python. He had given up asking these questions a long time ago. "The real question we have here is exactly how do you want to go in?"

Lyons had been giving that a lot of thought. It was high noon on Wall Street on a mild and sunny winter afternoon. People flooded forth from the towers of the financial empire in the lunch rush to frequent the high-end restaurants or the latest cool places in other parts of Manhattan. Going in hard and pulling a snatch-and-grab didn't strike him as the best course. Ideally what Lyons wanted was shock and awe—shock and awful enough to make Papas voluntarily comply. "We're sure he's at home?"

"It's lunch hour and, like any good business executive, he is surfing porn on the internet," Schwarz observed dryly. "Nothing illegal, but neither do you really want to know."

"Of course I do." Lyons leaned in and looked at the screen monitoring Demi Papas's personal internet activity. The Able Team leader watched several seconds of the activities of a man and a woman and someone who appeared to be a bit of both. "Exploring gender roles and boundaries… They say it's perfectly natural."

Schwarz snorted. "You know, for as long as I have known you, your boundaries seem to have consisted of one long, uninterrupted chain of extremely heterosexual blondes."

"It's a burden." Lyons holstered his revolver. "I live with it."

Blancanales laughed. "I think it's magic time."

Lyons snorted. "Pol's right. Let's make it magic. Like rabbit-out-of-a-hat magic with a spectacular act of auto-erotic interruptus."

Schwarz laughed, as well. "All right, then. What you want to do is walk right in on him unannounced, and to do that you will want to bypass the security desk in the foyer, have every door opened and avoid the private security and his secretary, as in a cascade of security failures preceding."

"That'd be great."

"I suppose you want all the security cameras turned off?"

"Cascading failure has such a lovely ring to it," Blancanales quipped.

"All right, I figured that might be the case." Schwarz started pulling up icons and one of his screens began filling with the squares of security camera footage. "Okay, that's your route, and I'll be talking you through it every step of the way." He opened his link to the Farm. "Bear, you getting all this?"

"Copy that, Gadgets. Could have done without the internet feed."

"Exploring gender roles and boundaries, they say it's perfectly natural," Schwarz said, parroting Lyons's earlier remark. "Be advised we are going in."

"Copy that. Do you need anything else on this end?"

"Not currently, but thanks. Will advise."

Schwarz turned his attention to target number one: the security guard sitting at the desk in the foyer. His name was Donald Blakely. Currently taking online business classes, he frequently did his homework on his laptop while on duty. Blakely also happened to be six foot six and a decorated United States Marine who had come back from Afghanistan a year ago. Schwarz liked Blakely. He was vet who was getting by and striving to get ahead. Schwarz decided to take it easy on him and kill two birds with one stone.

He watched as Blakely looked up from his Generally Accepted Principles of Accounting homework when his security console pinged. The message, from his manager, told him there was a problem in the security suite and his presence was required immediately. Blakely bounced up from his chair and charged through the foyer.

Schwarz nodded. "Go."

His Able Team teammates inserted their ear buds and deployed straight for the huge, shining glass doors. Schwarz turned off the camera watching the front of the building and in another window watched Blakely slide his card key through the lock on the security suite door. The next window showed Blakely entering the suite. It had banks of screens and Blakely's manager was frowning at the blank screen for the front door and then he frowned at Blakely. The door closed automatically behind Blakely, and Schwarz triggered the lock, froze it and turned off the cameras watching the foyer.

"Foyer is clear," Schwarz advised through the com link. "Proceed to elevators. Go to the fourteenth floor."

"Copy that," Lyons responded.

Schwarz programmed the elevator to not stop at any other floors, routed the feed from the camera to him and denied it to the building security recorder. Lyons and Blancanales rode up undisturbed.

Schwarz turned off the cameras in the hallway. There were a few people in the hall, but everyone knew that anyone coming out of the public elevators had already gone through security.

Lyons and Blancanales were dressed in business suits and actually looked as if they belonged there. They each wore an ear bud in one ear but a lot of people in all walks of life were doing that these days. "Go straight down the hall to the private elevators. Take the one on the right. It goes directly to Papas's office suite."

The two Able Team men walked to the private elevator. Schwarz waited until the hallway was clear and then opened the doors. He killed the camera and the two warriors stepped inside. The interior was far swankier than the public elevator. Blancanales ran a finger down the deep, rich, wood paneling of some exotic and probably endangered tropical hardwood. "Plush ride."

Schwarz spoke in their ear buds. "Here we go. When you go in, there's a foyer with a large meet-and-greet area behind it, but Papas's secretary appears to be out taking her lunch. Be advised there is a big guy sitting on the couch texting. He's security. Jay "Dukes" LeDuc. He was a bouncer at Papas's favorite slumming club and Papas poached him. No military or police training, but he's a brawler and licensed to carry a firearm in the State of New York. A registered Glock 17."

"Copy that. Status on Papas?"

"Still enthusiastically engaged."

"Copy. We're going in."

Schwarz opened the elevator door. The Able Team computer genius had been kind enough to turn off the ping and the swanky private conveyance was nearly silent. Dukes was a huge, tall, dark and handsome kind of guy who spent a lot of time at the gym. He showed his lack of training as he gaped at the two men walking across the foyer toward him.

Lyons had a charming, boyish smile when he was in a rare jovial mood. "Hi! Is Demi around?"

"Hey, wait! What?" LeDuc looked at his watch. "No, no, nah. No meetings and no calls. Mr. Papas is unavailable until two." LeDuc made the fatal mistake of filling his other hand with a tablet and squinting at it. "I got no one on the list, not even canceled wannabes and supplicants."

"Wannabes?" Lyons asked.

"Supplicants," Blancanales agreed. "Nice."

LeDuc started to rise. "Listen up. There must be some kind of mistake. I— Hey! Wait!"

The mistake was all Leduc's. Blancanales hit him low and Lyons hit him high. LeDuc failed to block either attack. The two men from Able Team switched high and low, and Leduc fell back in a destroyed heap onto the couch. Blancanales confiscated his Glock and ripped out the standing lamp's electrical cord and hog-tied him. "Leduc is down. What's the status on Papas?"

"He just finished."

Lyons shook his head. "I was looking forward to that."

"Well, do onto others..." Blancanales advised.

"There is that." Lyons and Blancanales strode through the opulent office suite. The amount of marble, exotic wood, gold gilding and objets d'art were worthy of a Russian oil oligarch or one of Saddam Hussein's sons.

The only way to enter Demi Papas's personal office was if he pushed a button and opened the door for you.

Schwarz pushed the button for Papas.

Lyons and Blancanales walked right in.

Papas nearly launched out his chair like a rocket and he reverted to the Greek of his childhood. *"Christos!"* He slapped his laptop shut in a panic and reverted to English. "Holy Christ!"

"Transsexuals, huh?" Lyons nodded acceptingly. "Well, you know. Exploring gender roles and boundaries… they say it's perfectly natural."

Papas turned a spectacular shade of purple. "Fuck you!"

Blancanales shrugged. "That's not what LeDuc said."

Demi Papas lost some color. "Duke…"

"You need to be cognizant of the fact," Blancanales continued softly, "that we walked into this building off the street and walked into your private office. At no point were we stopped or asked for identification, and not a single alarm has gone off." Blancanales knew that wasn't quite true. Good Mr. Blakely and his manager, locked up in the dark as they were, had to be dialing all sorts of numbers on their cell phones. "Why don't you have a seat?"

"I—"

Lyons roared. "Sit!"

Demi Papas slammed butt to leather.

Good cop/bad cop had been firmly established. Blancanales took a seat opposite Papas. Lyons stood, glaring. Blancanales took an unopened bottle of water from the desk and cracked it for himself. Lyons took out his gleaming, .357 Magnum Python revolver. Blancanales nodded. "Let us have words, like reasonable men."

Papas had gone from purple to pale and now he was going green.

Blancanales gestured with the water bottle amiably. "Go ahead, use the wastebasket."

Demi Papas, Wall Street's Perfect Weapon, threw up in stone-cold fear.

The Belle Nymphe

THE *NYMPHE* WAS HAUNTED. Or at least that was what the crew was starting to believe. The Baltic Sea was small

and bottlenecked as seas went, but it was bordered by
Sweden, Finland, Russia, Estonia, Latvia, Lithuania, the
long-disputed Kaliningrad oblast, Poland, Germany and
Denmark. For a small sea it was awash in the sea-faring
lore from myriad cultures ancient and modern. The sailors looked up Baltic ghost stories online and swapped
them like trading cards at mess and compared symptoms.
Sailing was in many ways a great deal like soldiering; it
mostly consisted of long periods of boredom and manual
labor followed by spurts of action and danger. Sailors had
a lot of time on their hands, were superstitious by nature,
and the stories grew and grew. One sailor discovered that
the *Nymphe* had once sailed under Malaysian registry and
the cook had died of food poisoning. This had turned the
galley into spook central.

Most everyone above the rank of steward was fairly
certain some member of the crew had far too much time
on their hands, as in enough time to take up the time-
honored mantle of ship's prankster. The captain had seen
to filling the crew's waking hours with all sorts of tasks
to cut down on the mischief.

Nevertheless, strange things were happening.

Some items had disappeared. Cookie couldn't swear
to it, but he was sure someone was pilfering food. Some
sailors were sure someone, or something, had disturbed
their belongings. Several of the men swore they had seen
the "phantom crewman," always at night, and pursued
him, only to find the apparition mysteriously disappear.

The idea of a stowaway had been almost universally
discarded. The actual living areas on a container ship were
very small and concentrated. Living anywhere else on the
ship in the Baltic winter would be a cold, hard and most
likely short existence. The ship's other anomaly was that
the *Nymphe* had passengers. Taking on passengers was an
ancient merchant ship tradition that had all but died out in

the late twentieth century with the rise of container ships and bulk vessels.

The *Nymphe's* passengers were mysterious. They did not fraternize with the crew and only rarely emerged from their converted container-module habitats. The ship's main liaison with the passengers was "the Korean." He scared the living hell out of everybody and dealt almost exclusively with the captain and the steward when he wanted something.

The ghost of the *Belle Nymphe* watched as the Korean walked down a gangway. Two crewmen just about dived out of his way. A third was carrying two large cans of diesel lubricant and was too slow. The Korean walked through the sailor as if he wasn't even there; shouldering him aside and making him drop his burden to the deck. The other two sailors helped the third and muttered imprecations in their native languages.

"What a dick," Hawkins muttered. The young soldier returned his attention to the galley. Hawkins was hungry. He couldn't steal any real quantity of anything at any given time. Scrounging was a time-honored tradition and a deservedly appreciated talent in all armies. Hawkins himself had been a semi-legendary past master at it in the United States Army Rangers, and his abilities had gone on to serve him and Phoenix Force well. He was appalled to find out that once you got on board a ship they had the bad taste to call it stealing and make it a severely punishable offense. They no longer rigged a grate and gave you a hundred lashes, but Hawk was a stowaway, and if he was caught he had very bad feeling that no matter what story he concocted it was the Korean rather than the captain who would decide his fate. He watched the door to the galley hungrily from his hiding spot. His scrounging instincts spoke to him.

He was going to the well too many times.

Despite the massive size of the ship, in the end it was a very small place. He had had already been spotted on three occasions. After surviving the first night he had carefully spent the next one mapping the ship from stem to stern, picking his escape and evasion routes from the galley, the crew's quarters and the engine room. Usually eluding his pursuers was simply a matter of pulling a Spider-Man up between two container vessels. The fact was people only very infrequently looked up.

Life aboard the *Belle Nymphe* without a berth wasn't a pleasure cruise. The Baltic was bitterly cold in winter and the wind never stopped blowing, but then again Hawkins had survived the twenty-one-day mountain phase of Ranger training in winter. There in the mountains of Georgia there had been no pantry to raid, no panty raids for down jackets and fresh fuzzy wool socks and gloves, nor a laundry room where he could throw his things in the dryer or smoke stack to lean against when it got bad. Save a constant gnawing hunger, he felt pretty good. Hawkins was intellectually aware that he really needed a shower but he wasn't willing to risk it. Ships and sailors frequently smelled bad, and it wasn't so bad he was attracting gulls yet.

Hawkins watched the galley from the darkness under the stairs and waited for Cookie to leave his post. Cookie was a huge, fat, black man from Trinidad, and Hawkins just didn't want to deal with the man when he had a cleaver in his hands. Cookie suddenly left his post. He put a wiggle in his walk and his fat jiggled as he sped toward the officer's quarters. That told Hawk that the overlords in the container vessels wanted something. They usually sent their orders through the steward and the steward summoned the cook, and Cookie was as frightened of the Korean as everyone else.

Hawkins descended silently.

He slipped into the galley and resisted sagging as real oven and stove warmth washed over him. His body craved fat and protein and he went for the gold. Hawkins took two mostly full water bottles from his pockets, poured powdered milk into them and shook them up for later. He stared at two cubes of butter on trays. Hawk grabbed one, shoved it into his mouth and snapped his head back twice like an alligator, sliding the cube down his throat. "Oh." He sighed. "That's what I'm talking about."

He was severely tempted by the second cube, but licked the first plate clean and put it back in the cupboard to make Cookie doubt himself. Hawk sucked two eggs and put the shells in his pockets for later disposal over the side. He took a massive risk and stole an apple. Hawk stared long and hard at the massive coffee machine that was slowly filling a mess-hall-size serving urn. He considered filling a water bottle with it but the smell might betray him. He poured himself a quick cup instead.

The door to the galley opened and Hawkins found himself face-to-face with the Korean. The big man's black eyes stared at Hawkins out of his dead mask of a face and, this close, Hawk knew exactly why the whole crew was terrified of the man. The Korean spoke with almost uninflected English. "What the hell are you doing drinking coffee when we haven't been served yet?"

Hawkins blinked stupidly and mentally considered the distance to the array of knives and cleavers hanging on a magnetic strip next to sink. He wouldn't have been surprised if the black eyes had rolled back and the Korean had opened his mouth wide to display giant shark-like teeth. Instead the man snorted in disgust. "You don't speak English?"

T. J. Hawkins performed the worst impression of the Swedish chef from the Muppets. "English? Ummm... Nay?" He suddenly grinned like a Swedish bumpkin that had fallen off a gravlax truck and nodded at the urn. "Café!"

The Korean took a step forward. Hawkins took a step back and got ready to hurl his cup into the dead eyes. The Korean sniffed the air. "You stink. Don't you Euro-trash assholes ever bathe?"

"Café?" Hawkins suggested.

The Korean exploded into motion faster than Hawkins could react, and Hawkins was fast. His coffee went flying as two ham-like hands slammed into his chest and projected him with childlike ease across the galley and into the double doors of the huge refrigerator unit. The Korean was once more instantly upon him. "What are you going to do about that, Stinko?"

Hawkins considered the tactical knife clipped to his back pocket and knew he would never make it. He met the Korean's death gaze. Hawkins's brows pulled together. His eyes nearly squeezed shut. His chin retracted and his lips pursed. His entire face moved toward the middle and made a fist like he was about to start crying.

"Oh for—" The Korean's palms exploded into Hawkins's chest again and slammed him so hard against the vault-like unit it rattled in its moorings. Hawkins slid down it limp as a squid. The Korean spun on his heel. "I should have stayed in Seoul. Never should have left the Church. I'd be in the High Priest's Quorum by now. I'd have thirteen bitches and a hundred and sixty-nine kids by now. Now? Now I'm on a boat surrounded by Baltic hillbillies who smell like feet. Christ wept."

The Korean slammed the door behind him.

Hawkins cocked his head. "Wow, a Korean, Mormon, Frankenstein. You don't see that every day." Hawkins filed that away for tonight's text session with the Farm. He shook his head slowly in disgust. "You're still a dick."

The Hamptons

FOR A GUY who wasn't married, Demi Papas required an awful lot of real estate, and real estate in the Hamptons was some of the most expensive in the United States. His house was nothing short of palatial and gazed out over the dark waters of the Atlantic. The escape from Manhattan had been a fairly simple affair. Blancanales had instructed Papas to call for his private helicopter. Papas had done so and they had simply gone to the roof, climbed aboard and headed to his beach house.

"Let's go to your office," Blancanales suggested.

Papas sounded almost eager. "Sure! Okay!"

He had tried to initiate a dialogue several times on the flight out and had been given the silent treatment except for terse orders.

He led them through the house. The decor was far more tasteful and subdued than Wall Street aerie. "So, what's this all about, fellas?"

"You," Lyons replied.

"Well, yeah, duh, but I mean, what can I do you for? I mean this is an awfully weird kidnapping."

Lyons kept his voice low, angry, yet amused. "Who said you're being kidnapped?"

"Listen, if you want money, we—"

"Who said we want money?"

"So—" Papas was starting to sweat "—what do you want?"

"We have what we want."

"And that is…"

"You," the Able Team leader reiterated.

Papas swallowed a frog in his throat. "My office… it's here."

Blancanales took point and Lyons pointed his revolver at the back of Papas's head as his teammate entered. The office looked like an old Victorian mansion's library complete with shelves of old books and a running ladder on rails. An unseen servant had already stoked a fire in the fireplace.

Papas followed Blancanales in and walked toward the desk. "Brandy? Cigars?"

Lyons cocked back the hammer on his Magnum and Papas froze. "Sit on the couch," Lyons ordered. Papas went and sat on the couch.

"What kind of gun do you have in the desk?" Blancanales asked.

Papas smiled sheepishly. "MAC-10?"

"That's a grand old piece," Blancanales observed.

"Yeah, well." Papas shrugged. "Chuck Norris had one."

"Yeah, but what movie?" Lyons asked.

Papas's face went flat, as though he found the question offensive. "*Lone Wolf McQuade.* I had the .44 Magnum and the sawed-off shotgun, too, but I couldn't hit shit with them." Papas suddenly smiled winningly. "I can't hit shit with the MAC, either, but at least it's fun to shoot. Sometimes I take it down to the beach and shoot clays with it."

The Able Team duo looked at each other.

"Listen, fellas. You said you want me? You got me, dead to rights. If this isn't a kidnapping, or extortion or about money, then it's gotta be revenge. Do what you gotta do, but do me a favor."

"What?" Lyons asked.

"Just not the face. I'm Greek Orthodox. For my mom's sake."

Lyons and Blancanales looked at each other.

Papas was just starting to crawl into some loathsome yet vaguely lovable gray area, and Blancanales's psych-war instincts were starting to tell him that Papas was probably more pawn than player in what was going on.

"What makes you think we want revenge?" Lyons asked.

Papas clapped his hands together as if in prayer. "Then tell me! What do you want?"

"We told you," Blancanales repeated. "We want to know everything about you."

"I got an autobiography." Papas pointed at the bookcase behind his desk. "I got three of them. First editions. I'll sign them for you."

"Might take you up on that. Meantime, I want your every financial transaction record, on and off the books, for the past five years."

Papas's mouth slowly dropped open. "Every one of them?"

"Legal, illegal, gray-area. I want to know where every dollar you have or had went and who and when it went through."

"Do you have any idea how much data that is? We're talking...shit, terahertzes, and that is just what I can lay my hands on from here."

Blancanales nodded. "I have all night, and friends who can help. Maybe you can have the help make sandwiches."

Papas turned and looked at Lyons's revolver. It was still pointed as his head. "You IRS guys have really upped your game."

Neither Able Team warrior said anything.

Papas sagged in further defeat. "You just want me to hand over the keys to the kingdom? You take my whole empire."

"We're not going to take anything. We just want to know every last thing about it. You won't be prosecuted. You won't lose a dime. Your information will never be shared with anyone except several people we know who have no interest in doing you any harm, either."

Papas tried to process this. "You know, I know I'm

going out on a huge limb here, but can I ask what all this is about? I mean like even a hint?"

Papas stiffened as Blancanales sat next to him on the couch.

"Sure!" he said, taking out his phone and pulling up a video file.

Papas frowned at the sight of a bloody and battered Rafael Encizo handcuffed to a chair in his underwear with a nude Propenko in the same predicament next to him. "And you guys break my balls for the stuff I watch?"

"Keep watching."

Branko walked up with his knife and took off Propenko's little finger with one curving cut that stopped on bone for half a heartbeat and sheared through. "Oh, God!" Papas recoiled. "Oh, God! No! You said you weren't! You said you wouldn't! You—"

"That's a friend of mine in that chair, so is the guy next to him," Lyons snarled. "Keep watching."

Papas watched in horrified fascination as Branko tossed the finger in Encizo's lap. "Jesus, that naked guy is hardcore."

"You have no idea," Blancanales said.

Encizo's phone rang and they listened to the conversation with Kurtzman. "I know that voice," Papas declared.

Lyons and Blancanales looked at each other. "The guy on the phone?" Blancanales asked.

"Nah, the guy we can't see. I swear I've heard his voice before." The verbal chess between Kurtzman and the unseen voice went on for a few more moments. "Jesus, that guy on the phone is hardcore."

In the video, the door suddenly smashed open and the flash-bang went off. McCarter and Lyons stormed in shooting. Papas's head snapped around on Lyons. "Jesus, that's you!"

"Keep watching."

Branko and his one pal went down in sprays of blood while the other guy surrendered.

"Jesus! This shit's really real!"

Blancanales clicked it off. "Yes, yes, it is." He decided to start taking some very big chances with Papas that the Farm would probably not approve of. "This started with an anti-terror operation in Prague. Then the trail led to the Kaliningrad oblast, then to Poland, where this took place."

Papas's face went slack. "Then to here?"

"Yes."

"To...me?" Papas was incredulous.

Blancanales read Papas. Whatever else was said about him, he was a shark and a master negotiator, but Blancanales had smelled the fear sweat on him and he genuinely seemed to be rattled. The Able Team interrogator decided to take another chance. "We have reason to believe it leads to your money."

Papas started doing math. "You think I've been..."

"We can't be sure, that's why we want everything. Keys to the kingdom, but with luck we won't be staying long and we'll leave them under the garden gnome for you when we're done."

"Who are you guys?"

"We're the good guys," Lyons declared.

Papas looked askance at Lyons and then back at Blancanales. "I'm going to go out another limb here."

Blancanales shrugged. "Go ahead. It's your house."

"What if I say no?"

Blancanales considered his answer. "If you really, knowingly, had nothing to do with any of what's going on, it's really in your best interest to help us willingly. Otherwise, a lot of the kingdom is gonna get smashed up and a lot of your information will get exposed as we get what we need anyway, but do it the hard way."

"And if I'm actively involved?"

Blancanales held up his phone meaningfully. "Then it is absolutely in your best interest to cut a deal with us right now. You don't want to meet the naked guy in the chair. He's really angry right now and he doesn't play by the same rules we do. He will appear, out of nowhere, just like we did, only he will do all the things we promised we wouldn't."

Papas stared into the fire.

Blancanales smiled in a fatherly fashion and clapped Papas on the shoulder. "What do you say? Want to roll with the good guys."

Papas nodded soberly. "I'll have the help make sandwiches."

CHAPTER THIRTEEN

Stony Man Farm

Aaron Kurtzman was deeply disappointed. He had looked forward to bringing down the Demi Papas empire and bringing the Perfect Weapon to his knees. Now Demi Papas was rolling with the good guys and Kurtzman found himself having to work with him. He was forced to speak with Papas over a link and endure his whoo-hooing and his motivational boardroom speak during conference calls. The consolation prize was that being privy to every aspect of the life of a renegade financial scumbag was frankly fascinating.

Beneath Papas's media empire he was involved in a vast swathe of gray-area business ventures. He didn't sell drugs or pimp little girls, but he was involved in a lot of things that were strictly non-kosher. He'd hurt a lot of people and made deals with very bad government officials in far-off countries, making off with a lot of wealth and rights to resources the people in those countries desperately needed.

He was a highly intelligent man and he hid most of it well, very well. To clean up his image he had given up taking controlling interest in American companies and then savaging them. However, strangely enough, as he couldn't stop telling anyone who would listen, he considered himself a patriot, the son of immigrants and there was nothing he didn't owe this country or that he wouldn't do for it. The statement might seem delusional to an outside observer, but Papas had hurled himself wholeheartedly into the investigation, and he appeared to be holding back nothing. Demi Papas had called his accountants and lawyers both aboveboard and below and they had been horrified as he had started opening up the Papas kingdom, and possibly exposing and implicating them, as well.

None of Papas's minions seemed able to object in the presence of Carl Lyons. Blancanales spent time smoothing ruffled feathers and making reassuring noises. The Stony Man cybernetics team pored over vast amounts of data trying to make it correlate with anything that had occurred from Prague to Poland. It was a monumental task. Papas also had a number of blind trusts and don't-ask-don't-tell business relationships that were proving very difficult to investigate. They had been at it for nearly forty-eight hours straight.

Hunt Wethers pushed himself away from his workstation. "I don't know."

Akira Tokaido was tired, frustrated and had inhaled so many energy drinks he might has well just hook up an IV unit and start squeezing a tennis ball. "What do you mean you don't know?"

Kurtzman had known Wethers and his ways for a very long time, and he felt a sudden glimmer of hope. Wethers was giving the multiple files on his screen a very professorial frown. "What is it you don't know, Hunt?"

"I'm not big on all this financial stuff. I'm a professor of cybernetics, an egghead. Though I do love doing intelligence analysis."

"And you're very good at it," Kurtzman prompted. "What's bothering you?"

"This guy Papas. I've only seen five minutes of his TV show by accident, and other than that, until recently? All knew about him was what I saw in the headlines, and I never had any interest in reading any further."

"Is this going someplace?" Tokaido asked.

Wethers ignored the young hacker. "It's just this. Demi Papas is an asshole."

"Well…" Kurtzman's brow furrowed. "We have kind of established that already."

"Right, but Papas is an *uber* asshole, a genuine Wolf of Wall Street. A certified, bona fide, qualified, genuine twenty-first-century robber baron. A self-professed Perfect Weapon with billions of dollars earned by means both fair and foul to back up the claim."

"Right…" Kurtzman agreed. "But I still don't see where this is going."

"That's just it. It's not going anywhere. I mean who is going to fool this guy? In his world he's an alpha predator. The alpha predator."

"Everyone makes mistakes, Hunt. Once in a while even us," Kurtzman cautioned.

"Agreed, but how likely is it in this situation? You think someone could hand him a dirty deal and he wouldn't know about it? Papas loves dirty deals. He'd smell one a mile off. Even if you did fool him, do you think you could get away with it for long? You think someone in his organization could be siphoning off money, or stealing from him on any sort of scale and get away with it? For long?"

Tokaido scratched his head. "So you're saying he's in on it?"

"Please say yes," Kurtzman pleaded.

"No, sorry to disappoint, but I'm thinking we might be looking in the wrong place."

Tokaido waved a hand at his bank of monitors. "What place would that be, Professor?"

"The place we are not looking," Wethers replied.

Kurtzman echoed Tokaido. "That would be…?"

Wethers smiled slyly. "The happy place."

"The happy place?"

"Demi Papas is an asshole who ruthlessly built an empire and made himself a billionaire. Then spent over ten years and hundreds upon hundreds of millions of dollars remaking himself into a media darling and a national figure. He had to turn over a new leaf, clean up his image. He had to get cuddly."

Carmen Delahunt sauntered into the room and chimed in. "Puppies, unicorns, kissing babies 'n' stuff."

Kurtzman snorted as he saw it. "Save the children, save the whales."

"He had to prove himself a friend to the world," Wethers continued.

Tokaido held up a knowing finger. "Friendship is magic!"

"Yes, it is," Wethers affirmed.

"Good works," Delahunt suggested. "Charities."

Kurtzman held up a finger of his own. "Foundations."

Delahunt clapped her hands. "Oh! Even better!"

Tokaido had been punching keys. He stopped and stared at his screen. "Big ideas for a better tomorrow…" he intoned.

"Akira," Kurtzman asked. "What are you looking at?"

Tokaido looked up from his screen. "You guys should come over here and take a look at this."

The North Sea

"Goddamn it!" Junior Pyle waved his arms and shouted in the face of the *Nymphe's* engineer. "It's freezing in there! Fix it!"

The ship's engineer was a lanky Dane who always had an electronic cigarette in his mouth. He, like everyone else aboard ship, was growing very tired of Pyle. "I have fixed it three times. Perhaps you have faulty equipment."

"The equipment is top of the line." Pyle's voice rose. "I picked it myself."

"Perhaps it is the ghost."

The Ghost of the good ship *Belle Nymphe* was gone. What it had now was a gremlin, an invisible tormentor of man and machine. The gremlin lay atop the habitation unit in question and grinned.

"Just goddamn fix it!"

The engineer turned, shaking his head. "I will fetch my tools. Go to the galley. It is warm there and there is coffee."

Pyle grabbed his laptop and stomped off to the galley. He left the door open for the engineer. Hawkins swung down and slipped inside. He figured he had five minutes. The engineer appeared to be in no hurry whatsoever. Hawkins had turned into Junior Pyle's personal, invisible, imp of Satan. He didn't feel bad about it at all. The ghost routine was reaching the end of its shelf life and it was only a matter of time before he got caught pilfering from the galley and the crew's quarters.

Hawkins had gone proactive and made Pyle his prey. Pyle kept having problems with his environmental unit. People were messing with his stuff. People were stealing food from his personal stash. Junior Pyle was shrilly and vocally sure people were doing this on purpose.

People didn't give a shit. People were not interested in investigating. People just wanted Junior Pyle to shut the hell up and quit whining.

Hawkins went to work. This was the most dangerous part of the raid. He had to keep his phone charged, and tech types were very anal about their equipment. The habitation unit had outlets ringing the walls. On the first raid Hawkins had pilfered one of a dozen spare USB adapters, pulled out Junior Pyle's gaming couch and hidden his charging phone behind it. Then it had been a matter of getting Pyle in and out of his habitation at regular intervals. Hawkins scanned the room to see if any of the computer monitor cameras were on but he gauged their field of view and chose his crawl path to retrieve his fully charged phone. There was the very real possibility that Pyle had microphones on but the door was open and the wind was howling. Hawkins decided to go shopping for dinner.

He found Junior Pyle had taped a sign to his mini-fridge threatening bodily harm to anyone who touched his food.

"Sorry," Hawkins whispered. His one fear was that Pyle would set up his own little security suite, but Hawkins had listened as Pyle had begged the other Asian man on the ship for some spare cameras. Pyle had been told in so many words what to go do with himself.

Hawkins examined the fridge. Pyle had applied a piece of Scotch tape under the bottom edge of the door as a hidden seal. He had taken the extra precaution of attaching a piece of his own hair to it so that it would break if the door was opened. Hawkins snapped out his tactical knife. "You're getting better…"

The former Ranger performed a lovely bit of surgery and lifted the tape and the hair intact. He opened the door to be confronted with a pyramid of snacks. Pyle had arranged it so that if a thief took anything from anywhere except the top it would fall over.

"Amateur hour." Hawkins cracked his red, swollen knuckles and with the care of a scrounger extraordinaire removed a Twinkie and a PowerBar ProteinPlus like an Olympic gold medal Jenga champion while leaving the structure intact. He took his treasures and ninja'ed back among the containers, secreting himself into one of the crane operator booths for the rest of the evening. They were a death trap if he was discovered, but they were currently covered with tarps against the wet and salt and wouldn't be uncovered until something needed loading or unloading.

Hawkins ate his dinner and considered his options. He knew he couldn't keep this up much longer. He was getting weaker and he could feel it. His great big plan had been that once the Farm had satellite tracking on the *Belle Nymphe*, he would eject into the night on a life raft and wait for extraction from Phoenix Force on the *Coronado*. That plan had gone straight down the shitter. Hawkins had miscalculated.

The *Belle Nymphe* was a thoroughly modern feeder vessel. She didn't carry containerized, ready-to-self-inflate life rafts. Container ships and bulk carriers faced the prospect of sinking very rapidly if they ran into trouble. They didn't have time for that. The *Nymphe* carried a free-fall lifeboat on the stern. It was bright orange, fully enclosed and vaguely shaped like a submarine. When the order to abandon ship was given, one of the officers would unlock it, the crew would load in as a unit and the lifeboat would drop fifty feet to the water below. It had a tiny screw for maneuvering, and the survival rations it carried were a terrible temptation.

But it was locked in place in its fall frame and Hawk was fairly sure that even if he could break into the lifeboat, release the gantry and chalks, and eject over the side, it would set off a number of alarms. He was sitting in the only other option, and that meant using the crane to swing the motor launch over the side, lower it, slide down, detach all the cables and try to speed away.

Hawkins was keeping that as plan Z.

Plan A was to keep doing what he was doing. The Game Room had pulled a disappearing act before and he had to make sure that didn't happen again, or, if possible, pull a stowaway hat trick.

Hawkins considered the man he referred to as "the Other Korean." He was clearly in charge. Hawkins had stalked him as he had gone out on deck and smoked, and listened to snatches of his phone conversations.

Getting into his habitation module, or the Game Room itself, was a terrible temptation. Though either one of those options would probably be a one-shot deal and he didn't like the look of the Other Korean, much less the big one. The slightest screwup would start the real gremlin hunt from stem to stern.

Hawkins checked his watch and decided it was time to check in and get some fatherly advice.

McCarter answered on the first ring.

"Hawk, how are you holding up?"

"Good news?" Hawkins scratched his filthy, matted beard. "The facial armor is coming in, and I am talking rainforest lush. I'm thinking it might just stop a bullet. Bad news is it smells like the rain forest, and it's camping under my nose."

McCarter made a noise.

"And don't tell my mom but I haven't been flossing."

"I need a no-bollocks assessment, Hawk."

"Bollocks..." Hawkins, like the overwhelming majority of Americans, found British English pleasing. "Truth is I feel like I'm back at the Florida phase of Ranger school. I'm hungry, I'm tired and I'm losing weight. Nearly all food supplies have been cut off, like I'm down to a Twinkie. I haven't taken sick yet, but I feel the outriders. One more night outside and I think I'm going to be in trouble."

"Bitch, bitch, bitch..." McCarter cajoled.

Hawk smiled very wearily. "You said honest assessment. All I wanted was dental floss, and that was mostly for my mom."

McCarter didn't hand out praise lightly or often. "You're doing yeoman's work, Hawk. Don't think everyone doesn't know it, either. You've got some bloody big bragging rights. I think it's time to extract you."

"Can you?"

"Well, there's the rub. The *USS Coronado* has no excuse to the stop the *Belle Nymphe* on the high seas, and the God's truth is we don't want to. Nor do we want to assault it with Phoenix. We know where the *Nymphye's* manifest says it going, but we don't know where it is actually going. The plan is to track them there, wherever that may be, with them left none the wiser."

"Okay, so where's the *Nymphe* supposedly headed, anyway?" Hawkins asked.

"The port of Miami, Florida."

Hawkins sagged back in the chair and felt the covered, crane operator's booth closing in on him as he contemplated crossing the entire breadth of Atlantic in winter. "Well, eventually it should start to get warmer."

"Actually, they are having problems with frost in the orange groves."

Hawkins rubbed his temples and was disturbed to find he was slightly feverish. He wished he hadn't made this call. He wanted to curl up fetal on the floor of the booth and eat his Twinkie. "Fine. Word to the wise. You haven't figured something out by the Azores? I'm taking the ship."

"Duly noted, but do me a favor. Hang on for twenty-four. All we have is what we have on hand, but what we have is Phoenix Force and the *Coronado* is currently the most modern warship on earth. We will get you out of there."

"Twenty-four?"

"You have my word. Worst case we assault anyway and taking the Game Room is worth the price of admission."

"Okay." Hawkins found himself fighting his eyes to keep them from closing. "Then I am eating my Twinkie."

"What?"

"Never mind, I'll save it for later." Hawkins took a deep breath, felt the soreness in his throat worsening and resolved himself to the very dangerous business of sleeping on the *Belle Nymphe* during the day. And tonight he would try to break into the extremely abbreviated medical bay of the *Nymphe*.

USS Coronado, the North Sea

"WE HAVE TO extract Hawk, now," McCarter declared. "His situation is deteriorating."

Phoenix Force sat at the captain's table with the captain of the *Coronado* and the XO. The captain was a very short, redheaded going to gray, permanently red-faced fireplug of a man. There were rumors that he might be one of the best sailors in the United States Navy.

"Gentlemen, this situation is highly irregular, and I'll have you know I have done some very irregular things with some very irregular men. You boys take the cake. However, I am told I have to extend you every possible courtesy. I have also been told under no circumstances am I to stop or hinder the *Belle Nymphe*. If you decide to assault it, I am instructed to hang back and extract you afterward if possible. If not, I am supposed to sail on."

"Thank you, Captain," McCarter said. "You have been more than patient."

The captain looked McCarter up and down again. "Forgive me, but why is an Englishman in command of American soldiers again?"

"You're not still upset about 1812, are you?" McCarter countered.

The captain burst out laughing. "No, the 'Star Spangled Banner' was worth it."

"Captain, how close can you sneak up on the *Belle Nymphe*?"

"Well, you happen to be aboard an Independence Class littoral combat ship. I believe I can say without undue braggadocio that we are currently one of, if not the stealthiest commissioned ship of war on earth. Particularly in the dark in winter seas? That feeder tub your guy is on? With her radar? I can crawl right up her ass and she'll never know it. The problem is what to do next. I got a Seahawk helicopter in the hangar and two Fire Scout drones sitting on the deck in the rain because your helicopter is taking up their berth. None of them are stealthy. How is that high-tech wreck of yours taking up my space?"

McCarter turned to Grimaldi. "How is our high-tech wreck?"

"I was able to patch a lot of it up." Grimaldi nodded at the captain. "And thanks, but they just don't have a lot of the parts I need on board. I cannibalized, and we have one happy engine, but there is no way I can fly anywhere close to the *Nymphe* without them knowing about it."

The captain looked at his Table of Equipment. "I got two RHIBs."

Calvin James looked at a copy of the TOE. "You have a Fleet-Class Common USV."

"I do." The captain looked at the status of the stealthy, unmanned 12-meter surface vessel. "But she's currently configured for mine warfare. We were coordinating with NATO forces on mine-sweeping exercises in the Baltic." He raised an eyebrow at McCarter. "Until I got diverted to this little excursion."

"Can you unconfigure the USV?" McCarter asked.

"Sure." The captain let out a long breath. "But the *Coronado* isn't currently carrying a manned mission module."

"Can you put a man in it, anyway?"

"Sure. I can have my guys just swap out the module bay—doesn't take more than an hour or two—but the passenger won't have any controls."

"But the *Coronado* could remotely direct the USV to the *Nymphe*." McCarter pressed. "Hawk could abandon ship, given the signal, wearing a life vest, and the man on the USV could spot him with night-vision equipment and coordinate via com link with the *Coronado* to vector the USV to Hawk, and then pull him out of the water. Correct?"

A sailor stared at a man who wasn't. "Mister? You don't get it. We are currently in Sea State Four. That is considered moderate weather, and I already have people throwing up. By nightfall we expect it to rise to Sea State Five or Six. That's rough to very rough seas. We're talking waves of four to six meters, with heavy rain expected. In the dark. The man riding the USV will be sitting in an open slot, with nothing but his dick in his hand. No canopy. No cockpit, and nothing to hold on to except what we can jury rig—and you want him to coordinate a rescue out of it? The man in the goddamn USV is the one who is going to need rescuing. None of my men are stupid enough to do that, even if I ordered them to do it, which I won't. And, by the way, I am fresh out of suicidal Navy SEALs today."

McCarter nodded as the plan came together. "I'm not."

Calvin James kept his expression neutral. His inner ear was messed up. He had gotten seasick for the first time in twenty years. Now McCarter wanted to put him in a robot bathtub in Sea State Six, at night, in a thunderstorm. James didn't hesitate. "I'm in."

McCarter gave his teammate a worried look and an out. "You sure?"

"What did I just say?"

"We can work out something else."

James stared at McCarter pointedly. "You got someone else in mind for the job?"

McCarter didn't. "You're sure you're up for this?"

"I might need some Dramamine."

The captain of the *Coronado* gave James a long, appraising look. "Son? You have serious sand."

"Not as much as Hawk," James corrected. "Not this week."

"Jesus Christ on a crutch." The captain of the *Coronado* was impressed. "You really are a sailor."

"Speaking of, I'll need a dry suit and a suppressed weapon, preferably something rifle caliber if I have to reach out ship to ship in the rolling waves. NVGs and com gear that will function in a storm, and spares. Hawk's going to be in shit shape when I drag him out of the drink. Assume that he has drowned and needs de-fib and emergency gear."

The captain was all in. "I will launch my RHIBs but keep them out of radar range, and I'll deploy both Fire Scout helicopter drones with thermal imaging observation packages. Screw orders. It doesn't leave this room but I'll have my chopper ready, armed and the *Coronado's* full weapons suite ready. I will assault or sink that *Nymphe* son of a bitch if it comes to it."

James gazed upon the captain with approval. "Don't do that unless I ask, and I won't ask. Neither will Hawk."

"That boat reaches its destination, Captain," McCarter reiterated.

"Fine. I am your eyes, then. I have some really good guys and gals in my crew. You won't lack. You won't lack for anything."

"I appreciate that, Captain."

The captain looked at his laptop and the state of his ship and its assets. "I need to swap modules, sneak up on that dizzy bastard and pre-deploy surveillance. When do you want to do it?"

"My guy is sick, starving and running out of options," McCarter said. "The sooner, the better."

"The sea should be just starting to get really shitty around midnight. I feel sorry for your friend, but that's when the *Nymphe* will be battening down, no one on deck.

She'll be effectively blind and just be taking it on the chin on autopilot with GPS. We nuzzle up to their bung and get the *Coronado's* eyes up in the air." The captain looked at James. "We deploy our search and rescue unit, and with luck your boy Hawk takes the plunge at—" he checked his watch "—zero two hundred?"

James looked at McCarter.

McCarter picked up his phone. "That'll do."

CHAPTER FOURTEEN

"Liberty City?" Delahunt asked.

Kurtzman was highly intrigued. "People, particularly in Libertarian circles, have been talking about the concept of a free city for a long time."

"A free city?" Tokaido asked.

"On paper it is fairly simple," Kurtzman said. "You find a small country basically willing to rent you some of their sovereign territory, and you drop a town, or a reasonable facsimile thereof, into their country. You pay them for the pleasure, either a flat fee or a percentage of the profits, or both, and theoretically for the most part they leave you alone. You don't have to deal with their or anyone else's tax laws, labor laws, regulations or treaties. You run your city any way you want, and as long as you don't break any of their federal statutes or speak out against the government, you are mostly your own jurisdiction."

"Sounds awesome." Tokaido liked the sound of it. "How come everyone isn't doing it?"

"Most attempts have failed spectacularly before they even got started. Like you say, it sounds awesome on paper, but the problems are baked in, and most investor know it, and so far the only countries that are tempted are Third World, and then you are forced to kowtow to dictators. Sooner or later, El Presidente for Life starts feeling the need to meddle.

"Another problem is the locals. Imagine living in a hut, struggling to make a living and your government sells a chunk of the land to foreigners, and it might be yours. They build a town, lights, install running water, proper sewage, schools, the whole bit, but they don't hire you or your people and they don't let you visit. The country makes money on it, but it goes straight to the corrupt government. It can make for severely hard feelings in a country that is already afraid of an uprising. On top of that? One civil war or even a peaceful election? And instead of Capitalist El Presidente you have Socialist Comrade Big Brother, and he nationalizes everything, including your free city. Almost every attempt has failed."

"Except Liberty City."

Kurtzman had read about Liberty City when it was first launched in the 1980s and had been highly excited about it at the time.

"Oh, on paper they had everything. They were going to be a model city for the future. A worldwide future of free city-states without borders. Financially self-sufficient, completely run by in-house green energy, they intended to be a high-tech dynamo attracting the world's best and brightest. They wanted to spawn a thousand like them, all freely competing, creative destruction. It was very exciting. It was the libertarian dream, and the first new idea to come along in a long time. On top of that, they chose Belize, an English-speaking country in Central America with no standing army, no revolutionary problems and mostly off the radar with the drug cartels at the time. They intended to become the shining city on the hill. 'Big Ideas for a Better Tomorrow.' They had a lot of investors. I even thought of throwing a few k their way back in the day. It didn't work out."

Tokaido swiped his screen, bringing up files and flinging them away as if he were tossing a Caesar salad. "But they're still there."

"They are, but they're not a city by any stretch of the imagination. They're kind of a high-tech exclave cult. They've launched a few exciting products, and far more boondoggles. It's like a really weird, transnational tech incubator. Millionaire maniacs still give them money, and go down there with their off-the-grid pet projects."

"Millionaire maniacs. I like the sound of that," Tokaido said, enthused. "But so does a certain billionaire butthole we know. What's up with that?"

Kurtzman steeled himself. There was nothing for it. "Well, let's just ask that lower end of the alimentary canal himself."

"You have the soul of a poet, Aaron," Carmen Delahunt remarked.

Kurtzman punched a key to open up a com link with the Papas end of the Able Team operation.

Demi Papas answered enthusiastically on the first electronic peep. "Papa Bear! How's it hanging, brother?"

Kurtzman forced his voice to remain neutral. "What can you tell me about your relationship with Liberty City, Mr. Papas?"

"Judas Priest! Liberty City?"

"Yes. You've had dealings with them. What is it—?"

"It's like that TV show *Lost* meets Jonestown, Bear! Only they don't drink the Kool-Aid, they drink other people's money. My money!"

Kurtzman peered at a file. "So why do you keep giving them money, Mr. Papas?"

"Why do you keep calling me Mr. Papas? Call me Papa Bear, Bear!"

"I'm not going to call you that."

"Okay. It's a Bear thing, I get it." Papas sounded hurt. "Call me Demi?"

Kurtzman struggled. Despite all efforts by all concerned, Demi Papas was growing on the Farm team. "Demi? What's up with you and Liberty City?"

"Oh, man, where do I start? I'll admit I was excited about it at first. I loved the whole free-city concept. No government? How awesome is that? I always try to avoid getting involved with the government. I mean our government. Other governments? Particularly small ones in faraway places? Them? They are often very reasonable and accommodating business partners, let me tell you. Free city in Belize? It sounded like a marriage made in heaven. Now, our government?" Papas snorted. "I mean, I am considering a presidential run, but other than that? I do everything I can to avoid it."

Kurtzman just let that one lie. "But you have ongoing business dealings with them."

"It's like having an idiot savant step-cousin. They've flirted with some interesting developments in solar panels over the years. Algae as biofuel, but the boys in California are beating them on that one. I don't believe in any of that shit, but I get to put green energy credits on the Papas brand, and with their weirdo nonnational status, I actually make money. A few of their patents have worked out. I'm talking pocket change, but it's all about the brand."

Papas paused. "But I'll tell you, they've come up with some 3-D printing technology that is nothing short of amazing. I gave them a shitload of money. I mean I was so impressed I even went down to Liberty City and looked at it." Papas snorted again. "Liberty City, total freak show, but the tech was amazing."

Everyone in the Annex looked at each other and thought of a certain fallen UAV helicopter lying like a dissected frog in the Farm workshop.

"And...?" Kurtzman prompted. "The 3-D stuff?"

"So their stuff was, and will be, for the foreseeable future, too expensive to put into mass production. It's the story of their life. They make these incredible toys but unless you are a First World nation…? And even then it's easier to knock it together off the shelf and let your boys figure out how to do it better five years from now.

"The 3-D shit? They should just sell it to the Chinese before they steal it and let them make Happy Meal toys for three cents on the dollar. But, no, they are all about keeping their shit their own. They are so secretive, always talking about some new big thing they can't talk about, and they are always, always, always asking for more money."

Delahunt, Tokaido, Wethers and Kurtzman looked at each other.

Kurtzman silenced his microphone. "Nice work, Hunt."

Wethers shrugged. "I live to serve."

Kurtzman uncovered his mike. A thought occurred to him. "Demi?"

"Bear?"

The Stony Man cybernetics chief decided to go out on limb. "You like rolling with the good guys?"

"This has been the most exciting forty-eight hours of my life, Bear. I think I hear a proposition. Bring it."

"How do you feel about fieldwork?"

Papas's voice rose in excitement. "You mean like undercover?"

"My guys will be undercover. You will make the introduction."

"When I am not making deals? I am brokering them, Baby Bear!"

Kurtzman was getting a headache. "I need my guys to go to Liberty City and look around, and they need a Golden Wonka ticket to get in. You say Liberty City is always sniffing around for money. I need to turn my guys into mad-money men. I'll need you to help cement the cover, consult on the back story and make the handshake."

There was a long pause on the other side of the link. "Bear?"

"Demi?"

"I have an erection."

The North Sea

T. J. HAWKINS AWOKE SICK. He had been sleeping in the operator's chair and the moment he moved he found his joints and muscles ached like tetanus. One swallow told him his throat was on fire. He blinked, trying to open eyes that were gummed shut. Despite the icebox-cold interior of the crane booth he was sweating with fever.

High seas rolled the *Nymphe* like a rocking horse. Rain hammered and the wind rattled and flapped the tarp covering the booth. Beyond the booth the world whistled and moaned and rolled. Hawkins coughed, coughed and coughed again. Despite his fever and the stolen down jacket he was shivering.

It wasn't good.

Hawkins sat in the pitch-black of the booth and addressed no one in particular, or perhaps the entire planet. "Screw y'all," he croaked. "Wanna know why?" The soldier reached into his jacket and pulled out his Twinkie. "'Cause I got this!"

The planet howled and rolled in response.

"Haters be hatin'…" Hawkins unwrapped his snack cake and very deliberately chewed every bite forty times, the way his mother had always told him to, and laboriously forced the mostly liquefied confection past his turgid, infected esophagus and finished the last of his bottle of water. He smacked his cracked lips. "Like a new man." Hawkins rose from the operator's chair and sat back down as the darkness spun around him. He took a deep breath and decided to check his messages.

McCarter had called him five times and texted him three.

Hawkins haltingly checked his messages with cold, stiff fingers. It was two in the morning and rescue had been waiting since midnight. Hawkins tapped his phone and McCarter responded instantly.

"Hawk! Are you all right?"

Hawk's voice scraped painfully over his vocal chords. "I overslept."

McCarter's voice went grim. "Hawk, are you all right?"

The young soldier took a deep breath and it cost him a coughing fit. "I took sick."

"Can you go extract? Cal is in a USV off the bow ready to fish you out. You could throw a rock at the *Coronado* if you could see it."

Hawkins shivered with infection and thought about stepping out of the crane booth into the wind and rain and jumping into the North Sea. Throwing himself naked into the *Nymphe's* boilers had far more appeal. However, he'd suffered hypothermia before and he knew within minutes of stepping outside he might just go fetal and start to feel warm again. Given his condition, the cold shock of diving into the North Sea would be a fine jump-start to the process. "I'm excited about this plan. I'm thankful to be a part of it. Let's do it!"

"Listen, we are in Sea State Six. The *Nymphe* is a big, flat-bottomed son of a bitch. She'll shove you out rather than suck you into the screws. We're counting on that. We don't want you bobbing and flipping around in the engine froth in the stern. Make your way to the starboard bow. Cal has done this before. When he gives you the signal, jump. The bow wake will push you right to him."

"Starboard bow, right." Hawkins sighed.

"Hawk?"

"Yeah?"

"Go. Go now."

"Okay. Extracting," Hawkins pulled the life vest he had stolen out from under the operator's chair and shrugged into it. He buttoned it up and was thankful that the tabs were Velcro. "Okay…" Hawkins cracked the booth door and shoved up the tarp high enough to let himself squeeze out. His boots hit the deck and the wind buckled him. The rain and cold went into his bones like knife cuts and seemed to shrivel his heart and lungs. The deck was mostly darkness save for the running lights. The ship rolled and Hawkins fell against the rail. He found himself gazing out across the heaving, seemingly infinite dark. He pulled himself along the long gangway toward the prow as the huge ship was tossed. The stacks of containers scraped and groaned in their locks and eclipsed what little light there was. He reached the prow and looked around. He coughed loud and hard and did fuzzy-headed math.

"Starboard…"

Hawkins hobbled his way from port to starboard. He passed the massive mechanical anchor capstan and reached the starboard rail. He rested while the rain and wind smashed him, and waited for James to signal that he had seen him.

The Korean spoke directly behind him.

"Hey, Stinko." Hawkins flinched despite himself and considered the tactical knife in his back pocket. He wondered if his numb fingers could open it. "Turn around, real slow," the Korean commanded.

Hawkins turned. The Korean would have looked ridiculous in the lemon-yellow oilskin jacket and matching sou'wester hat except that he was so goddamn big, and Hawk was frankly jealous of his ensemble. There was nothing ridiculous at all about the tricked-out AR carbine he held, much less the green laser dot it currently printed on Hawkins's chest. The dot never wavered despite the pitch and roll of the ship. It was as if the Korean were a human, stabilized gun mount. He seemed to feel no need to keep a hand on the rail or anything else, either.

The young Texan raised a feverish eyebrow at the Korean's oilskins. "Nice gear, Gorton," he rasped. "You get fish sticks with that?"

The Korean's dead eyes sized Hawkins up and down in the rain. "You don't sound good."

"I feel pretty good. Not scared at all. I feel kind of invincible. 'Course I just had a Twinkie."

The Korean's dead smile arranged itself on his face. "Yesterday we had a genuine *Caine Mutiny* conference about that missing Twinkie. Junior is just about at the mental meltdown point."

"You know?" Hawkins hacked. "I never liked him."

"Me, either. I wanted to kill him, but someone else has dibs. Then I started thinking. The Ghost of the *Nymphe*? Food disappearing? The crew seeing apparitions? And let's be honest, would any of the crew dare to start a campaign of terror on Junior, annoying as he is, if I'm around?"

"To be honest? I was a little nervous about it myself."

"And you should be," the Korean averred. "I really should have figured it out earlier, but I enjoyed shoving you into the refrigerator and watching you cry so much that I didn't connect the dots. Then you know what happened?"

Hawkins realized he had gone from shivering to shaking with cold. It took him two tries to clear his throat. "You told the ship's steward to tell Stinko man to take a bath," A ragged fit of coughing tore through his chest. "And he said…who?"

"Right!"

"So what happens now?"

"You are going to talk to me, but you make me a little nervous. You're just not the pussy I pushed around in the galley. Tell me the truth. Have you been riding my ass since the Oder Lagoon?"

"Since the cabin in the woods," Hawkins rasped.

"Nice. You know, I've met Force Recon Marines, Navy SEALs, Spetsnaz, you name it, but no one knows how to suck it and suffer like a United States Army Ranger. You a Ranger who went Delta?"

Hawkins shrugged, but it was more of twitched hunching of his shoulders.

"So, we both know you're going to have to try something, and I don't want to shoot you unless I have to. I want to talk to you and so will some people I know. So what I am going to do? I'm just going to stand here. So are you. Until you fall down. Then I am going let you lay there for another half hour in case you are faking. Then? We go medieval. We give you antibiotics, but we go medieval." The dead smile came back. "You can try to draw your gun, or your knife, or whatever you've got, or come over here and take a swing any old time in between."

Hawkins felt himself going from shaking to shuddering. His teeth were clacking together. "You're not a good Mormon, are you?"

The Korean blinked in the rain. He lifted his chin. "Your phone is ringing."

Hawkins looked down and a tiny bit of light was flashing out of the collar of his jacket. James had spotted him on the rail. Hawkins doubted he could see the Korean. "You want me to answer that?"

The Korean twitched his pistol. "Why don't you come over here and hand it to me?"

"Okay…"

"Slowly," the Korean cautioned.

Hawkins opened his jacket and felt the wind and cold smash into his throat and chest. He pulled out his phone. It was vibrating and peeping plaintively. Hawkins held the phone upside down but the text message from Calvin James was plain.

Now now now

"Over here. Slowly."

Hawkins tottered forward. He figured he had three last acts left on earth. He put his will into his thumb for the first one. He managed to squeeze the extra button beneath the minus on the volume, and the stun gun prongs snapped out against his palm. The ship rolled to starboard and the water on deck sloshed around the Korean's feet. Hawkins gave the button a doubled squeeze in his second act on earth and tossed the phone. The double squeeze was a hold-down function. The Farm phone had the most powerful phone battery in the world. The snap-snap-snapping of the voltage was lost in the gale but the sparking between the two probes was unmistakable.

The Korean dodged and that was why his shot missed. Hawkins didn't miss. The phone fell sparking into the two inches of water around the Korean's feet and conducted 950,000 volts into him. The phone was water resistant, but it was not waterproof and it had been thrown in water with its prongs deployed and sparking.

Hawkins charged the Korean with the speed and coordination of one of the Walking Dead.

It was enough.

His mass met the Korean's and the Korean was so tall it bent him backward over the rail and toppled him over it. Hawkins followed the momentum and went over with him. The two men tumbled through space.

Hawkins lost contact with the Korean. He hit the North Sea and as he had expected the cold shock hit him like a hammer as he went under. He couldn't stop himself from gasping reflexively and he breathed in two good lungsful of seawater. The ocean heaved and roiled. The salt water burned his lungs and throat. He could barely move his numb limbs and he couldn't tell whether he was above or below the surface as he was smashed around.

Hawkins ceased struggling and gave himself to the sea.

CHAPTER FIFTEEN

Super Palm Resort, Belmopan, Belize

Able Team geared up for war. They were not shrugging into armor or strapping on web gear, but their battle suits were impressive nonetheless.

Blancanales's approximately nine thousand dollars of Savile Row bespoke tropical weight, French-blue wool, cut in the English style. His hand-painted Italian silk tie perfectly matched his pocket square and tied together with his black leather Italian driving mocs and belt. He made no attempt to do anything to control his white wavy hair. He looked like a man who designed one-off, million-dollar sports cars, a very successful drug dealer or the kind of physicist who got laid regularly. He looked mad, bad and dangerous to know.

Lyons wore a navy-blue blazer cut to fit his physique and charcoal-gray slacks. Product slicked back his blond hair like a close-fitting golden helmet around his head. In throwback *Miami Vice* style he wore neither a tie nor socks. He slid on blue-mirrored sunglasses and looked like the absolute worst sort of muscle that the best sort of money could buy.

Schwarz, wearing an American-cut gray suit that would not have been out of place in an episode of *Mad Men*, looked like a very dangerous personal assistant.

Able Team all agreed that Demi Papas's fashion con-

sultant consortium did good work, and the billionaire had
spared no expense. They were about to go into battle, and
the battlefield was a business proposition.

Papas walked in and grinned. He wore his signature
pinstriped double-breasted suit, and it fit his swaggering
style. "You boys look like a million bucks!"

Blancanales grinned back. "You look like a billion."

Papas laughed happily. He had stopped just short of
opening his pocketknife to become blood brothers and of-
fering Blancanales his sister, but the Perfect Weapon was
man crushing pretty hard on Blancanales. Papas checked
his watch. "Five point six billion last time I checked, and
that was half an hour ago. Things may have changed. Last
year? I had a personal best of six, but of course..." Papas
sighed. "That was last year."

"You'll always be the six billion dollar man to me,
Demi," Blancanales intoned consolingly.

Papas actually blushed. "Oh, Jesus, who needs Viagra
when I got you around! You sweet man!"

Blancanales shrugged demurely. He was a master of
psychological warfare. He had gotten into the heads of
drug lords, fanatical terrorists, corrupt politicians, as well
as revolutionaries, dictators and heads of state. He'd never
had a billionaire BFF before.

Lyons slid his .357 Magnum Colt Python into the shoulder rig. The rig was Swedish deer-suede and fit like the
proverbial glove. His jacket had been cut to accommodate
the rig and when he buttoned it, Lyons for the life of him
could not detect that he was armed. All of this had been
done without a single fitting.

Papas literally had a device like a tanning booth that
weighed and laser measured you and then he sent the di-
mensions to his tailors, who had worked 24/7 to have the
garments sent by courier jet. Lyons had no desire for great
personal wealth, but he liked to think he cleaned up pretty

good and had decent taste in a sporty kind of way. This was Star Wars fashion technology, and Demi Papas could personally call czars of the fashion world to fly the Death Star for him.

"It's perfect. All of it," Lyons conceded.

Papas stopped short of squealing like a schoolgirl. For the past seventy-two hours Lyons had made a production number of very slowly warming up to the billionaire. Anytime he said anything to Papas that wasn't a snarl, you could hear the man's tailbone wagging. Papas stabbed out a fervent finger at Lyons. "You deserve the best, buddy. They call you the Ironman? You don't need any flying-robot armor. You wear your superhero suit on the inside. It shows in every move you make! I can see it!"

Lyons actually felt himself warming to the billionaire—slightly. "Thank you, Mr. Papas."

"Mr. Papas? Still? Call me Demi!"

"You'll always be Mr. Papas to me."

"You know that kinda turns me on, too?"

Demi Papas had turned into Santa Claus. Being a billionaire who knew everybody, there were things he could pull off that even the Farm couldn't dream of. Schwarz had given him a shopping list of surveillance equipment and esoteric electronic devices and Papas had delivered. He had also gotten them guns, and he had coordinated with the Farm to produce passports, fake IDs and built portfolios for Able Team that could stand up to federal bureaucratic scrutiny for several days. He had also loaded their wallets with massive amounts of cash and no-limit credit cards.

"And, you guys? When this is over? You're keeping all of it, I insist!"

Lyons was about to protest but Schwarz, drooling over his electronic haul on the bed, cut him off. "Oh, hell, yes! Thanks, Demi!"

Lyons was secretly pleased. He was kind of keen on the clothes and the holster in particular.

"Okay, you fellas ready?" Papas asked, knowing. Able Team had spent twenty-four hours, a flight to Belize and the next twenty-four hours working on their covers and studying their prey. "This isn't a board meeting. It's not even a pitch. It's a meet and greet, and the people you're meeting are sort of squirrely and off the grid. Let me do the talking."

Blancanales raised one eyebrow in bemusement.

"Okay, okay, okay. I don't know what kind of undercover, James Bond stuff you guys have done before. Fine, you do the talking. I'm just saying this, if for any reason the negotiations stall, or God forbid, someone farts in church or steps on someone's toes? Look to me. I've dealt with these open source, bitcoin, Linux system-loving, Liberty City assholes before. All I'm saying is that Big Papa is here for you. I'll tell you, I'm loving this shit! I have never felt so alive! And when this is all over? The best steaks in New York, on me, and I want to hear the story behind all this. Names changed to protect the innocent and all that shit, but you boys are having dinner with me and bending my ear and breaking my balls."

Blancanales nodded. "That's a date."

"Well, all right, then. Let's go meet the Magistrate."

Med Unit, USS Coronado

HAWKINS SLOWLY TRANSITIONED from oblivion to a mass of cells aware of light and dark and heat and cold, to a cognizant though thoroughly messed-up primate. He became aware of McCarter, James and Propenko standing around his gurney. McCarter looked down upon Phoenix Force's current favorite son. "How are you doing, Hawk?"

Hawkins's feverish mind spun like the reels of a slot

machine and hit on the only good thing that had happened to him recently. "I ate a Twinkie."

"Right." McCarter looked at his youngest warrior askance. "You mentioned something about that during your last check-in."

"It saved me."

"No, Cal saved you."

Recent events passed through Hawkins's brain like celluloid film burning and coming apart in the projector. "I ate the Twinkie. I got out of the booth. I made it from the stern to the prow. I fought the Korean. I took him over the side." Hawkins's voice became a little firmer and the room became a little more solid. "I won."

"That's a big Twinkie," James observed.

Hawkins felt the need for another one. "What's the diagnosis?"

"You've got pneumonia."

Hawkins blinked. His eyes felt as if they were full of sand. "Walking pneumonia?"

McCarter and James laughed. McCarter shook his head. "Well, it was 'taking the Korean over the side and winning' kind of pneumonia, but now it's full-blown. You're also suffering from exhaustion and malnutrition. You are in hospital until further notice."

"So…"

"So the good news is you took the Korean with you over the side. The *Nymphe* has not changed course, gone to battle stations or sent out any alarm that we can detect. The *Coronado* is going to continue to shadow the *Nymphe* to the gates of hell if need be, and this ship has some interesting assets. The other good news is that you get bed rest all the way across the Atlantic. With luck we may get you back to walking and fighting pneumonia status before we reach the next stop."

"I could catch up on some Netflix." Hawkins felt himself becoming more and more lucid, and more and more and more wanting to go back to sleep. "The Korean?"

"No sign of him." James shook his head. "I had to keep my eyes on you only. Was he wearing flotation gear?"

"He was dressed like the Gorton's Fisherman."

"Then I think you got away clean," James said.

Hawkins's stomach dropped, and he already felt nauseous. "Aw, damn."

"What?" McCarter asked.

"My phone."

"What about it?"

"I doubled pumped the stun gun and threw it in the puddle he was standing in. Fried him and tackled him over the side."

"Nice," James admitted.

Propenko spoke for the first time. "The little Fruit Rabbit has proved himself," he said reluctantly. "I give him this."

There was nothing little about Hawkins, and while Phoenix Force broke his balls constantly he believed he had earned temporary godhood and he wasn't going to let some Russian penitentiary storm trooper pull rank. "You know, I don't have to prove myself to you."

"Yes," Propenko contradicted. "Yes, you do."

McCarter rolled his eyes and changed the subject. "Hawk, did you get jolted when you hit the Korean?"

Hawkins had to stop to think about that. "No?"

"Then the phone shorted out. If it didn't go out in a scupper during the storm, all they are going to find is a salt-soaked, burned-out phone, and even if they can resuscitate it, it is all Farm encrypted.

"We're thinking your giant Korean is a merc. With luck the Game Room guys on the *Nymphe* he was assigned to protect will think the Korean went out in the middle of a storm to make some kind of very private call and went over the side in the storm. As far as I can tell, you left no trace." McCarter leaned in over the gurney. "Besides the phone, Hawk, did you leave a trace?"

"I left my trace on Junior…"

"We're running that down. Bear is going to be very sad to hear you sacrificed your phone, but you did send us a lot of pictures. We're hoping the gamers come up on our radar presently."

"So what's the plan now?"

"The plan is until further notice Phoenix Force enjoys the hospitality of the good ship *Coronado*. We get rest, heal up and wait to see what Able Team digs up."

"What's Able been doing?"

"Oh, Able? They spent some time in Manhattan, then they spent a few days in the Hamptons enjoying the hospitality of a billionaire and last I checked they had been forced to fly to a hotel spa resort in Belize. And, might I add, they all got Savile Row suits and unlimited credit card accounts." McCarter paused. "I'm not bitter."

"Now—" Cal pointed to the crude $$$Luffy-Land$$$ logo stretched across his chest "—we got T-shirts."

"There is that."

"I got a Twinkie and pneumonia?" Hawkins suggested.

Propenko held up a bandaged hand with three fingers and a thumb sticking out of it. "Nine is lucky number in Russia."

"You're right. Able Team, poor bastards." McCarter sipped United States Navy coffee. "They get all the hard jobs…

Liberty City

"IT'S LIKE THE Disneyland that Uncle Walt forgot," Lyons observed.

Blancanales had to agree. Liberty City suddenly erupted

out of the jungle as if by magic. It certainly wasn't a city. It didn't really qualify as a town. It was more of a weird, high-low-tech hamlet. A lot of the tech, particularly the structures, was literally from other decades.

Blancanales hadn't seen a geodesic dome in a while, and he observed everything from buildings that looked like small college dormitories to little hillsides with doors in that might have belonged to Hobbits. Central to all stood a three-ring-size, blinding-white, circus-tent-like structure with the flag of Liberty City flying over it. The flag consisted of a blue field with planet earth with what could have been misconstrued as atomic symbol arcs girding it. The earth had an eye in its center staring out and emitting golden rays.

"Atlas Shrugged meets the Masons anybody?" Schwarz suggested.

"You have no bloody idea," Papas confirmed.

Solar panels covered every rooftop and electric golf carts seemed to be the main form of transportation, though mountain bikes were in abundance and Blancanales noted a few horses. He saw no combustion-engine vehicles save for the Land Rover Defender that Able and Papas rode in.

Papas had driven Able out of Belmopan and kept up a constant patter while they flew along the private, two-lane, semi-truck-rated connector road that led through the rain forest. Blancanales saw clear blue ocean through the trees. It looked as though Liberty City owned a very nice little slice of Belizean beachfront property.

As Able Team pulled into the Liberty City town proper, he could see beach bungalows and even tree houses with catwalks in between them. Someone had taken the time and effort to dig a canal from the beach that divided the little hamlet in two, and several charming footbridges crossed it at intervals.

Able had carefully studied the satellite images of Liberty City the Farm had acquired. Just out of sight of town, Liberty City boasted a small airstrip and two of the larger buildings had helipads. Also out of sight and beneath the trees were the warehouses and workshops.

Papas pulled the Rover up to the Circus Tent that Blancanales was guessing was city hall.

Magistrate Tan Van Staafl stepped out on cue. He looked exactly how one might picture a social and technological visionary. He was tall and lean. Decades under the Central American sun had burned his skin a permanent ruddy-rust color. He wore a faded denim shirt and pants and sandals, and had the thick, flowing white hair of an Albert Einstein who had a style consultant. The magistrate had sleepy-looking eyes that on second glance were keenly alert.

A tall, attractive, though harried and concerned-looking redhead flanked him on one side. Blancanales's eyebrows rose as he noted that on the Magistrate's six was the Central American version of Lurch from the Addams Family. A short man who was built like a circus strongman stood by the door.

Papas nodded through the tinted windows. "So the gal is Julie Curl. She's head of the Liberty City city council, but from everything I can figure out the council seems to be mostly ceremonial and they mostly just report to the Magistrate. The gigantic son of a bitch is Señor Ixchel-lupa-something. I'm Greek, and even I can't pronounce it, but it means blood moon in Mayan. Everyone just calls him Moon, except that no one has ever called him that to his face that I know of except the Magistrate and, as far as I know, me. From what little I've seen, Moon just scares the shit out of people and people just do what Moon says. The guy in the back in Thaniel Maier. He's rumored to be ex-Israeli special forces and can Krav Maga you to death in a heartbeat."

Blancanales and Lyons looked at each other. Neither man had showed up in any of the Farm intel and they looked like trouble with a capital T. Lyons took a picture of the big man through the tinted glass and fired it off to the Farm. Papas parked and Able Team disembarked.

The Magistrate beamed. "Big Papa!"

"The Tan-Man!"

They hugged vigorously. Magistrate Staafl turned and looked Blancanales up and down. "And you must be this nearly mythic Señor Blanca I have been hearing about."

Blancanales walked right up and hugged the Magistrate and kissed him on the cheek old-school Latin style. From behind his sunglasses Blancanales noticed Moon tense. The Able Team warrior stepped back and clasped the Magistrate's arms happily. The master of role camouflage adopted a thick Mexican accent. "Mythological, *Magistrado*? You honor me too much, though I have been called a *fantasma* upon occasion."

The Magistrate smiled and squeezed Blancanales's arms in return. His cover was that of a "ghost" investor, a mix of bag man and broker reputed to have some very illegitimate clients with piles of illegitimate money who were looking to launder it through legitimate enterprises. Papas had assured Able Team that Liberty City had taken dirty money before.

Councilwoman Curl was doing everything in her power not to glare at Blancanales. He had the distinct impression she did not like the character role Blancanales was playing or his reputed money at all.

Moon was eyeing Lyons like one predator sizing up another. Lyons simply grinned at the giant from behind his mirrored shades.

Blancanales gestured backward.

"*Magistrado*, may I introduce Señor Hermann, my personal assistant, and Señor Irons, he is…well, you know."

"Welcome, welcome. Welcome all." The Magistrate gave both Able Team men a firm handshake. He turned back to Blancanales. "And let us not stand on formalities. Call me Tan, my friends do."

"Well then, call me Blanco." Blancanales oozed love. "My friends do."

"But isn't Blanca your name?" the Magistrate asked.

"Blanca is my surname." Blancanales pointed at his flowing white hair. "But Blanco is also my nickname, because of my hair. Between you and me? We shall drop the *señor*."

The Magistrate beamed. "Thank you, Blanco."

"You seem to have a very interesting little city here, Tan."

The Magistrate gazed upon his kingdom and sighed wistfully. "We never quite became the self-sufficient city I and the others founders dreamed of. We had such great dreams back then." He suddenly bucked up and smiled. "But we have endeavored to persevere."

"Forgive me—" Blancanales smiled shyly "—but I do not detect much of a manufacturing base to invest in."

"Actually we have a small but very interesting manufacturing base that I am eager to show you. However, you are right. We are not exactly what you would call a factory town."

"Forgive me once again for my impertinence, but what sort of town are you?"

"Not impertinent at all, my friend. You have come many miles to make a possible investment. If I were to describe Liberty City as succinctly as possible, perhaps in a single word, I would describe her, in her current incarnation, as an incubator."

"Ah, an *incubadora*!" Blancanales made a pleased noise. "I have heard this term. They use it in Silicon Valley in California."

"Correct, my friend. In recent years we have specialized in taking in big ideas and, with private investments, giving them the funding, taxation and regulatory freedom, as well as the creative license they need, to come to fruition.

"You have undoubtedly noticed all the solar panels. As you may know, as an energy source, solar is extremely expensive. In the United States and other developed nations, most citizens cannot afford it without massive subsidization by the government. The majority of the citizens of the planet cannot afford it all. It has been our dream to produce solar electricity that the average middle-class First World citizen can afford and that the developed nations could afford to put into foreign aid packages in large quantities."

"A noble sentiment. And I understand there is green in this green energy. Even if it does not work, one understands there is money to be siphoned from these subsidies." Blancanales leered slightly. "Governments, you know."

Councilwoman Curl visibly bit back a retort.

Staafl gave Blancanales a knowing look. "I will not deny it, Blanca. We have not perfected the technology. Yet we have profited from it. However we have a number of other projects."

"Forgive me once more, but if a project cannot find typical venture capital or attract government subsidies, why would you take it in?"

"A good question, and I will admit some of the projects we have put our time and money into have turned out to be absolute boondoggles. However, sometimes an idea cannot find investment because it is too bold, too risky for standard investors or they simply to do not have the vision to see its potential to change the very world."

Blancanales put some cupidity in his eyes. "You have such projects?"

Staafl looked Blancanales straight in the eye. "Several, promising rewards beyond the dreams of avarice."

Blancanales slowly shook his head and let a slow smile light up his face. "I have never met a visionary before. I am very glad Demi convinced me to come."

Magistrate Staafl blinked and beneath his mahogany tan Blancanales thought he might be blushing. "Thank you, Blanco. That is very kind of you to so say. Come. Come in. I am sure you and your people have had a long trip, and despite having stayed at the Super Palm resort, I can assure you my chef is better than theirs. After a lunch and siesta I will give you the grand tour and, with luck, we will talk business."

Papas grinned. "Well, you guys appear to be getting along like gangbusters. You want me to stick around or...?"

Blancanales looked at the Magistrate.

Staafl smiled benevolently. "If my new friend and his people would like to accept our hospitality, perhaps a stay of a day or two might convince him of Liberty City's worthiness. I can arrange a flight back to the capital whenever he wishes."

Blancanales smiled sunnily at the idea. "Few things would please me more."

Lyons spoke for the first time. "Was that a shooting range I saw when we drove in?"

The Magistrate nodded. "It is. We have been given charter city status, and in our charter we are guaranteed protections by the Belize Defense Force. However, they consist of little more than a thousand men and we are very close to the southern border of Mexico. As you know, there has been violent unrest in the south of Mexico over the years, as well as the drug cartels. I—" Magistrate Staafl suddenly backpedaled. "Señor Blanca, I... Forgive me."

Blancanales raised a calming hand. "It is nothing. I can easily imagine you having such problems, and man must protect his interests—" Blancanales nodded knowingly "—and his investments."

"Yes, well, we do have a small security force, licensed by the government of Belize, but with no authority or jurisdiction beyond Liberty City's immediate borders."

The Magistrate turned back to Lyons. "Would you like to avail yourself of our range?"

The Able Team leader smiled behind his shades. "Few things would please me more."

CHAPTER SIXTEEN

Liberty City

"I am very disheartened," the Magistrate said. He sat in Liberty City's larger equivalent of the Game Room, and spoke on a secure line to Kun on board the *Belle Nymphe*. "And I find it nearly impossible to believe Mr. Ji-Hoon was washed overboard."

"It is very hard to believe, yet we have carefully examined his quarters. His pistol is missing, and so is a set of the ship's foul-weather gear. We found his phone. For whatever reason, it appears he went out on deck during the storm to the unsheltered prow. If for some reason he was escaping from the ship, he did not take his laptop, his wallet, money or any of his personal effects with him as far as we can tell."

"So you are telling me he went out into the storm to make a phone call?"

"I did not say that, Magistrate. I said we found his phone. It was of some note that his phone has a hidden stun gun feature and the delivery prongs were deployed. However, if the phone was being washed about on the deck, it is not out of the realm of possibility that it experienced the stun-feature equivalent of a 'butt dial,' as you Americans like to call it."

The Magistrate's snowy-white brows furrowed. "His phone had a stun gun feature?"

Kun paused. "The phone is not one of yours?"

"Oh, I issued Ji-Hoon a phone. One printed in Liberty City and protected with our best encryption. But it certainly didn't have a stun gun feature."

"So Mr. Ji-Hoon had two phones. The most obvious answer is that he wanted to make calls that neither you nor I could monitor."

"This is which also begs the question, why would Ji-Hoon have a stun gun on his phone when he has his hands?"

"That is a very good question," Kun admitted. "Perhaps he thought it was an interesting toy?"

"Ji-Hoon is not interested in toys," the Magistrate observed. "Much less nonlethal ones."

"Perhaps it simply was an extraneous part of the package the phone came with when Ji-Hoon acquired it?"

"What kind of phone is it?" the Magistrate asked.

"Salt water has shorted it out, but it appears to be some kind of highly modified Apple."

The Magistrate blinked. "Ji-Hoon genuinely despised Apple products and anyone who used them."

"I believe I have heard him state such an opinion on several occasions."

"I would very much like to see this phone."

Kun held the phone up to his computer camera. It did indeed appear to be an Apple product and a pair of small, stainless-steel, vaguely insectile barbs jutted out near the ear bud jack.

"I would very much like to see this phone," the Magistrate repeated.

"The *Nymphe* is currently in the North Sea," Kun advised.

"You have a helicopter?"

"We do."

"As soon as you are in range of a suitable country, I would like you to have the helicopter pilot fly you and the phone there. Pick one of Ji-Hoon's men to be your bodyguard and I want you to get to Liberty City as quickly as possible by any means possible."

Kun checked his computer. "The Netherlands is currently closest."

"Amsterdam should do elegantly for all your needs. I will have Hans coordinate with you."

"I will leave immediately when we are in range."

"Very good."

The Magistrate pondered then asked, "Didn't you mention something about the *Belle Nymphe* having a ghost some days back?"

"I did, but only because I thought you might find it amusing. The cook complained that the men were stealing food. It was blamed on some kind of hybrid, Baltic phantasm. Some of the ship's crew claimed to have seen a phantom crewman. I..." Kun trailed off as he caught the implication.

"Didn't you also say in your last report that Junior was complaining that someone was stealing food from his private stash and messing with his equipment?"

"I did. However, I mostly blamed it on paranoia, cabin fever and possibly some of the crew messing around. None of ship's complement like Junior and, to my shame, I took personal pleasure in his discomfiture."

"I can well imagine, Kun. To my own shame I might have enjoyed it myself."

"Thank you, Magistrate. Had any of our equipment turned up missing, I had resolved to let Ji-Hoon teach the crew a collective lesson."

"And yet Ji-Hoon is now disappeared. Have there been any ghost sightings reported since the night of the storm?"

"It appears the ghost has become quiet."

"Who is in charge of security now? Gert?"

"Yes, Mr. Von Sprack has taken over."

The Magistrate considered Gert Von Sprack. He was as German and as anally retentive as his name sounded. "Have Gert search the ship from stem to stern. Look for any clue that might lead one to suspect an intruder. Have him interview every member of the crew right up to the captain about all ghost stories, ship's anomalies and missing food or equipment. Also have him ask every crewman about any interaction they had with Ji-Hoon."

"I will institute this immediately."

"After you have been dropped off in Amsterdam, have Von Sprack ready the Game Room to be airlifted at a moment's notice."

"At once. How do you find the new clients you spoke of?"

The Magistrate considered Liberty City's newest possible investors. "Very interesting. I am having dinner with them tonight. Moon is currently keeping them entertained."

The Range

"Fire!" Moon shouted. Thaniel Maier drew his Glock and steel plates rang and rocked back and forth on their springs with incredibly rapid double taps on the 25-meter range. The merc was clearly using the Israeli shooting technique. He worked the six targets and worked back, emptying his 13-round magazine. Maier cleared his weapon and grinned back at Lyons and Moon. Earlier he had buzz-sawed silhouette targets at the same range on full auto with a SIG-Sauer MPX submachine gun.

"Nice," Lyons admitted.

"Thanks!" Maier shrugged. "It wasn't bad."

Lyons had been surprised by their choice of caliber. "A .357 SIG?"

Maier nodded. He spoke with hardly any accent. "Citizens of Belize are mostly barred from owning firearms. When they are given a permit to own a weapon, they have to be of nonmilitary caliber. Liberty City's charter says we can have a security force, but they have to follow the same rules. Nothing that can fire out of an AK or an AR or any Belize Defense Force weapon, so no 9 mm or .45s, either." He hefted his Glock 32. "We found a way to retain a little firepower. Letter of the law and all that."

"I approve." Lyons nodded. "I mean it's the loserest of losearian .357s, like sacrificing everything that makes it beautiful and good to cycle semi-auto .357, but, at least it's .357."

Maier snorted. "We try."

Moon spoke in a surprisingly soft sibilant English with a Mayan-accented voice. "Haven't seen you shoot for shit, Irons."

"Oh." Lyons made a show of being taken aback. "You want to see me shoot?"

"You're awfully pretty." Moon looked Lyons up and down and smiled for the first time, exposing huge teeth with gaps in between that belonged on a llama or some other sort of large Central American ungulate rather than a man. "Can you?"

Lyons nodded and sighed. "We try." He drew his Colt Python.

"Oh, for—" Maier gazed upon the revolver happily. "You win. That is a real .357."

Moon maintained his mocking tone. "That is a grand old piece, *abuelo poco*. Can you do anything with it? Or are you *compensando*?"

Lyons gave a very rare smile of his own. He was not a grandfather, there was nothing little about him and, as for compensating for something, women he had been with called him Ironman, as well. "Is he always like this?"

"Oh, no." Maier laughed. "You're a guest, this is Moon being nice. But if you want his respect, you got to beat it into him. And since neither you, me nor any man walking the earth can beat it into him, you have got to at least impress him a little. And you? So far?" The Israeli laughed and looked at Lyons's clothes. "I mean, me and Moon both admire your taste in pocket squares, but…"

Lyons spun his revolver around his trigger finger. He gave it two revolutions forward and then two back. He gave the pistol threes and sixes and then turned his wrist to put the pin-wheeling pistol into the horizontal plane.

Maier threw back his head and laughed. "Oh, shit man, here we go!"

Lyons's twirled his pistol as though he was in Tombstone. He suddenly released, caught the pistol in his left hand and seamlessly continued the revolver ballet.

"Oh, my God!" Maier exhorted.

Lyons pulled an over-the-shoulder catch first left, then right and then left again. The satin-polished stainless steel was a blur.

"Oh, my God!"

"Watch for it," Lyons cautioned. "This part happens fast…" He tossed the whirling revolver high up into the air. This was the hard part and it took perfect timing. Many gun aficionados considered the Colt Python the ultimate revolver.

Dropping one on the ground while trying to show off ranked right up with a French kiss at a family reunion.

Gravity took its inevitable course. The spinning revolver reached its apex and fell back toward earth. Lyons snapped his hand out, caught the revolver in the firing position, lunged like a fencer in the same motion and the Python detonated like a six-stick string of dynamite in as many heartbeats. The six lead-smeared black iron plates waggled back and forth on their springs. A shoulder holster wasn't ideal for it, but Lyons did a credible job of spinning the smoking, empty pistol one more time and returning it to the suede.

"Oh, my God!" Maier was laughing so hard he was crying.

Lyons felt a tiny part of him might regret having to pop the Israeli killer's head like a cyst. "You impressed?"

"Oh, God, yes!"

"What about you, big man?" Lyons turned to regard the giant. "Fuck, fight or wrestle?"

Moon burst out laughing. He held up giant, spatulate hands. "We can hold off on that, Señor Irons."

"Well, then, I guess the first beer is on me."

"Beer here is free." Moon laughed. "But if you like tequila? I have a bottle of the good stuff."

"I like both."

"He is a guest," Maier remarked.

"You like girls, Irons?" Moon asked. "We have girls."

The plan was for Schwarz to go for a walk tonight, and to electronically and possible physically break into Liberty City's sensitive databases. Getting Liberty City's two apparently most dangerous men drunk and debauched would be a good start at covering Schwarz's action. "I prefer seven-foot-tall Mayan men of mystery, but what the hell, when in Rome?"

The giant burst out laughing again. It was almost choked and awkward and Lyons got the impression the giant psychopath wasn't used to it. Moon pointed a finger the size of a bratwurst at him. "You are starting to grow on me."

Blancanales was the master of role camouflage and psychological warfare, but Lyons was a detective who had been undercover many times in his police career, and far more as the leader of Able Team. He went all-in. "This whole place is starting to grow on me. I'll tell you, I got real tired of deserts and goat men wearing suicide vests. And Mexico? I left the Middle East work because of the beheadings, burnings and crucifixions, and now Mexico? It's like they're in a race with these Islamist extremists and they think they can win. And I'm not betting against them."

Maier looked at Lyons thoughtfully. "You like this Blanca asshole?"

"I like him a lot. He pays good and he treats the help well."

"But?"

"It's goddamn Mexico, man. And Blanca is a money-man for some real shit-birds. One minute you're on the beach in Mazatlan and its liquor and whores, and next you know you're in the limo and are being pinned by three SUVs in an alley in Nuevo Laredo pouring in fire. Don't get me wrong, Blanca is for real. He can deliver the money, but him and his bosses? They are currently having a high turnover rate, and the guys guarding them usually go down first. Unless of course you turncoat, and once you do that your days are numbered, anyway." Lyons glanced around at the rainforest surrounding the shooting clearing. "Tree houses, chicks, sloths, free beer and your own firing range? You saying you're hiring?"

Maier and Moon looked at each other. Moon straightened to his full height and stared down at Lyons. "Let's go get a lot of drinks and talk."

Lyons paused. "My guy, Blanca, and his assistant. They're safe?"

Moon's voice grew faraway and strange. "Liberty City is probably the safest place on earth, and may be the last safe place in the foreseeable future."

Lyons noted the weirdness and met it with a grin. "Then let's fire it up!"

Stony Man Farm

KURTZMAN NODDED DECISIVELY. "Do it."

Barbara Price, after conferring with Hal Brognola in Washington, had given Kurtzman the go-ahead.

Tokaido began very gently inviting the Liberty City security suite to dance. "These guys are weird." It was a very odd setup; some of it was top of the line and some of it was ancient. It had been very recently upgraded, but all the new top-of-the-line stuff was guarding the manufacturing wing. Security in town was positively decrepit. The security cameras were of 1990's vintage, and you could actually see them with your eyes in their mounting positions. Tokaido shook his head at the grainy black-and-white pictures with the occasional line skewing down through the footage. "These guys are Cro-Magnons."

Wethers peered over Tokaido's shoulder. "Nevertheless, the cameras are pervasive. If Gadgets goes walkabout? We are going to have to pick him one hell of a route to avoid detection, and I don't know if we can pick one that will take him to anything of any interest. We want to get him to the manufacturing wing or the Circus Tent without being seen, so he'll need to hit the roof. And since we have no air assets he's going to need a hang-glider and a running start off of Doyle's Delight."

Kurtzman frowned. Doyle's Delight was the highest peak in Belize and several hundred miles away. Liberty City was on the flat northern coast.

Tokaido looked back at Kurtzman. "You want a cascade of surveillance failure? It will be a lot easier than the one we pulled in Papas's Tower of Profit on Wall Street."

"That would work once, and we would have to assume our guys would have to bug out directly from the target area. The jig would be up, whether we get what we want or not. I want Gadgets going in like a ninja, unseen, unheard, unsuspected, and I want him to leave the same way."

"Then he needs darkness," Wethers declared. "Liberty City is a solar Mecca by day, but what happens when the sun sinks over the mountains in the west?"

Tokaido pounded keys. "It looks like they get their power at night and during some parts of the rainy season from the gas turbine at Belize City."

Wethers shrugged at Kurtzman. "It's Belize. Charming place, but they have to be used to power outages."

"True, but Liberty City will have emergency generators. You have a read on that, Akira?"

"There is nothing in the schematics that I can pull up. I'm thinking when the lights go off someone in each building has to literally go downstairs and flip a switch. That may be different in the manufacturing wing or the Circus Tent, but that will take a hard hack. Like I said, their encryption is top of the line."

Huntington Wethers walked over to a large screen and swiped his finger on the satellite photo of Liberty City. "We cut the power. Gadgets goes ninja straight through town and heads for the beach. He runs a buttonhook back through the forest. Assuming he makes it? When they turn on their generators, Gadgets is in the woods making his way to the manufacturing wing. When he's in range, we turn the power back on. They turn their generators off, we cut the power again. Gadgets goes in. I think we can play that game a couple of times. Rolling blackouts. I bet Liberty City has experienced them before, and with any luck their main reaction will be a whole lot of swearing and not much suspicion."

Tokaido nodded. It could work. "I can walk into the Belize City power station's net and own it, and the only thing that will get turned off is Belize City. All they will think is that they have a bug in their system."

Delahunt made an approving noise. "And that still leaves us with the hard hack into Liberty City in our back pocket."

Kurtzman made an approving noise of his own at Wethers. "It's not bad."

The Magistrate's mansion

"YOUR MAN IRONS is very impressive," the Magistrate remarked.

Blancanales nodded. "I like to think so."

The Magistrate had a smaller, circus-tent-like structure of his own and it looked down on the ocean. His dining room was an open-air affair, and the dining was magnificent. Blancanales feasted on what appeared to be a rack of baby back ribs except they were barbecued with Belizean spices with lime and the ribs were tapir rather than beef.

Blancanales was a firm believer that if you really wanted to eat well you needed to cross the Rio Grande and eat your way all the way down to Ushuaia on the southern tip of Argentina. The shrimp-stuffed corn tamales were some of the best he had ever had. The meal was course after candlelit course with the sound of the surf in the background. Chilean whites and Argentine reds flowed depending on what was being served. Blancanales considered himself a gourmet and a gourmand, and if Schwarz got the green light to go for a walk, Blancanales considered it his duty to get the Magistrate food-stunned and, with any luck, drunk.

The Magistrate swirled the wine in his glass. "Where did you find him?"

"Oh, I always use ex-United States military men."

"Doesn't using mercenaries break the blood rule, and let no one in from outside the family?"

"That is just the point. I am outside the family. I am a broker. In effect, I am a mercenary. If you are Sinaloa

Cartel, and I show up with Zeta muscle? Well, you see. But if I tell you I will transport your money or broker your transaction, and I am surrounded by American mercenaries? Strangely, you would feel more secure. Also, I find the Americans are extremely loyal. They quickly form cohesive teams, they come exquisitely trained, I tell you—" Pol made a cutting motion across his throat "—like a hot knife through butter. I work for very bad men, and they are scared of them."

The Magistrate nodded thoughtfully.

Blancanales tilted his glass at him. "I tell you, Tan. If you need men, I recommend a few. Not that I am saying you do. Your man Maier seems very competent, and this *gigante*, Moon? He gives my man Irons pause."

"I will tell you honestly. In light of recent events it has come to my attention that I may need to upgrade my security apparatus, particularly abroad."

"Well, I know men." Blancanales weighed risks, health, hemispheres and who they had some certainty the enemy had never seen. "A Navy SEAL. An Englishman. How do they say it—SAS? I have worked with them before, but, given the pleasures of my current task?" Pol waved his wineglass at his pleasing surroundings. "I need no protection save that I keep Irons near me always. They are in Mexico City. Would you like me to make a phone call?"

"Forgive me, Blanco, but what sort of scruples do these men have?"

"Are you running cocaine or pimping little girls?" Blancanales countered.

"No." Magistrate Staafl made a face. "We do not do that here."

"Well, then, in that case, I might describe these men, as they describe themselves, 'down for anything.' What that might be?" Blancanales took a judicious sip of his wine. "That is between you and them."

"You are too kind, Blanco."

"I live to serve." Blancanales smiled another shy smile. "And I will take a small commission."

"Your man Irons drinks with my men. May I ask where your assistant is?"

Blancanales regarded his red wine by the candlelight. "He is not so much an assistant as a pet geek. I suspect you know of such things."

"I have met them."

"You take him to Belize and he immediately gets on his computer. It is really quite sad, but he is useful."

"I understand completely, Blanco. I must have Moon run herd on my—"

The constellation of lights that described Liberty City at night suddenly went out. The city dropped into inky blackness only interrupted by the breaks in the trees that allowed the stars.

Magistrate Staafl uncharacteristically lost his cool. "Goddamn it!"

"Do not worry, my friend." Blancanales shrugged as though it was nothing. "I am from Mexico. These things are common."

"This will be fixed immediately," Staafl snarled.

"Allow me to say, Tan, I am unruffled. I enjoy the sound of the surf, the company of new friends and the candlelight."

Staafl grabbed Blancanales's words like a lifeline. "You are too kind."

Blancanales held up his nearly empty glass. "Kindness, hell. Pour the wine. Let us see what this evening presents us."

Magistrate Staafl took up the carafe and poured. "I believe this evening might be quite productive."

Blancanales smiled like a kid on Christmas. "I am banking on it."

CHAPTER SEVENTEEN

Schwarz went for a walk. It was more of a serpentine lope through Liberty City. It struck him again that despite a distinctly low population level, Liberty City was extremely heavy on security personnel. Men with .357-caliber submachine guns were spilling into the night. However most of them had tactical lights on their weapons rather than NVGs strapped to their faces, and most of them looked either irritated or bored and slow-walked to their emergency stations or to their patrol patterns.

The lights suddenly snapped on at the Circus Tent. They were joined by the glare of perimeter security floodlights that threatened to solarize Schwarz's night-vision goggles. The Able Team computer whiz took a detour through the little Hobbit Hill district and the deep darkness in the tiny vales. Throughout the districts of the tiny town he mostly heard swearing in a number of languages. Schwarz made unerringly for the sea.

Lights began popping on throughout Liberty City.

Schwarz found himself ensconced in the blackness of the beach with only starlight to betray him. He crossed the canal and headed north across the sand. He noted that Liberty City had a lagoon, and it must have been dredged because the pier looked as though it could service an ocean-going ship of decent size, though it lacked cranes and a serious loading facility.

He was also reminded that the lost *Maria Cecilia* and T. J. Hawkins's home away from home, the *Belle Nymphe,* were both feeder ships that came with their own cranes for loading and unloading. Schwarz jogged another kilometer up the beach and then started his buttonhook back through the forest.

He could see the lights of Liberty City's little industrial park lighting up the night in lunar glare ahead. Schwarz turned down the gain on his NVGs and drew a silenced Ruger .22 pistol. His phone was his main communication link and he had an ear bud taped in place in one ear and a mike taped to his throat. "I am on approach to the factory. It is lit up like the sun."

"Copy, Gadgets," Kurtzman replied. "We have eyes on. You want another blackout?"

"Copy that, Bear. Give the industrial park their power back. Let's get them to turn off their generators, then cut power again."

"Copy. Returning power to Liberty City in five, four, three…"

Schwarz continued his run through the trees and stopped well short of the manufacturing wing's fence. Slightly to the south all the lights popped back on in Liberty City. He actually heard a few cheers. Schwarz watched as the emergency lights in the factory wing blinked out. The perimeter lights stayed on. "Give them a few minutes."

"Copy that."

Schwarz scanned the factory fence. It was twelve feet tall and topped with razor wire. His NVGs didn't pick up any infrared perimeter lasers to break, but the fence glowed slightly hotter than the surroundings. "The fence is electrified. If it's electrified, it sets off the alarm if it gets touched."

"Copy. Are you in position?"

Schwarz took off his jacket. "Ready."

"Shutting down the Liberty City power grid in five, four, three, two, one…"

The factory wing went jungle-dark save for the stars above. Schwarz scrambled up the fence and tossed his jacket over the coils of razor wire. He rolled over the fence top and dropped to the soft earth. The ground between the fence and the factory warehouses had been cleared to make a twenty-meter dead zone, but no shots rang out.

Schwarz moved for the front door of the four interconnected warehouses. According to Tokaido, the security suite could put the manufacturing quad into lockdown, but in a blackout, the last thing the buildings did was unlock the doors so no one would be trapped inside.

Schwarz walked in the front door.

It was late and no one appeared to be around. Unlike most of Liberty City's eccentric dwellings, the manufacturing quad was not filled with windows and skylights. It was a series of dark, windowless vaults hiding its secrets from the world. Schwarz flicked the flashlight function on his phone to infrared. It would burn up his battery fast but he didn't intend to stay long. He walked through a hallway of offices and entered the first factory cube.

The technology was impressive as hell.

The Able Team computer genius had seen 3-D printing machines before. Most were the size of household appliances. The ones that were being used in mass production in the airline industry were the size of pickup trucks. Liberty City's printing machines were like the arms of giant Japanese battle robots poised over printing plates the size of school buses. They were supplemented by untold dozens of smaller printing appendages like the legs of a vast mechanical centipede. Row after row of container vessels containing the raw-powdered materials of plastics and metals were connected to the arms large and small by vast bundles of umbilicals.

By Schwarz's lights, Liberty City had the most impressive 3-D printing facility on earth, and they had the scope to build things far larger than Go-pro helicopter drones. Some of the printing surface plates looked big enough to print helicopter gunships. Schwarz swiftly began photographing all of it.

"Gadgets, this is Farm. The last time we shut down the power, the lights in the manufacturing wing came back on in three minutes. You have sixty seconds, and we have security movement all over Liberty City."

"Copy that, Farm." Schwarz went to the massive central printing plate. He took a walk across it, swiping his finger in the printing material residue and wiping it into a small Ziploc plastic bag. He noted large steel braces to the sides and mounted in the ceiling that could hold his imagined gunship or something even larger in place while the printers layered up the product micron-by-micron of steel, or aluminum or plastic.

Schwarz started to get a very bad feeling.

"Gadgets. You have a thirty-second window on manufacturing quad emergency generators. Security elements moving into your area. Recommend you extract."

"Copy that, Farm. Am advised." Schwarz moved toward a machine that looked some kind of giant, angry, adamantine mantis shrimp. It struck him that it might suddenly come forward and do work on top of whatever was happening on the printing plate. Magistrate Staafl hadn't lied. Liberty City was doing things other people were afraid to try, and very bad money was paying for it.

Liberty City was building things from scratch. Things no one could afford, unless they pumped millions of dollars into a small, private facility with technology on loan from God.

Kurtzman's voice registered increasing urgency. "Gadgets, get out. Get out now!"

"Extracting!" One wing of the manufacturing quad would have to be enough. Schwarz thought it might be plenty for Kurtzman to work with. He hit Send and sent his pictures to the Farm.

Schwarz broke into a run for the back door. Lights popped on in the manufacturing wing catty-corner to him. When the lights went on, the security cameras went on. He ran into the next wing, ignored the arachnid-like machines and ran for his life.

The lights snapped on inside the wing he had just vacated.

Schwarz hit the back door and ran down the loading dock. He headed for the trees as the facility lights snap-snap-snapped on behind him. Schwarz sprinted for the fence. An alarm buzzed along the fence and it suddenly crackled. The jacket he'd laid over the razor wire rose like a ghost from the static and fell back smoldering.

Schwarz ran straight for it. "Cut the power! Cut the power now! Cut it! Cut it! Cut it!"

"They still have their generators on. It won't—"

"Cut the power! The electricity for the fence comes from the main grid! I am extracting!"

"Copy that! Cutting power in five, four, three, two…"

Schwarz hit the fence. His fingers curled through links but no juice burned through his body. Some but not all of the lights behind him cut out. He scrambled up the twelve feet of storm fencing like an ape and took a few minor scorchings as he seized his smoldering jacket and went over the razor wire. He tried to take the blackened burning jacket with him but it shredded and tore. With luck the remaining shreds would burn up when the fence turned back on and whatever blackened remnants remained would wash away in tomorrow's rain.

Schwarz hit the ground and snarled as he broke through the trees for the ocean. The fact was, he had left tracks behind and he knew it. He burned for the beach, burst out of the trees and headed south down the beach for the canal.

His head snapped around at the sound that chilled the hearts of operators around the world.

Schwarz heard the baying of dogs.

"Gadgets, be advised," Kurtzman warned. "You have pursuit."

"Copy!"

"Dogs," Schwarz muttered to himself. "And how come no one mentioned dogs?" He knew he was a new, smoky, foreign smell, and the dogs would beeline toward him. Schwarz considered the sea. A little swim would take off his stink but if that was where his trail stopped that was where the dogs would stop, and Liberty City happened to have a little marina, boats and a lot of guys with inordinately powerful submachine guns. Schwarz lengthened his stride and headed for the canal.

Liberty City was his only hope for freedom.

The sound of the dogs increased behind him and he knew they had hit the beach. Schwarz ran up the concrete pier and dived into the canal. The canal was wide and deep enough to allow a decent-size motorboat to motor right up to the main Circus Tent.

He immediately learned that the canal appeared to be a major part of the Liberty City sewage system. Resigning himself to a broad-spectrum program of antibiotics, he resisted throwing up under water and swam inland. It wasn't a bad system, the tide came in and the tide came out and took it all away. The poo-eating filter feeders in the lagoon probably loved it. It did not make his swim any easier. The canal had been dug deep enough to be available twenty-four hours a day, and the tide was coming into the lagoon and the gentle surge helped push him along. As the tide came in it would also erase his tracks on the beach.

Schwarz kicked along the slimed canal wall and nearly

puked twice. He knew if he opened his eyes he would be giving himself multiple ocular infections, and he knew he couldn't swim all the way back to their lodgings. Even if he could he would be trying to enter the Circus Tent slimed with the waste of Liberty City, human and otherwise. Schwarz rose up gasping like the Creature from the Crap Lagoon. He still heard dogs barking. Whoever was running them figured they had a bite. Schwarz no longer smelled like special operator, manufacturing wing and smoking blanket.

He smelled like poo.

Schwarz sighed and breathed through his mouth. And what dog didn't like that?

He breast-stroked on the surface to the next footbridge and hauled himself out. His NVGs and electronic gear were all toast and he gave them to the canal to let the outgoing tide take away. The Circus Tent was still lit up like the sun. His chances of getting in to his quarters tonight in his current state were null and void. He considered the darkness of Hobbit Hill and scratched it off his list.

Schwarz heard a radio crackle twenty meters away. "We have a possible security breach, possibly from beach side."

A security man spoke back. "Copy. Refugee, criminal or citizen flight?"

Schwarz noted the words *citizen flight*.

The man on the other end replied. "Undetermined. Possible trail stopped at the pier. They may be going for a boat. I need a beat-the-bushes sweep down toward the water."

"Copy."

Security men shouted and coordinated. Liberty City security was forming a skirmish line and heading Schwarz's way. He saw a light at the head of the canal and the sound of a motorboat put-put-putting on low throttle. The Able Team warrior heaved himself up and ran for the trees. The sounds of dogs and men forced him to veer off. Schwarz ran for the tree houses. Like Hobbit Hill the tree houses formed their own little district of micro-domiciles and had been constructed to coincide with the giant hardwoods they were built around. Catwalks connected the tree houses, and the Christmas lights strewn along the ropewalks and stairs kept going on and off as the Farm messed with the power.

Schwarz scrambled up a steep wooden gangway with rope rails and made his way along the tree scaffolding. It creaked with every step but there was already plenty of background noise as Liberty City ran its security sweep. He picked the largest, darkest quietest tree house. He tried the door and discovered it had no lock. Schwarz slipped inside as silent as a ghost.

Schwarz froze as Councilwoman Curl lit a candle, sniffed the air, turned and stared at him. Schwarz pointed his pistol between the councilwoman's eyes and put a finger to his lips. The councilwoman's hair was wet and she was naked save for a bathrobe. She chewed her lip for one heartbeat and then gave Schwarz one of the coldest female looks he had ever been exposed to. "You are Señor Blanca's asshole assistant."

"His assistant?" Schwarz shook his head and spoke the truth. "I mean, don't get me wrong, he needs my assistance to wipe his butt when it comes to anything bigger than downloading an app on his phone. But, his assistant? Hell, no. And I can make him admit it."

Many women were beautiful when they were angry. Redheads by candlelight had a leg up on it. "You have a gun."

Dogs barked and the sound of men and radios got closer. Flashlight beams cut through the forest floor below. Councilwoman Curl glared defiantly. Schwarz thought about everything he had seen of the councilwoman in the two minutes he had met her and everything he had read in her file. The words *citizen flight* rang through his mind again.

He took a giant chance, flicked on the Ruger's safety and tossed it onto the table next to the candle. "No, I don't."

Curl was mildly shocked. Schwarz was mildly taken aback as the councilwoman took the opportunity to pull a snub-nosed .38 out of her robe pocket and point it at his groin. Her nose wrinkled. "You smell like poo."

"I went for a swim. And, for a green city? Your sanitation system isn't what it could be. Can I borrow your shower?"

"I've tried to take a shower three times. This is a tree house. You have to pump the water up, and the power keeps going off."

"I apologize." Schwarz threw down another card. "That's my fault."

"For some strange reason, I find myself believing you."

The sounds outside said the searchers had entered the little tree house district. Schwarz decided to roll the dice and let it ride. "Councilwoman, may I be frank with you?"

"You have five seconds to start being frank with me or I am going to shoot you in the dick and scream rape. And, speaking of rape, God help you when Moon lays his hands on you. It's rumored he has certain predilections."

"I have been bad. I do not trust your magistrate at all, and I went on a walkabout in your manufacturing wing. I was unsubtle but I managed to make it look like it came from the outside, from the sea, rather than inside. But it is a thin ruse. I am covered with poo. I have dogs on my trail, and the guys with the leashes have .357-Magnum-caliber submachine guns. I need a shower, some way to clean and dry my clothes, a place to sleep and some way to insert myself back into that Circus Tent like I never left it. What do you say, want to be bunkies?"

Councilwoman Curl snapped her revolver toward an open door with a dripping noise coming out of it. "Strip, and squeeze your clothes out in the bucket."

Schwarz didn't ask questions. He moved into the tiny dark shower stall and stripped. He squeezed his septic clothes into the bucket. The tree house shook slightly as boots in force hit the catwalks. "Councilwoman, I—"

"Give me the bucket!" she barked.

Schwarz handed over his watery bucket of bilge. He also retrieved his silenced pistol and disappeared into the shadows.

A fist pounded on the door. "Councilwoman Curl, we—"

Curl stomped over and flung open the door. "Goddamn it!"

A powerful-looking black man in body armor backed up before Curl's fury. An even larger blond man backed him up. "Madame Councilman, we—"

"First the shower stops three times! Now the toilet is overflowing?" Curl hurled the wastewater out over the catwalk barely missing the blond man. Her voice rose to a scream as she hurled the bucket after the effluvium. She pointed her finger in the black man's face. "Screw you, Dirk!"

Councilwoman Curl slammed the door in Dirk's face.

Dirk's voice was just audible outside as he walked away. "God, I hate that bitch."

"Me, too," Blondie replied. "I'd still do her."

"Me, too," Dirk replied. His voice went ugly. "And we will before this is over."

The catwalk creaked as the two security men descended to ground level.

Curl turned to Schwarz and appraised his naked form in the candlelight. "I will shower with you, sleep with you, clean your clothes, cook your breakfast and get you back in the main tent if you promise to get me the hell out of here when you go."

The lights in the tree house suddenly popped on and

despite its extremely limited floor space it was a very charming living space. Schwarz was dripping wet, naked as the day he was born and still smelled like poo. He gave Councilwoman Curl his best grin and put his pistol back on the table. It was the best offer he'd had since this mission had started. "I'll scrub your back if you scrub mine. Everything else is negotiable, and I get you out of here no matter what."

"Bathing is good clean fun," Curl remarked.

"You really want to get out of here, don't you?" Schwarz asked.

"You have no idea."

CHAPTER EIGHTEEN

USS Coronado

Commanding Officer Regina Hitch burst into the cabin Phoenix Force temporarily called HQ. She was a short, stout, extremely competent-looking woman. She was also slightly out of breath and appeared to have run from the bridge. "The *Belle Nymphe* has launched a helicopter!"

McCarter looked up from his coffee. The past few days of rest and relaxation while the *Coronado* used her stealth features to ghost the *Nymphe* across the North Sea had been a godsend. It looked as if it was time to get back to work, though. "What heading?"

"Due south, on a straight vector for the Netherlands and Amsterdam. She's currently cruising at eighty-seven knots. She'll hit the Netherlands coast in about ninety minutes."

McCarter looked at Grimaldi. "Can you catch her?"

Jack Grimaldi regarded his coffee gravely. "I'm on one engine and my girl isn't happy. Word is the Farm is trying to leapfrog me the parts I need using an aircraft carrier in the Atlantic, but that is days away. I hate to say it, but taking her on a full sprint with one engine over the ocean might just end up with some people swimming."

The CO smirked. "I got a Hawk in the hangar that will leave your hinky bird in the dust."

Grimaldi froze in mid-sip. "Did you just call my girl a hinky bird?"

The CO's smirk went up a notch. She had flown Navy choppers before deciding she wanted her own ship. "Yes, I believe I just did."

"It's cold," the Stony Man ace remarked. "It's cold on this ship…"

The Commanding Officer continued. "If that chopper is a sky-crane like you said, about a hundred miles per hour will be her ideal cruising speed, maybe a quarter more at full throttle."

"What if she's carrying a loaded container?" Manning asked.

"Oh, jeez." The CO did some aeronautical math. "Probably less than half that, a quarter, maybe less. A bird like that is built for torque, not for speed."

"She's right," Grimaldi confirmed.

"Thank you."

"You're welcome."

Calvin James pulled up a map of the North Sea on his tablet. "It's a safe bet they're transporting somebody. Have you intercepted any communications from the *Nymphe* or the chopper?"

"None yet, but they won't have to contact Netherlands coastal authority for another hour. It's slightly unusual, but then again she's a sky crane flying off a feeder ship. They could claim any sort of major or minor emergency, and if their papers are all in order the Dutchies won't bat an eye. If they don't have any cargo there probably won't even be an inspection."

McCarter found himself liking the CO. "You think you can catch them?"

"At emergency war power and stripped for speed? My girl can do two hundred plus in a sprint for the coast, but if we're going, you need to say one, two, three, go, and you need to say it now."

"One, two, three, go," McCarter said.

"She'll be ready in twenty."

"Thank you, Commander."

The CO spoke over her shoulder as she headed out for the hangar deck. "I live to serve..."

"I like her," Manning announced.

"She called my girl hinky..."

The rest of the team ignored the pouting pilot.

"How do you want to play it?" James asked McCarter.

The Phoenix Force leader considered his assets. Hawkins was in the infirmary and currently gurgling between sentences. Encizo had been released but advised to rest. He was taking that advice and racking up rest time. McCarter himself was still coughing as if he had never given up smoking, and he was painfully aware that if Phoenix Force suddenly found themselves having to assault the *Belle Nymphe*, the assault force would be thin on the ground and most of them wheezing. Now he had to pare down Phoenix even further.

Manning and James sighed. They both knew it was down to one of them and even without slight cases of cabin fever, both men would leap at the opportunity to return to action, their injuries notwithstanding.

"We could always send Nick?" Manning suggested.

Everyone at the table laughed.

Propenko had been frustrated in his attempt to go deep-sea fishing with his finger, so he ingratiated himself with the crew of the *USS Coronado* by setting himself semi-permanently in state in the mess hall and telling tales of Russian penitentiary wonder and horror that set even the most debauched sailors aboard squealing like cartoon housewives that had seen a mouse.

"Okay, maybe not such a good idea," Manning admitted.

"It's Cal," McCarter announced.

Manning was mildly appalled. "You're kidding."

James scowled.

"You have cracked ribs." McCarter had made his decision. "He runs faster than you."

"I run faster than him when he doesn't have cracked ribs," James remarked.

"When you not falling on your face, dizzy bastard," Manning scoffed and poured himself more coffee. "Who the hell ever heard of a seasick SEAL, anyway?"

Manning had a mild point. McCarter eyed James. "No shit assessment, mate. How are you doing?"

"I'm better, and as a sailor, I hate to say it, but I think some time on solid ground would do me good. On top of that, I may be the only one that none of the enemy had any contact with, even by proxy."

"Right, then. Pack light. The Farm will arrange whatever you need in Amsterdam. With luck we can have you land at almost the same time as their chopper. If they're dropping someone off, be ready for a planes, trains and automobiles tail job."

James rose. He'd be armed with his fists, a phone and his credit card until his quarry went to ground. Calvin James had worked with far less. "I'll need a couple of GPS trackers."

Liberty City

"So," SCHWARZ asked, "you have no idea what they are building in the manufacturing quad?" He had to admit it wasn't the most romantic pillow talk. Then again, he and Councilwoman Curl had stopped short of actually sleeping together, but bath time had been a great deal of fun and so was the snuggling after. He figured it was just as well. Sleeping with the enemy nearly always turned out badly, though he was fairly sure that while she might betray him to save her life, he had turned her into an ally. If one had to lay low, there were worse places than the bed of a good-looking redhead.

"I know lots of things they are building in there. The problem is there are lots of things that I don't." Curl shook her head bitterly against Schwarz's chest. "And despite being head of the Liberty City city council, I no longer have the security clearance to enter or find out."

"Let me guess, you lost it when Liberty City started taking in large amounts of suspect money."

"I complained loudly and bitterly about it. Tan finally told me to shut up or leave. That was very uncharacteristic of him. In fact, he's changed a lot over the past two years."

"In what way?"

"He was depressed. Liberty City never quite fulfilled its charter, much less his dream. Then about three years ago he got his groove back, genuine missionary zeal, and then people started needing security clearances. A lot of people were fired. A lot of people left."

"And Moon showed up."

"Yeah, we have had incursions by refugees. Some of the fighting in Mexico got a little too close for comfort. There have been spats with the locals, protests because we mostly don't hire locally. We had some of our people beaten up in the nearest town. And we did have one very frightening experience with some guys who must have been cartel who walked in and started acting as if they owned the place—and us." Curl shuddered. "They had the local police scared and apparently the Belizean State Police paid off."

"Moon took care of that?"

"Yes, he did, and for the most part everything else, as well. Then Maier, with a small but very heavily armed security army and some guys even scarier."

"One of them a Korean, almost as big as Moon but with death mask for a face?"

Curl lifted her head. "Um…yeah. Mr. Ji-Hoon. How do you know about that?"

"I can't tell you that right now, but I can tell you that you don't have to worry about him anymore."

"How so?"

Schwarz looked steadily into Curl's big green eyes. "Nobody has to worry about Mr. Ji-Hoon anymore."

Curl's big green eyes grew very wide.

Schwarz changed the subject. "So why didn't you just leave?"

"I was going to. I'd bought my ticket and was packing my bags. I was going to say with my sister for a little while, then head to Silicon Valley and see what I could do to help save the world from there. I stepped out of the bedroom and Moon was sitting at my table drinking my tea. He smiled that donkey-toothed smile of his and spoke to me in that baby whisper of his. He said Wyoming was beautiful this time of year and my sister's ranch was lovely, and that my niece even lovelier and how lucky I was. He said he had never been to Wyoming and wondered aloud if he might just have to take a trip up there soon."

"And then?"

"Then he got up, thanked me for the tea and went back downstairs. I heard him and Maier laughing as they walked away."

"And so you—"

"And so I went into the bathroom, threw up, unpacked my bags and went back to work the next day."

"I'm sorry."

"I'm sorry, too. I mean, I do love the work, there are some projects here I still really believe in. But it is scary around here. People show up who no one has ever heard of, they don't comingle and then they disappear. Did you know we have a brothel?"

Curl was scared and venting. Schwarz rolled with it. "I heard a rumor."

"Rumor, hell. A year ago I went for a walk on the beach and discovered to my wondering eyes that Liberty City has its own bikini team. There's an old British Colonial back in the forest left over from the logwood trade. The males around here have dubbed it Casa Happy. I've never been, but apparently it's been renovated up to Playboy mansion grotto standards. The Liberty City privileged and the pleasing get to spend time there, and almost always guests. The girls frolic on the beach all day and go on weekly shopping excursions in Belmopan. Me? I haven't been out of this dump in six months." Curl gave Schwarz a bitter look. "I think your buddy Irons is up there right now."

"I believe he is, or was, and I am betting he drank the two most dangerous men in Liberty City under the table to give me some elbow room."

Curl smiled despite herself. "You know I think I saw that in an episode of *Star Trek*."

"So you're a nerd," Schwarz mused.

"Of course I'm a nerd. Nerds are hot."

Schwarz ran his eye up and down the naked redhead spooning into him. "Yes, they are."

"You say sweet things."

"So things are getting scary?"

"We've lost about three quarters of our population, and nearly all of the original Liberty City believers are gone. Some just flat-out disappeared. It is very obvious that illegitimate money is being laundered through the legitimate projects. Culturally? Liberty City has gotten downright tribal. We definitely have inner and outer circles. It's like *Lost* meets *Lord of the Flies* meets Scientology. And, Moon? Moon is no Tom Cruise."

"No," the Able Team warrior agreed. "No, he's not."

"I'm just waiting for Staafl and his new acolytes to start

wearing white robes. And throw in an unhealthy dose of *1984* while you're at it."

"Staafl is up to something?"

"Yes. Yes, he is."

Schwarz sighed. "Well, someone is going to have to put a stop to it, whatever it is."

"And that someone is you?"

"Me and a few good friends."

"Are you saying that Señor Blanca is not a cartel bagman-slash-broker?"

Schwarz went cards-on-the-table time; at least most of them save for an ace or two. "No, he is not."

"And this guy Irons isn't some badass ex-merc?"

"He is certainly badass. Gotta give him that." Schwarz ran his fingers through luxurious red hair. "Let me ask you a question. How are we going to get me back into the Circus Tent undiscovered?"

"We're not. You and I are going to take a cart, drive over to the dining commons and walk in bold as brass. It's Sunday Morning Mimosas—the place will be packed."

A slow smile crept across Schwarz's face. "So…?"

"So we let everyone think you spent the night with me."

"Well, I can live with that, but how does that work out for you?"

"Tan and I were lovers."

"Oh."

"It was years ago, when I was younger and more foolish and I really thought he was a visionary. It didn't work out. He goes through Gal Fridays in cycles. But since then I have been sort of forbidden fruit around here. As Liberty City's resident redheaded hottie and ex-flame of our fearless leader, I get hit on a lot, and I haven't been with anyone in a very long time. You show up for breakfast with me all google-eyed and hanging on your arm? You will have counted serious coup. It will throw Tan off his game, and even Moon and Maier will look at you in a new light."

Schwarz grinned. "I want pancakes."

Stony Man Farm

HUNT WETHERS LOOKED up from his files. "These guys are bad news, Bear."

Kurtzman was reading the same files. Moon was a very, very bad man. He had been involved in the indigenous Zapatista uprisings in the Mexican state of Chiapas. Only he was an indigenous Mayan who had turned against his own people. While the Mexican army hunted Zapatista guerillas in the mountains and the forests, Moon had put his tendencies to work. He and other loyalist "militias" had looted, pillaged and terrorized the Zapatista rebels' home villages and towns. Mexican military forces had turned a benevolent and blind eye to the atrocities. In the twenty-first century much of the hostilities had died down. Human rights organizations and the United Nations were now involved and much of the struggle was political.

Moon had moved on.

He was known to have done strong-arm work for the southern chapters of the Los Zetas drug cartels, and while many cartel executioners gloried in slowly sawing someone's head off, Moon was famous for being able to do it with one swing of a machete. There was a gap in his recent history, and now he appeared to have become Liberty City's town tamer.

Thaniel Maier had served in the Israeli Maglan commando unit, which specialized in fighting behind enemy lines. Kurtzman could not confirm it without hacking into IDF databases, but his sources told him that Maier had then been recruited by the Mossad for the Kidon department, which was widely alleged to be responsible for the assassination of terrorists. Maier had been booted out for reasons that were redacted, though what he would have to have done to get kicked out of that club gave Kurtzman pause. His sources in Israel informed him that Maier's name was mud, and worse, that he was unofficially banished from Israeli soil. He had been a private contractor for the past five years.

Moon was the goon, and Liberty City's one-man Brute Squad. Maier was commander of Liberty City's Republican Guard. From everything Able Team had gleaned, the two men shared the same tendencies that had gotten them exiled from their homelands. In Liberty City they had found a new home, though why they would serve a man like Magistrate Staafl was the question. Money was the obvious answer, but Aaron Kurtzman's instincts told him there was something more going on. Liberty City, for all the recent excitement, seemed like pretty tame work, and Moon and Maier seemed like the kind of borderline psychopaths who wanted to watch the whole world burn.

The Stony Man cyber chief pulled up the photos Schwarz had taken inside the manufacturing quad before losing his phone in the canal. He snorted to himself. Phoenix Force and Able Team were going through some very expensive phones and fast, and the Farm wasn't printing money. Kurtzman snorted bemusedly again. Liberty City was printing something. He marveled again at the sheer size of the printing units. Three-D printing was very popular in the aerospace industry, but even the big boys had nothing on this scale. It was nothing short of incredible. It must have been hideously expensive. It kept coming back to a state actor, but they couldn't find any connections.

Kurtzman spoke aloud. "Where did they get the money?"

Wethers and Tokaido wandered over and looked the

photos covering the big screen like a mosaic. It was an assembly line right out of one of the *Terminator* movies.

"Drugs," Tokaido announced. "Papas sauntered in wearing Pol like a cheap suit and stinking of cartel money. Magistrate Staafl jumped to attention."

"Correct," Kurtzman agreed. "But from what we can gather, the cartels have laundered money through Liberty City. Most likely so have other criminal enterprises, and that can be very lucrative. But it is not direct investment. The illegitimate concerns want their money cleaned up, Liberty City gets a cut, and probably a hefty one, but then the money flows out again. It doesn't stay in solar panels that aren't selling."

Wethers nodded. "Of course you have your sugar daddy's like Demi Papas."

"Right," Kurtzman acknowledged. "Then again he's doing it in a similar vein except he is laundering his reputation. He's given them some real money, but Papas never had any real faith in Liberty City as a moneymaker. He got his green energy street cred and he tosses them a bone once in a while. What we are looking at in this one wing has never been done before. This stuff was built from scratch without the financial backing of Uncle Sam or Mother Russia. It's like a high-tech company that doesn't have a bottom line. If this has been going on for the past three years, it would take massive and consistent infusions of capital. Everything else we've seen? Papas? The bait Pol is throwing? That's almost small potatoes. That's the stuff that keeps the lights on and the girls at Casa Happy in lingerie. This stuff we are looking at here is the kind of stuff that breaks piggy banks."

"I can't say that you're wrong," Wethers said. "But where are they getting it? I mean, unless they have their own secret diamond mine on the premises or they secretly broke into Fort Knox and stole everything without anyone knowing... I don't see it. If big oil or big corporations were involved, I think we would have found the link days ago."

"Drugs," Tokaido repeated. "Gotta be drugs."

Kurtzman sighed.

"No," Wethers said and raised a finger. "Let's follow the lad's logic. If the Mexican and South American cartels are not directly investing, that mostly eliminates cocaine, marijuana money in any substantial form and Mexican brown heroin." Wethers nodded at Tokaido. "What does that leave?" he prompted.

Tokaido snapped his fingers. "China white!"

"And you, Bear?"

Kurtzman hated it when Wethers made him feel as if he were back in school, though he was also inordinately pleased with himself when he answered one of the professor's questions correctly.

Kurtzman pulled up a map of the world and panned in to expand the mountains that overlapped Myanmar, Laos and Thailand. "I, for one, do not believe anyone in the Golden Triangle is investing their drug money directly into Liberty City."

Wethers nodded. "Correct."

Kurtzman was pleased, and the answer stood in front of them. He swiped to the Golden Crescent. The crescent-shaped swath of mountains and valley was at the crossroads of central, south and western Asia, encompassing the borders of Afghanistan, Iraq and Pakistan.

Tokaido frowned. "So Central Asian opium is paying for Liberty City?"

"Last I checked, Afghanistan's cut of the trade alone was worth over four billion last year—and this was your idea," Wethers mentioned.

"They're not paying for Liberty City. They're paying Liberty City to build something for them, and Liberty City had to build the tools first."

"So what are they building? A bomb? You can't just print up plutonium, can you?"

"No, you can't. We were looking at the Russians. We were looking at the Iranians. We were looking at the drug cartels and renegade corporations. We were looking in the wrong places."

Kurtzman typed in two key words and a chunk of Asia encompassing Kazakhstan, Uzbekistan, Turkmenistan, Kyrgyzstan and Afghanistan was highlighted as a unit. Put together, it was enough real estate to easily qualify as a continent.

"I don't know what they're building down there in Liberty City, but if it's printed three-dimensionally from scratch, it's untraceable. For that matter, they can even print it to make it look as though it belongs to someone else."

The Stony Man computer genius stared at the map of Central Asia. "I don't know what Liberty City is building," he reiterated. "But that patch of earth has the money, and rumor is some of them want their own Caliphate."

CHAPTER NINETEEN

Philip S. W. Goldson International Airport
Belize City

Calvin James had traded dizziness and the long-forgotten thrill of seasickness for extreme jet lag. Nonetheless, he was pleased with his progress.

A man Hawkins had called the "Other Korean" and a blond bodyguard who acted as if he had stick up his butt had disembarked the Sikorsky sky crane helicopter at Amsterdam Airport Schiphol.

The *Coronado's* Seahawk helicopter had landed James in the helipark literally thirty seconds later and one hundred meters away. A quick sprint that had left him slightly queasy had gotten James on the same shuttle bus to the main terminal. The Korean had gone to the Aeroméxico desk and bought a first-class ticket on the next flight to Belize City with a connecting flight through Mexico City. James had waited five minutes and bought a ticket on the same flight and had a two-hour wait. He had shepherd's pie and then whiled away an hour at the Rijksmuseum's airport annex taking in the showing of Dutch Masters.

He bought a carry-on bag, two off-the-rack suits and accessories. Calvin James grinned to himself as he went to the airport's shipping service and Federal Express priority overnight mailed $$$Luffy-Land$$$ T-shirts to Kurtzman, Wethers, Delahunt and Tokaido. He figured Delahunt might wear hers to bed. Tokaido would be the only one willing, if probably not eager, to wear his in public.

The flight across the Atlantic had been uneventful. He'd eaten three times, slept twice, watched two movies and had flirted rather successfully with the surgically enhanced flight attendant. His one fear was that the Other Korean might suddenly rabbit in Mexico City to lose any suspected tail. It was an excellent place to get lost in. However the Korean and his bodyguard had faithfully taken the connecting flight to Belize and so had James. He had watched them go the car rental park and rent a Jeep. While they had filled out the paperwork, James had casually walked up as the valet delivered the vehicle to the front and attached a GPS unit under the rear bumper. James was fairly sure it was a waste of time.

He thought he had a very good idea of where the Other Korean and Stick-up-his-Butt were going.

Calvin James rented a black Toyota Land Cruiser, started his tail and made a call. "Bear, I'm heading out of Belize City." He brought up the GPS window on the tablet in his lap. "The Korean and his muscle are in a rental Jeep heading north. Do you have them?"

"Copy that, Cal. We have tracking. It looks like they are heading straight for Liberty City."

"Yeah, that's the way I figure it."

"That was two continents, one sea and an ocean, Cal. Nice tail."

James smiled wearily. "Yeah, I get that a lot, and I'm pretty good at following people, too."

Kurtzman laughed. "How you holding up?"

"Little weary, but assuming they drive straight into Liberty City I can probably afford a nap. How is Phoenix doing?"

"Still aboard the *Coronado*. The *Nymphe* has reached the Atlantic and is bearing southwest. I have a suspicion that you, Able Team and the rest of Phoenix are about to have a conjunction of the stars in Belize. At their present speed following the *Nymphe* it will be about a week and a half before they arrive. Then again, if we decide they need to hit Liberty City and fast? The *Coronado* is one of the fastest major warships in the world. She can do fifty knots plus in a pinch, and by all accounts her crew is pretty excited about Phoenix Force and this mystery mission. From her position right now she could sprint to Belize in four days."

"Ironman in command?"

"Able is in the country. As it stands now it is their show. If someone calls in the amphibious invasion it's going to be him."

"Copy."

"I will inform Ironman you are in country and have him contact you. Right now he is in a pretty high-power meeting."

"I'm going to make sure our boys reach Liberty City safe and sound. Until I hear from Able, how do you want me to proceed?"

"Well, Cal, right now you are kind of a free agent. What do you think?"

James had had a nice long flight to think about it. He had studied and restudied everything they had on Liberty City and examined the satellite photos with the zeal of a SEAL planning a mission. "I was thinking I might take a detour to the embassy in Belmopan. You think you can arrange for them to loan me some hardware? Right now all I have is a tire iron."

"I already have, but as you might imagine the weapon selection at the Embassy armory in Belize is—how shall we say?—sparse. A Marine M-16 and a Beretta is about the most they can do for you. They can probably scrounge you up a bayonet if you ask nicely."

"Tear gas? Smoke?" James asked hopefully.

"Most US Embassies carry both these days. I will make sure they are told to extend you every courtesy."

"Thanks, Bear."

"So what are you thinking?"

"Well, once I am armed up, I was thinking Corozal is the closest town of any size near Liberty City. It's a resort town, and it's on the Caribbean. I figured maybe someone has some scuba gear to rent. Liberty City has beachfront property and a canal that leads through the center of town and to that manufacturing quad of theirs. So I'm thinking I rent a boat, as well, and when I get the call I mount an amphibious invasion of Liberty City."

Kurtzman was pleased. "Nice. I'll have Carmen rent you two places in Corozal and locate the boat and scuba rental outfits for you."

"Thanks, Bear. So what is Able's status?"

"Their cover appears to be holding. Gadgets went walkabout last night. He almost got caught. Be advised Liberty City is on a high state of alert right now."

"Is he all right?"

"He apparently took the opportunity to seduce the head of the Liberty City city council."

"Eew."

"No, she's a redhead and hot."

"Oh, well, didn't know the old Radio Shack nerd had it in him."

"Your thing for redheads is well known, Cal," Kurtzman advised. "And jealousy is an ugly emotion."

Carmen Delahunt sang out in the background of the Annex. "Redheads rule!"

James pulled out onto the coastal road. "You know you love me best, Bear."

"I love all my wayward children equally, Cal."

"You know you love me best."

Kurtzman was silent.

James rolled his eyes as the afternoon rain shower suddenly hammered the Land Cruiser. "Okay, after Mack, you love me best."

"You do dress the best."

"Yeah, and I am wearing off-the-rack and I hear Able is having Savile Row shit sent to them by private courier. I need to hang out with this Papas dude."

"You know, he's still in Belize, and that is almost not a bad idea. He is gung-ho for this operation and he could buy you a yacht, a mansion…hell, he could probably buy you Belize if you need it."

"I am a black man, and a black Federal Express card would look real good on me, Bear."

"I know it would, but be advised, Papas is seriously man-crushing on Ironman."

"Nah." James shook his head. "Once Papas goes black, he'll never go back."

James was rewarded by the sound of Kurtzman strangling on his coffee. "You win." He laughed. "I will set it up. Before you go amphibious you posing as one of his bodyguards is just about perfect cover while you're in Belize."

Visions of lobster dinners, custom couture and unlimited expenses danced through Calvin James's head. "Now that's what I'm talking about."

Liberty City

"AN INCURSION?" Carl Lyons glared balefully around the lunch table. The daily rainstorm lashed the trees outside the open-air dining area and hammered the roof of the big tent. "I was told this is some kind of free city! I was told this is the safest place on earth! I'm told Señor Blanca is fine and go ahead, have a shooting holiday and get drunk with Bigfoot and Wonder-Jew in Casa Happy!"

Moon and Maier looked both hungover and genuinely penitent. The support wires of the Circus Tent stopped just short of shaking as Lyons roared, "And we have a goddamn incursion?"

Blancanales thought Lyons was laying it on a little thick but it wasn't bad.

Magistrate Staafl raised a hand. "Mr. Irons, please, I—"

Lyons whirled on Blancanales. "And where were you, prick-face?"

"I was getting laid."

Lyon's face went flat and his eyes went deadly. "I've never liked you."

Blancanales raised his glass of wine and drank.

"Mother—"

"Mr. Irons, please sit down. We have incursions, but none have been hostile in years. We get refugees, destitute locals, even boat people from Haiti and Cuba drawn by our name. The last hostile incursion we had was a jaguar. Moon and the dogs treed it and it now adorns my bed. As far as we can tell, nothing was stolen, nothing was broken into and we found no tracks. We had a series of blackouts last night that originated at the power station. It is quite possible the security suite malfunctioned and that we had no incursion at all."

Lyons looked at Blancanales. "Señor Blanca?"

"I do admire you fervor for my protection, Irons, but we are guests here. You are berating our hosts, and I gave you permission to join Moon and Maier for some recreation. I was safe here all night, surrounded by men with guns. Not a shot was fired. Nothing happened, and you and I have survived far, far worse. I feel safe here. Please, sit."

Lyons slammed himself back into his chair and glared at nothing in particular.

"Magistrate?" A willowy, platinum-haired girl in a peasant dress entered the dining area. According to Curl, she was the latest groupie/assistant Tan Staafl was grooming. "Your guests have arrived."

Staafl gestured. "Send them in."

The Able Team duo arranged looks of mild interest on their faces as the Other Korean entered with his bodyguard.

The Korean bowed curtly. "Magistrate."

"Kun, how are you? How was your flight?"

"Excellent, and a refreshing rest from the sea, but I am glad to be back here in Liberty City."

"And we are well pleased to have you."

Kun ran his gaze over the Able Team pair. "Investors?"

"Indeed. Do you have anything for me?"

Kun glanced around again. Maier almost said something.

Staafl waved their concerns away. "We are among friends."

Lyons and Blancanales watched as Kun set a Farm phone in front of the Magistrate. Staafl picked up the phone and turned it over in his hand. "Interesting. Kun, after you have refreshed yourself, why don't you—?"

"I would like to take the phone to the lab and begin dissecting it now."

"As you say, dear friend." The Magistrate looked to the stiff-looking blond man. "Gert?"

Gert spoke with a clipped, German accent. "We found nothing, *Herr* Staafl. Nevertheless, I believe we should talk, in private."

"Very well. Gentlemen, if you will excuse me?"

"Please," Blancanales encouraged. "Take your time."

"Enjoy your meal. Perhaps you would like to go out and enjoy the water, or, have you been to Casa Happy?"

Blancanales nodded at Lyons. "My man has. I am eager to see it."

"Oh, well, take one of the golf carts, avail yourself and, let's say, shall we meet for an early dinner?"

"Indeed, Tan, a pleasure."

"Until then." Lyons and Blancanales watched as the Magistrate and his cyber and security guys left the tent. The team rose and went to the cart park outside of the Circus Tent.

"So how is Casa Happy, Carl?" Blancanales asked.

"Well, it's no Luffy-Land," Lyons growled. "And thank God for that."

Blancanales thought about the mission pictures he had seen. "I still want the T-shirt."

Corozal, Belize

"Wow, a black spy!" Papas was ecstatic. "I've never seen a black spy."

Calvin James tried to be offended, but there was nothing in Demi Papas's big Greek eyes except childlike awe. The billionaire was wearing nothing but a black Speedo and enough body hair to qualify as a sweater and leggings. He did not appear to believe in man-scaping. James held out his hand. "Call me Cal."

"Demi!" Papas shook happily and had a surprisingly strong grip. "Come in! Come in!"

James was slightly disappointed they weren't staying at the Copa Cabana or some of the other swankier Corozal hotels. Papas had rented or mostly likely had just flat out bought a dilapidated beach shack just outside town. The advantage was that it was about a stone's throw from the shore and boasted a little private pier.

"I got everything!" The billionaire pointed at the couch. James observed a pair of scuba tanks that looked old but serviceable, a compressor unit and two sets of fins, goggles, weight belts and snorkels. James noted with some amusement a pair of diving knives with old-fashioned, strap-on, ankle sheaths on the coffee table. Of interest, as well, was a sharpening stone sitting on newspaper. Apparently, Papas was all-in on this mission. "Oh, and I got spear guns! You want a spear gun? I got spear guns."

"You never can tell when one will come in handy," James observed.

"They're still on the boat, but they are really cool."

"We have a boat?" James asked.

Papas pointed out proudly toward the pier. James took in the majesty of an ancient, wooden, paint-peeling fishing boat. It was about thirty feet long and the only amenity it appeared to boast was a bridge the size of a phone booth. Papas had done something correctly. There were about one million boats just like it in the Caribbean. No one would look at it twice. "It'll do."

"Oh, hey!" Papas had remembered something. "I asked the Bear what sizes you wear. I hope you don't mind, but I bought you some clothes."

James perked up. "Now we're cooking with gas."

Papas went into the bedroom and came out with a brown paper grocery bag. "Check it out, Cal."

James kept severe disappointment off his face as he examined the contents. Papas had acquired him a matching black Speedo, an ancient pair of faded and torn carpenter's jeans that appeared to have become Capri pants through natural erosion, and a ribbed undershirt that someone had washed in a colored load and turned slightly pink. A bedraggled-looking straw hat and blue flip-flops completed the ensemble. Except for the Speedo, the garments looked and smelled as if Papas had bought them from the previous owners down on the beach with spare change.

"Get it? We're fishermen," Papas hooted. "Remember *Dr. No*?"

"I've seen it…"

"Bond and that black guy—Quarrel? They posed as fishermen to get close to the private island. We're like that!"

"We are?"

"Right. Except you're Bond and I'm Quarrel."

James regarded the billionaire dryly. "You're saying you're my black boat driver."

Papas blinked, and then his smile broke out like the sun. "I am!"

In a very reluctant and disappointed way, James had to admit it wasn't bad.

"Oh, I didn't know if you'd be hungry, so I got us a box of empanadas. Oh, and there's a twelver of Belikin Premium in the fridge." Papas pulled up short. "Do you drink beer on a spy mission?"

"If my cover requires it."

"Right."

"Right. Now I could use a nap."

"I figured. I strung a hammock out back. Go ahead and put your feet up. I was about to fill the tanks."

James appraised the man-tanned man in Speedos. "You know your way around boats and diving gear?"

"Oh, yeah. Look at me." Papas spread in his arms to let James take in the majesty.

He took in a man who was a lot older than the cosmetic surgery on his face let on. His arms and shoulders were still powerful, but he'd never had nor ever would have six-pack abs. There was nothing aristocratic about him. Except for his face, he was built like a Greek peasant.

"If it wasn't for the miracle of American opportunity, I'd be in a boat just like that one on the pier, dressed just like this, fishing, with my cousins. You know…sometimes? When I can't take it anymore? I still do."

James was finding Papas hard not to like.

Papas sighed wistfully. He suddenly perked up. "Oh, I was also thinking!"

"I hear its dangerous work, but what you got?"

"Well, I'm Demi Papas!"

"I know that. I've seen you on TV."

"Right! So I was thinking if we need to go in through Liberty City's front door rather than swim up the back? I figured our best bet would be you posing as one of my bodyguards. So, anyway, like I said, I asked the Papa Bear for your sizes. I got some clothes sent. They're on the bed."

James forced himself to walk casually into the bedroom rather than sprint. Laid out the bed were two gorgeous, tropical-weight, American-cut suits; one dark blue and the other charcoal-pinstripe gray. A small assortment of exquisitely matched ties, shirts, socks, belts and accessories was laid out to match each suit. Several gleaming pairs of shoes sat lined up at the foot of the bed, and James detected casual wear hanging off the back of the room's single chair. A black suede shoulder holster hung off the bedpost.

"The Bear said you'd be picking up a Beretta. So I had you fitted for a Beretta. You picked up a Beretta?"

"I did."

Papas shot James a wary look. "Listen, don't get me wrong, but I didn't know you were black. I mean, if we need a do-over? It'll take another twenty-four hours."

"No." James took in his haul. "That'll do, Papas. That'll do."

Stony Man Farm

"I DON'T THINK we have a choice." Wethers shook his head. "We need to find out what they are building in there. I think Gadgets is going to have to go for another walk in the moonlight."

Kurtzman didn't like it at all. "Dangerous, he almost got caught once, Liberty City is on high alert and still not sure if they had an intruder or not. If we institute another series of blackouts they will come out in full force. Their dogs caught a scent last time, and they are half convinced it was a false alarm, but the manufacturing quad is going to be the first place they go."

Tokaido threw out the obvious choice. "Have Cal do it. He's a SEAL. Swimming up canals and infiltrating stuff is the kinda stuff he does in his sleep."

Kurtzman had been thinking it. So had everyone else. He had also been thinking about keeping team Zorba and Quarrel, as he had found himself thinking of them, as an ace in the hole or even better yet emergency extraction in case it all went south for Able Team before the rest of Phoenix Force showed up.

"Our other choice is a hard hack right into the Liberty City mainframe. And, unlike the rest of the place? It is absolutely state-of-the-art. They really have had geniuses building them things from scratch, including their computer architecture. Their stuff is like the Martians donated it to them. They design it for themselves and no one else. We will be tap-dancing through minefields trying to get in and get out without being detected."

"You're saying Akira can't do it?"

Tokaido suddenly shot Wethers a desperate look.

"I'm not saying he can't, but it might just be the biggest challenge the Stony Man cybernetic team has ever faced. We almost always have the technological edge. Now we are facing guys like us. They have the home field advantage and we're not just sneaking through their firewall or breaking their encryption. Liberty City's home field is a deliberately closed and alien system. Breaking in? Maybe. But taking a step in any direction once inside without being detected? It will be like *Invasion of the Body Snatchers*, every single program high to low will be ready to point its finger and pod scream."

Tokaido stared in awe. "Nice."

Kurtzman stared at the satellite photo of the manufacturing quad. "So, either a hard infiltration or a hard hack. Like you said, Hunt. Both are minefields, and we're running out of time."

"No!" Carmen Delahunt leaned out of her workstation. "No, no and no!"

Kurtzman's brows bunched but he felt internally hopeful. Delahunt was ex-FBI and data analysis was her specialty. "What've you got, Carm?"

Delahunt hedged. "Listen, I'm not the cyber guy here."

"No duh," Tokaido scoffed.

The redhead's brows veed dangerously. "You remember when you declared you needed to learn how to fight? Do you remember the first person that kicked your ass in the dojo? Honey, I got plenty more where that came from. You want me to pull up the Tokaido Taps Out highlight reel? I don't think we've watched it since the Christmas party two years ago, and we could all use a laugh right about now."

Tokaido's shoulders sagged. "That was needlessly hurtful."

Wethers ignored the shamed hacker. "What Bear said, what have you got, Carm?"

"How about a soft infiltration and a soft hack?"

The cyber men stared at one another.

"The hard hack into the Liberty City mainframe is problematic. I'm with you, Hunt. Turning off all the lights again? Bear's right, its trouble. Besides, Gadgets got through two of the four quad buildings and they were empty except for the 3-D printing machines. I think we all suspect whatever they built is being stored in the other two buildings, and they are on lockdown."

"So?" Wethers prompted.

Delahunt pointed at the central monitor and the pictures from the Liberty City manufacturing quad Kurtzman had been using for wallpaper. "So, I have been staring at those machines of loving grace Bear has been all goo-goo eyed over for the past forty-eight hours. Those robo arms, large and small, are creatures onto themselves. They have to have their own little central processing units, don't they?"

"Probably," Kurtzman conceded.

"So they got their orders and printed up what they were supposed to print up. I'm sure the files of what exactly was built and the specs are classified up the wazoo and stored in the Liberty City mainframe or double secret mainframe, but wouldn't each printing arm's tiny CPU have some kind of record of the movements it had made?"

Wethers nodded thoughtfully. "Unless they purged it, probably. Why?"

Delahunt put her hands to her ample chest in false modesty. "I am but a single mother and a humble data analyst. But you brain trusts? Forgive me if I'm wrong, but if you had a record of every movement that every printing arm in that facility has made over the past, say, two years? Couldn't you create some kind of a program that would reverse engineer their movements and build you some kind of model that would allow you to extrapolate what they might've been building? I mean, how hard is to hack into a robotic arm? And they can't be expecting anyone to do it from the inside."

The cyber men stared at each other.

"So," Delahunt continued, "the key is to get Cal into the quad soft, somehow, and then Tokaido can talk him through the hack. After that he can just scamper away through the trees like a good little SEAL and drink champagne cocktails with Demi. God knows I wish I was." She opened her suit jacket and pointed her fingers at the $$$Luffy-Land$$$ logo stretched across her chest. "So far all I've gotten is a T-shirt."

"Hey!" Tokaido's jealousy was palpable. "Where did you get that?"

"We all got them. Courtesy of Cal." Delahunt turned her attention to Kurtzman. "What do you say, Bear?"

"We need to start working up a plan to get Cal into the quad."

CHAPTER TWENTY

Corozales Beach

"Hit it!" James shouted. He tensed as Papas rammed the throttle full forward on the water-ski rental boat. The rope from the boat to James's harness went tight and he ran as fast as he could. The lights of the boat tore ahead of him across the dark Caribbean. Behind him the rental hang glider suddenly took wind and his feet became lighter and lighter.

James white-knuckled his control bar as the barely discernible surf came toward him and he half expected to hit the water and ski on his face while his sail turned into a sea anchor and tried to drown him in the dark. His boots barely hit spume and James was airborne. It had been a while since he had been hang gliding, much less at night, and he let Papas and his boat simply pull him up like a kite until he ran out of tow rope.

James shoved his legs back into the leg sack. The rope went taut and he unhooked his umbilical. He was flying.

James could dimly hear him woo-hooing over the sound of the speedboat's engine and the ocean wind. There was a good evening breeze and the wind gave him good lift. James kept his nose into it and kept rising. Below him he could see the boat's running lights and the white wake churning as the billionaire turned sharply back for shore. Papas grew on people, maybe like a bad rash, but James was starting to see how the boy from Mykonos had made his way to the top.

James checked the altimeter on his wrist and gave himself five thousand feet to work with before turning back toward the coast of Central America. The wind off the ocean gave him lots of air to play with and it was a fairly short jaunt to Liberty City. It was two o'clock in the morning and he was in no particular hurry. He felt no nausea or dizziness; just the wind in his face and the joy of earth and sea below. James felt good. The ocean was dark save for bits of bioluminescence and reflected starlight. Belize was a black mass broken by fewer and fewer lights as he left Corozal behind.

Kurtzman spoke in James's ear bud. "How you doing, Cal?"

"Good. Real good." He pulled his NVGs out of his knapsack and the night beauty went harsh and lunar-gray. "Making my approach."

"Copy that, Cal. So far we have no movement around the quad. Akira has been ghosting around the edges of Liberty City security. We don't think they have cameras or motion sensors on the roof. We have a good two hours of satellite imaging on the quad. Recommend you land on the helipad and take your time. Papas is on the way. ETA forty-five minutes."

"Copy that, Bear." In James's NVGs the nearly uninterrupted beach formed an easy road to follow straight to Liberty City. He could see the glow of the main town and associated compounds ahead. James spoke into the link. "Able, this is Phoenix, I am about to make final approach."

"Copy that," Lyons returned. "Gadgets is in tree city with Curl. Pol and I are in circus central. We are ready if it comes to a hostile breakout."

"Copy, Able. Will contact you when I touch down." As far as they had ascertained, Liberty City didn't have an air defense system, but James skirted the town and used the updraft coming off the hills to rise higher. "Beginning final approach, Bear."

"Copy that."

James tucked his knees into his chest and pulled his legs out of the sack and harness. The hang glider immediately stalled as his legs dropped. As he swung to vertical and hung from the control bar by his hands, the nose started tipping down precipitously. "Girl? It was fun."

James let go and arched hard into free fall.

Playtime was over. He waited a few seconds to make sure the ghost glider was nowhere near him and pulled the rip cord on the British military surplus MC-4 Ram Air parachute Papas had bought from the Corozal skydiving club.

James's straps cinched against him hard as the canopy filled. He took up his control toggles and began his descent into the free city. The quad was dark save for low ground lights around its immediate perimeter. As he got lower he became aware of two men with dogs walking patrol around the electrified fence. Neither man nor beast looked up as James passed over them. He flared his chute just about perfectly and alighted featherlight on the orange square of the helipad right in the center of the white landing crosshairs. He waited but no alarms went off and no stalag lights snapped on.

"Whenever there's trouble, or in case of attack, have no fear, because Bond is black," he intoned smugly. James spoke into the link. "I am on top, about to go in."

"Copy that."

James changed frequencies. "Bond in position. How you doing, Quarrel?"

"ETA thirty minutes, Bond!" Papas sounded positively giddy. "Will hold on the coordinates Papa Bear gave me."

"Copy that." James shrugged out of his suit and harness.

He took out his multitool, opened up a panel on one of the air-conditioning units and jammed his jump gear between two ducts and sealed the unit back up again. James went to the roof access door. He took out his phone and a key card from his wallet. One corner of the card flared out to form a USB hub. James connected the phone to card and slid the card into the lock. "Ready for handshake, Bear."

"Copy. We have handshake. Breaking the door."

Code scrolled down the phone's screen as Akira Tokaido pulled a Vulcan mind meld on the roof access lock.

Back at Stony Man Farm, Tokaido told the door to unlock and that the act of unlocking the door was nobody's business and should not appear on any security suite or even be recorded in the log.

Calvin James slipped inside the quad. He descended the stairs to the factory level. He slipped through the silent foyer and a lounge and stole a lab coat off a coat rack. His card now had top quad clearance and it let him onto the factory floor.

James stared for a moment in awe. He'd seen the pictures on his phone but they hadn't done what had been accomplished here justice. He had been on assembly lines and the robot machines were clunky, greasy and painted hazard yellow. The smaller printing machines here looked like something that a comic book superhero might fight or a mad scientist might graft one or more of their arms onto him. If you mated a few of the giant printing machines together and gave them a helmet they looked as if they might defend Japan from giant reptiles with atomic breath. "You boys do good work, give you that," He held up his phone so the Farm could see. "What's my plan of attack?"

Tokaido spoke on the link. "Go to any workstation."

James picked one overlooking a school-bus-size printing plate and sat. All the monitors were dark but numerous little green LED lights told him there was power going through the system. "Now what?"

"Disconnect your card. Just connect your phone through any USB hub, preferably directly into the monitor or the desktop unit."

"Copy that." James felt around behind the gorgeously huge monitor and connected his Farm phone. "I'm in."

"I know."

"Now what?"

"Now nothing. They're all on. They're just in sleep mode. I'll just—"

Calvin James just about jumped out of his seat as printing arms all over the floor suddenly snapped up and coiled as though they were about to beat the shit out him. He found his pistol in his hand. "Holy shit! What the hell is happening?"

"No." Tokaido seemed unconcerned. "No, you're good. The good news is that even though these printing machines have been used on all sorts of assorted jobs, they are all connected to a central hub. I just needed to coordinate."

"Yeah, well, coordinate with the brother first. It's like we've got a 'Skynet becoming self-aware' situation down here."

"Nice."

James eyed the gleaming machines and their arms warily. He fully expected one to sprout legs and scuttle forward. "So what else do I do?"

"Nothing. I just have to download the printing arm movements."

"How many of those are there?"

"Millions."

"Swell."

"No, no, you're good. Do you know how much data an individual arm movement and a material squirt takes up? This isn't a movie or a song. We are talking about the electronic record of an arm movement. We're talking barely a kilobyte per. This will not take long."

"Good to know."

"Hang tight."

James shook his head. Hang tight was right.

Stony Man Farm

"WE HAVE TWO TRUCKS!" Delahunt stated. "They are diverting from the main highway to the Mexican border crossing. They are taking Liberty Road straight to town."

"A bit late at night for it," Wethers commented.

"Downright suspicious," Kurtzman agreed. "Akira, how are we coming with the downloads?"

"Working on it. Almost there."

Kurtzman spoke into the link. "Cal, be advised we have two loaded trucks inbound. Very likely they are coming to your location."

"Copy that," James responded. "Keep me advised."

Kurtzman brought up the window Delahunt was looking at. "What are they carrying? Can you tell?"

Delahunt zoomed in. It was at night, using thermal imaging, and this was a satellite that specialized at mapping the earth for agricultural purposes. But it was still pretty obvious. "Intermodal containers—who would have guessed?"

"It's like they cornered the market," Tokaido commented.

Kurtzman watched the trucks. It wasn't a bad corner to market. There were literally millions upon millions of them, on ships, trucks, planes and railroads moving to, from and across every continent on earth including Antarctica.

The Game Room had led them a merry chase out of one, and now it looked as if more were coming to join the party. Kurtzman was starting to get a very bad feeling that the party was about to start for real. It was time to make a command decision. He touched an icon and called Barbara Price. She was a thousand feet away in the Farmhouse proper.

She answered immediately. "What is it, Bear?"

"I think we need the *Coronado* to break off tailing the *Belle Nymphe* and get Phoenix Force within striking range of Liberty City. It's that time."

Price paused on her end of the line. "That is an awfully big risk. The *Nymphe* is currently in the middle of the Atlantic. I can try to scramble another military ship to pick up the tail but that could take up to forty-eight hours. The *Nymphe* is currently sailing in a major Atlantic shipping lane. She could meet up with any one of a thousand ships at any moment and transfer cargo or personnel. We would have no way to stop it and stand a very good chance of losing the tail.

"For that matter, according to Dutch customs authority, that sky crane helicopter refueled and flew back on a heading straight for the *Nymphe*. They can relaunch that helicopter carrying the Game Room or God knows what else at any time, to any one of thousands of aforementioned ships in the night, and without the *Coronado's* over-the-horizon radars we will never know about it."

"I know, it's a risk, and a big one, but I would bet anything that the *Belle Nymphe* and her cargo are headed straight for Liberty City. I believe the Korean is the guy they keep calling Game Master, and they extracted him in the North Sea. There hasn't been any exciting activity since. Assuming nothing spooks them, it just doesn't seem to me they are willing to attract attention to expedite the Game Room or the Game Master's minions to Liberty City. There was no reason they couldn't have sent all three of them—apparently they didn't care enough to."

Price let out a long breath. The Farm had chalked up one hell of a lot of wins trusting Kurtzman's instincts. "All right. I'll tell the *Coronado* to break off and sail at all speed for Belize. The good news about this is that I think I can arrange for the parts Jack needs for *Dragonslayer* to be waiting for him."

"That is good news."

Price calculated. "There's got to be an aircraft carrier in the Atlantic somewhere within a thousand miles that can break off a frigate or one of its support ships to pick up the *Nymphe's* tail. Meantime we'll see if they can also launch a Hawkeye airborne early-warning plane to keep an eye on the *Nymphe* in the interim. Failing that, there is almost nothing better at sneaking up on unsuspecting ships like a US attack submarine. I'll talk to Hal in DC and somehow we'll get eyes on the *Nymphe*."

"Thanks, Barb."

"You're welcome. Oh, and I happen to be looking at my computer. What's this about trucks?"

Liberty City, Manufacturing Quad

CALVIN JAMES WATCHED from the roof as the truck convoy pull into the quad's main loading docks. The download was complete and he had extracted from the factory floor. The trucks were Mercedes-Benz semis carrying what outwardly looked like a standard ISO container each, though James found those were hardly ever what they seemed on this mission. The problem was that the trucks were beeping and flashing their taillights as they backed into the docks, and, from the overhang of the roof, blocked him from seeing what was being unloaded. Neither did he have any view of the docks from the two manufacturing floors he had access to. The other two buildings were locked down, not just with electronic locks, but genuine, massive metal locks on the doors that he doubted he could blow off with his Beretta, even if he was willing to leave the evidence, which he wasn't.

James teeth flashed in the dark. "Mrs. James didn't raise no fools..." He swiftly went to the ventilation unit he had violated earlier and pulled out his chute. James snapped out his tactical knife and began removing the suspension lines. He stuffed the shrouds and straps back in and concealed them.

Moving to the edge of the roof over the dock, James began weaving and knotting himself a climbing line. He listened as he worked. He could hear men talking below; some in English, some in Spanish, some others muttered in a language he didn't recognize. Two men who appeared to be drivers and not involved with loading or unloading stepped out into the night and lit cigarettes.

James checked his creation. As a sailor and a SEAL it ranked as one the worst bits of rope work of his career, but with luck it would rappel him to the loading docks unseen and back up if need be. He anchored one end to a solar panel frame that looked as though it would hold and stepped over the edge. It was two stories down to the dock entrance and, as fortune had it, the front of one of the truck cabs stuck out a few feet.

James walked down the back of the warehouse. It all came down to security cameras. He could see two of them to either side of him on the building face but they were pointed at the approach road and the grounds immediately in front of the docks. James silently stepped onto the cab of the truck and went flat as he peered into the loading bay.

The trucks were unloading men.

It appeared to be at least a platoon of them. Most were bearded and appeared to be of some kind of Middle East or Central Asia origin. Whatever they were speaking, it wasn't Arabic. They didn't seem to be on a high state of alert. The men stretched stiffly, lit cigarettes and cracked jokes in their language as would men who had spent a long journey in the back of a container vessel.

James watched as men kept exiting as though the trucks were clown cars in the circus. He took up his phone and started video recording. Men had opened up the third truck down the dock, and they began unloading crates. James couldn't read the writing on them but he had seen those kinds of crates a thousand times in his life as a soldier. They were military and, by their size and shape, they contained weapons.

Thaniel Maier stepped out onto the dock and James was surprised that it appeared he had unknowingly spent most of the night with the Israeli. He wondered who might else come crawling out of the woodwork or where all the new guys might go. He felt a terrible temptation to try to sneak into the wings he hadn't seen but he bit it back. He had gotten what he had come for and more. Mission creep could kill.

It was time to get out.

James hit Send and quickly scaled the wall and hid his rope. He donned the lab coat he had stolen and considered two very bad options. He could walk out the front door. The security cameras were on, but he would be a man walking out the door in a lab coat, though, he grudged, there was a chance that black men in lab coats might be like a unicorn sighting around here. That assumed anyone was watching the camera. Given the state of events and last night's excitement and the clandestine activity this evening, the assumption was going to have to be yes.

"Bear, you got the data and the footage?"

"Copy that."

"I need you to cut the power for ten seconds. I am extracting into town with the convoy. Prepare to cut all the lights if it gets hairy and tell Papas to be ready. I may be coming in hot if this doesn't work."

"Copy. Are you ready?"

"Do it."

"On my mark. Five, four, three, two, one…"

The building went dark and James went out the front door. He hugged the wall as he ran around the quad for the loading dock. James heard sounds of consternation and ran straight toward them. He made for the two truck drivers who were smoking as he pulled off his NVGs and shoved them into his knapsack.

James walked up to the drivers as the lights snapped on, keeping a truck directly between him and the loading bay. He smiled and approached with his bag over his shoulder like a sailor. *"¡Hola!"*

The drivers nodded. *"¡Hola!"* One kindly offered James a smoke and he accepted. *"¿Habla usted inglés?"*

One of the drivers lit the cigarette and smiled. "You know English is the official language of Belize?"

James smiled sheepishly. "I keep forgetting that. Hey, can you give me a ride back into town? My cart is still charging." The other driver jerked his head at the cabs without hesitation.

James grinned. "Thanks, man."

Despite speaking English, the driver gave a very Latin shrug. "It is nothing."

James climbed up into the cab. "Bond is black," he reiterated to no one in particular.

Men shouted on the docks and the driver climbed up behind the wheel. "Archibaldo. Call me Archie. You?"

"Call me Jimmy."

"Let's go, *muchacho*!"

The truck pulled out onto the gravel road. An armored guard with a .357 Magnum submachine gun and a large, black-furred and vicious-looking Belgian Malinois waved the truck through the perimeter gate without even looking at it. The driver gave James a look. "Forgive me for asking, Jimmy, but, since I am dropping you off… Are you an Ewok? Or a Hobbit?"

James burst out laughing. "Is that how you think of us?"

Archie shrugged in a live-and-let-live sort of way. "Living in trees? Living in little hills? Living in circus tents? Me, I just drive."

James laughed again and thought about his extraction. He didn't want to walk through the center of town, nor did he have a good feeling about swimming the canal in the Speedo he was wearing.

"Actually, I'm feeling kind of Happy."

"Casa Happy!" The driver got excited. "You are lucky!"

James gave Archie a shit-eating grin. "Luck has nothing to do with it."

"Ha!" Archie punched James in the shoulder in a comradely fashion. "I have only heard rumors about that place. Next time—when I am on a day run and having lunch in the commissary? You are telling me stories!" He glanced back and forth as if someone might be watching or listening. "We're not supposed to pick up citizens. You? You owe me!"

James glanced furtively from side to side, as well. "Tell you what, Archie. Give me your phone number. I'll send you pictures."

"You are my true friend." Archie dug out his phone and gleefully handed it over. James added Archie to his address book and felt slightly bad sending it to the Farm. Archie pulled over to the little logging road that led to Casa Happy. "I would tell you good luck, but I don't think you need it."

"Thanks, Arch!"

Archibaldo pulled away. James waited for the truck's taillights to disappear and began loping back down the road. They had put him on the roof at Luffy-Land. He had a sneaking suspicion he would never see the wonders of Casa Happy for himself. He put his ear bud back in and tapped the icon for the Team Zorba frequency. "Quarrel, this is Bond."

"Good evening, Mr. Bond."

James rolled his eyes as he ran. Papas needed to work on his secure communications skills. "I am extracting by sea."

"You got a boat?"

"This is going to be self service. Are you at the rendezvous point?"

There was a pause while Papas doubted himself and checked his GPS. "I am Papas on the spot!"

"Quarrel." James rolled his eyes for real. "Quarrel on the spot, and the response is affirmative."

Papas vocally snapped to attention. "Copy that!"

James saw the headlights of the other two trucks coming up the road and broke for the trees. The enemy had just brought in well more than a platoon of muscle that sure stank like jihadists of some sort, and when it came to the manufacturing quad, Phoenix Force still didn't know what Liberty City was building in there. That was for the Farm cybernetics team to figure out.

James had done his job. He had a five-mile swim ahead of him and his next goal was to work Papas for the most expensive breakfast in Corozal, and then the most expensive lunch, and then dinner, and repeat with shopping excursions in between until the mighty services of Calvin James were called upon again. He figured he had forty-eight hours before the rest of Phoenix Force showed up and ruined his Caribbean dining and shopping spree.

The thought kept him warm as he hit the Caribbean Sea and swam.

He put that thought away as he resigned himself to re-inserting tomorrow and become the Ghost of Liberty City.

He was going to show Hawkins how haunting the enemy was done.

CHAPTER TWENTY-ONE

USS Coronado

The *Coronado* roared toward the territorial waters of Belize. McCarter was SAS, Her Majesty's Royal Navy. He'd been invited up to the bridge and he marveled. The United States Littoral Combat Ships were extremely controversial, but whatever you said about them, they were fast, like a two-thousand-plus metric-ton speedboat fast. The captain had given her the full throttle toward the end and taken the *Coronado* up to her never-exceed sprint speed of fifty knots.

Crewmen were checking the internet in fast and furious fashion to see if any ship, civilian or military, had ever done an Atlantic Ocean run faster. Bragging rights were on the line. A Sea Stallion helicopter from the *USS Theodore Roosevelt* had delivered a load of parts for Grimaldi, and the maintenance crew of the *Coronado* huddled in amazement and awe at the wonders of *Dragonslayer*.

All of them had been forced to sign nondisclosure agreements.

McCarter turned to the captain. "That was sailing, Captain."

The captain grinned. So did the XO. "I always wanted to see what the new girl on the block could really do."

McCarter broke into a fresh bout of coughing. The captain gave him an appraising look. "How are you and your team? You just want me to initiate shore bombardment of Liberty City now and end this farce?"

McCarter drank tea with lemon and was severely tempted. "Like the way you think, Captain."

"Oh, well, you know. American sailors hear a British accent and we get all excited."

McCarter raised his cup. The United States Navy was his second favorite navy on earth, and he liked navies. "How far from Belize, then?"

"Just over the horizon. Not too worried about shore detection. Unless the enemy has a satellite window."

"They might."

"In that case, I am hard to see."

Stony Man Farm

"OH…MY…GOD." It wasn't something that Hunt Wethers said often, but his reconstruction software of the log of the 3-D printer movements had been spot-on.

In a matter of minutes it had tracked and located the patterns that had built every component of the UAV they had captured in the fight outside Kaliningrad from both movement and material. That base of data turned cruising the millions of movements from a needle in a haystack to a doorway into the Liberty City Enigma machine. They could backtrack and now knew which commands printed powdered copper, silver, gold, carbon-reinforced plastic and steel. They knew which commands were building up solid structure and which were creating computer components.

Kurtzman watched the screens all around the Computer Room that were displaying the different projects the Liberty City manufacturing quad had been working on. Once they had been able to break individual combinations of movement and printing, Wethers's program built the outline of the project up in schematic form one line at a time. Stealing the printing movements with Calvin James's help had been a matter of minutes. Rebuilding the movements and printing and trying to guess what they were was taking up immense amounts of the Farm's computing power, and the Farm had more than most on the planet.

Some of the laser models were a total loss. It was clear they were small computer parts, CPUs, hard drives and video cards, but a laser diagram of their shape could not discern what they were doing. Nonetheless, all had to be run for any possible clue. Other laser models revealed thousands of printed mechanical parts, and the Farm was ripping their shape against millions of similar shapes around the planet to determine their function.

The key to all of it was the movements of the big arms on the giant printing plates; they were gross movements and, with luck, the laser model would be obvious just by its shape. The hitch was that it turned out the big arms had their own little foreign language onto themselves.

Wethers and Tokaido had been forced to go back to the drawing board, but there were two things Kurtzman was sure of in this life. In the cybernetic world, Huntington Wethers knew how to see things and Akira Tokaido knew how break things. Aaron Kurtzman watched as the first big plate project declared itself as a green laser model schematic. Wethers had beat him by ten seconds, and Wethers was right. "They're printing missiles."

The distinguished former Berkeley professor pulled up a file even before his program finished Etch A Sketching the model. "We have a match. The Russians have a missile—the 3M-54 Klub. NATO code name Sizzler. Depending on variation, it is an antiship missile, antisubmarine missile or land-attack cruise missile."

Kurtzman saw the worst possible scenario coming to pass. "What kind of warhead?"

"Depends on the variant. Nuclear, chemical or conventional." Wethers looked up from his monitor. "Rumored biological."

"Launch platforms?" Kurtzman asked.

"It was originally designed with Russian Kilo-class submarines as the primary launch platform. It has been adapted for launch from surface warships and a version is being developed for air launch from Russian Federation 'Bear' heavy bombers."

"Anything else?"

Wethers spoke without an ounce of humor. "You'll laugh."

"No, I won't."

"The shorter range Klub-K variant can be disguised with its launch unit as a standard ISO shipping container that can be placed on a truck, train or merchant vessel. The Klub-K was thought to be just a concept until a mock-up was displayed at the Russian MAKS 2011 air show. US Intelligence doesn't believe the Russian military had put the Klub-K variant into mass production."

"Bastards." Delahunt glared at her screen as the missile came to life. "But they got the schematics. They didn't need to set up an assembly line and hire hundreds if not thousands of workers to produce thousands of missiles. They're just printing the shit up—the ones they need, just enough to fulfill the mission."

Kurtzman knew Delahunt was right. A private facility with that kind of *Star Wars'* worthy 3-D printing technology, beholden to none except whoever who had hundreds of millions to burn? It sold itself. "You know I am a free-market capitalist, but theoretically, there can be a downside."

Delahunt gave a predatory grin. "I love it. I love capitalism. It's how single redheads get ahead."

Wethers stared. "You have worked for the government your entire life."

"I don't care. And I like sailors, too. What did the captain of the *Coronado* say? Let's pull Able and start the shore bombardment ASAP."

"I wish. Listen, we need to get Able to somehow—"

Calvin James spoke across the com link. "Farm, this is Cal."

"Go ahead, Cal."

"I have movement in the manufacturing quad. The loading bay is open and the mystery assholes are pouring out."

"What are they doing?"

"They are putting on gas masks. They're rolling out cylinders on dollies."

The blood of everyone in the Annex froze.

Calvin James's voice went ice-cold with the clarity of the situation. "They are going Jim Jones. They're going to scorch-earth the citizens of Liberty City, and then do whatever they're going to do. Tell Able it's coming out of the quad and to expect chemical or biological. I need Able to converge here now—whatever the cost. Bear, talk to Barb. I am requesting the *Coronado's* missiles and guns."

Kurtzman's chest tightened. His worst-case scenarios were when the mission controller had to tell the Stony Man teams no. The mission parameters were clear and until Brognola called them from Washington to notify them otherwise, their hands were tied.

"Cal! Be advised, *Coronado* has no permission to attack Liberty City or the sovereign territory of Belize. If you can get out of the two-mile limit they can extract you, but fire support is not available. Repeat, not available! Recommend you extract now. The enemy is too strong."

"Then load whatever is left of Phoenix into *Dragonslayer*. Full assault on the manufacturing quad. Whatever they are doing doesn't leave. The quad has only one gate."

Kurtzman heard James flick the safety off his rifle. "I'll hold it as long as I can."

Kurtzman hit the open com link. "Able. Phoenix. Cal at the quad. Enemy at platoon strength and attempting a breakout with chemical weapons! Will vector you in. Go! Go! Go!"

The Quad, Liberty City

CALVIN JAMES SHOT and shot and shot. His M-16/A-2 was Marine Corps old-school issue with a long barrel and no optical sight. ARs were an accurate platform from the get-go, and while it grieved him to admit that Gary Manning was a better shot than him and Mack Bolan was even better, even by his own lights he was a damn good shot. He had already decided on a philosophy of none shall pass. He rolled behind a tree as an RPG rocket ripped toward his position.

He rolled up behind the next tree as the second truck tried to make a run for the gate. He flicked his selector to 3-round burst and burned triple-shot after triple-shot into the truck's grille and windshield.

Calvin James was running out of ammo.

The enemy burned AK rounds at him as if they had a waterfall of ammunition from on high. The truck stopped as the driver and engine died at about the same time. The little gatehouse was a burning ruin. The guard was dead and the attack dog in a fit of good sense had gone walkies west for Guatemala post haste. Another rocket screamed from the loading dock. James hunched as it directly hit the tree he was hiding behind.

"Oh, shit!" James hunched as the besieged tree gave up and fell across the road right behind the burning gatehouse. None of the trucks, much less the electric carts, could roll over that. "Thanks," he muttered.

Two more rockets and several hundred tracers screamed toward him. James rolled onto the road behind the fallen tree as his stump exploded. He slapped in his last magazine. James slammed the bolt home on a fresh round and spoke across the link. "Farm! Requesting fire support! On my signal!"

"Negative, Cal." Kurtzman came back. "Get out of there!"

James watched as the enemy deployed by squads. Behind their skirmish line they had loaded their gas equipment into carts. All of which they could lift over the tree he was hiding behind. James snapped on the bayonet the US Embassy had kindly given him.

"Able! Phoenix! Quarrel! I need immediate backup! Now or not at all!"

McCarter came across the link. "ETA five, Cal. Get out of there!"

The enemy roared *"Allāhu Akbar!"* and charged.

James eased his Beretta in its holster and flicked off the safety. "Negative, Phoenix Leader. We cannot let them into Liberty City. We have innocents." The black Phoenix Force warrior thought of the day-care center he had seen and the children playing on the beach. "We have children. Repeat, requesting *Coronado* missiles or artillery on the quad and my position."

"Negative!" Kurtzman snarled. "I have eyes. We have nothing for five minutes. Get out of there!"

"Negative, Bear." James spun up and began firing over his log.

Demi Papas ran out of the trees in a Speedo and body armor gasping under a bulging rifle bag. "I got you, buddy! I got you!"

He tottered up, the enemy fire ripping all around him. James yanked Papas down as tracers streaked. "You're supposed to be my extraction!"

"You said you were going to hold them as long as you could." Papas gasped. "Screw that!"

James ignored the breach of command. "What'd you bring me?"

"Everything!"

James ripped open the bag and pulled out the ancient ARWEN 37 mm grenade launcher that US embassies had issued decades ago after the Iranian Embassy takeover. It seemed the enemy had brought poison gas to kill the citizens of Liberty City. They had thrown off their gas masks to facilitate killing James.

Calvin James gave them a 5-round spread of tear gas across their skirmish line.

"Can I shoot them?" Papas asked.

James plucked red-hot shells out of the ARWEN's smoking breech. "Shoot as many as you can!"

"Eat shit, shit eaters!" Papas roared. He crouched and sprayed his MAC-10 into the stumbling, gas-staggered enemy line. "Who's your papa? Who's your papa?"

James ignored that, too. He rolled up and gave the enemy line three more gas shells and sent two soaring into the loading bay.

"They ain't stopping!" Papas observed.

"No!"

"Allāhu Akbar!" The war cry was ragged in the gas but the enemy came forward in a wave.

James snapped in the three smoke rounds and clacked the cylinder shut. He pumped the smoke grenades into the enemy charge, figuring, let them be disoriented and let them suck particulate. The bag contained six hand grenades, but they were all smoke. James pulled them and hurled the smoking munitions into the miasma of smoke and gas. The enemy wasn't shouting anymore but they still staggered forward shooting.

Papas dropped his weapon. "I'm out."

James took up his M-16 and made his last five rounds count. He laid the weapon on the log with the bayonet ready. "What else we got?"

Papas pulled out a weapon of plastic, steel and rubber bands. "Spear guns?"

"Gimme." Papas tossed him the loaded spear gun and took up its mate. He tossed four spears between them. "That's it. That's all we got. Let's mess 'em up!"

"Don't have to tell me twice..." James aimed his spear gun as a man came out of the smoke and gas shouting and choking and spraying his AK in all directions. James squeezed his trigger and the man's shouting turned to screaming as the barbed spear took him in the belly.

Papas howled in victory. "You know who I am?" He fired his spear gun and hit a man in the chest. His spear still had the line attached. Papas put his foot against the log and yanked. The man screamed and scrabbled at the barbed steel shaft in his chest as he was yanked facedown in the dirt. "I'm Demi fucking Papas!"

James let it go.

This was the Alamo.

He hauled back on the rubber, recocked and put a spear in the guide. James aimed and fired, and a man spun and took it in the throat. Papas fired and missed. They both dropped down behind the log as more of the enemy came out of the smoke and poured fire on their position. Papas triggered his last spear blindly over the tree trunk. James fired his spear over the top and took up his empty rifle and bayonet. Papas reached down pulled both diving knives out of the rifle bag. He also dug out another smoke grenade and handed it to James. Papas put a blade in each hand.

"We do them! Greek style! Gut them like sheep! I never wanted to go out like Howard Hughes!"

James pulled the pin on the last smoke grenade and tossed it. "Demi?"

"Yeah?"

"You are an American hero."

"Aw, *Christos*…"

James went over the top and Papas followed.

Dragonslayer scudded over the trees, both door guns blazing. James grabbed Papas by the hair. "Down!" One non-combat-oriented part of Calvin James's mind was surprised as Papas's hair came up in a mass in his hand. James shoved down hard. "Down!"

Lyons shouted from behind the gate. "Cal! Cal!"

James raised his arm and waved over the tree trunk. He saw Able Team assaulting the quad in a golf cart.

"Cal! Stay down!"

That suited James down to the ground. Able Team leaped out of the cart and hit the tree trunk. Each of them had a stolen SIG .357 submachine gun and began pouring in fire. A weapon clattered in the gravel next to James. He tossed the hairpiece back to Papas. "Here."

"No, Cal. I need a gun."

James took a prone position and fired into the retreating shapes in the smoke. He couldn't tell who was door-gunning but they were making murder. "Gun!"

A Liberty City security SIG pistol landed in the gravel. Papas snatched it up and began firing. James saw the shape of a man with a launch tube over his shoulder in the strobing, security-lighted smoke and gas. "Jack! Rocket! Rocket! Rocket! Three o'clock!"

Dragonslayer banked steeply to her nine. The rocket sizzled upward and missed but the proximity fuse went off and orange fire lit the sky. The chopper shook as she took shrapnel right up her hindquarters beneath the tail boom. *Dragonslayer* did three crazy spins and then suddenly her spins tightened and the helicopter dropped under control to a very hard landing on the lawn. The enemy gave a ragged cheer and unleashed on the chopper. To their misfortune, Hawkins now had a stable firing platform with a .50-caliber machine gun and he ripped right back into them.

McCarter's voice came over the link. "Give it to them. Give them all of it. Fish? Burn it down."

The rest of Phoenix Force deployed. Encizo had a grenade launcher but it wasn't a 37 mm British antiriot weapon. His was 40 mm and it wasn't loaded with tear gas or smoke. Encizo squeezed off a round and sent white-phosphorus into the loading dock. He fired again and the quad's glass front doors smashed inward and immediately began filling the area with white-hot smoke and burning metal. He put one on the roof and the last of the assholes charged screaming, *"Allāhu Akbar!"*

Encizo's voice came over the link. "Should've said uncle." He fired low and popped a Willie Pete into the last charge. Men disappeared, screaming in the burning mix. James rose. "Mag!" Blancanales tossed him a 6-round bandolier and James reloaded. He slowly started going forward.

Papas croaked. "Hey, Bond!" James turned to find Papas with a round through his shoulder and one through his belly. "Hey!"

James bent and put pressure on both his wounds. "Medic!"

Manning charged forward with the medical bag out of *Dragonslayer*.

Encizo put another five rounds of Willie Pete into the quad. The decision had been made. None shall pass. If the Magistrate and his minions had decided to gas the good citizens, the Farm didn't have enough men on the ground to contain it. So they just burned the quad to the ground.

Phoenix Force was beat to hell and *Dragonslayer*

was down. They heard sirens and alarms and shouts and screams in town. There was nothing they could do about that, either. All that was to be done was to wait for the rocket engines of the 3-D cloned missiles to start giving them secondary explosions and the Farm teams would let the Belizean military sweep up the ashes.

"Bear?" McCarter asked.

"I have no movement. The quad is turning into a massive heat signature. Burning in earnest. Anyone who retreated into it…"

"Copy that."

Lyons took a knee by Papas and James. "How you doing, Demi?"

Calvin James grinned. "This man is an American hero."

Demi clenched his teeth and grinned up at James. "And Bond is black."

Lyons shook his head. "I just lost my billionaire BFF."

James nodded knowingly. "I've told you before, Carl. Once they go black, they—"

"Bloody hell!" McCarter roared raggedly and raised his weapon.

Out in the trees beyond Casa Happy two sky-crane helicopters rose into the air. Both of them carried an ISO container cabled beneath their bellies. McCarter opened fire and every member of Able and Phoenix followed suit. The range was well more than a kilometer. The two massive choppers dipped their noses unconcernedly and swung out of Liberty City's pool of light. They cut their running lights and disappeared in the general direction of Guatemala.

McCarter spoke into his link. "Bear, I have two choppers leaving Liberty City. Do you have eyes?"

"No."

"The *Coronado*?"

"She did, but her radar just lost them in the hills."

McCarter stared into the massive flames rising out of the quad. The good news was that the screaming had mostly stopped, and they had ended the massacre of Liberty City. The bad news was that the combined forces of Able Team and Phoenix Force had failed the mission. "Bear? Broken arrow. Repeat, broken arrow. Assume Liberty City missiles are missing."

CHAPTER TWENTY-TWO

Stony Man Farm

"Does that qualify as pulling defeat from the jaws of victory?" Delahunt asked.

Kurtzman watched satellite footage of the quad burning. Police and fire from Corozal were on the scene, and state police and soldiers were showing up in droves.

Wethers shook his head. "They were going to exterminate the population of Liberty City. We stopped a massacre. That's what we do."

Kurtzman nodded. Wethers was right. So was Delahunt. No one would be breaking out the champagne on this one. He clicked on the link to Phoenix. "What is your status, Phoenix Leader?"

"We're back on board the *Coronado*. Jack got *Dragonslayer* off the ground enough to limp back. Papas was the only casualty. He took two bullets. The doctor on board has him stabilized and says he should be all right, but he needs to be taken to real hospital ASAP."

"Did you manage to bring back anything from the quad?"

"Jack said he didn't have the lift to bring any prisoners. In fact, we had to dump all our weapons and ammo to get airborne. Though I did get you this…"

Kurtzman's computer pinged and a picture popped up. It was a picture of a backpack-style cylinder with a sprayer attached, similar to something an exterminator might wear. It chilled the Stony Man cybernetics chief to think that was exactly what it was—only this rig was for exterminating one's fellow humans.

"Here's another."

A second picture popped up and it was a close-up of the markings on the cylinder.

"Cynosil?" Tokaido asked.

"Cyanide gas," Wethers said.

"Does anyone even make that anymore?"

Kurtzman nodded. It just kept getting worse.

"Cyanide gas developed a very bad name after the Nazis used it to murder over a million people as part of their Final Solution at Auschwitz. It didn't help its reputation that the United States used it for the execution of Death Row prisoners. Most countries have banned it."

"Sadly enough," he continued, "not to play Devil's advocate, but it started off as a pesticide called Zyklon B. It's an effective one. Cyanide gas is extremely lethal in the right concentrations and is nonpervasive. If you had termites in your house? You could tent it and use cyanide, no problem. In fact, the Czech Republic and a few other countries still produce it for that exact purpose, only they renamed it Cynosil. I would bet you dollars to doughnuts the writing on the side of that cylinder is Czech.

"Akira, why don't you look up the company and see who might have bought enough within the last year to exterminate an entire town?"

"On it, Bear."

McCarter spoke. "We saw no sign of Maier, Moon, the Korean or Von Sprack, much less the Magistrate."

"That's to be expected. I think we all know where they are, or at least where they aren't. You got anything else?"

"Nothing sticks out, but I'll have a full after-action report for you within the hour."

Barbara Price burst into the Annex. "Bear. We have a problem."

Kurtzman's heart sank at the expression on Price's face. "Don't tell me it's the *Belle Nymphe*."

"The Navy just got a report from the observation plane."

Kurtzman closed his eyes. "And?"

"The *Belle Nymphe* appears to be sinking, rapidly."

"How long ago did we get eyes on the *Nymphe*?"

"There was no distress call. The Hawkeye got within range with forward-looking infrared radar five minutes ago." Price sighed. "They report no outward damage to the *Nymphe* is visible and no wreckage. No lifeboats. No one in the water. She's going down as if someone just pulled the plug."

Kurtzman's clenched his fists around the arms of his wheelchair. The Game Room was gone. "I need some kind of list of any known ships that could have been within a loaded sky crane's range of the *Nymphe*."

"Bear, I don't think there is a list like that."

"Well, make one!"

Everyone in the Annex was dumbstruck by Kurtzman's outburst. His heavy shoulders sagged.

"Barb, I'm sorry. It's my job to make lists, not yours."

Price understood the pressure they were all operating under. "Bear, we gambled. We lost. It happens. If we hadn't surged the *Coronado* we would have hundreds of dead Liberty City citizens, and Able would have had to fight Maier's little army plus the imported foreign fighters. You always compare this stuff to chess. We made a move, and it was a good one. We took some of their pieces. They countered. Now it's our move again. We need to work something up, and we need to do it fast. We need anything. Any thread or pattern we can put together with what we have."

The Farm's mission controller smiled at her cybernetics genius. "I'll take wild guesses at this point."

Kurtzman straightened in his chair. "You're right."

"Ha!" Delahunt snarled in triumph. "Here's a little somethin' I've been working on."

"What?" Price asked.

"Not what—who. And it's Gert Von Sprack."

"What about him?" Price queried. "From what little we know he's Game Room security."

"Well…before that he *was* German Federal Police. GSG 9, special operations and counterterrorism unit."

Not only had Able Team and Phoenix Force worked with GSG 9 on several occasions, but Gary Manning had also been an explosives instructor for the elite unit. They were among the best of the best.

"Until?" Kurtzman had noticed Delahunt's emphasis of the word *was*.

"Until he found God."

"I'm betting he didn't become a born again-Christian?" Wethers surmised.

"Oh, no. He found Allah. He started preaching it. Started preaching it to his fellow operators. Started questioning orders and stating his absolute refusal to operate against fellow Muslims. They let him go. It looks like he drifted into private contract work in the Middle East and Central Asia, working for some very dodgy clients."

"The newly converted are more pious than the Prophet himself," Wethers said.

"No one's more moral than a reformed whore," Delahunt countered. "At least, that's what my mother always said."

Tokaido sat up. "Hey!"

"Hay is for horses," Delahunt said. "But what have you got?"

"Maier? You think?"

Kurtzman was taken aback. "An Israeli Mossad agent converting to Islam? It's a bit of stretch."

"Yeah, but your contacts said he had a stink on him, and there were red flags before they let him go. And when they did? He was, like, banished from Israel and tacitly from the Middle East in general. You said no one will talk about it and the information had been redacted in official files. Have you even heard of such a thing? Would Maier radicalizing qualify?"

Wethers raised an eyebrow. "You saying Moon is a Muslim, too?"

"No, he's just a psycho."

Price turned her eyes to the burning buildings on the screen. "And the Magistrate?"

Kurtzman and Wethers looked at each other. Kurtzman pondered. "Able Team was in Liberty City for over seventy-two hours. We got no reports of minarets or morning calls to the faithful and there were no prayer rugs in sight. For that matter, Maier took a decent stab at drinking Carl under the table at Casa Happy, and the Magistrate seemed to like wine a little too much with every meal."

"The faithful can be given dispensations during a time of war," Wethers pointed out. "Particularly if it is jihad."

Delahunt pulled up Tan Van Staafl's file. "He's an aging visionary whose vision never quite came true. From what we got out of Councilwoman Curl, Staafl was always a little unstable. Whether he was radicalized, self-radicalized or some combination thereof aided by an influx of untold millions of dollars? No matter what, the Magistrate seems to be all-in when it comes to mass murder of his citizens."

Kurtzman turned his attention to the schematic missile model on one of his screens. "It's an interesting thought, and it ties in with our theory about Central Asian money and connection with the Caliphate movement. But he has gotten away scot-free out of Liberty City, and we have to assume he took a load of missiles with them, and we have no idea what their final objective is."

"Their objective is to gas the crap out of someone," Tokaido piped up. "It's kind of obvious."

Kurtzman frowned. "No, I don't think so."

"They have cyanide?"

"Cyanide isn't all that good a war gas. You need heavy concentrations, and it disperses quickly. The Germans tried it in World War I and went with other options." Kurtzman pointed at the missile model and a picture of an actual example on the screen. "A Klub-K missile? It's small in the scheme of things. Even if they have a full container silo of, say, eight to twelve missiles, the amount of cyanide they could deliver would be ridiculously small. You wouldn't spend hundreds of millions of dollars to custom print your own missiles just to hurl pesticide at someone."

Price was grim. "So we are looking at nuclear or biological."

Delahunt shrugged. "We have zero evidence they have either. They had no bio-lab we know about. I don't know, Bear? Nukes?"

"They could easily print the mechanical components to make a bomb. What they can't print is the fissionable material. Without a source of plutonium to slam together, the bomb is just a mechanical device that claps its hands."

Wethers stood and stared at the missile. "Then let's just go with a Klub-K's primary mission. It's a cruise missile, capable of a short supersonic sprint, whose primary mission is to deliver about 450 pounds of high explosive."

"Not exactly apocalyptic," Tokaido scoffed.

"The weapon, no. So we have to start looking at targets."

Kurtzman went back to square one. "These guys' MO is container boxes and the transportation systems that love them, and they are never safer than when they are on a container ship in international waters. They could put the boxes on a train or trucks, but Mexico enforces its southern border a lot more stringently than we enforce ours and that's a long trip across the entire breadth of Mexico."

"Let's stick with container vessels for the moment," Price suggested.

Wethers pulled up a map of Guatemala and put it on the main screen. "Guatemala has two coasts, Caribbean and Pacific, and it has one major shipping port on each side. Puerto Barrios on the Caribbean, and Puerto San José on the Pacific. They ship a lot coffee and it is surprising how many clothes and other products have Made in Guatemala on the label. So they'll have a decent number of container vessels going in and out. We can take a big stab at breaking into the Guatemalan port authority data base to see who has gone in our out from, say, six hours ago and for the next twenty-four hours."

"That could be hundreds of ships." Tokaido made an unhappy face. "We can't tail them all."

"No, we can't," Kurtzman agreed. "But we can make that list I was shouting about on a much smaller scale. We can't tail them all, but we can make a list of who comes in and goes out on Hunt's time table, and we can check in on them at least by satellite to see who's on their scheduled course and if anyone has deviated from it."

"What if they're laying low?" Tokaido asked. "That's what I'd do."

"No." Kurtzman shook his head. "No. My gut tells me these guys aren't laying low. Last night they were about to Final Solution their citizenry. They scorched earth and got out. And, despite our efforts, got out on their own timeline. Whatever they're doing, they're doing it now. The only advantage we have is that if we are right and they are in a container vessel, then that is the speed of their operation and it gives us a little time."

"It's not bad." Wethers chewed his lip. "But I don't think these guys will be deviating from course unless we force them to. I think they have their destination firmly in mind. They are going to sail up, all their papers and registry in order, and let fly when they are in range of their target."

Kurtzman nodded. "Agreed, which means I need you to make me a list."

Price gazed upon Kurtzman bemusedly.

"A list of viable Klub-K missile targets launched off the coast," Kurtzman put his palms together. "Pretty please, Barb? With sugar on top."

"Well, since you used the magic word…"

USS Coronado

"I'M SORRY TO have put your crew through all of this, Commander." McCarter sat in the officer's mess with the CO. He raised his coffee mug. "You have all of our thanks."

Commander Regina Hitch scoffed. "Are you kidding? The crew is having a ball. After that run across the Atlantic they're calling the ship the Millennium Falcon. We broke a record. We may never be able to tell anyone about it, but the crew is pretty damn smug about it. The crew also wants me to build a stage in the main mess and have Propenko perform nightly."

McCarter laughed. "He is something."

"And let me tell you," Hitch continued, "my aircrew? They have never seen a chopper like that one of yours— hell, neither have I—and they have learned more from that Jack guy of yours this week than they have in their past five shore trainings. Having you and your men on board? The pleasure has been all ours. You guys are welcome back anytime."

"Thank you, Commander."

"And even if none of that was true? You pulled the *Coronado* out of the Baltic in midwinter. That alone earned you the keys to the kingdom."

McCarter would have thought the CO was chatting him up, but as a sailor himself he knew it was all true. Any distraction at sea was welcome, and the presence of Able Team and Phoenix Force qualified as a genuine break from routine.

"So where to next?" the CO asked.

"We don't know. I can tell you this much. You know we were tailing a suspect ship. We surged to Belize because we thought we had a lead. We were right, but the bad guys got away into Guatemala. We have two ports on both sides of Central America to worry about and possibly hundreds of ships as likely targets. And that is if—and that is a mighty big if, mind you—they didn't take truck, train or a plane, or if the buggers split up." McCarter blinked at the CO. "What?"

"Oh, I just like listening to men who have English accents."

McCarter smirked. "We are aware of the fact that our accents make Americans think we are smarter than we actually are."

"It's working!" Commanding Officer Hitch refilled their mugs. "So what do you think the target is?"

"I have been thinking on that. The obvious answer is to sail up the Potomac and fire a spread at the White House, but they have to figure we might be expecting that. It looks like Central Asian jihadists are involved, and the Lord bloody knows they are always sporting a biggie for New York."

"'Sporting a biggie'?"

"I think you get the gist of it."

"I do."

"Well, then. They sail into port of New York, fire off a salvo of missiles that can literally maneuver between buildings and Bob's your uncle. It's a target-rich environment."

"Bob's my uncle..." The CO smirked.

"Yes, he is, Commander."

"So what's bothering you?"

"I don't know." McCarter had been worrying it like a bone but he couldn't come up with a solution. "They've gone to an awful lot of time, trouble and expense. They have scuttled two container vessels with all hands. They were about to destroy Liberty City, and who knows how many millions they put into that printing facility.

"Whatever they are doing has to be big. Like, start-a-world-war big, and all of that is just assuming an American target. If they could get close to a US fleet, or even better sail in while the fleet is in port, they could pull a Pearl Harbor. A full spread of missiles would sink a US aircraft carrier. That would certainly make a statement, but..." McCarter heaved a sigh. "Then again, what's to stop them from sailing to Hong Kong and launching on mainland China? Or putting a broadside into Buckingham Palace?"

"You say they are jihadists." CO Hitch waggled her eyebrows. "I hate to disrespect a guest in my mess, but America is the Great Satan and proud of it. England? You're kind of an imp of Satan, or our homunculus, or something."

McCarter just about shot coffee out his nose. "Homunculus, then?"

"Sorry, not to be a size-queen, but it's true, and I am just not buying China. Plus, I think Beijing is out of range."

"No." The Phoenix leader set down his coffee and nodded. "No, you're not wrong at all. It has to be the Great Satan or nothing. They had two choppers, and we caught none of the big fish. One had to be personnel, while the other had to be the equipment."

"What choppers?"

"What matters, Commander, is that I believe the enemy has one box of eight missiles. With small conventional warheads. They can't fire just one missile and sail on to the next target. They'll have one opportunity, one salvo, to make the biggest possible impression."

The CO brandished her mug excitedly. "Like a full spread of photon torpedoes!"

"You had me until you went all Trekkie, luv."

"Did you just call me 'luv'?"

"Yes, Commander Hitch, I believe I did."

"So what are you thinking?"

"As you said, a full spread of photon torpedoes, then, and like I said, a target-rich environment, and then at least one target that make the whole thing worthwhile."

The CO waggled her thumbs. "By the pricking of your thumbs, something wicked this way comes," she paraphrased. Hitch jerked her thumbs in opposite directions, east and west. "But which way?"

"There are a lot more targets on the east coast of the United States, and it is also a lot more heavily defended, and, to my knowledge, there has never been a terrorist attack on the west coast."

"Seattle, San Francisco, Los Angeles. Those are your biggies. But I don't see your big target?"

"Maybe it hasn't arrived yet."

"And so?"

"And so I am wondering what kind of record this tub of yours can set transiting the Panama Canal to make the California coast."

Container vessel, Hallelujah Jordan, Pacific Ocean

"WE ARE PASSING the Sea of Cortez," Captain Raheel announced. "This is Baja, Mexico. It will not be long until we raise the coast of the United States."

Thaniel Maier stood on the bridge and nodded at the

Egyptian sea captain and dedicated, radicalized Islamist extremist. "Thank you, Captain."

Gert Von Sprack came onto the bridge. "I have completed the inspection. All is in readiness."

"Thank you, brother." Despite his conversion and radicalization, Von Sprack scowled in a very Germanic manner. Maier nodded. "What troubles you?"

"The Magistrate. He is drinking heavily. He was distraught when he learned of the plan to exterminate the citizens. He is even more upset about the attack on the manufacturing quad. I am not sure if his faith is strong."

"What are you saying about Brother Staafl?"

"I am not sure he is completely reliable, and we are almost within reach of Glory and Martyrdom."

"If it pleases you, my brother, and Allah, let me tell you that the Magistrate is not only unreliable, but at this juncture he is also completely irrelevant."

A very ugly smile passed over Von Sprack's face.

Maier smiled back. Germans had not invented the concept of schadenfreude, or the pleasure derived from misfortune of others, but he liked the fact that they had cared enough to actually come up with a name for it. Maier was extremely pleased that the word literally meant *harm-joy*. It had been his mantra all his life and now that harm-joy he had inflicted on others all his life no longer needed the cover of a military organization to allow him to inflict it. Now his harm-joy was directed with purpose.

In God's name.

"I would have given him to Ji-Hoon and Kun to play with, or even Moon."

Von Sprack scowled. "Moon is an infidel of the worst sort."

"I understand you own an attack dog," Maier commented.

Von Sprack flinched. Dogs were deemed to be filthy animals. "He has his uses."

"But he is not a Muslim?"

Von Sprack gave a rare smile. "No, brother. He is not."

"Neither is Moon, and so does he."

"So, the Magistrate—"

"There is no Magistrate, and nothing left to be Magistrate of, but he was needed until we extracted from Liberty City. I believe he is not strong, but it was he who seduced Kun into this. Kun still worships him as a technological God who gave him money for all his toys. I see no reason to upset Kun until it is required. We need his expertise. Speaking of which, how goes the conversion of the Game Room?"

"It is complete. Kun seems pleased."

Maier nodded. The Game Room had been transformed from a command-and-control station for small-unit ground operations to a battle bridge most major warships would have envied. "The men?"

"It is a shame so many brothers were martyred at the quad. However, your men are fit and in good spirits. They are ready for what is to come." Van Sprack paused and looked sidelong at Maier. "Am I to assume you are in command now?"

"Do you object, brother?"

"I would say it is about time."

"If Allah wills, but it pleases me to hear you say that." Maier watched the Baja Peninsula come into view. The sea was calm and beautiful, and the blue water and desert coast beaches of Baja reminded him of Israel. He longed to watch it burn. It would, but he would most likely not be alive to see it.

Maier tapped the date function on his watch. He knew it was compulsive but he couldn't help it.

Von Sprack read his mind and smiled. "I checked

the website an hour ago, brother. His schedule has not changed."

Maier grinned ruefully at himself. "Thank you, brother."

"Even if for some reason he does not show, the death of tens of thousands of unbelievers sinning against God shall be a glorious start, and a lesson to them all of what is to come."

"I know, I know." For a sociopath, Maier was almost wistful. "Yet, Allah forgive me for my arrogance, I yearn for this man to die in fire, and by my hand."

"If Allah wills it," Von Sprack intoned.

Maier shrugged and nodded happily. "I believe he does. However, just in case he tests our resolve, I think we should move to plan B."

Von Sprack agreed. "We have already been forced to sink two ships. The enemy knows this. The sooner we are off this tub, the better."

CHAPTER TWENTY-THREE

Barbara Price gave Kurtzman "the look."

Kurtzman cringed as she glared down at him.

"So, you gave the *Coronado* permission to transit the Panama Canal and go for another speed record up the west coast?"

"I didn't give anyone permission to do anything. David is on command on the ground. And that means that ship."

"And you didn't tell me?"

"You were asleep."

"We were all asleep, except you. You just stay down here. Lurking."

"Well, I thought if I woke you up in the middle of the night there was a very good chance you would have said no, and David would have done it, anyway. So you both win and...you can both blame me."

The look returned. "Oh, we will."

Kurtzman steeled himself. "Go ahead, say it."

"The last time we surged the *Coronado* we had mixed results. I liked them, mind you, but we have Able and Phoenix together on one ship, and we have hundreds of ships and two coastlines, assuming the bad guys didn't go by land. I was thinking of getting them someplace central, with a jet nearby. Preferably something fast, so they could deploy in any direction. You have put all our eggs in one basket."

"I'm with David. I think if we have to scramble Able or Phoenix by jet someplace it's already over. I trust his instincts more than yours or mine. If Mack were here and said David is wrong, that would force me to reconsider. As I understand it, air defense destroyers are positioning themselves in the Potomac and New York harbor. San Diego has done the same and is sending ships with anti-missile capability to Los Angeles."

"So that leaves…"

"San Francisco!" Carmen Delahunt declared. "And the President of the United States!"

"What are you saying?" Price asked.

"The President will be at a fund-raiser in San Francisco, and all kinds of west coast royalty will be there. Business leaders. Film directors. Music and movie stars. And, I might add, one United States senator and two congress-men! Well, one congressman and one congresswoman, but that's not the point."

"Oh…my…God…" Price intoned.

"Oh, and let's talk about your target rich-environment. Or was it McCarter's? That doesn't matter. You know what else is happening in the City by the Bay? The San Francisco 49ers have a playoff game, at home. Sold out, mind you, and Levi's stadium can accommodate up to 75,000 fans.

"You remember how they lit up Poland with that ther-mobaric weapon? That was an antitank missile. A Klub-K? That's a five-hundred-pound, fuel-air warhead. Every single person including the President will fry at that fund-raiser. At every event venue? Thousands killed outright, tens of thousands horribly burned, limbs blasted off and everyone poisoned by the ethylene and propylene oxide. They will all just be sitting there in their seats, in the open, when it happens. And that's just four missiles—we figure they have between eight and twelve." Delahunt took a deep breath.

"San Francisco had no naval presence," Kurtzman mused and began hitting keys. "We can scramble jets, but a fighter shooting down a cruise missile doing a supersonic sprint on the deck is problematic."

"Then we just have to stop the launch in the first place," Price said. "First thing we do is pull the President."

Delahunt shook her head. "They'll be watching. If the President suddenly cancels, these thugs could pull a big fade and wait for their next chance. We lose them."

Kurtzman frowned as he put innocent lives in danger. "We pull the President, but we fake his attendance—body double, whatever it takes—we have to reel the bad guys in."

"Agreed, the problem is we can't stop or search every container vessel going into San Francisco Bay, and if we just bar everything within Klub-K range? Once again, we've tipped off the enemy."

Kurtzman pulled up a map of North America's west coast and watched a surprisingly fast-blinking green light. "The *Coronado* has already outstripped every ship on our list. She can be in San Francisco Bay with none the wiser."

Price pulled up the *Coronado's* specs. "*Coronado* has one, eleven-cell SeaRAM missile launcher, and it is designed to defend the ship against incoming missiles. It is not a combat-arena, air-defense weapon that can defend the entire Bay area."

Akira Tokaido appeared like an apparition in possibly the ugliest, threadbare, red-plaid bathrobe in history. "I think they're already there."

Everyone in the room just stared.

"No, they sank two of their own ships. They know if they do a third the jig is up. Even at full steam? A container ship making it to the Bay in time for the President's fundraiser—they would have to push the ship at full speed, and they must know we are watching for anomalies. They jumped ship."

"To what?" Kurtzman asked.

"Probably trucks. California really doesn't have coastal defense batteries. I mean, if two helicopters took off from a container ship, flying nap of the ocean, and delivered two container vessels to a pair of trucks waiting on the Pacific Coast Highway, in the middle of the night, outside of… oh, Lompoc? It would be dumb luck if the Coast Guard or law enforcement stumbled on them. They shoot up the road. The choppers have a false flight plan they filed days ago. They shoot ahead up to the Bay area. They load up and take ISO containers out to the waiting launch ship. Which was already in position before they ever took off from Guatemala."

Kurtzman watched everything go to hell in a handbasket. "Thanks, Akira. Thanks for that."

"You're welcome."

Kurtzman suddenly felt his weariness. He had been going nonstop for days and his needles and haystacks kept multiplying. "We need a list of every possible helicopter landing and refueling at every airport and airstrip from Mexicali to San Francisco. Or a miracle." The phone application on Kurtzman's desktop chimed. He looked at his Caller ID. It was from a private phone currently located in a private clinic in Manhattan and had been routed through a military satellite and passed the Farm's security protocols.

It was from Demi Papas.

Kurtzman punched a key and put it on speaker. "Demi?"

"Papa Bear!"

Kurtzman searched for strength. "What can I do for you?"

"Well, you know I was just lying here…you know, shot."

"You're an American hero, Demi. But I am kind of busy."

"Well, I've had a lot of time to think…you know, about our problem."

"What are you thinking?"

"Well…it's just that Liberty City was this free city thing I invested in—you know, for the street cred rather than profit—and it was a freak show before it turned into a total freak show."

"Right…"

"Well, I don't know if there is any connection, but a couple of years ago I got an invite to invest in *Innovation One*. I was already trying to scrape off Liberty City and I took a pass, but, you know, it's the same sort of weird, extra-territorial setup. Maybe you should look into it."

Alarms and marching bands began sounding off in the computer genius's head. He began hammering his keyboard. "Demi?"

"Papa Bear?"

"You're an American hero. I gotta go. I'll let you know how it turns out."

"Thanks. I—"

Kurtzman terminated the call and hit a key.

Innovation One appeared on the wall-size main screen.

"God's miracles great and small," Delahunt announced.

Kurtzman grinned exultantly. "*Innovation One!* Converted bulk tanker. Custom-built dormitory, cafeteria, gym facilities, two helicopter pads and a drop-down deck devoted to plug-and-play custom ISO container boxes."

Price frowned. "Yes, but what is it?"

"Like Liberty City, it's an experiment. The Bay area—South Bay and Silicon Valley in particular—are dependent to a large degree on an influx of foreign engineers. Those engineers are at the mercy of the United States worker visa program. You have to jump through hoops and it can take years. Used to be the easiest way to bypass was to marry an American. Failing that, you have to apply for a temporary visa again and again and again.

"*Innovation One* is a ship that sits just outside California's territorial limit, right off the Farallon Islands. The engineers can commute into the Bay area in the morning and leave at night, and telecommute from the ship, as well. It was a very expensive idea, but it was thought it would be cheaper if enough valley companies invested in it. A lot of them did, but the record has been spotty and at the end of the day you have to be an engineer who is willing to live more time than not on a ship. It's changed hands a few times and was almost scrapped. The State of California isn't pleased with it but there isn't much to be done."

"Can we send in the Coast Guard?" Delahunt asked

Price marveled at the gall of the plan. "No," the mission controller answered. "The Coast Guard has no authority, and we have no proof of anything and the Navy has nothing in range before the fund-raiser. And…what if we're wrong?"

"Wrong, hell." Delahunt pulled up a news article. "According to the San José *Mercury News*—and I quote—*'Innovation One* is dealt another blow as it is forced to debark its population while it deals with dangerous gas leaks and structural cracking.'"

"When was that?" Price asked.

"It was announced two days ago, and *Innovation One's* press release says the repairs will take at least two weeks."

"How far out is the *Coronado*?"

Tokaido pulled up the map charting its movement and every other ship on the list out of Guatemala. "At full speed? She could sneak up *Innovation One's* ass by tomorrow night."

USS Coronado

PHOENIX FORCE CUT the Zodiac's engine and paddled for *Innovation One*. Their TOE was very low at this point, but the *Coronado* was just about the most modern ship in the US Navy.

Unlike most ship's armories where God only knew what sort of WW II to Vietnam relics you might come across, she had a small but tidy assortment of the Navy's latest small arms. Everyone had an M-4 rifle with an optic except for Manning. He had a .50-caliber Grendel rifle. It looked like an M-16 on growth hormones and the Navy used it to detonate floating mines from helicopters.

Phoenix Force was missing Hawkins and Encizo, but had Propenko. Able Team was tip-top and back aboard ship. The plan was simple. Phoenix Force was to board *Innovation One* and have a look around. If needed, Able Team would pull an air-cavalry assault out of *Dragonslayer.*

Innovation One was a big ship; a bulk tanker rather than container vessel. That meant she had large internal spaces rather than an open framework for stacking containers. Her abbreviated container deck was customized for swapping in power supplies and other specialized units.

Phoenix Force moved in under human paddle power. Luckily the ocean conditions weren't bad. *Innovation One's* deck lights were on, but it outwardly seemed as though no one was home.

Phoenix Force came up alongside. "Cal?"

James stood and braced himself as he took out his grapnel. He pushed the button and the padded, folding spikes snapped out. He took his time arranging his rope and slowly began swinging the grapnel in larger and larger arcs.

It was about a forty-meter vertical throw to the rail, but the rope imparted him massive leverage. James sent his grapnel skyward and rope paid upward. That was the downside. The rope was instant drag and it added slog with every inch deployed.

The grapnel sailed over the rail with ease. He very slowly began reeling rope back in. He felt the grapnel bumping and scraping things and he slowed his pull. The rope suddenly went taut and he leaned back and put his weight into it.

The grapnel held.

"Should've joined the rodeo..." James took point and pulled a Spider-Man up the side of the ship. He stopped at the top of the rail and hung by his hands, looking around. Nothing moved, so he slid over the rail. He shot the thumbs-up.

McCarter tied off the Zodiac and he and the rest of the team climbed up.

"Phoenix on board," McCarter whispered into his com.

Lyons replied, "Copy that, Phoenix. Able hot on the pad."

McCarter looked down nearly three football pitches of ship. "Well, lads, the missiles and the Game Room should be to stern in front of the bridge. Quick's the word and quiet the action."

James moved forward down the long, lit path along the rail. He passed the helicopter pad and then was followed by Propenko and McCarter. Manning took their six with the big rifle.

They passed a volleyball sand pit and a full-size basketball court. The swimming pool was covered. *Innovation One* was a bulk transport but all but two of her cranes had been removed and they were both over the ISO units.

James stopped and crouched and the line behind him stopped, as well. "Farm, this is Cal. The lights are on but nobody is home. I have no movement." He put a hand down and pressed his palm against the deck. "I don't even have a hum or vibration. This ship isn't alive."

"Be advised," Kurtzman returned, "*Innovation One* does not need to have her engines on. Any number of the ISO containers can be power units and she uses solar power to charge her batteries."

"Copy."

James continued forward on his own. It was a long ship and a long, nerve-racking walk. He could swear the darkened windows of the bridge were looking at him. He approached the container deck, which had been cut into the ship and was flush with the deck. It could hold three containers across by six down, and descended three containers deep into the hold. The spaces were all filled. James looked at a container that appeared to have twelve hatches. He waved the team forward. McCarter stared down at the container.

"Looks like the Klub-K picture right out of Wikipedia," the Phoenix Force leader commented.

Propenko made a noise. "What? We kill no one? I am still owed for finger."

McCarter reported in. "Farm, be advised. *Innovation One* is target. Missiles are on board. Launch Able."

"Copy that, Phoenix. Able—"

Floodlights snapped on in a chain of luminescent detonations from stem to stern. Shouts erupted from the bridge and belowdeck. Boots rang on steel.

Several of Thaniel Maier's men in black ran out to the bridge rail. Their laser pointers swept the deck around Phoenix Force and the sound of a .357 Magnum on full auto was something to hear as strobing muzzle-flashes lit the night.

McCarter fired and one of the gunmen jerked back. He knelt and fired blind over the rail. The rail was a solid steel partition and Phoenix Force's rifles sparked off it. The only cover was the cranes for loading and unloading ISO units and Phoenix Force dove for them.

"Gummer! Covering fire!" McCarter yelled.

Manning raised his Grendel rifle and popped three times with thunder that dwarfed the buzz saws of the Liberty City men. Three black holes punched through the rail and two of the men firing behind it dropped their weapons and fell out of sight.

A grenade clanked to the deck two meters away.

James flicked his selector to semiauto and fired as fast as he could pull the trigger. Sparks shrieked off the deck as the grenade skittered away spinning across the deck. "Down!"

Phoenix Force hit the deck as the grenade went off and shrapnel sparked against the crane and shattered the operator's window.

McCarter snapped his head up. The missile hatches hadn't opened but he could hear mechanical things going on underneath them. "Farm! Enemy is initiating launch procedures!"

CHAPTER TWENTY-FOUR

Hallelujah Jordan bridge

Kun spoke from the Game Room. "I hear them, above me."

"You do," Maier confirmed. He listened as gunfire ripped across the night. A bullet struck one of the bridge windows and it cracked. "Proceed with launch. Secondary targets." It would not be what he had hoped for, but it would still be gorgeous beyond words, and he savored giving the order. "Full San Francisco spread. Burn the city of Sodom."

"Launch sequence is initiated. System is not hot, changing targeting parameters. It will take a few moments."

"I understand." Maier turned to the captain. "Raheel, martyrdom is at hand. Have your crew drive the commandos away from the missile container at any cost. I will send men behind them. Nothing must impede the launch."

Captain Raheel took up an AK and snapped out the bayonet. "If Allah wills!" Raheel got on the horn and roared in Arabic. "All crew. Take up your weapons. Attack the infidels beneath the bridge. Let nothing stop you."

"Allāhu Akbar!" Raheel ran down the stairs to join his crew.

Magistrate Tan Staafl shook like milk. He stank of liquor. "Oh, God, oh, God, oh, God…"

Maier turned to Moon. "It is meaningless now."

"Yes?" Moon seemed pleased.

"But the fools will try to take the bridge."

"Yes?"

"Make them suffer for it."

Moon's voice went sick and baby-like. "Yes."

"But before you do, twist this fool's head off. I have been waiting to watch that for a year."

The Magistrate's head snapped back and forth between the two killers. "Wait, what?"

Moon loomed over Tan Staafl, closed his massive hands around Staafl's skull and slowly twisted. The Magistrate of Liberty City keened like a guinea pig being killed.

MANNING WATCHED in horror as a missile hatch flipped open. "Oh, for—" He bellowed at his team. "Go over the side! Go over the side!"

McCarter roared. "Gummer!"

Manning made his peace and ran to the open hatch. He began firing .50-caliber rounds into the nose cone of the missile staring up at him. "Oh, my God!" He staggered backward as heat washed up out of the silo and tried to burn his eyebrows off. The fuel of the fuel-air weapon screamed like the teakettle of the damned and sent fitful streams of flame into the air as the rocket engines fired, but the high explosive stubbornly refused to detonate.

Manning sat as the Klub-K missile rose into the air in slow motion, squirting fire out of multiple orifices. It suddenly pulled a violent cartwheel that sent it spinning out over the ocean. The missile slammed into the water and detonated. A one-hundred-foot geyser of ocean erupted lit from within with orange fire. *Innovation One* rocked with the blast.

Manning got to his feet. "That worked out well."

Another hatch flipped open.

"Oh, for—"

"Allāhu Akbar!" Men in civvies burst out onto the deck in a bayonet charge with AKs blazing. Phoenix engaged

them from behind the crane. Manning had no cover to take. The Canadian rifleman just took a knee and started firing. The crew came in screaming their God's name. Manning knocked them down like bowling pins and knew he wasn't going to make it.

Dragonslayer thundered overhead and the machine guns mounted over the pontoons tore into the *Hallelujah Jordan* suicide squad reaping them like wheat. Manning rose unsteadily and went back to his job. Bullets cracked all around him. He fired down into the next open missile silo. No streamers of fire erupted. The rocket engines didn't detonate. "Oh, for… Oh!" Manning realized one of his bullets had lobotomized the missile. Another missile hatch popped open next to it. "Now if I can do that twice, six more times—"

A bullet slammed into Manning's back. He staggered as he got hit again and fell to the deck.

Another hatch flipped open.

"Oh, for…"

Dragonslayer

"Go! Go! Go!" Jack Grimaldi shouted.

Able Team fast-roped right on top of the bridge.

Jack Grimaldi's girl was a little lighter with the Able Team operatives out his cabin, but she was not a happy camper. He pulled back on the stick and hit the throttle to get altitude. *Dragonslayer* thundered but she also audibly whined and clanked. She also started attracting gunfire.

The *Coronado* had received the parts Grimaldi wanted off Belize and their host had given him a precious gift. Grimaldi had but one engine and it was cranky, and he was wearing pontoons because he absolutely expected to go into the drink if he wasn't blown out of the sky. Even so, he had his stub wings, and he had four of the *Coro-*

nado's Hellfire missiles attached to them. Grimaldi had wanted the full eight but in practice he couldn't take off with them and Able Team at the same time.

Intellectually the ace Stony Man pilot knew his best option was to put all four Hellfires into the launching module and send them and *Innovation One* sky high. That would also send Able Team and Phoenix Force to the Old Place in the deep. Spiritually, Jack Grimaldi knew that just wasn't going to happen. He veered out over the ocean to give himself a little distance.

Grimaldi had read up all about Klub-K missiles. They were capable of a Mach 1-plus sprint toward their final destination. But missiles were not like bullets out of the barrel of a gun. They fired their rocket motors and then gained momentum. He was in the unique, first-time-in-history situation to be in a gunship over a war ship waiting for them to fire.

Theoretically it was ducks in a barrel, and he was goddamn sick and tired of getting hammered this entire mission. It was time to hammer back.

He flicked his Hellfires to hot and the helmet-mounted sight clicked into life on his visor. Wherever he looked his Hellfire would go. It was very possible that combat pilots were the cockiest people on earth. Jack Grimaldi was quite possibly the greatest combat pilot on earth. He looked at the giant clawfoot tub that was *Innovation One* and saw a pitifully inferior opponent.

"Bring it."

Another Klub missile rose up on a column of fire. The joy was that the Klub-K launched with rocket motors and then, when it picked up enough speed, its ramjet engine kicked in. The rocket motor lit the night. All Grimaldi had to do was to keep his helmet sight on it. Hellfire missiles were small and agile and accelerated to Mach 1 almost instantly.

The Stony Man ace squeezed his missile trigger. "See ya!"

The Hellfire ripped off its rail. The Klub wasn't like a slow-motion Cape Canaveral launch, but it still wasn't hard to follow. Hellfire and Klub coincided and the Farallon Islands got their own supernova.

Grimaldi fought his controls as the blast wave rolled over *Dragonslayer*.

A second missile rose on a violent column of fire.

Grimaldi kicked his collective and tracked with his helmet sight at the same time. He squeezed his trigger. "Lather, rinse, repeat..."

His Hellfire obliterated another missile but it didn't achieve fuel-air detonation. It was still a magnificent fireworks display, but math was not on the ace pilot's side. He spoke to both teams across the link.

"Someone do something. I am running out of missiles."

LYONS JUMPED FROM the top of the bridge to the balcony below. He landed and it jolted up his bones. He whirled and took a rifle butt to the jaw that loosened teeth and threw him against the solid rail. Lyons felt his shotgun slip from his hands.

Moon threw back his head and laughed. "I remember you, *abuelo poco*!" The Mayan's size-fifteen boot crashed into Lyon's chest. "I remember thinking you were compensating for something!" Moon's boot hit Lyons again with the horrific power of a man who was seven feet tall. Only Lyons's armor kept his sternum from cracking. Moon cocked his foot. "Go ahead, spin your pistol!"

Lyons didn't bother going for his pistol. He knew he would never make it.

The giant's huge boot thrust for Lyon's face to knock him over the rail. Lyons ducked just beneath it, and Moon's massive leg violently slid over his shoulder. Lyons roared with effort and stood beneath Moon's massive weight. Moon's momentum helped with the procedure as Lyons went with it and tipped the big man over the rail. Moon screamed as he fell to the burning, erupting missile hatches below.

Lyons limped into the bridge as Blancanales and Schwarz engaged from the roof. Magistrate Tan Staafl was lying on his stomach but staring up at the roof. Lyons gazed at the controls and gave the wheel an experimental turn. He wasn't a sailor but he had assaulted ships before. One look told him *Innovation One's* controls had been killed. There was no taking her anywhere.

"This is Able Leader. *Innovation One* is dead in the water."

"Copy that," Kurtzman confirmed.

Lyons went out, grabbed up his shotgun and prepared to shoot skeet at launching missiles.

The Game Room

"I HAVE FOUR missiles left," Kun reported. His hair was a mess and his suit was drenched in blood. "I have seen the enemy gunship on camera. He has two missiles left. He is waiting for me to fire. I suggest I reassign all four missiles for one target and launch simultaneously. Two, possibly three, will escape and ensure total annihilation."

Maier was annoyed at the state of the situation but hopeful. Rong and Junior Pyle lay dead on the carpeting in massive pools of vivisected blood. Maier admired Kun's artistry, but he really wanted some people to die on a massive scale. "Do you have a target in mind?"

"I have done a quick search of the internet. Today is Thursday. The President's fund-raiser, the 49er game, the concert and all secondary targets were scheduled for Saturday and are all null."

"But you have something in mind?"

Kun was pleased with himself. "There is a World Wrestling Entertainment event at the Shark Tank tonight. It is called Thursday Night Smackdown. And the coordinates for the Shark Tank are already in the targeting computer."

"We could lay the smackdown," Maier savored the poetry. "What are the casualties again?"

"Seventeen thousand plus. It is sold out."

"Do it."

"Recalibrating."

PHOENIX FORCE was being attacked on all sides. Able Team engaged from the bridge but the numbers game was against the Farm tonight. They had managed to pull Manning out of the line of fire but they had lost the big rifle. McCarter slammed home his next-to-last magazine and called in fire support.

"*Coronado*. This is Phoenix. Requesting fire mission. All available guns and missiles. On my position. Sink *Innovation One*. Repeat, sink *Innovation One*."

The captain sounded sick to his soul. "Phoenix, this is *Coronado* I am waiting permission."

"Bloody hell…"

Propenko was staring at his hand. He had lost his ring and middle finger on top of the little one. He pointed the remaining thumb and forefinger of his mangled hand at McCarter like a gun. "We could just step on missile hatches. Dead? We fall across them. Four of them? Four of us. We will exceed missile takeoff weight. Perhaps we jam hatches. Pilot shoot down anything that gets past. I give it five chances out of ten."

McCarter found himself laughing as bullets ripped against the crane housing. Nikita Propenko was genuinely the toughest man on earth. "You beautiful bastard."

"I am handsome in mine own way," Propenko agreed.

"I heard that!" Grimaldi's voice came across the link. "I will do you one better. Able, Phoenix, abandon ship. I repeat, abandon ship!"

"Jack, what are you bloody going on about?"

"Four missiles we might just live through. If I fire into the missile deck, it's Armageddon. But we've seen some of the missiles not detonate. I'm going to jam them shut and see what happens. Tell the *Coronado* we need immediate sea extraction."

"Jack, you—"

"Get off the ship!"

Dragonslayer swung into sight of the ship's lights and turned into a bullet magnet. Von Sprack and his men clustered by the ventilation units for cover. Grimaldi fired both his missiles into the enemy position, and Von Sprack and the Liberty Security brigade went non-relevant. *Dragonslayer* was smoking and tilting as it came down.

McCarter bellowed out, "You heard the man!"

Phoenix Force charged down the rail.

Able Team disappeared from the bridge and appeared moments later.

Phoenix Force reached the rope and simply leaped overboard.

Able Team followed.

Dragonslayer spun down, dying half out of control. She crash-landed on top of the launch container with genius precision. Grimaldi leaped out and ran for the rail. "Wait for me, fellas!"

The Game Room

"LAUNCH," MAIER ORDERED.

Kun hit the launch key.

Four made-from-scratch Klub-K missiles fired their boosters. Their hatches did not open. Three of the missiles spent several heartbeats sizzling in their launch boxes as they filled with violently expanding rocket propellant. One ripped upward past the hatch, met a sixteen-thousand-pound helicopter and detonated in a spectacular fashion.

The thermobaric warhead and the four rocket boosters detonated. That set off the other three warheads, but they didn't have any time to deploy their fuel. It was more than enough. The blast wave assumed the shape of the mostly hollow ship and the Game Room was incinerated.

Von Sprack and his men attempted to rise to heaven but their charred bodies failed to reach escape velocity and fell to feed the fish.

Innovation One's back broke and her guts twisted open. Technically *Innovation One* was larger than the Titanic. But she went down in fire rather than ice.

MCCARTER KNEW HE had to get his teams away before the massive, sinking ship made a hole in the water that sucked them down. He watched the bow of the *Hallelujah Jordan* rise and reached out to pull Propenko into the Zodiac. James, Manning and Able Team were already aboard. He shouted across the water, "Jack! I saw you jump, Jack!"

After only a moment the Stony Man warriors heard Grimaldi call out of the darkness. "C'mon in! The water's fine!"

McCarter ripped the Zodiac's engine into life as Lyons pulled out a flashlight and located Grimaldi.

The Phoenix Force leader pulled around and they hauled him in.

Lyons regarded the wet pilot. "You seem happy. *Dragonslayer* is going down with that ship."

Jack Grimaldi lay back in the Zodiac. "You know? I have been wanting to upgrade for a while."

EPILOGUE

The relief was apparent on Barbara Price's face as she surveyed the Stony Man cybernetics staff in the Computer Room.

"That was close," she acknowledged. "And close to home. Hal just called to say the President extends his thanks to all of you. The Man is aware that he was personally targeted in this operation."

Price knew it had been a team effort, even more so this time around. And she knew that the solidarity and selflessness—both in the field and here at the Farm—was the difference between victory and defeat.

Able Team and Phoenix Force were on their way back to the Farm, with Jack Grimaldi flying them home in a Navy loaner. She had already heard the rumors about equipment upgrades. And the mission controller was preparing her response; Brognola would be back at Stony Man in time to deal with all procurement requests...

* * * * *

COMING SOON FROM

GOLD EAGLE®

Available July 7, 2015

THE EXECUTIONER® #440
KILLPATH – *Don Pendleton*

After a DEA agent is tortured and killed by a powerful Colombian cartel, Bolan teams up with a former cocaine queen in Cali to obliterate the entire operation.

SUPERBOLAN® #175
NINJA ASSAULT – *Don Pendleton*

Ninjas attack an American casino, and Bolan follows the gangsters behind the crime back to Japan—where he intends to take them out on their home turf.

DEATHLANDS® #123
IRON RAGE – *James Axler*

Ryan and the companions are caught in a battle for survival against crocs, snakes and makeshift ironclads on the great Sippi river.

ROGUE ANGEL™ #55
BENEATH STILL WATERS – *Alex Archer*

Annja uncovers Nazi secrets—and treasure—in the wreckage of a submerged German bomber shot down at the end of WWII.

COMING SOON FROM

GOLD EAGLE®

Available August 4, 2015

THE EXECUTIONER® #441
MURDER ISLAND – *Don Pendleton*
On an uncharted island, a psychotic hunter stalks the ultimate prey: man. His newest targets are an international arms dealer—a criminal who was in CIA custody when his plane was shot down—and Mack Bolan, the Executioner.

STONY MAN® #138
WAR TACTIC – *Don Pendleton*
Tensions between China and the Philippines are on the rise, and a series of pirate attacks on Filipino ports and vessels only makes things worse. Phoenix Force discovers that the pirates are armed with American weapons, while Able Team must hunt down the mastermind behind the attacks.

OUTLANDERS® #74
ANGEL OF DOOM – *James Axler*
The Cerberus fighters must battle Charun and Vanth, alien gods intent on opening a portal to bring their kind to earth. If the alien forces succeed, an invasion from a barbaric dimension will lay siege to Europe…and beyond.

THE EXECUTIONER DON PENDLETON'S

Bolan charged down the hall, greeting every challenge with a snarl of bullets, blasting craters into the torsos of El Tiburon's fighters. Some of them wore body armor, but the M4's deadly sputter struck with enough force to slow them down, allowing Bolan to adjust aim and put bullets into their exposed heads and throats.

The Executioner surged across the ground floor, his senses fine-tuned to everything around him. Between Rojas's sniping, Bolan's blitz and the gunmen's agitated state, Los Soldados de Cali Nuevos didn't stand a chance in this tenement.

It took all of a minute and two 30-round magazines to completely clear the first story. The second story was alive with breaking glass and screams of terror and pain. Rojas wasn't allowing the Soldados a moment of respite.

Bolan had supplied the woman with low-light and magnification optics which could squeeze every ounce of accuracy out of the rifle, and from the sounds of it, she was taking advantage of her concealed position.

She'd obviously done a lot of long-range shooting, even though the distance wasn't great. At most, her shots would have to travel forty yards, but even so, her accuracy and the sheer amount of destruction she was

wreaking on the tenement were impressive. By the time
Bolan reached the second-floor corridor, only a few men
remained within sight. They were cowering in a corner,
seeking protection against the drywall.

The Executioner shouldered his rifle and drilled one
of the men through the side of his head with a single
round. The other Soldado let out a scream as he saw his
friend's head go to pieces, and waved his machine pistol
wildly. In the dark hallway, Bolan was a wraith among
the shadows.

Bolan ripped the terrified gunman open with a tri-burst
from his compact rifle, eliminating that threat before
continuing across the floor.

"On two," Bolan told Rojas. "Don't shoot me."

"Wouldn't dream of it," La Brujah replied. "I'm saving
all my ammo and hatred for the enemy."

Don't miss
KILLPATH
by Don Pendleton,
available July 2015 wherever
Gold Eagle® books and ebooks are sold.